The Sisters — Complete

by

Georg Ebers

Double 9
BOOKS

The Sisters — Complete
by Georg Ebers

ISBN: 978-93-67149-24-9

Published by

DOUBLE 9 BOOKS
2/13-B, Ansari Road
Daryaganj, New Delhi – 110002
info@double9books.com
www.double9books.com
Tel. 011-40042856

ABOUT THE AUTHOR

Georg Moritz Ebers was a German Egyptologist and author who was born in Berlin on March 1, 1837, and died in Tutzing, Bavaria, on August 7, 1898. He bought the Ebers Papyrus, which is one of the oldest medical records from Egypt and is what made him famous. Georg Ebers was born in Berlin. He was the fifth child in a wealthy family of bankers and someone who made ceramics. After their father killed himself soon after Ebers was born, the children were raised by their mother alone. Smart people like Georg Wilhelm Friedrich Hegel, the Grimm Brothers, and Alexander von Humboldt liked going to the club that his mother ran. Ebers studied law in Gottingen and Oriental languages and history in Berlin. Egyptology was something he studied in depth, so in 1865 he was made Dozent in Egyptian language and antiquities at Jena. In 1868 he was made professor. In 1870, he was hired as a professor at Leipzig to teach these topics. He went to Egypt twice for research reasons. His first important work, Ägypten und die Bücher Moses, came out in 1867 and 1868. In 1874, he edited the famous medical tablet called tablet Ebers, which he had found in Thebes (H. Joachim, 1890).

CONTENTS

DEDICATION TO HERR EDUARD von HALLBERGER

Allow me, my dear friend, to dedicate these pages to you. I present them to you at the close of a period of twenty years during which a warm and fast friendship has subsisted between us, unbroken by any disagreement. Four of my works have first seen the light under your care and have wandered all over the world under the protection of your name. This, my fifth book, I desire to make especially your own; it was partly written in your beautiful home at Tutzing, under your hospitable roof, and I desire to prove to you by some visible token that I know how to value your affection and friendship and the many happy hours we have passed together, refreshing and encouraging each other by a full and perfect interchange of thought and sentiment.

PREFACE

By a marvellous combination of circumstances a number of fragments of the Royal Archives of Memphis have been preserved from destruction with the rest, containing petitions written on papyrus in the Greek language; these were composed by a recluse of Macedonian birth, living in the Serapeum, in behalf of two sisters, twins, who served the god as "Pourers out of the libations."

At a first glance these petitions seem scarcely worthy of serious consideration; but a closer study of their contents shows us that we possess in them documents of the greatest value in the history of manners. They prove that the great Monastic Idea—which under the influence of Christianity grew to be of such vast moral and historical significance—first struck root in one of the centres of heathen religious practices; besides affording us a quite unexpected insight into the internal life of the temple of Serapis, whose ruined walls have, in our own day, been recovered from the sand of the desert by the indefatigable industry of the French Egyptologist Monsieur Mariette.

I have been so fortunate as to visit this spot and to search through every part of it, and the petitions I speak of have been familiar to me for years. When, however, quite recently, one of my pupils undertook to study more particularly one of these documents—preserved in the Royal Library at Dresden—I myself reinvestigated it also, and this study impressed on my fancy a vivid picture of the Serapeum under Ptolemy Philometor; the outlines became clear and firm, and acquired color, and it is this picture which I have endeavored to set before the reader, so far as words admit, in the following pages.

I did not indeed select for my hero the recluse, nor for my heroines the twins who are spoken of in the petitions, but others who might have lived at a somewhat earlier date under similar conditions; for it is proved by the papyrus that it was not once only and by accident that twins were engaged in serving in the temple of Serapis, but that, on the contrary, pair after pair of sisters succeeded each other in the office of pouring out libations.

I have not invested Klea and Irene with this function, but have simply placed them as wards of the Serapeum and growing up within its precincts. I selected this alternative partly because the existing sources of knowledge give us very insufficient information as to the duties that might have been required of the twins, partly for other reasons arising out of the plan of my narrative.

Klea and Irene are purely imaginary personages, but on the other hand I have endeavored, by working from tolerably ample sources, to give a faithful picture of the historical physiognomy of the period in which they live and move, and portraits of the two hostile brothers Ptolemy Philometor and Euergetes II., the latter of whom bore the nickname of Physkon: the Stout. The Eunuch Eulaeus and the Roman Publius Cornelius Scipio Nasica, are also historical personages.

I chose the latter from among the many young patricians living at the time, partly on account of the strong aristocratic feeling which he displayed, particularly in his later life, and partly because his nickname of Serapion struck me. This name I account for in my own way, although I am aware that he owed it to his resemblance to a person of inferior rank.

For the further enlightenment of the reader who is not familiar with this period of Egyptian history I may suggest that Cleopatra, the wife of Ptolemy Philometor—whom I propose to introduce to the reader—must not be confounded with her famous namesake, the beloved of Julius Caesar and Mark Antony. The name Cleopatra was a very favorite one among the Lagides, and of the queens who bore it she who has become famous through Shakespeare (and more lately through Makart) was the seventh, the sister and wife of Ptolemy XIV. Her tragical death from the bite of a viper or asp did not occur until 134 years later than the date of my narrative, which I have placed 164 years B.C.

At that time Egypt had already been for 169 years subject to the rule of a Greek (Macedonian) dynasty, which owed its name as that of the Ptolemies or Lagides to its founder Ptolemy Soter, the son of Lagus. This energetic man, a general under Alexander the Great, when his sovereign—333 B.C.— had conquered the whole Nile Valley, was appointed governor of the new Satrapy; after Alexander's death in 323 B.C., Ptolemy mounted the throne of the Pharaohs, and he and his descendants ruled over Egypt until after the death of the last and most famous of the Cleopatras, when it was annexed as a province to the Roman Empire.

This is not the place for giving a history of the successive Ptolemies, but I may remark that the assimilating faculty exercised by the Greeks over other nations was potent in Egypt; particularly as the result of the powerful influence of Alexandria, the capital founded by Alexander, which developed with wonderful rapidity to be one of the most splendid centres of Hellenic culture and of Hellenic art and science.

Long before the united rule of the hostile brothers Ptolemy Philometor and Euergetes—whose violent end will be narrated to the reader of this story—Greek influence was marked in every event and detail of Egyptian life, which had remained almost unaffected by the characteristics of former conquerors—the Hyksos, the Assyrians and the Persians; and, under the Ptolemies, the most inhospitable and exclusive nation of early antiquity threw open her gates to foreigners of every race.

Alexandria was a metropolis even in the modern sense; not merely an emporium of commerce, but a focus where the intellectual and religious treasures of various countries were concentrated and worked up, and transmitted to all the nations that desired them. I have resisted the temptation to lay the scene of my story there, because in Alexandria the Egyptian element was too much overlaid by the Greek, and the too splendid and important scenery and decorations might easily have distracted the reader's attention from the dramatic interest of the persons acting.

At that period of the Hellenic dominion which I have described, the kings of Egypt were free to command in all that concerned the internal affairs of their kingdom, but the rapidly-growing power of the Roman Empire enabled her to check the extension of their dominion, just as she chose.

Philometor himself had heartily promoted the immigration of Israelites from Palestine, and under him the important Jewish community in Alexandria acquired an influence almost greater than the Greek; and this not only in the city but in the kingdom and over their royal protector, who allowed them to build a temple to Jehovah on the shores of the Nile, and in his own person assisted at the dogmatic discussions of the Israelites educated in the Greek schools of the city. Euergetes II., a highly gifted but vicious and violent man, was, on the contrary, just as inimical to them; he persecuted them cruelly as soon as his brother's death left him sole ruler over Egypt. His hand fell heavily even on the members of the Great Academy— the Museum, as it was called—of Alexandria, though he himself had been devoted to the grave labors of science, and he compelled them to seek a new home. The exiled sons of learning settled in various cities on the shores of the Mediterranean, and thus contributed not a little to the diffusion of the intellectual results of the labors in the Museum.

Aristarchus, the greatest of Philometor's learned contemporaries, has reported for us a conversation in the king's palace at Memphis. The verses about "the puny child of man," recited by Cleopatra in chapter X., are not genuinely antique; but Friedrich Ritschl—the Aristarchus of our own days, now dead—thought very highly of them and gave them to me, some years ago, with several variations which had been added by an anonymous hand, then still in the land of the living. I have added to the first verse two of these, which, as I learned at the eleventh hour, were composed by Herr H. L. von Held, who is now dead, and of whom further particulars may be learned from Varnhagen's 'Biographisclaen Denkmalen'. Vol. VII. I think the reader will thank me for directing his attention to these charming lines and to the genius displayed in the moral application of the main idea. Verses such as these might very well have been written by Callimachus or some other poet of the circle of the early members of the Museum of Alexandria.

I was also obliged in this narrative to concentrate, in one limited canvas as it were, all the features which were at once the conditions and the characteristics of a great epoch of civilization, and to give them form and movement by setting the history of some of the men then living before the reader, with its complications and its denouement. All the personages of my story grew up in my imagination from a study of the times in which they lived, but when once I saw them clearly in outline they soon stood before my mind in a more distinct form, like people in a dream; I felt the poet's pleasure in creation, and as I painted them their blood grew warm, their pulses began to beat and their spirit to take wings and stir, each in its appropriate nature. I gave history her due, but the historic figures retired into the background beside the human beings as such; the representatives of an epoch became vehicles for a Human Ideal, holding good for all time; and thus it is that I venture to offer this transcript of a period as really a dramatic romance.

Leipzig November 13, 1879. GEORG EBERS.

CHAPTER I

On the wide, desert plain of the Necropolis of Memphis stands the extensive and stately pile of masonry which constitutes the Greek temple of Serapis; by its side are the smaller sanctuaries of Asclepios, of Anubis and of Astarte, and a row of long, low houses, built of unburnt bricks, stretches away behind them as a troop of beggar children might follow in the train of some splendidly attired king.

The more dazzlingly brilliant the smooth, yellow sandstone walls of the temple appear in the light of the morning sun, the more squalid and mean do the dingy houses look as they crouch in the outskirts. When the winds blow round them and the hot sunbeams fall upon them, the dust rises from them in clouds as from a dry path swept by the gale. Even the rooms inside are never plastered, and as the bricks are of dried Nile-mud mixed with chopped straw, of which the sharp little ends stick out from the wall in every direction, the surface is as disagreeable to touch as it is unpleasing to look at. When they were first built on the ground between the temple itself and the wall which encloses the precincts, and which, on the eastern side, divides the acacia-grove of Serapis in half, they were concealed from the votaries visiting the temple by the back wall of a colonnade on the eastern side of the great forecourt; but a portion of this colonnade has now fallen down, and through the breach, part of these modest structures are plainly visible with their doors and windows opening towards the sanctuary—or, to speak more accurately, certain rudely constructed openings for looking out of or for entering by. Where there is a door there is no window, and where a gap in the wall serves for a window, a door is dispensed with; none of the chambers, however, of this long row of low one-storied buildings communicate with each other.

A narrow and well-trodden path leads through the breach in the wall; the pebbles are thickly strewn with brown dust, and the footway leads past quantities of blocks of stone and portions of columns destined for the construction of a new building which seems only to have been intermitted the night before, for mallets and levers lie on and near the various materials. This path leads directly to the little brick houses, and ends at a small closed wooden door so roughly joined and so ill-hung that between it and the threshold, which is only raised a few inches above the ground, a fine gray cat contrives to squeeze herself through by putting down her head and rubbing through the dust. As soon as she finds herself once more erect on her four legs she proceeds to clean and smooth her ruffled fur, putting up her back, and glancing with gleaming eyes at the house she has just left, behind which at this moment the sun is rising; blinded by its bright rays she turns away and goes on with cautious and silent tread into the court of the temple.

The hovel out of which pussy has crept is small and barely furnished; it would be perfectly dark too, but that the holes in the roof and the rift in the door admit light into this most squalid room. There is nothing standing against its rough gray walls but a wooden chest, near this a few earthen bowls stand on the ground with a wooden cup and a gracefully wrought jug of pure and shining gold, which looks strangely out of place among such humble accessories. Quite in the background lie two mats of woven bast, each covered with a sheepskin. These are the beds of the two girls who inhabit the room, one of whom is now sitting on a low stool made of palm-branches, and she yawns as she begins to arrange her long and shining brown hair. She is not particularly skilful and even less patient over this not very easy task, and presently, when a fresh tangle checks the horn comb with which she is dressing it, she tosses the comb on to the couch. She has not pulled it through her hair with any haste nor with much force, but she shuts her eyes so tightly and sets her white teeth so firmly in her red dewy lip that it might be supposed that she had hurt herself very much.

A shuffling step is now audible outside the door; she opens wide her tawny-hazel eyes, that have a look of gazing on the world in surprise, a smile parts her lips and her whole aspect is as completely changed as that of a butterfly which escapes from the shade into the sunshine where the bright beams are reflected in the metallic lustre of its wings.

A hasty hand knocks at the ill-hung door, so roughly that it trembles on its hinges, and the instant after a wooden trencher is shoved in through the wide chink by which the cat made her escape; on it are a thin round cake of bread and a shallow earthen saucer containing a little olive-oil; there is no more than might perhaps be contained in half an ordinary egg-shell, but it looks fresh and sweet, and shines in clear, golden purity. The girl goes to the door, pulls in the platter, and, as she measures the allowance with a glance, exclaims half in lament and half in reproach:

"So little! and is that for both of us?"

As she speaks her expressive features have changed again and her flashing eyes are directed towards the door with a glance of as much dismay as though the sun and stars had been suddenly extinguished; and yet her only grief is the smallness of the loaf, which certainly is hardly large enough to stay the hunger of one young creature—and two must share it; what is a mere nothing in one man's life, to another may be of great consequence and of terrible significance.

The reproachful complaint is heard by the messenger outside the door, for the old woman who shoved in the trencher over the threshold answers quickly but not crossly.

"Nothing more to-day, Irene."

"It is disgraceful," cries the girl, her eyes filling with tears, "every day the loaf grows smaller, and if we were sparrows we should not have enough to satisfy us. You know what is due to us and I will never cease to complain and petition. Serapion shall draw up a fresh address for us, and when the king knows how shamefully we are treated—"

"Aye! when he knows," interrupted the old woman. "But the cry of the poor is tossed about by many winds before it reaches the king's ear. I might find a shorter way than that for you and your sister if fasting comes so much amiss to you. Girls with faces like hers and yours, my little Irene, need never come to want."

"And pray what is my face like?" asked the girl, and her pretty features once more seemed to catch a gleam of sunshine.

"Why, so handsome that you may always venture to show it beside your sister's; and yesterday, in the procession, the great Roman sitting by the queen looked as often at her as at Cleopatra herself. If you had been there too he would not have had a glance for the queen, for you are a pretty thing, as I can tell you. And there are many girls would sooner hear those words then have a whole loaf—besides you have a mirror I suppose, look in that next time you are hungry."

The old woman's shuffling steps retreated again and the girl snatched up the golden jar, opened the door a little way to let in the daylight and looked at herself in the bright surface; but the curve of the costly vase showed her features all distorted, and she gaily breathed on the hideous travestie that met her eyes, so that it was all blurred out by the moisture. Then she smilingly put down the jar, and opening the chest took from it a small metal mirror into which she looked again and yet again, arranging her shining hair first in one way and then in another; and she only laid it down when she remembered a certain bunch of violets which had attracted her attention when she first woke, and which must have been placed in their saucer of water by her sister some time the day before. Without pausing to consider she took up the softly scented blossoms, dried their green stems on her dress, took up the mirror again and stuck the flowers in her hair.

How bright her eyes were now, and how contentedly she put out her hand for the loaf. And how fair were the visions that rose before her young fancy as she broke off one piece after another and hastily eat them after slightly moistening them with the fresh oil. Once, at the festival of the New Year, she had had a glimpse into the king's tent, and there she had seen men and women feasting as they reclined on purple cushions. Now she dreamed of tables covered with costly vessels, was served in fancy by boys crowned with flowers, heard the music of flutes and harps and—for she was no more than a child and had such a vigorous young appetite—pictured herself as selecting the daintiest and sweetest morsels out of dishes of solid gold and eating till she was satisfied, aye so perfectly satisfied that the very last mouthful of bread and the very last drop of oil had disappeared.

But so soon as her hand found nothing more on the empty trencher the bright illusion vanished, and she looked with dismay into the empty oil-cup and at the place where just now the bread had been.

"Ah!" she sighed from the bottom of her heart; then she turned the platter over as though it might be possible to find some more bread and oil on the other side of it, but finally shaking her head she sat looking thoughtfully into her lap; only for a few minutes however, for the door opened and the slim form of her sister Klea appeared, the sister whose meagre rations she had dreamily eaten up, and Klea had been sitting up half the night sewing for her, and then had gone out before sunrise to fetch water from the Well of the Sun for the morning sacrifice at the altar of Serapis.

Klea greeted her sister with a loving glance but without speaking; she seemed too exhausted for words and she wiped the drops from her forehead with the linen veil that covered the back of her head as she seated herself on the lid of the chest. Irene immediately glanced at the empty trencher, considering whether she had best confess her guilt to the wearied girl and beg for forgiveness, or divert the scolding she had deserved by some jest, as she had often succeeded in doing before. This seemed the easier course and she adopted it at once; she went up to her sister quickly, but not quite unconcernedly, and said with mock gravity:

"Look here, Klea, don't you notice anything in me? I must look like a crocodile that has eaten a whole hippopotamus, or one of the sacred snakes after it has swallowed a rabbit. Only think when I had eaten my own bread I found yours between my teeth—quite unexpectedly—but now—"

Klea, thus addressed, glanced at the empty platter and interrupted her sister with a low-toned exclamation. "Oh! I was so hungry."

The words expressed no reproof, only utter exhaustion, and as the young criminal looked at her sister and saw her sitting there, tired and worn out but submitting to the injury that had been done her without a word of complaint, her heart, easily touched, was filled with compunction and regret. She burst into tears and threw herself on the ground before her, clasping her knees and crying, in a voice broken with sobs:

"Oh Klea! poor, dear Klea, what have I done! but indeed I did not mean any harm. I don't know how it happened. Whatever I feel prompted to do I do, I can't help doing it, and it is not till it is done that I begin to know whether it was right or wrong. You sat up and worried yourself for me, and this is how I repay you—I am a bad girl! But you shall not go hungry—no, you shall not."

"Never mind; never mind," said the elder, and she stroked her sister's brown hair with a loving hand.

But as she did so she came upon the violets fastened among the shining tresses. Her lips quivered and her weary expression changed as she touched the flowers and glanced at the empty saucer in which she had carefully placed them the clay before. Irene at once perceived the change in her sister's face, and thinking only that she was surprised at her pretty adornment, she said gaily: "Do you think the flowers becoming to me?"

Klea's hand was already extended to take the violets out of the brown plaits, for her sister was still kneeling before her, but at this question her arm dropped, and she said more positively and distinctly than she had yet spoken and in a voice, whose sonorous but musical tones were almost masculine and certainly remarkable in a girl:

"The bunch of flowers belongs to me; but keep it till it is faded, by mid-day, and then return it to me."

"It belongs to you?" repeated the younger girl, raising her eyes in surprise to her sister, for to this hour what had been Klea's had been hers also. "But I always used to take the flowers you brought home; what is there special in these?"

"They are only violets like any other violets," replied Klea coloring deeply. "But the queen has worn them."

"The queen!" cried her sister springing to her feet and clasping her hands in astonishment. "She gave you the flowers? And you never told me till now? To be sure when you came home from the procession yesterday you only asked me how my foot was and whether my clothes were whole and then not another mortal word did you utter. Did Cleopatra herself give you this bunch?"

"How should she?" retorted Klea. "One of her escort threw them to me; but drop the subject pray! Give me the water, please, my mouth is parched and I can hardly speak for thirst."

The bright color dyed her cheeks again as she spoke, but Irene did not observe it, for—delighted to make up for her evil doings by performing some little service—she ran to fetch the water-jar; while Klea filled and emptied her wooden bowl she said, gracefully lifting a small foot, to show to her sister:

"Look, the cut is almost healed and I can wear my sandal again. Now I shall tie it on and go and ask Serapion for some bread for you and perhaps he will give us a few dates. Please loosen the straps for me a little, here, round the ankle, my skin is so thin and tender that a little thing hurts me which you would hardly feel. At mid-day I will go with you and help fill the jars for the altar, and later in the day I can accompany you in the procession which was postponed from yesterday. If only the queen and the great foreigner should come again to look on at it! That would be splendid! Now, I am going, and before you have drunk the last bowl of water you shall have some bread, for I will coax the old man so prettily that he can't say 'no.'"

Irene opened the door, and as the broad sunlight fell in it lighted up tints of gold in her chestnut hair, and her sister looking after her could almost fancy that the sunbeams had got entangled with the waving glory round her head. The bunch of violets was the last thing she took note of as Irene went out into the open air; then she was alone and she shook her head gently as she said to herself: "I give up everything to her and what I have left she takes from me. Three times have I met the Roman, yesterday he gave me the violets, and I did want to keep those for myself—and now—" As she spoke she clasped the bowl she still held in her hand closely to her and her lips trembled pitifully, but only for an instant; she drew herself up and said firmly: "But it is all as it should be."

Then she was silent; she set down the water-jar on the chest by her side, passed the back of her hand across her forehead as if her head were aching, then, as she sat gazing down dreamily into her lap, her weary head presently fell on her shoulder and she was asleep.

CHAPTER II

The low brick building of which the sisters' room formed a part, was called the Pastophorium, and it was occupied also by other persons attached to the service of the temple, and by numbers of pilgrims. These assembled here from all parts of Egypt, and were glad to pass a night under the protection of the sanctuary.

Irene, when she quitted her sister, went past many doors—which had been thrown open after sunrise—hastily returning the greetings of many strange as well as familiar faces, for all glanced after her kindly as though to see her thus early were an omen of happy augury, and she soon reached an outbuilding adjoining the northern end of the Pastophorium; here there was no door, but at the level of about a man's height from the ground there were six unclosed windows opening on the road. From the first of these the pale and much wrinkled face of an old man looked down on the girl as she approached. She shouted up to him in cheerful accents the greeting familiar to the Hellenes "Rejoice!" But he, without moving his lips, gravely and significantly signed to her with his lean hand and with a glance from his small, fixed and expressionless eyes that she should wait, and then handed out to her a wooden trencher on which lay a few dates and half a cake of bread.

"For the altar of the god?" asked the girl. The old man nodded assent, and Irene went on with her small load, with the assurance of a person who knows exactly what is required of her; but after going a few steps and before she had reached the last of the six windows she paused, for she plainly heard voices and steps, and presently, at the end of the Pastophorium towards which she was proceeding and which opened into a small grove of acacias dedicated to Serapis—which was of much greater extent outside the enclosing wall—appeared a little group of men whose appearance attracted her attention; but she was afraid to go on towards the strangers, so, leaning close up to the wall of the houses, she awaited their departure, listening the while to what they were saying.

In front of these early visitors to the temple walked a man with a long staff in his right hand speaking to the two gentlemen who followed, with the air of a professional guide, who is accustomed to talk as if he were reading to his audience out of an invisible book, and whom the hearers are unwilling to interrupt with questions, because they know that his knowledge scarcely extends beyond exactly what he says. Of his two remarkable-looking hearers one was wrapped in a long and splendid robe and wore a rich display of gold chains and rings, while the other wore nothing over his short chiton but a Roman toga thrown over his left shoulder.

His richly attired companion was an old man with a full and beardless face and thin grizzled hair. Irene gazed at him with admiration and astonishment, but when she had feasted her eyes on the stuffs and ornaments he wore, she fixed them with much greater interest and attention on the tall and youthful figure at his side.

"Like Hui, the cook's fat poodle, beside a young lion," thought she to herself, as she noted the bustling step of the one and the independent and elastic gait of the other. She felt irresistibly tempted to mimic the older man, but this audacious impulse was soon quelled for scarcely had the guide explained to the Roman that it was here that those pious recluses had their cells who served the god in voluntary captivity, as being consecrated to Serapis, and that they received their food through those windows—here he pointed upwards with his staff when suddenly a shutter, which the cicerone of this ill-matched pair had touched with his stick, flew open with as much force and haste as if a violent gust of wind had caught it, and flung it back against the wall.—And no less suddenly a man's head-of ferocious aspect and surrounded by a shock of gray hair like a lion's mane—looked out of the window and shouted to him who had knocked, in a deep and somewhat overloud voice.

"If my shutter had been your back, you impudent rascal, your stick would have hit the right thing. Or if I had a cudgel between my teeth instead of a tongue, I would exercise it on you till it was as tired as that of a preacher who has threshed his empty straw to his congregation for three mortal hours. Scarcely is the sun risen when we are plagued by the parasitical and inquisitive mob. Why! they will rouse us at midnight next, and throw stones at our rotten old shutters. The effects of my last greeting lasted you for three weeks—to-day's I hope may act a little longer. You, gentlemen there, listen to me. Just as the raven follows an army to batten on the dead, so that fellow there stalks on in front of strangers in order to empty their pockets—and you, who call yourself an interpreter, and in learning Greek have forgotten the little Egyptian you ever knew, mark this: When you have to guide strangers take them to see the Sphinx, or to consult the Apis in the temple of Ptah, or lead them to the king's beast-garden at Alexandria, or the taverns at Hanopus, but don't bring them here, for we are neither pheasants, nor flute-playing women, nor miraculous beasts, who take a pleasure in being stared at. You, gentlemen, ought to choose a better guide than this chatter-mag that keeps up its perpetual rattle when once you set it going. As to yourselves I will tell you one thing: Inquisitive eyes are intrusive company, and every prudent house holder guards himself against them by keeping his door shut."

Irene shrank back and flattened herself against the pilaster which concealed her, for the shutter closed again with a slam, the recluse pulling it to with a rope attached to its outer edge, and he was hidden from the gaze of the strangers; but only for an instant, for the rusty hinges on which the shutter was hanging were not strong enough to bear such violent treatment, and slowly giving way it was about to fall. The blustering hermit stretched out an arm to support it and save it; but it was heavy, and his efforts would not have succeeded had not the young man in Roman dress given his assistance and lifted up the shutter with his hand and shoulder, without any effort, as if it were made of willow laths instead of strong planks.

"A little higher still," shouted the recluse to his assistant. "Let us set the thing on its edge! so, push away, a little more. There, I have propped up the wretched thing and there it may lie. If the bats pay me a visit to-night I will think of you and give them your best wishes."

"You may save yourself that trouble," replied the young man with cool dignity. "I will send you a carpenter who shall refix the shutter, and we offer you our apologies for having been the occasion of the mischief that has happened."

The old man did not interrupt the speaker, but, when he had stared at him from head to foot, he said: "You are strong and you speak fairly, and I might like you well enough if you were in other company. I don't want your carpenter; only send me down a hammer, a wedge, and a few strong nails. Now, you can do nothing more for me, so pack off!"

"We are going at once," said the more handsomely dressed visitor in a thin and effeminate voice. "What can a man do when the boys pelt him with dirt from a safe hiding-place, but take himself off."

"Be off, be off," said the person thus described, with a laugh. "As far off as Samothrace if you like, fat Eulaeus; you can scarcely have forgotten the way there since you advised the king to escape thither with all his treasure. But if you cannot trust yourself to find it alone, I recommend you your interpreter and guide there to show you the road."

The Eunuch Eulaeus, the favorite councillor of King Ptolemy—called Philometor (the lover of his mother)—turned pale at these words, cast a sinister glance at the old man and beckoned to the young Roman; he however was not inclined to follow, for the scolding old oddity had taken his fancy—

perhaps because he was conscious that the old man, who generally showed no reserve in his dislikes, had a liking for him. Besides, he found nothing to object to in his opinion of his companions, so he turned to Eulaeus and said courteously:

"Accept my best thanks for your company so far, and do not let me detain you any longer from your more important occupations on my account."

Eulaeus bowed and replied, "I know what my duty is. The king entrusted me with your safe conduct; permit me therefore to wait for you under the acacias yonder."

When Eulaeus and the guide had reached the green grove, Irene hoped to find an opportunity to prefer her petition, but the Roman had stopped in front of the old man's cell, and had begun a conversation with him which she could not venture to interrupt. She set down the platter with the bread and dates that had been entrusted to her on a projecting stone by her side with a little sigh, crossed her arms and feet as she leaned against the wall, and pricked up her ears to hear their talk.

"I am not a Greek," said the youth, "and you are quite mistaken in thinking that I came to Egypt and to see you out of mere curiosity."

"But those who come only to pray in the temple," interrupted the other, "do not—as it seems to me—choose an Eulaeus for a companion, or any such couple as those now waiting for you under the acacias, and invoking anything rather than blessings on your head; at any rate, for my own part, even if I were a thief I would not go stealing in their company. What then brought you to Serapis?"

"It is my turn now to accuse you of curiosity!"

"By all means," cried the old man, "I am an honest dealer and quite willing to take back the coin I am ready to pay away. Have you come to have a dream interpreted, or to sleep in the temple yonder and have a face revealed to you?"

"Do I look so sleepy," said the Roman, "as to want to go to bed again now, only an hour after sunrise?"

"It may be," said the recluse, "that you have not yet fairly come to the end of yesterday, and that at the fag-end of some revelry it occurred to you that you might visit us and sleep away your headache at Serapis."

"A good deal of what goes on outside these walls seems to come to your ears," retorted the Roman, "and if I were to meet you in the street I should take you for a ship's captain or a master-builder who had to manage a number of unruly workmen. According to what I heard of you and those like you in Athens and elsewhere, I expected to find you something quite different."

"What did you expect?" said Serapion laughing. "I ask you notwithstanding the risk of being again considered curious."

"And I am very willing to answer," retorted the other, "but if I were to tell you the whole truth I should run into imminent danger of being sent off as ignominiously as my unfortunate guide there."

"Speak on," said the old man, "I keep different garments for different men, and the worst are not for those who treat me to that rare dish—a little truth. But before you serve me up so bitter a meal tell me, what is your name?"

"Shall I call the guide?" said the Roman with an ironical laugh. "He can describe me completely, and give you the whole history of my family. But, joking apart, my name is Publius."

"The name of at least one out of every three of your countrymen."

"I am of the Cornelia gens and of the family of the Scipios," continued the youth in a low voice, as though he would rather avoid boasting of his illustrious name.

"Indeed, a noble gentleman, a very grand gentleman!" said the recluse, bowing deeply out of his window. "But I knew that beforehand, for at your age and with such slender ankles to his long legs only a nobleman could walk as you walk. Then Publius Cornelius—"

"Nay, call me Scipio, or rather by my first name only, Publius," the youth begged him. "You are called Serapion, and I will tell you what you wish to know. When I was told that in this temple there were people who had themselves locked into their little chambers never to quit them, taking thought about their dreams and leading a meditative life, I thought they must be simpletons or fools or both at once."

"Just so, just so," interrupted Serapion. "But there is a fourth alternative you did not think of. Suppose now among these men there should be some shut up against their will, and what if I were one of those prisoners? I have asked you a great many questions and you have not hesitated to answer, and you may know how I got into this miserable cage and why I stay in it. I am the son of a good family, for my father was overseer of the granaries of this temple and was of Macedonian origin, but my mother was an Egyptian. I was born in an evil hour, on the twenty-seventh day of the month of Paophi, a day which it is said in the sacred books that it is an evil day and that the child that is born in it must be kept shut up or else it will die of a snake-bite. In consequence of this luckless prediction many of those born on the same day as myself were, like me, shut up at an early age in this cage. My father would very willingly have left me at liberty, but my uncle, a caster of horoscopes in the temple of Ptah, who was all in all in my mother's estimation, and his friends with him, found many other evil signs about my body, read misfortune for me in the stars, declared that the Hathors had destined me to nothing but evil, and set upon her so persistently that at last I was destined to the cloister—we lived here at Memphis. I owe this misery to my dear mother and it was out of pure affection that she brought it upon me. You look enquiringly at me—aye, boy! life will teach you too the lesson that the worst hate that can be turned against you often entails less harm upon you than blind tenderness which knows no reason. I learned to read and write, and all that is usually taught to the priests' sons, but never to accommodate myself to my lot, and I never shall.—Well, when my beard grew I succeeded in escaping and I lived for a time in the world. I have been even to Rome, to Carthage, and in Syria; but at last I longed to drink Nile-water once more and I returned to Egypt. Why? Because, fool that I was, I fancied that bread and water with captivity tasted better in my own country than cakes and wine with freedom in the land of the stranger.

"In my father's house I found only my mother still living, for my father had died of grief. Before my flight she had been a tall, fine woman, when I came home I found her faded and dying. Anxiety for me, a miserable wretch, had consumed her, said the physician—that was the hardest thing to bear. When at last the poor, good little woman, who could so fondly persuade me—a wild scamp—implored me on her death-bed to return to my retreat, I yielded, and swore to her that I would stay in my prison patiently to the end, for I am as water is in northern countries, a child may turn me with its little hand or else I am as hard and as cold as crystal. My old mother died soon after I had taken this oath. I kept my word as you see—and you have seen too how I endure my fate."

"Patiently enough," replied Publius, "I should writhe in my chains far more rebelliously than you, and I fancy it must do you good to rage and storm sometimes as you did just now."

"As much good as sweet wine from Chios!" exclaimed the anchorite, smacking his lips as if he tasted the noble juice of the grape, and stretching his matted head as far as possible out of the window. Thus it happened that he saw Irene, and called out to her in a cheery voice:

"What are you doing there, child? You are standing as if you were waiting to say good-morning to good fortune."

The girl hastily took up the trencher, smoothed down her hair with her other hand, and as she approached the men, coloring slightly, Publius feasted his eyes on her in surprise and admiration.

But Serapion's words had been heard by another person, who now emerged from the acacia-grove and joined the young Roman, exclaiming before he came up with them:

"Waiting for good fortune! does the old man say? And you can hear it said, Publius, and not reply that she herself must bring good fortune wherever she appears."

The speaker was a young Greek, dressed with extreme care, and he now stuck the pomegranate-blossom he carried in his hand behind his ear, so as to shake hands with his friend Publius; then he turned his fair, saucy, almost girlish face with its finely-cut features up to the recluse, wishing to attract his attention to himself by his next speech.

"With Plato's greeting 'to deal fairly and honestly' do I approach you!" he cried; and then he went on more quietly: "But indeed you can hardly need such a warning, for you belong to those who know how to conquer true—that is the inner—freedom; for who can be freer than he who needs nothing? And as none can be nobler than the freest of the free, accept the tribute of my respect, and scorn not the greeting of Lysias of Corinth, who, like Alexander, would fain exchange lots with you, the Diogenes of Egypt, if it were vouchsafed to him always to see out the window of your mansion— otherwise not very desirable—the charming form of this damsel—"

"That is enough, young man," said Serapion, interrupting the Greek's flow of words. "This young girl belongs to the temple, and any one who is tempted to speak to her as if she were a flute-player will have to deal with me, her protector. Yes, with me; and your friend here will bear me witness that it may not be altogether to your advantage to have a quarrel with such as I. Now, step back, young gentlemen, and let the girl tell me what she needs."

When Irene stood face to face with the anchorite, and had told him quickly and in a low voice what she had done, and that her sister Klea was even now waiting for her return, Serapion laughed aloud, and then said in a low tone, but gaily, as a father teases his daughter:

"She has eaten enough for two, and here she stands, on her tiptoes, reaching up to my window, as if it were not an over-fed girl that stood in her garments, but some airy sprite. We may laugh, but Klea, poor thing, she must be hungry?"

Irene made no reply, but she stood taller on tiptoe than ever, put her face up to Serapion, nodding her pretty head at him again and again, and as she looked roguishly and yet imploringly into his eyes Serapion went on:

"And so I am to give my breakfast to Klea, that is what you want; but unfortunately that breakfast is a thing of the past and beyond recall; nothing is left of it but the date-stones. But there, on the trencher in your hand, is a nice little meal."

"That is the offering to Serapis sent by old Phibis," answered the girl.

"Hm, hm—oh! of course!" muttered the old man. "So long as it is for a god—surely he might do without it better than a poor famishing girl."

Then he went on, gravely and emphatically, as a teacher who has made an incautious speech before his pupils endeavors to rectify it by another of more solemn import.

"Certainly, things given into our charge should never be touched; besides, the gods first and man afterwards. Now if only I knew what to do. But, by the soul of my father! Serapis himself sends us what we need. Step close up to me, noble Scipio—or Publius, if I may so call you—and look out towards the acacias. Do you see my favorite, your cicerone, and the bread and roast fowls that your slave has brought him in that leathern wallet? And now he is setting a wine-jar on the carpet he has spread at the big feet of Eulaeus—they will be calling you to share the meal in a minute, but I know of a pretty child who is very hungry—for a little white cat stole away her breakfast this morning. Bring me half a loaf and the wing of a fowl, and a few pomegranates if you like, or one of the peaches Eulaeus is so judiciously fingering. Nay—you may bring two of them, I have a use for both."

"Serapion!" exclaimed Irene in mild reproof and looking down at the ground; but the Greek answered with prompt zeal, "More, much more than that I can bring you. I hasten—"

"Stay here," interrupted Publius with decision, holding him back by the shoulder. "Serapion's request was addressed to me, and I prefer to do my friend's pleasure in my own person."

"Go then," cried the Greek after Publius as he hurried away. "You will not allow me even thanks from the sweetest lips in Memphis. Only look, Serapion, what a hurry he is in. And now poor Eulaeus has to get up; a hippopotamus might learn from him how to do so with due awkwardness. Well! I call that making short work of it—a Roman never asks before he takes; he has got all he wants and Eulaeus looks after him like a cow whose calf has been stolen from her; to be sure I myself would rather eat peaches than see them carried away! Oh if only the people in the Forum could see him now! Publius Cornelius Scipio Nasica, own grandson to the great Africanus, serving like a slave at a feast with a dish in each hand! Well Publius, what has Rome the all conquering brought home this time in token of victory?"

"Sweet peaches and a roast pheasant," said Cornelius laughing, and he handed two dishes into the anchorite's window; "there is enough left still for the old man."

"Thanks, many thanks!" cried Serapion, beckoning to Irene, and he gave her a golden-yellow cake of wheaten bread, half of the roast bird, already divided by Eulaeus, and two peaches, and whispered to her: "Klea may come for the rest herself when these men are gone. Now thank this kind gentleman and go."

For an instant the girl stood transfixed, her face crimson with confusion and her glistening white teeth set in her nether lip, speechless, face to face with the young Roman and avoiding the earnest gaze of his black eyes. Then she collected herself and said:

"You are very kind. I cannot make any pretty speeches, but I thank you most kindly."

"And your very kind thanks," replied Publius, "add to the delights of this delightful morning. I should very much like to possess one of the violets out of your hair in remembrance of this day—and of you."

"Take them all," exclaimed Irene, hastily taking the bunch from her hair and holding them out to the Roman; but before he could take them she drew back her hand and said with an air of importance:

"The queen has had them in her hand. My sister Klea got them yesterday in the procession."

Scipio's face grew grave at these words, and he asked with commanding brevity and sharpness:

"Has your sister black hair and is she taller than you are, and did she wear a golden fillet in the procession? Did she give you these flowers? Yes—do you say? Well then, she had the bunch from me, but although she accepted them she seems to have taken very little pleasure in them, for what we value we do not give away—so there they may go, far enough!"

With these words he flung the flowers over the house and then he went on:

"But you, child, you shall be held guiltless of their loss. Give me your pomegranate-flower, Lysias!"

"Certainly not," replied the Greek. "You chose to do pleasure to your friend Serapion in your own person when you kept me from going to fetch the peaches, and now I desire to offer this flower to the fair Irene with my own hand."

"Take this flower," said Publius, turning his back abruptly on the girl, while Lysias laid the blossom on the trencher in the maiden's hand; she felt the rough manners of the young Roman as if she had been touched by a hard hand; she bowed silently and timidly and then quickly ran home.

Publius looked thoughtfully after her till Lysias called out to him:

"What has come over me? Has saucy Eros perchance wandered by mistake into the temple of gloomy Serapis this morning?"

"That would not be wise," interrupted the recluse, "for Cerberus, who lies at the foot of our God, would soon pluck the fluttering wings of the airy youngster," and as he spoke he looked significantly at the Greek.

"Aye! if he let himself be caught by the three-headed monster," laughed Lysias. "But come away now, Publius; Eulaeus has waited long enough."

"You go to him then," answered the Roman, "I will follow soon; but first I have a word to say to Serapion."

Since Irene's disappearance, the old man had turned his attention to the acacia-grove where Eulaeus was still feasting. When the Roman addressed him he said, shaking his great head with dissatisfaction:

"Your eyes of course are no worse than mine. Only look at that man munching and moving his jaws and smacking his lips. By Serapis! you can tell the nature of a man by watching him eat. You know I sit in my cage unwillingly enough, but I am thankful for one thing about it, and that is that it keeps me far from all that such a creature as Eulaeus calls enjoyment—for such enjoyment, I tell you, degrades a man."

"Then you are more of a philosopher than you wish to seem," replied Publius.

"I wish to seem nothing," answered the anchorite.

"For it is all the same to me what others think of me. But if a man who has nothing to do and whose quiet is rarely disturbed, and who thinks his own thoughts about many things is a philosopher, you may call me one if you like. If at any time you should need advice you may come here again, for I like you, and you might be able to do me an important service."

"Only speak," interrupted the Roman, "I should be glad from my heart to be of any use to you."

"Not now," said Serapion softly. "But come again when you have time — without your companions there, of course — at any rate without Eulaeus, who of all the scoundrels I ever came across is the very worst. It may be as well to tell you at once that what I might require of you would concern not myself but the weal or woe of the water-bearers, the two maidens you have seen and who much need protection."

"I came here for my parents' sake and for Klea's, and not on your account," said Publius frankly. "There is something in her mien and in her eyes which perhaps may repel others but which attracts me. How came so admirable a creature in your temple?"

"When you come again," replied the recluse, "I will tell you the history of the sisters and what they owe to Eulaeus. Now go, and understand me when I say the girls are well guarded. This observation is for the benefit of the Greek who is but a heedless fellow; but you, when you know who the girls are, will help me to protect them."

"That I would do as it is, with real pleasure," replied Publius; he took leave of the recluse and called out to Eulaeus.

"What a delightful morning it has been!"

"It would have been pleasanter for me," replied Eulaeus, "if you had not deprived me of your company for such a long time."

"That is to say," answered the Roman, "that I have stayed away longer than I ought."

"You behave after the fashion of your race," said the other bowing low. "They have kept even kings waiting in their ante-chambers."

"But you do not wear a crown," said Publius evasively. "And if any one should know how to wait it is an old courtier, who—"

"When it is at the command of his sovereign," interrupted Eulaeus, "the old courtier may submit, even when youngsters choose to treat him with contempt."

"That hits us both," said Publius, turning to Lysias. "Now you may answer him, I have heard and said enough."

CHAPTER III

Irene's foot was not more susceptible to the chafing of a strap than her spirit to a rough or an unkind word; the Roman's words and manner had hurt her feelings.

She went towards home with a drooping head and almost crying, but before she had reached it her eyes fell on the peaches and the roast bird she was carrying. Her thoughts flew to her sister and how much the famishing girl would relish so savory a meal; she smiled again, her eyes shone with pleasure, and she went on her way with a quickened step. It never once occurred to her that Klea would ask for the violets, or that the young Roman could be anything more to her sister than any other stranger.

She had never had any other companion than Klea, and after work, when other girls commonly discussed their longings and their agitations and the pleasures and the torments of love, these two used to get home so utterly wearied that they wanted nothing but peace and sleep. If they had sometimes an hour for idle chat Klea ever and again would tell some story of their old home, and Irene, who even within the solemn walls of the temple of Serapis sought and found many innocent pleasures, would listen to her willingly, and interrupt her with questions and with anecdotes of small events or details which she fancied she remembered of her early childhood, but which in fact she had first learnt from her sister, though the force of a lively imagination had made them seem a part and parcel of her own experience.

Klea had not observed Irene's long absence since, as we know, shortly after her sister had set out, overpowered by hunger and fatigue she had fallen asleep. Before her nodding head had finally sunk and her drooping eyelids had closed, her lips now and then puckered and twitched as if with grief; then her features grew tranquil, her lips parted softly and a smile gently lighted up her blushing cheeks, as the breath of spring softly thaws a frozen blossom. This sleeper was certainly not born for loneliness and privation, but to enjoy and to keep love and happiness.

It was warm and still, very still in the sisters' little room. The buzz of a fly was audible now and again, as it flew round the little oil-cup Irene had left empty, and now and again the breathing of the sleeper, coming more and more rapidly. Every trace of fatigue had vanished from Klea's countenance, her lips parted and pouted as if for a kiss, her cheeks glowed, and at last she raised both hands as if to defend herself and stammered out in her dream, "No, no, certainly not—pray, do not! my love—" Then her arm fell again by her side, and dropping on the chest on which she was sitting, the blow woke her. She slowly opened her eyes with a happy smile; then she raised her long silken lashes till her eyes were open, and she gazed fixedly on vacancy as though something strange had met her gaze. Thus she sat for some time without moving; then she started up, pressed her hand on her brow and eyes, and shuddering as if she had seen something horrible or were shivering with ague, she murmured in gasps, while she clenched her teeth:

"What does this mean? How come I by such thoughts? What demons are these that make us do and feel things in our dreams which when we are waking we should drive far, far from our thoughts? I could hate myself, despise and hate myself for the sake of those dreams since, wretch that I am! I let him put his arm round me—and no bitter rage—ah! no—something quite different, something exquisitely sweet, thrilled through my soul."

As she spoke, she clenched her fists and pressed them against her temples; then again her arms dropped languidly into her lap, and shaking her head she went on in an altered and softened voice:

"Still-it was only in a dream and—Oh! ye eternal gods—when we are asleep—well! and what then? Has it come to this; to impure thoughts I am adding self-deception! No, this dream was sent by no demon, it was only a distorted reflection of what I felt yesterday and the day before, and before that even, when the tall stranger looked straight into my eyes—four times he has done so now—and then—how many hours ago, gave me the violets. Did I even turn away my face or punish his boldness with an angry look? Is it not sometimes possible to drive away an enemy with a glance? I have often succeeded when a man has looked after us; but yesterday I could not, and I was as wide awake then as I am at this moment. What does the stranger want with me? What is it he asks with his penetrating glance, which for days has followed me wherever I turn, and robs me of peace even in my sleep? Why should I open my eyes—the gates of the heart—to him? And now the poison poured in through them is seething there; but I will tear it out, and when Irene comes home I will tread the violets into the dust, or leave them with her; she will soon pull them to pieces or leave them to wither miserably—for I will remain pure-minded, even in my dreams—what have I besides in the world?"

At these words she broke off her soliloquy, for she heard Irene's voice, a sound that must have had a favorable effect on her spirit, for she paused, and the bitter expression her beautiful features had but just now worn disappeared as she murmured, drawing a deep breath:

"I am not utterly bereft and wretched so long as I have her, and can hear her voice."

Irene, on her road home, had given the modest offerings of the anchorite Phibis into the charge of one of the temple-servants to lay before the altar of Serapis, and now as she came into the room she hid the platter with the Roman's donation behind her, and while still in the doorway, called out to her sister:

"Guess now, what have I here?"

"Bread and dates from Serapion," replied Klea.

"Oh, dear no!" cried the other, holding out the plate to her sister, "the very nicest dainties, fit for gods and kings. Only feel this peach, does not it feel as soft as one of little Philo's cheeks? If I could always provide such a substitute you would wish I might eat up your breakfast every day. And now do you know who gave you all this? No, that you will never guess! The tall Roman gave them me, the same you had the violets from yesterday."

Klea's face turned crimson, and she said shortly and decidedly:

"How do you know that?"

"Because he told me so himself," replied Irene in a very altered tone, for her sister's eyes were fixed upon her with an expression of stern gravity, such as Irene had never seen in her before.

"And where are the violets?" asked Klea.

"He took them, and his friend gave me this pomegranate-flower," stammered Irene. "He himself wanted to give it me, but the Greek—a handsome, merry man—would not permit it, and laid the flower there on the platter. Take it—but do not look at me like that any longer, for I cannot bear it!"

"I do not want it," said her sister, but not sharply; then, looking down, she asked in a low voice: "Did the Roman keep the violets?"

"He kept—no, Klea—I will not tell you a lie! He flung them over the house, and said such rough things as he did it, that I was frightened and turned my back upon him quickly, for I felt the tears coming into my eyes. What have you to do with the Roman? I feel so anxious, so frightened—as I do sometimes when a storm is gathering and I am afraid of it. And how pale your lips are! that comes of long fasting, no doubt—eat now, as much as you can. But Klea! why do you look at me so—and look so gloomy and terrible? I cannot bear that look, I cannot bear it!"

Irene sobbed aloud, and her sister went up to her, stroked her soft hair from her brow, kissed her kindly, and said:

"I am not angry with you, child, and did not mean to hurt you. If only I could cry as you do when clouds overshadow my heart, the blue sky would shine again with me as soon as it does with you. Now dry your eyes, go up to the temple, and enquire at what hour we are to go to the singing-practice, and when the procession is to set out."

Irene obeyed; she went out with downcast eyes, but once out she looked up again brightly, for she remembered the procession, and it occurred to her that she would then see again the Roman's gay acquaintance, and turning back into the room she laid her pomegranate-blossom in the little bowl out of which she had formerly taken the violets, kissed her sister as gaily as ever, and then reflected as to whether she would wear the flower in her hair or in her bosom. Wear it, at any rate, she must, for she must show plainly that she knew how to value such a gift.

As soon as Klea was alone she seized the trencher with a vehement gesture, gave the roast bird to the gray cat, who had stolen back into the room, turning away her head, for the mere smell of the pheasant was like an insult. Then, while the cat bore off her welcome spoils into a corner, she clutched a peach and raised her hand to fling it away through a gap in the roof of the room; but she did not carry out her purpose, for it occurred to her that Irene and little Philo, the son of the gate-keeper, might enjoy the luscious fruit; so she laid it back on the dish and took up the bread, for she was painfully hungry.

She was on the point of breaking the golden-brown cake, but acting on a rapid impulse she tossed it back on the trencher saying to herself: "At any rate I will owe him nothing; but I will not throw away the gifts of the gods as he threw away my violets, for that would be a sin. All is over between him and me, and if he appears to-day in the procession, and if he chooses to look at me again I will compel my eyes to avoid meeting his—aye, that I will, and will carry it through. But, Oh eternal gods! and thou above all, great Serapis, whom I heartily serve, there is another thing I cannot do without your aid. Help me, oh! help me to forget him, that my very thoughts may remain pure."

With these words she flung herself on her knees before the chest, pressed her brow against the hard wood, and strove to pray.

Only for one thing did she entreat the gods; for strength to forget the man who had betrayed her into losing her peace of mind.

But just as swift clouds float across the sky, distracting the labors of the star-gazer, who is striving to observe some remote planet—as the clatter of the street interrupts again and again some sweet song we fain would hear, marring it with its harsh discords—so again and again the image of the young Roman came across Klea's prayers for release from that very thought, and at last it seemed to her that she was like a man who strives to raise a block of stone by the exertion of his utmost strength, and who weary at last of lifting the stone is crushed to the earth by its weight; still she felt that, in spite of all her prayers and efforts, the enemy she strove to keep off only came nearer, and instead of flying from her, overmastered her soul with a grasp from which she could not escape.

Finally she gave up the unavailing struggle, cooled her burning face with cold water, and tightened the straps of her sandals to go to the temple; near the god himself she hoped she might in some degree recover the peace she could not find here.

Just at the door she met Irene, who told her that the singing-practice was put off, on account of the procession which was fixed for four hours after noon. And as Klea went towards the temple her sister called after her.

"Do not stay too long though, water will be wanted again directly for the libations."

"Then will you go alone to the work?" asked Klea; "there cannot be very much wanted, for the temple will soon be empty on account of the procession. A few jars-full will be enough. There is a cake of bread and a peach in there for you; I must keep the other for little Philo."

CHAPTER IV

Klea went quickly on towards the temple, without listening to Irene's excuses. She paid no heed to the worshippers who filled the forecourt, praying either with heads bent low or with uplifted arms or, if they were of Egyptian extraction, kneeling on the smooth stone pavement, for, even as she entered, she had already begun to turn in supplication to the divinity.

She crossed the great hall of the sanctuary, which was open only to the initiated and to the temple-servants, of whom she was one. Here all around her stood a crowd of slender columns, their shafts crowned with gracefully curved flower calyxes, like stems supporting lilies, over her head she saw in the ceiling an image of the midnight sky with the bright, unresting and ever-restful stars; the planets and fixed stars in their golden barks looked down on her silently. Yes! here were the twilight and stillness befitting a personal communion with the divinity.

The pillars appeared to her fancy like a forest of giant growth, and it seemed to her that the perfume of the incense emanated from the gorgeous floral capitals that crowned them; it penetrated her senses, which were rendered more acute by fasting and agitation, with a sort of intoxication. Her eyes were raised to heaven, her arms crossed over her bosom as she traversed this vast hall, and with trembling steps approached a smaller and lower chamber, where in the furthest and darkest background a curtain of heavy and costly material veiled the brazen door of the holy of holies.

Even she was forbidden to approach this sacred place; but to-day she was so filled with longing for the inspiring assistance of the god, that she went on to the holy of holies in spite of the injunction she had never yet broken, not to approach it. Filled with reverent awe she sank down close to the door of the sacred chamber, shrinking close into the angle formed between a projecting door-post and the wall of the great hall.

The craving desire to seek and find a power outside us as guiding the path of our destiny is common to every nation, to every man; it is as surely innate in every being gifted with reason—many and various as these are—as the impulse to seek a cause when we perceive an effect, to see when light visits the earth, or to hear when swelling waves of sound fall on our ear. Like every other gift, no doubt that of religious sensibility is bestowed in different degrees on different natures. In Klea it had always been strongly developed, and a pious mother had cultivated it by precept and example, while her father always had taught her one thing only: namely to be true, inexorably true, to others as to herself.

Afterwards she had been daily employed in the service of the god whom she was accustomed to regard as the greatest and most powerful of all the immortals, for often from a distance she had seen the curtain of the sanctuary pushed aside, and the statue of Serapis with the Kalathos on his head, and a figure of Cerberus at his feet, visible in the half-light of the holy of holies; and a ray of light, flashing through the darkness as by a miracle, would fall upon his brow and kiss his lips when his goodness was sung by the priests in hymns of praise. At other times the tapers by the side of the god would be lighted or extinguished spontaneously.

Then, with the other believers, she would glorify the great lord of the other world, who caused a new sun to succeed each that was extinguished, and made life grow up out of death; who resuscitated the dead, lifting them up to be equal with him, if on earth they had reverenced truth and were found faithful by the judges of the nether world.

Truth—which her father had taught her to regard as the best possession of life—was rewarded by Serapis above all other virtues; hearts were weighed before him in a scale against truth, and whenever Klea tried to picture the god in human form he wore the grave and mild features of her father, and she fancied him speaking in the words and tones of the man to whom she owed her being, who had been too early snatched from her, who had endured so much for righteousness' sake, and from whose lips she had never heard a single word that might not have beseemed the god himself. And, as she crouched closely in the dark angle by the holy of holies, she felt herself nearer to her father as well as to the god, and accused herself pitilessly, in that unmaidenly longings had stirred her heart, that she had been insincere to herself and Irene, nay in that if she could not succeed in tearing the image of the Roman from her heart she would be compelled either to deceive her sister or to sadden the innocent and careless nature of the impressionable child, whom she was accustomed to succor and cherish as a mother might. On her, even apparently light matters weighed oppressively, while Irene could throw off even grave and serious things, blowing them off as it were into the air, like a feather. She was like wet clay on which even the light touch of a butterfly leaves a mark, her sister like a mirror from which the breath that has dimmed it instantly and entirely vanishes.

"Great God!" she murmured in her prayer, "I feel as if the Roman had branded my very soul. Help thou me to efface the mark; help me to become as I was before, so that I may look again in Irene's eyes without concealment, pure and true, and that I may be able to say to myself, as I was wont, that I had thought and acted in such a way as my father would approve if he could know it."

She was still praying thus when the footsteps and voices of two men approaching the holy of holies startled her from her devotions; she suddenly became fully conscious of the fact that she was in a forbidden spot, and would be severely punished if she were discovered.

"Lock that door," cried one of the new-comers to his companion, pointing to the door which led from the prosekos into the pillared hall, "none, even of the initiated, need see what you are preparing here for us—"

Klea recognized the voice of the high-priest, and thought for a moment of stepping forward and confessing her guilt; but, though she did not usually lack courage, she did not do this, but shrank still more closely into her hiding-place, which was perfectly dark when the brazen door of the room; which had no windows, was closed. She now perceived that the curtain and door were opened which closed the inmost sanctuary, she heard one of the men twirling the stick which was to produce fire, saw the first gleam of light from it streaming out of the holy of holies, and then heard the blows of a hammer and the grating sound of a file.

The quiet sanctum was turned into a forge, but noisy as were the proceedings within, it seemed to Klea that the beating of her own heart was even louder than the brazen clatter of the tools wielded by Krates; he was one of the oldest of the priests of Serapis, who was chief in charge of the sacred vessels, who was wont never to speak to any one but the high-priest, and who was famous even among his Greek fellow-countrymen for the skill with which he could repair broken metal-work, make the securest locks, and work in silver and gold.

When the sisters first came into the temple five years since, Irene had been very much afraid of this man, who was so small as almost to be a dwarf, broad shouldered and powerfully knit, while his wrinkled face looked like a piece of rough cork-bark, and he was subject to a painful complaint in his feet which often prevented his walking; her fears had not vexed but only amused the priestly smith, who whenever he met the child, then eleven years old, would turn his lips up to his big red nose, roll his eyes, and grunt hideously to increase the terror that came over her.

He was not ill-natured, but he had neither wife nor child, nor brother, nor sister, nor friend, and every human being so keenly desires that others should have some feeling about him, that many a one would rather be feared than remain unheeded.

After Irene had got over her dread she would often entreat the old man—who was regarded as stern and inaccessible by all the other dwellers in the temple—in her own engaging and coaxing way to make a face for her, and he would do it and laugh when the little one, to his delight and her own, was terrified at it and ran away; and just lately when Irene, having hurt her foot, was obliged to keep her room for a few days, an unheard of thing had occurred: he had asked Klea with the greatest sympathy how her sister was getting on, and had given her a cake for her.

While Krates was at his work not a word passed between him and the high-priest. At length he laid down the hammer, and said:

"I do not much like work of this kind, but this, I think, is successful at any rate. Any temple-servant, hidden here behind the altar, can now light or extinguish the lamps without the illusion being detected by the sharpest. Go now and stand at the door of the great hall and speak the word."

Klea heard the high-priest accede to this request and cry in a chanting voice: "Thus he commands the night and it becomes day, and the extinguished taper and lo! it flames with brightness. If indeed thou art nigh, Oh Serapis! manifest thyself to us."

At these words a bright stream of light flashed from the holy of holies, and again was suddenly extinguished when the high-priest sang: "Thus showest thou thyself as light to the children of truth, but dost punish with darkness the children of lies."

"Again?" asked Krates in a voice which conveyed a desire that the answer might be 'No.'

"I must trouble you," replied the high-priest. "Good! the performance went much better this time. I was always well assured of your skill; but consider the particular importance of this affair. The two kings and the queen will probably be present at the solemnity, certainly Philometor and Cleopatra will, and their eyes are wide open; then the Roman who has already assisted four times at the procession will accompany them, and if I judge him rightly he, like many of the nobles of his nation, is one of those who can trust themselves when it is necessary to be content with the old gods of their fathers; and as regards the marvels we are able to display to them, they do not take them to heart like the poor in spirit, but measure and weigh them with a cool and unbiassed mind. People of that stamp, who are not ashamed to worship, who do not philosophize but only think just so much as is necessary for acting rightly, those are the worst contemners of every supersensual manifestation."

"And the students of nature in the Museum?" asked Krates. "They believe nothing to be real that they cannot see and observe."

"And for that very reason," replied the high-priest, "they are often singularly easy to deceive by your skill, since, seeing an effect without a cause, they are inclined to regard the invisible cause as something supersensual. Now, open the door again and let us get out by the side door; do you, this time, undertake the task of cooperating with Serapis yourself. Consider that Philometor will not confirm the donation of the land unless he quits the temple deeply penetrated by the greatness of our god. Would it be possible, do you think, to have the new censer ready in time for the birthday of King Euergetes, which is to be solemnly kept at Memphis?"

"We will see," replied Krates, "I must first put together the lock of the great door of the tomb of Apis, for so long as I have it in my workshop any one can open it who sticks a nail into the hole above the bar, and any one can shut it inside who pushes the iron bolt. Send to call me before the performance with the lights begins; I will come in spite of my wretched feet. As I have undertaken the thing I will carry it out, but for no other reason, for it is my opinion that even without such means of deception—"

"We use no deception," interrupted the high-priest, sternly rebuking his colleague. "We only present to short-sighted mortals the creative power of the divinity in a form perceptible and intelligible to their senses."

With these words the tall priest turned his back on the smith and quitted the hall by a side door; Krates opened the brazen door, and as he gathered together his tools he said to himself, but loud enough for Klea to hear him distinctly in her hiding-place:

"It may be right for me, but deceit is deceit, whether a god deceives a king or a child deceives a beggar."

"Deceit is deceit," repeated Klea after the smith when he had left the hall and she had emerged from her corner.

She stood still for a moment and looked round her. For the first time she observed the shabby colors on the walls, the damage the pillars had sustained in the course of years, and the loose slabs in the pavement.

The sweetness of the incense sickened her, and as she passed by an old man who threw up his arms in fervent supplication, she looked at him with a glance of compassion.

When she had passed out beyond the pylons enclosing the temple she turned round, shaking her head in a puzzled way as she gazed at it; for she knew that not a stone had been changed within the last hour, and yet it looked as strange in her eyes as some landscape with which we have become familiar in all the beauty of spring, and see once more in winter with its trees bare of leaves; or like the face of a woman which we thought beautiful under the veil which hid it, and which, when the veil is raised, we see to be wrinkled and devoid of charm.

When she had heard the smith's words, "Deceit is deceit," she felt her heart shrink as from a stab, and could not check the tears which started to her eyes, unused as they were to weeping; but as soon as she had repeated the stern verdict with her own lips her tears had ceased, and now she stood looking at the temple like a traveller who takes leave of a dear friend; she was excited, she breathed more freely, drew herself up taller, and then turned her back on the sanctuary of Serapis, proudly though with a sore heart.

Close to the gate-keeper's lodge a child came tottering towards her with his arms stretched up to her. She lifted him up, kissed him, and then asked the mother, who also greeted her, for a piece of bread, for her hunger was becoming intolerable. While she ate the dry morsel the child sat on her lap, following with his large eyes the motion of her hand and lips. The boy was about five years old, with legs so feeble that they could scarcely support the weight of his body, but he had a particularly sweet little face; certainly it was quite without expression, and it was only when he saw Klea coming that tiny Philo's eyes had lighted up with pleasure.

"Drink this milk," said the child's mother, offering the young girl an earthen bowl. "There is not much and I could not spare it if Philo would eat like other children, but it seems as if it hurt him to swallow. He drinks two or three drops and eats a mouthful, and then will take no more even if he is beaten."

"You have not been beating him again?" said Klea reproachfully, and drawing the child closer to her. "My husband—" said the woman, pulling at her dress in some confusion. "The child was born on a good day and in a lucky hour, and yet he is so puny and weak and will not learn to speak, and that provokes Pianchi."

"He will spoil everything again!" exclaimed Klea annoyed. "Where is he?"

"He was wanted in the temple."

"And is he not pleased that Philo calls him 'father,' and you 'mother,' and me by my name, and that he learns to distinguish many things?" asked the girl.

"Oh, yes of course," said the woman. "He says you are teaching him to speak just as if he were a starling, and we are very much obliged to you."

"That is not what I want," interrupted Klea. "What I wish is that you should not punish and scold the boy, and that you should be as glad as I am when you see his poor little dormant soul slowly waking up. If he goes on like this, the poor little fellow will be quite sharp and intelligent. What is my name, my little one?"

"Ke-ea," stammered the child, smiling at his friend. "And now taste this that I have in my hand; what is it?—I see you know. It is called—whisper in my ear. That's right, mil—mil-milk! to be sure, my tiny, it is milk. Now open your little mouth and say it prettily after me—once more—and again—say it twelve times quite right and I will give you a kiss—Now you have earned a pretty kiss—will you have it here or here? Well, and what is this? your ea-? Yes, your ear. And this?—your nose, that is right."

The child's eyes brightened more and more under this gentle teaching, and neither Klea nor her pupil were weary till, about an hour later, the re-echoing sound of a brass gong called her away. As she turned to go the little one ran after her crying; she took him in her arms and carried him back to his mother, and then went on to her own room to dress herself and her sister for the procession. On the way to the Pastophorium she recalled once more her expedition to the temple and her prayer there.

"Even before the sanctuary," said she to herself, "I could not succeed in releasing my soul from its burden—it was not till I set to work to loosen the tongue of the poor little child. Every pure spot, it seems to me, may be the chosen sanctuary of some divinity, and is not an infant's soul purer than the altar where truth is mocked at?"

In their room she found Irene; she had dressed her hair carefully and stuck the pomegranate-flower in it, and she asked Klea if she thought she looked well.

"You look like Aphrodite herself," replied Klea kissing her forehead. Then she arranged the folds of her sister's dress, fastened on the ornaments, and proceeded to dress herself. While she was fastening her sandals Irene asked her, "Why do you sigh so bitterly?" and Klea replied, "I feel as if I had lost my parents a second time."

CHAPTER V

The procession was over

At the great service which had been performed before him in the Greek Serapeum, Ptolemy Philometor had endowed the priests not with the whole but with a considerable portion of the land concerning which they had approached him with many petitions. After the court had once more quitted Memphis and the procession was broken up, the sisters returned to their room, Irene with crimson cheeks and a smile on her lips, Klea with a gloomy and almost threatening light in her eyes.

As the two were going to their room in silence a temple-servant called to Klea, desiring her to go with him to the high-priest, who wished to speak to her. Klea, without speaking, gave her water-jar to Irene and was conducted into a chamber of the temple, which was used for keeping the sacred vessels in. There she sat down on a bench to wait. The two men who in the morning had visited the Pastophorium had also followed in the procession with the royal family. At the close of the solemnities Publius had parted from his companion without taking leave, and without looking to the right or to the left, he had hastened back to the Pastophorium and to the cell of Serapion, the recluse.

The old man heard from afar the younger man's footstep, which fell on the earth with a firmer and more decided tread than that of the softly-stepping priests of Serapis, and he greeted him warmly with signs and words.

Publius thanked him coolly and gravely, and said, dryly enough and with incisive brevity:

"My time is limited. I propose shortly to quit Memphis, but I promised you to hear your request, and in order to keep my word I have come to see you; still—as I have said—only to keep my word. The water-bearers of whom you desired to speak to me do not interest me—I care no more about them than about the swallows flying over the house yonder."

"And yet this morning you took a long walk for Klea's sake," returned Serapion.

"I have often taken a much longer one to shoot a hare," answered the Roman. "We men do not pursue our game because the possession of it is any temptation, but because we love the sport, and there are sporting natures even among women. Instead of spears or arrows they shoot with flashing glances, and when they think they have hit their game they turn their back upon it. Your Klea is one of this sort, while the pretty little one I saw this morning looks as if she were very ready to be hunted, I however, no more wish to be the hunter of a young girl than to be her game. I have still three days to spend in Memphis, and then I shall turn my back forever on this stupid country."

"This morning," said Serapion, who began to suspect what the grievance might be which had excited the discontent implied in the Roman's speech, "This morning you appeared to be in less hurry to set out than now, so to me you seem to be in the plight of game trying to escape; however, I know Klea better than you do. Shooting is no sport of hers, nor will she let herself be hunted, for she has a characteristic which you, my friend Publius Scipio, ought to recognize and value above all others—she is proud, very proud; aye, and so she may be, scornful as you look—as if you would like to say 'how came a water-carrier of Serapis by her pride, a poor creature who is ill-fed and always engaged in service, pride which is the prescriptive right only of those, whom privilege raises above the common herd around them?—But this girl, you may take my word for it, has ample reason to hold her head high, not only because she is the daughter of free and noble parents and is distinguished by rare beauty, not because while she was still a child she undertook, with the devotion and constancy of the best of mothers, the care of another child—her own sister, but for a reason which, if I judge you rightly, you will understand better than many another young man; because she must uphold her pride in order that among the lower servants with whom unfortunately she is forced to work, she may never forget that she is a free and noble lady. You can set your pride aside and yet remain what you are, but if she were to do so and to learn to feel as a servant, she would presently become in fact what by nature she is not and by circumstances is compelled to be. A fine horse made to carry burdens becomes a mere cart-horse as soon as it ceases to hold up its head and lift its feet freely. Klea is proud because she must be proud; and if you are just you will not contemn the girl, who perhaps has cast a kindly glance at you—since the gods have so made you that you cannot fail to please any woman—and yet who must repel your approaches because she feels herself above being trifled with, even by one of the Cornelia gens, and yet too lowly to dare to hope that a man like you should ever stoop from your height to desire her for a wife. She has vexed you, of that there can be no doubt; how, I can only guess.

If, however, it has been through her repellent pride, that ought not to hurt you, for a woman is like a soldier, who only puts on his armor when he is threatened by an opponent whose weapons he fears."

The recluse had rather whispered than spoken these words, remembering that he had neighbors; and as he ceased the drops stood on his brow, for whenever any thing disturbed him he was accustomed to allow his powerful voice to be heard pretty loudly, and it cost him no small effort to moderate it for so long.

Publius had at first looked him in the face, and then had gazed at the ground, and he had heard Serapion to the end without interrupting him; but the color had flamed in his cheeks as in those of a schoolboy, and yet he was an independent and resolute youth who knew how to conduct himself in difficult straits as well as a man in the prime of life. In all his proceedings he was wont to know very well, exactly what he wanted, and to do without any fuss or comment whatever he thought right and fitting.

During the anchorite's speech the question had occurred to him, what did he in fact expect or wish of the water-bearer; but the answer was wanting, he felt somewhat uncertain of himself, and his uncertainty and dissatisfaction with himself increased as all that he heard struck him more and more. He became less and less inclined to let himself be thrown over by the young girl who for some days had, much against his will, been constantly in his thoughts, whose image he would gladly have dismissed from his mind, but who, after the recluse's speech, seemed more desirable than ever. "Perhaps you are right," he replied after a short silence, and he too lowered his voice, for a subdued tone generally provokes an equally subdued answer. "You know the maiden better than I, and if you describe her correctly it would be as well that I should abide by my decision and fly from Egypt, or, at any rate, from your protegees, since nothing lies before me but a defeat or a victory, which could bring me nothing but repentance. Klea avoided my eye to-day as if it shed poison like a viper's tooth, and I can have nothing more to do with her: still, might I be informed how she came into this temple? and if I can be of any service to her, I will-for your sake. Tell me now what you know of her and what you wish me to do."

The recluse nodded assent and beckoned Publius to come closer to him, and bowing down to speak into the Roman's ear, he said softly: "Are you in favor with the queen?" Publius, having said that he was, Serapion, with an exclamation of satisfaction, began his story.

"You learned this morning how I myself came into this cage, and that my father was overseer of the temple granaries. While I was wandering abroad he was deposed from his office, and would probably have died in prison, if a worthy man had not assisted him to save his honor and his liberty. All this does not concern you, and I may therefore keep it to myself; but this man was the father of Klea and Irene, and the enemy by whose instrumentality my father suffered innocently was the villain Eulaeus. You know—or perhaps indeed you may not know—that the priests have to pay a certain tribute for the king's maintenance; you know? To be sure, you Romans trouble yourselves more about matters of law and administration than the culture of the arts or the subtleties of thought. Well, it was my father's duty to pay these customs over to Eulaeus, who received them; but the beardless effeminate vermin, the glutton—may every peach he ever ate or ever is to eat turn to poison!—kept back half of what was delivered to him, and when the accountants found nothing but empty air in the king's stores where they hoped to find corn and woven goods, they raised an alarm, which of course came to the ears of the powerful thief at court before it reached those of my poor father. You called Egypt a marvellous country, or something like it; and so in truth it is, not merely on account of the great piles there that you call Pyramids and such like, but because things happen here which in Rome would be as impossible as moonshine at mid-day, or a horse with his tail at the end of his nose! Before a complaint could be laid against Eulaeus he had accused my father of the peculation, and before the Epistates and the assessor of the district had even looked at the indictment, their judgment on the falsely accused man was already recorded, for Eulaeus had simply bought their verdict just as a man buys a fish or a cabbage in the market. In olden times the goddess of justice was represented in this country with her eyes shut, but now she looks round on the world like a squinting woman who winks at the king with one eye, and glances with the other at the money in the hand of the accuser or the accused. My poor father was of course condemned and thrown into prison, where he was beginning to doubt the justice of the gods, when for his sake the greatest wonder happened, ever seen in this land of wonders since first the Greeks ruled in Alexandria. An honorable man undertook without fear of persons the lost cause of the poor condemned wretch, and never rested till he had restored him to honor and liberty. But imprisonment, disgrace and indignation had consumed the strength of the ill-used man as a worm eats into cedar wood, and he fell into a decline and died. His preserver, Klea's father, as the reward of his courageous action fared even worse; for here by the Nile virtues are punished in this world, as crimes are with you. Where injustice holds sway frightful things occur, for the gods seem to take the side of the wicked. Those who do not hope for a reward in the next world, if they are neither fools nor philosophers—which often comes to the same thing—try to guard themselves against any change in this.

"Philotas, the father of the two girls, whose parents were natives of Syracuse, was an adherent of the doctrines of Zeno—which have many supporters among you at Rome too—and he was highly placed as an official, for he was president of the Chrematistoi, a college of judges which probably has no parallel out of Egypt, and which has been kept up better than any other. It travels about from province to province stopping in the chief towns to administer justice. When an appeal is brought against the judgment of the court of justice belonging to any place—over which the Epistates of the district presides—the case is brought before the Chrematistoi, who are generally strangers alike to the accuser and accused; by them it is tried over again, and thus the inhabitants of the provinces are spared the journey to Alexandria or—since the country has been divided—to Memphis, where, besides, the supreme court is overburdened with cases.

"No former president of the Chrematistoi had ever enjoyed a higher reputation than Philotas. Corruption no more dared approach him than a sparrow dare go near a falcon, and he was as wise as he was just, for he was no less deeply versed in the ancient Egyptian law than in that of the Greeks, and many a corrupt judge reconsidered matters as soon as it became known that he was travelling with the Chrematistoi, and passed a just instead of an unjust sentence.

"Cleopatra, the widow of Epiphanes, while she was living and acting as guardian of her sons Philometor and Euergetes—who now reign in Memphis and Alexandria—held Philotas in the highest esteem and conferred on him the rank of 'relation to the king'; but she was just dead when this worthy man took my father's cause in hand, and procured his release from prison.

"The scoundrel Eulaeus and his accomplice Lenaeus then stood at the height of power, for the young king, who was not yet of age, let himself be led by them like a child by his nurse.

"Now as my father was an honest man, no one but Eulaeus could be the rascal, and as the Chrematistoi threatened to call him before their tribunal the miserable creature stirred up the war in Caelo-Syria against Antiochus Epiphanes, the king's uncle.

"You know how disgraceful for us was the course of that enterprise, how Philometor was defeated near Pelusium, and by the advice of Eulaeus escaped with his treasure to Samothrace, how Philometor's brother Euergetes was set up as king in Alexandria, how Antiochus took Memphis, and then allowed his elder nephew to continue to reign here as though he were his vassal and ward.

"It was during this period of humiliation, that Eulaeus was able to evade Philotas, whom he may very well have feared, as though his own conscience walked the earth on two legs in the person of the judge, with the sword of justice in his hand, and telling all men what a scoundrel he was.

"Memphis had opened her gates to Antiochus without offering much resistance, and the Syrian king, who was a strange man and was fond of mixing among the people as if he himself were a common man, applied to Philotas, who was as familiar with Egyptian manners and customs as with those of Greece, in order that he might conduct him into the halls of justice and into the market-places; and he made him presents as was his way, sometimes of mere rubbish and sometimes of princely gifts.

"Then when Philometor was freed by the Romans from the protection of the Syrian king, and could govern in Memphis as an independent sovereign, Eulaeus accused the father of these two girls of having betrayed Memphis into the hands of Antiochus, and never rested till the innocent man was deprived of his wealth, which was considerable, and sent with his wife to forced labor in the gold mines of Ethiopia.

"When all this occurred I had already returned to my cage here; but I heard from my brother Glaucus—who was captain of the watch in the palace, and who learned a good many things before other people did—what was going on out there, and I succeeded in having the daughters of Philotas secretly brought to this temple, and preserved from sharing their parents' fate. That is now five years ago, and now you know how it happens, that the daughters of a man of rank carry water for the altar of Serapis, and that I would rather an injury should be done to me than to them, and that I would rather see Eulaeus eating some poisonous root than fragrant peaches."

"And is Philotas still working in the mines?" asked the Roman, clenching his teeth with rage.

"Yes, Publius," replied the anchorite. "A 'yes' that it is easy to say, and it is just as easy too to clench one's fists in indignation—but it is hard to imagine the torments that must be endured by a man like Philotas; and a noble and innocent woman—as beautiful as Hera and Aphrodite in one—when they are driven to hard and unaccustomed labor under a burning sun by the lash of the overseer. Perhaps by this time they have been happy enough to die under their sufferings and their daughters are already orphans, poor children! No one here but the high-priest knows precisely who they are, for if Eulaeus were to learn the truth he would send them after their parents as surely as my name is Serapion."

"Let him try it!" cried Publius, raising his right fist threateningly.

"Softly, softly, my friend," said the recluse, "and not now only, but about everything which you under take in behalf of the sisters, for a man like

Eulaeus hears not only with his own ears but with those of thousand others, and almost everything that occurs at court has to go through his hands as epistolographer. You say the queen is well-disposed towards you. That is worth a great deal, for her husband is said to be guided by her will, and such a thing as Eulaeus cannot seem particularly estimable in Cleopatra's eyes if princesses are like other women—and I know them well."

"And even if he were," interrupted Publius with glowing cheeks, "I would bring him to ruin all the same, for a man like Philotas must not perish, and his cause henceforth is my own. Here is my hand upon it; and if I am happy in having descended from a noble race it is above all because the word of a son of the Cornelii is as good as the accomplished deed of any other man."

The recluse grasped the right hand the young man gave him and nodded to him affectionately, his eyes radiant, though moistened with joyful emotion. Then he hastily turned his back on the young man, and soon reappeared with a large papyrus-roll in his hand. "Take this," he said, handing it to the Roman, "I have here set forth all that I have told you, fully and truly with my own hand in the form of a petition. Such matters, as I very well know, are never regularly conducted to an issue at court unless they are set forth in writing. If the queen seems disposed to grant you a wish give her this roll, and entreat her for a letter of pardon. If you can effect this, all is won."

Publius took the roll, and once more gave his hand to the anchorite, who, forgetting himself for a moment, shouted out in his loud voice:

"May the gods bless thee, and by thy means work the release of the noblest of men from his sufferings! I had quite ceased to hope, but if you come to our aid all is not yet wholly lost."

CHAPTER VI

"Pardon me if I disturb you"

With these words the anchorite's final speech was interrupted by Eulaeus, who had come in to the Pastophorium softly and unobserved, and who now bowed respectfully to Publius.

"May I be permitted to enquire on what compact one of the noblest of the sons of Rome is joining hands with this singular personage?"

"You are free to ask," replied Publius shortly and drily, "but every one is not disposed to answer, and on the present occasion I am not. I will bid you farewell, Serapion, but not for long I believe."

"Am I permitted to accompany you?" asked Eulaeus.

"You have followed me without any permission on my part."

"I did so by order of the king, and am only fulfilling his commands in offering you my escort now."

"I shall go on, and I cannot prevent your following me."

"But I beg of you," said Eulaeus, "to consider that it would ill-become me to walk behind you like a servant."

"I respect the wishes of my host, the king, who commanded you to follow me," answered the Roman. "At the door of the temple however you can get into your chariot, and I into mine; an old courtier must be ready to carry out the orders of his superior."

"And does carry them out," answered Eulaeus with deference, but his eyes twinkled—as the forked tongue of a serpent is rapidly put out and still more rapidly withdrawn—with a flash first of threatening hatred, and then another of deep suspicion cast at the roll the Roman held in his hand.

Publius heeded not this glance, but walked quickly towards the acacia-grove; the recluse looked after the ill-matched pair, and as he watched the burly Eulaeus following the young man, he put both his hands on his hips, puffed out his fat cheeks, and burst into loud laughter as soon as the couple had vanished behind the acacias.

When once Serapion's midriff was fairly tickled it was hard to reduce it to calm again, and he was still laughing when Klea appeared in front of his cell some few minutes after the departure of the Roman. He was about to receive his young friend with a cheerful greeting, but, glancing at her face, he cried anxiously;

"You look as if you had met with a ghost; your lips are pale instead of red, and there are dark shades round your eyes. What has happened to you, child? Irene went with you to the procession, that I know. Have you had bad news of your parents? You shake your head. Come, child, perhaps you are thinking of some one more than you ought; how the color rises in your cheeks! Certainly handsome Publius, the Roman, must have looked into your eyes—a splendid youth is he—a fine young man—a capital good fellow—"

"Say no more on that subject," Klea exclaimed, interrupting her friend and protector, and waving her hand in the air as if to cut off the other half of Serapion's speech. "I can hear nothing more about him."

"Has he addressed you unbecomingly?" asked the recluse.

"Yes!" said Klea, turning crimson, and with a vehemence quite foreign to her usual gentle demeanor, "yes, he persecutes me incessantly with challenging looks."

"Only with looks?" said the anchorite. "But we may look even at the glorious sun and at the lovely flowers as much as we please, and they are not offended."

"The sun is too high and the soulless flowers too humble for a man to hurt them," replied Klea. "But the Roman is neither higher nor lower than I, the eye speaks as plain a language as the tongue, and what his eyes demand of me brings the blood to my cheeks and stirs my indignation even now when I only think of it."

"And that is why you avoid his gaze so carefully?"

"Who told you that?"

"Publius himself; and because he is wounded by your hard-heartedness he meant to quit Egypt; but I have persuaded him to remain, for if there is a mortal living from whom I expect any good for you and yours—"

"It is certainly not he," said Klea positively. "You are a man, and perhaps you now think that so long as you were young and free to wander about the world you would not have acted differently from him—it is a man's privilege; but if you could look into my soul or feel with the heart of a woman, you would think differently. Like the sand of the desert which is blown over the meadows and turns all the fresh verdure to a hideous brown—like a storm that transforms the blue mirror of the sea into a crisped chaos of black whirl pools and foaming ferment, this man's imperious audacity has cruelly troubled my peace of heart. Four times his eyes pursued me in the processions; yesterday I still did not recognize my danger, but to-day—I must tell you, for you are like a father to me, and who else in the world can I confide in?—to-day I was able to avoid his gaze, and yet all through long endless hours of the festival I felt his eyes constantly seeking mine. I should have been certain I was under no delusion, even if Publius Scipio—but what business has his name on my lips?—even if the Roman had not boasted to you of his attacks on a defenceless girl. And to think that you, you of all others, should have become his ally! But you would not, no indeed you would not, if you knew how I felt at the procession while I was looking down at the ground, and knew that his very look desecrated me like the rain that washed all the blossoms off the young vine-shoots last year. It was just as if he were drawing a net round my heart—but, oh! what a net! It was as if the flax on a distaff had been set on fire, and the flames spun out into thin threads, and the meshes knotted of the fiery yarn. I felt every thread and knot burning into my soul, and could not cast it off nor even defend myself. Aye! you may look grieved and shake your head, but so it was, and the scars hurt me still with a pain I cannot utter."

"But Klea," interrupted Serapion, "you are quite beside yourself—like one possessed. Go to the temple and pray, or, if that is of no avail, go to Asclepios or Anubis and have the demon cast out."

"I need none of your gods!" answered the girl in great agitation. "Oh! I wish you had left me to my fate, and that we had shared the lot of our parents, for what threatens us here is more frightful than having to sift gold-dust in the scorching sun, or to crush quartz in mortars. I did not come to you to speak about the Roman, but to tell you what the high-priest had just disclosed to me since the procession ended."

"Well?" asked Serapion eager and almost frightened, stretching out his neck to put his head near to the girl's, and opening his eyes so wide that the loose skin below them almost disappeared.

"First he told me," replied Klea, "how meagrely the revenues of the temple are supplied—"

"That is quite true," interrupted the anchorite, "for Antiochus carried off the best part of its treasure; and the crown, which always used to have money to spare for the sanctuaries of Egypt, now loads our estates with heavy tribute; but you, as it seems to me, were kept scantily enough, worse than meanly, for, as I know—since it passed through my hands—a sum was paid to the temple for your maintenance which would have sufficed to keep ten hungry sailors, not speak of two little pecking birds like you, and besides that you do hard service without any pay. Indeed it would be a more profitable speculation to steal a beggar's rags than to rob you! Well, what did the high-priest want?"

"He says that we have been fed and protected by the priesthood for five years, that now some danger threatens the temple on our account, and that we must either quit the sanctuary or else make up our minds to take the place of the twin-sisters Arsinoe and Doris who have hitherto been employed in singing the hymns of lamentation, as Isis and Nephthys, by the bier of the deceased god on the occasion of the festivals of the dead, and in pouring out the libations with wailing and outcries when the bodies were brought into the temple to be blessed. These maidens, Asclepiodorus says, are now too old and ugly for these duties, but the temple is bound to maintain them all their lives. The funds of the temple are insufficient to support two more serving maidens besides them and us, and so Arsinoe and Doris are only to pour out the libations for the future, and we are to sing the laments, and do the wailing."

"But you are not twins!" cried Serapion. "And none but twins—so say the ordinances—may mourn for Osiris as Isis and Neplithys."

"They will make twins of us!" said Klea with a scornful turn of her lip. "Irene's hair is to be dyed black like mine, and the soles of her sandals are to be made thicker to make her as tall as I am."

"They would hardly succeed in making you smaller than you are, and it is easier to make light hair dark than dark hair light," said Serapion with hardly suppressed rage. "And what answer did you give to these exceedingly original proposals?"

"The only one I could very well give. I said no—but I declared myself ready, not from fear, but because we owe much to the temple, to perform any other service with Irene, only not this one."

"And Asclepiodorus?"

"He said nothing unkind to me, and preserved his calm and polite demeanor when I contradicted him, though he fixed his eyes on me several times in astonishment as if he had discovered in me something quite new and strange. At last he went on to remind me how much trouble the temple singing-master had taken with us, how well my low voice went with Irene's high one, how much applause we might gain by a fine performance of the hymns of lamentation, and how he would be willing, if we undertook the duties of the twin-sisters, to give us a better dwelling and more abundant food. I believe he has been trying to make us amenable by supplying us badly with food, just as falcons are trained by hunger. Perhaps I am doing him an injustice, but I feel only too much disposed to-day to think the worst of him and of the other fathers. Be that as it may; at any rate he made me no further answer when I persisted in my refusal, but dismissed me with an injunction to present myself before him again in three days' time, and then to inform him definitively whether I would conform to his wishes, or if I proposed to leave the temple. I bowed and went towards the door, and was already on the threshold when he called me back once more, and said: 'Remember your parents and their fate!' He spoke solemnly, almost threateningly, but he said no more and hastily turned his back on me. What could he mean to convey by this warning? Every day and every hour I think of my father and mother, and keep Irene in mind of them."

The recluse at these words sat muttering thoughtfully to himself for a few minutes with a discontented air; then he said gravely:

"Asclepiodorus meant more by his speech than you think. Every sentence with which he dismisses a refractory subordinate is a nut of which the shell must be cracked in order to get at the kernel. When he tells you to remember your parents and their sad fate, such words from his lips, and under the present circumstances, can hardly mean anything else than this: that you should not forget how easily your father's fate might overtake you also, if once you withdrew yourselves from the protection of the temple. It was not for nothing that Asclepiodorus—as you yourself told me quite lately, not more than a week ago I am sure—reminded you how often those condemned to forced labor in the mines had their relations sent after them. Ah! child, the words of Asclepiodorus have a sinister meaning. The calmness and pride, with which you look at me make me fear for you, and yet, as you know, I am not one of the timid and tremulous. Certainly what they propose to you is repulsive enough, but submit to it; it is to be hoped it will not be for long. Do it for my sake and for that of poor Irene, for though you might know how to assert your dignity and take care of yourself outside these walls in the rough and greedy world, little Irene never could. And besides, Klea, my sweetheart, we have now found some one, who makes your concerns his, and who is great and powerful—but oh! what are three clays? To think of seeing you turned out—and then that you may be driven with a dissolute herd in a filthy boat down to the burning south, and dragged to work which kills first the soul and then the body! No, it is not possible! You will never let this happen to me—and to yourself and Irene; no, my darling, no, my pet, my sweetheart, you cannot, you will not do so. Are you not my children, my daughters, my only joy? and you, would you go away, and leave me alone in my cage, all because you are so proud!"

The strong man's voice failed him, and heavy drops fell from his eyes one after another down his beard, and on to Klea's arm, which he had grasped with both hands.

The girl's eyes too were dim with a mist of warm tears when she saw her rough friend weeping, but she remained firm and said, as she tried to free her hand from his:

"You know very well, father Serapion, that there is much to tie me to this temple; my sister, and you, and the door-keeper's child, little Philo. It would be cruel, dreadful to have to leave you; but I would rather endure that and every other grief than allow Irene to take the place of Arsinoe or the black Doris as wailing woman. Think of that bright child, painted and kneeling at the foot of a bier and groaning and wailing in mock sorrow! She would become a living lie in human form, an object of loathing to herself, and to me—who stand in the place of a mother to her—from morning till night a martyrizing reproach! But what do I care about myself—I would disguise myself as the goddess without even making a wry face, and be led to the bier, and wail and groan so that every hearer would be cut to the heart, for my soul is already possessed by sorrow; it is like the eyes of a man, who has gone blind from the constant flow of salt tears. Perhaps singing the hymns of lamentation might relieve my soul, which is as full of sorrow as an overbrimming cup; but I would rather that a cloud should for ever darken the sun, that mists should hide every star from my eyes, and the air I breathe be poisoned by black smoke than disguise her identity, and darken her soul, or let her clear laugh be turned to shrieks of lamentation, and her fresh and childlike spirit be buried in gloomy mourning. Sooner will I go way with her and leave even you, to perish with my parents in misery and anguish than see that happen, or suffer it for a moment."

As she spoke Serapion covered his face with his hands, and Klea, hastily turning away from him, with a deep sigh returned to her room.

Irene was accustomed when she heard her step to hasten to meet her, but to-day no one came to welcome her, and in their room, which was beginning to be dark as twilight fell, she did not immediately catch sight of her sister, for she was sitting all in a heap in a corner of the room, her face hidden, in her hands and weeping quietly.

"What is the matter?" asked Klea, going tenderly up to the weeping child, over whom she bent, endeavoring to raise her.

"Leave me," said Irene sobbing; she turned away from her sister with an impatient gesture, repelling her caress like a perverse child; and then, when Klea tried to soothe her by affectionately stroking her hair, she sprang up passionately exclaiming through her tears:

"I could not help crying—and, from this hour, I must always have to cry. The Corinthian Lysias spoke to me so kindly after the procession, and you—you don't care about me at all and leave me alone all this time in this nasty dusty hole! I declare I will not endure it any longer, and if you try to keep me shut up, I will run away from this temple, for outside it is all bright and pleasant, and here it is dingy and horrid!"

CHAPTER VII

In the very midst of the white wall with its bastions and ramparts, which formed the fortifications of Memphis, stood the old palace of the kings, a stately structure built of bricks, recently plastered, and with courts, corridors, chambers and halls without number, and veranda-like out-buildings of gayly-painted wood, and a magnificent pillared banqueting-hall in the Greek style. It was surrounded by verdurous gardens, and a whole host of laborers tended the flower-beds and shady alleys, the shrubs and the trees; kept the tanks clean and fed the fish in them; guarded the beast-garden, in which quadrupeds of every kind, from the heavy-treading elephant to the light-footed antelope, were to be seen, associated with birds innumerable of every country and climate.

A light white vapor rose from the splendidly fitted bath-house, loud barkings resounded from the dog-kennels, and from the long array of open stables came the neighing of horses with the clatter and stamp of hoofs, and the rattle of harness and chains. A semicircular building of new construction adjoining the old palace was the theatre, and many large tents for the bodyguard, for ambassadors and scribes, as well as others, serving as banqueting-halls for the various court-officials, stood both within the garden and outside its enclosing walls. A large space leading from the city itself to the royal citadel was given up to the soldiers, and there, by the side of the shady court-yards, were the houses of the police-guard and the prisons. Other soldiers were quartered in tents close to the walls of the palace itself. The clatter of their arms and the words of command, given in Greek, by their captain, sounded out at this particular instant, and up into the part of the buildings occupied by the queen; and her apartments were high up, for in summer time Cleopatra preferred to live in airy tents, which stood among the broad-leaved trees of the south and whole groves of flowering shrubs, on the level roof of the palace, which was also lavishly decorated with marble statues. There was only one way of access to this retreat, which was fitted up with regal splendor; day and night it was fanned by currents of soft air, and no one could penetrate uninvited to disturb the queen's retirement, for veteran guards watched at the foot of the broad stair that led to the roof, chosen from the Macedonian "Garde noble," and owing as implicit obedience to Cleopatra as to the king himself. This select corps was now, at sunset, relieving guard, and the queen could hear the words spoken by the officers in command and the clatter of the shields against the swords as they rattled on the pavement, for she had come out of her tent into the open air, and stood gazing towards the west, where the glorious hues of the sinking sun flooded the bare, yellow limestone range of the Libyan hills, with their innumerable tombs and the separate groups of pyramids; while the wonderful coloring gradually tinged with rose-color the light silvery clouds that hovered in the clear sky over the valley of Memphis, and edged them as with a rile of living gold.

The queen stepped out of her tent, accompanied by a young Greek girl—the fair Zoe, daughter of her master of the hunt Zenodotus, and Cleopatra's favorite lady-in-waiting—but though she looked towards the west, she stood unmoved by the magic of the glorious scene before her; she screened her eyes with her hand to shade them from the blinding rays, and said:

"Where can Cornelius be staying! When we mounted our chariots before the temple he had vanished, and as far as I can see the road in the quarters of Sokari and Serapis I cannot discover his vehicle, nor that of Eulaeus who was to accompany him. It is not very polite of him to go off in this way without taking leave; nay, I could call it ungrateful, since I had proposed to tell him on our way home all about my brother Euergetes, who has arrived to-day with his friends. They are not yet acquainted, for Euergetes was living in Cyrene when Publius Cornelius Scipio landed in Alexandria. Stay! do you see a black shadow out there by the vineyard at Kakem; That is very likely he; but no—you are right, it is only some birds, flying in a close mass above the road. Can you see nothing more? No!—and yet we both have sharp young eyes. I am very curious to know whether Publius Scipio will like Euergetes. There can hardly be two beings more unlike, and yet they have some very essential points in common."

"They are both men," interrupted Zoe, looking at the queen as if she expected cordial assent to this proposition.

"So they are," said Cleopatra proudly. "My brother is still so young that, if he were not a king's son, he would hardly have outgrown the stage of boyhood, and would be a lad among other Epheboi,—[Youths above 18 were so called]—and yet among the oldest there is hardly a man who is his superior in strength of will and determined energy. Already, before I married Philometor, he had clutched Alexandria and Cyrene, which by right should belong to my husband, who is the eldest of us three, and that was not very brotherly conduct—and indeed we had other grounds for being angry with him; but when I saw him again for the first time after nine months of separation I was obliged to forget them all, and welcome him as though he had done nothing but good to me and his brother—who is my husband, as is the custom of the families of Pharaohs and the usage of our race. He is a young Titan, and no one would be astonished if he one day succeeded in piling Pelion upon Ossa. I know well enough how wild he can often be, how unbridled and recalcitrant beyond all bounds; but I can easily pardon him, for the same bold blood flows in my own veins, and at the root of all his excesses lies power, genuine and vigorous power. And this innate pith and power are just the very thing we most admire in men, for it is the one gift which the gods have dealt out to us with a less liberal hand than to men. Life indeed generally dams its overflowing current, but I doubt whether this will be the case with the stormy torrent of his energy; at any rate men such as he is rush swiftly onwards, and are strong to the end, which sooner or later is sure to overtake them; and I infinitely prefer such a wild torrent to a shallow brook flowing over a plain, which hurts no one, and which in order to prolong its life loses itself in a misty bog. He, if any one, may be forgiven for his tumultuous career; for when he pleases my brother's great qualities charm old and young alike, and are as conspicuous and as remarkable as his faults—nay, I will frankly say his crimes. And who in Greece or Egypt surpasses him in grasp and elevation of mind?"

"You may well be proud of him," replied Zoe. "Not even Publius Scipio himself can soar to the height reached by Euergetes."

"But, on the other hand, Euergetes is not gifted with the steady, calm self-reliance of Cornelius. The man who should unite in one person the good qualities of those two, need yield the palm, as it seems to me, not even to a god!"

"Among us imperfect mortals he would indeed be the only perfect one," replied Zoe. "But the gods could not endure the existence of a perfect man, for then they would have to undertake the undignified task of competing with one of their own creatures."

"Here, however, comes one whom no one can accuse!" cried the young queen, as she hastened to meet a richly dressed woman, older than herself, who came towards her leading her son, a pale child of two years old. She bent down to the little one, tenderly but with impetuous eagerness, and was about to clasp him in her arms, but the fragile child, which at first had smiled at her, was startled; he turned away from her and tried to hide his little face in the dress of his nurse—a lady of rank-to whom he clung with both hands. The queen threw herself on her knees before him, took hold of his shoulder, and partly by coaxing and partly by insistence strove to induce him to quit the sheltering gown and to turn to her; but although the lady, his wet-nurse, seconded her with kind words of encouragement, the terrified child began to cry, and resisted his mother's caresses with more and more vehemence the more passionately she tried to attract and conciliate him. At last the nurse lifted him up, and was about to hand him to his mother, but the wilful little boy cried more than before, and throwing his arms convulsively round his nurse's neck he broke into loud cries.

In the midst of this rather unbecoming struggle of the mother against the child's obstinacy, the clatter of wheels and of horses' hoofs rang through the court-yard of the palace, and hardly had the sound reached the queen's ears than she turned away from the screaming child, hurried to the parapet of the roof, and called out to Zoe:

"Publius Scipio is here; it is high time that I should dress for the banquet. Will that naughty child not listen to me at all? Take him away, Praxinoa, and understand distinctly that I am much dissatisfied with you. You estrange my own child from me to curry favor with the future king. That is base, or else it proves that you have no tact, and are incompetent for the office entrusted to you. The office of wet-nurse you duly fulfilled, but I shall now look out for another attendant for the boy. Do not answer me! no tears! I have had enough of that with the child's screaming." With these words, spoken loudly and passionately, she turned her back on Praxinoa—the wife of a distinguished Macedonian noble, who stood as if petrified—and retired into her tent, where branched lamps had just been placed on little tables of elegant workmanship. Like all the other furniture in the queen's dressing-tent these were made of gleaming ivory, standing out in fine relief from the tent-cloth which was sky-blue woven with silver lilies and ears of corn, and from the tiger-skins which covered all the cushions, while white woollen carpets, bordered with a waving scroll in blue, were spread on the ground.

The queen threw herself on a seat in front of her dressing-table, and sat staring at herself in a mirror, as if she now saw her face and her abundant, reddish-fair hair for the first time; then she said, half turning to Zoe and half to her favorite Athenian waiting-maid, who stood behind her with her other women:

"It was folly to dye my dark hair light; but now it may remain so, for Publius Scipio, who has no suspicion of our arts, thought this color pretty and uncommon, and never will know its origin. That Egyptian headdress with the vulture's head which the king likes best to see me in, the young Greek Lysias and the Roman too, call barbaric, and so every one must call it who is not interested in the Egyptians. But to-night we are only ourselves, so I will wear the chaplet of golden corn with sapphire grapes. Do you think, Zoe, that with that I could wear the dress of transparent bombyx silk that came yesterday from Cos? But no, I will not wear that, for it is too slight a tissue, it hides nothing and I am now too thin for it to become me. All the lines in my throat show, and my elbows are quite sharp—altogether I am much thinner. That comes of incessant worry, annoyance, and anxiety. How angry I was yesterday at the council, because my husband will always give way and agree and try to be pleasant; whenever a refusal is necessary I have to interfere, unwilling as I am to do it, and odious as it is to me always to have to stir up discontent, disappointment, and disaffection, to take things on myself and to be regarded as hard and heartless in order that my husband may preserve undiminished the doubtful glory of being the gentlest and kindest of men and princes. My son's having a will of his own leads to agitating scenes, but even that is better than that Philopator should rush into everybody's arms. The first thing in bringing up a boy should be to teach him to say 'no.' I often say 'yes' myself when I should not, but I am a woman, and yielding becomes us better than refusal—and what is there of greater importance to a woman than to do what becomes her best, and to seem beautiful?

"I will decide on this pale dress, and put over it the net-work of gold thread with sapphire knots; that will go well with the head-dress. Take care with your comb, Thais, you are hurting me! Now—I must not chatter any more. Zoe, give me the roll yonder; I must collect my thoughts a little before I go down to talk among men at the banquet. When we have just come from visiting the realm of death and of Serapis, and have been reminded of the immortality of the soul and of our lot in the next world, we are glad to read through what the most estimable of human thinkers has said concerning such things. Begin here, Zoe."

Cleopatra's companion, thus addressed, signed to the unoccupied waiting-women to withdraw, seated herself on a low cushion opposite the queen, and began to read with an intelligent and practised intonation; the reading went on for some time uninterrupted by any sound but the clink of metal ornaments, the rustle of rich stuffs, the trickle of oils or perfumes as they were dropped into the crystal bowls, the short and whispered questions of the women who were attiring the queen, or Cleopatra's no less low and rapid answers.

All the waiting-women not immediately occupied about the queen's person—perhaps twenty in all, young and old-ranged themselves along the sides of the great tent, either standing or sitting on the ground or on cushions, and awaiting the moment when it should be their turn to perform some service, as motionless as though spellbound by the mystical words of a magician. They only made signs to each other with their eyes and fingers, for they knew that the queen did not choose to be disturbed when she was being read to, and that she never hesitated to cast aside anything or anybody that crossed her wishes or inclinations, like a tight shoe or a broken lutestring.

Her features were irregular and sharp, her cheekbones too strongly developed, and the lips, behind which her teeth gleamed pearly white—though too widely set—were too full; still, so long as she exerted her great powers of concentration, and listened with flashing eyes, like those of a prophetess, and parted lips to the words of Plato, her face had worn an indescribable glow of feeling, which seemed to have come upon her from a higher and better world, and she had looked far more beautiful than now when she was fully dressed, and when her women crowded round leer—Zoe having laid aside the Plato—with loud and unmeasured flattery.

Cleopatra delighted in being thus feted, and, in order to enjoy the adulation of a throng, she would always when dressing have a great number of women to attend her toilet; mirrors were held up to her on every side, a fold set right, and the jewelled straps of her sandals adjusted.

One praised the abundance of her hair, another the slenderness of her form, the slimness of her ankles, and the smallness of her tiny hands and feet. One maiden remarked to another—but loud enough to be heard—on the brightness of her eyes which were clearer than the sapphires on her brow, while the Athenian waiting-woman, Thais, declared that Cleopatra had grown fatter, for her golden belt was less easy to clasp than it had been ten days previously.

The queen presently signed to Zoe, who threw a little silver ball into a bowl of the same metal, elaborately wrought and decorated, and in a few minutes the tramp of the body-guard was audible outside the door of the tent.

Cleopatra went out, casting a rapid glance over the roof—now brightly illuminated with cressets and torches—and the white marble statues that gleamed out in relief against the dark clumps of shrubs; and then, without even looking at the tent where her children were asleep, she approached the litter, which had been brought up to the roof for her by the young Macedonian nobles. Zoe and Thais assisted her to mount into it, and her ladies, waiting-women, and others who had hurried out of the other tents, formed a row on each side of the way, and hailed their mistress with loud cries of admiration and delight as she passed by, lifted high above them all on the shoulders of her bearers. The diamonds in the handle of her feather-fan sparkled brightly as Cleopatra waved a gracious adieu to her women, an adieu which did not fail to remind them how infinitely beneath her were those she greeted. Every movement of her hand was full of regal pride, and her eyes, unveiled and untempered, were radiant with a young woman's pleasure in a perfect toilet, with satisfaction in her own person, and with the anticipation of the festive hours before her.

The litter disappeared behind the door of the broad steps that led up to the roof, and Thais, sighing softly, said to herself, "If only for once I could ride through the air in just such a pretty shell of colored and shining mother-of-pearl, like a goddess! carried aloft by young men, and hailed and admired by all around me! High up there the growing Selene floats calmly and silently by the tiny stars, and just so did she ride past in her purple robe with her torch-bearers and flames and lights-past us humble creatures, and between the tents to the banquet—and to what a banquet, and what guests! Everything up here greets her with rejoicing, and I could almost fancy that among those still marble statues even the stern face of Zeno had parted its lips, and spoken flattering words to her. And yet poor little Zoe, and the fair-haired Lysippa, and the black-haired daughter of Demetrius, and even I, poor wretch, should be handsomer, far handsomer than she, if we could dress ourselves with fine clothes and jewels for which kings would sell their kingdoms; if we could play Aphrodite as she does, and ride off in a shell borne aloft on emerald-green glass to look as if it were floating on the waves; if dolphins set with pearls and turquoises served us for a footstool, and white ostrich-plumes floated over our heads, like the silvery clouds that float over Athens in the sky of a fine spring day. The transparent tissue that she dared not put on would well become me! If only that were true which Zoe was reading yesterday, that the souls of men were destined to visit the earth again and again in new forms! Then perhaps mine might some day come into the world in that of a king's child. I should not care to be a prince, so much is expected of him, but a princess indeed! That would be lovely!"

These and such like were Thais' dreams, while Zoe stood outside the tent of the royal children with her cousin, the chief-attendant of prince Philopator, carrying on an eager conversation in a low tone. The child's nurse from time to time dried her eyes and sobbed bitterly as she said: "My own baby, my other children, my husband and our beautiful house in Alexandria—I left them all to suckle and rear a prince. I have sacrificed happiness, freedom, and my nights'-sleep for the sake of the queen and of this child, and how am I repaid for all this? As if I were a lowborn wench instead of the daughter and wife of noble men; this woman, half a child still, scarcely yet nineteen, dismisses me from her service before you and all her ladies every ten days! And why? Because the ungoverned blood of her race flows in her son's veins, and because he does not rush into the arms of a mother who for days does not ask for him at all, and never troubles herself about him but in some idle moment when she has gratified every other whim. Princes distribute favor or disgrace with justice only so long as they are children. The little one understands very well what I am to him, and sees what Cleopatra is. If I could find it in my heart to ill-use him in secret, this mother—who is not fit to be a mother—would soon have her way. Hard as it would be to me so soon to leave the poor feeble little child, who has grown as dear to my soul as my own—aye and closer, even closer, as I may well say—this time I will do it, even at the risk of Cleopatra's plunging us into ruin, my husband and me, as she has done to so many who have dared to contravene her will."

The wet-nurse wept aloud, but Zoe laid her hand on the distressed woman's shoulder, and said soothingly: "I know you have more to submit to from Cleopatra's humors than any of us all, but do not be overhasty. Tomorrow she will send you a handsome present, as she so often has done after being unkind; and though she vexes and hurts you again and again, she will try to make up for it again and again till, when this year is over, your attendance on the prince will be at an end, and you can go home again to your own family. We all have to practise patience; we live like people dwelling in a ruinous house with to-day a stone and to-morrow a beam threatening to fall upon our heads. If we each take calmly whatever befalls us our masters try to heal our wounds, but if we resist may the gods have mercy on us! for Cleopatra is like a strung bow, which sets the arrow flying as soon as a child, a mouse, a breath of air even touches it—like an over-full cup which brims over if a leaf, another drop, a single tear falls into it. We should, any one of us, soon be worn out by such a life, but she needs excitement, turmoil and amusement at every hour. She comes home late from a feast, spends barely six hours in disturbed slumber, and has hardly rested so long as it takes a pebble to fall to the ground from a crane's claw before we have to dress her again for another meal. From the council-board she goes to hear some learned discourse, from her books in the temple to sacrifice and prayer, from the sanctuary to the workshops of artists, from pictures and statues to the audience-chamber, from a reception of her subjects and of foreigners to her writing-room, from answering letters to a procession and worship once more, from the sacred services back again to her dressing-tent, and there, while she is being attired she listens to me while I read the most profound works—and how she listens! not a word escapes her, and her memory retains whole sentences. Amid all this hurry and scurry her spirit must need be like a limb that is sore from violent exertion, and that is painfully tender to every rough touch. We are to her neither more nor less than the wretched flies which we hit at when they trouble us, and may the gods be merciful to those on whom this queen's hand may fall! Euergetes cleaves with the sword all that comes in his way. Cleopatra stabs with the dagger, and her hand wields the united power of her own might and of her yielding husband's. Do not provoke her. Submit to what you cannot avert; just as I never complain when, if I make a mistake in reading, she snatches the book from my hand, or flings it at my feet. But I, of course, have only myself to fear for, and you have your husband and children as well."

Praxinoa bowed her head at these words in sad assent, and said:

"Thank you for those words! I always think only from my heart, and you mostly from your head. You are right, this time again there is nothing for me to do but to be patient; but when I have fulfilled the duties here, which I undertook, and am at home again, I will offer a great sacrifice to Asclepias and Hygiea, like a person recovered from a severe illness; and one thing I know: that I would rather be a poor girl, grinding at a mill, than change with this rich and adored queen who, in order to enjoy her life to the utmost, carelessly and restlessly hurries past all that our mortal lot has best to offer. Terrible, hideous to me seems such an existence with no rest in it! and the heart of a mother which is so much occupied with other things that she cannot win the love of her child, which blossoms for every hired nurse, must be as waste as the desert! Rather would I endure anything—everything—with patience than be such a queen!"

CHAPTER VIII

"What! No one to come to meet me?" asked the queen, as she reached the foot of the last flight of porphyry steps that led into the ante-chamber to the banqueting-hall, and, looking round, with an ominous glance, at the chamberlains who had accompanied her, she clinched her small fist. "I arrive and find no one here!"

The "No one" certainly was a figure of speech, since more than a hundred body-guards-Macedonians in rich array of arms-and an equal number of distinguished court-officials were standing on the marble flags of the vast hall, which was surrounded by colonnades, while the star-spangled night-sky was all its roof; and the court-attendants were all men of rank, dignified by the titles of fathers, brothers, relatives, friends and chief-friends of the king.

These all received the queen with a many-voiced "Hail!" but not one of them seemed worthy of Cleopatra's notice. This crowd was less to her than the air we breathe in order to live—a mere obnoxious vapor, a whirl of dust which the traveller would gladly avoid, but which he must nevertheless encounter in order to proceed on his way.

The queen had expected that the few guests, invited by her selection and that of her brother Euergetes to the evening's feast, would have welcomed her here at the steps; she thought they would have seen her—as she felt herself—like a goddess borne aloft in her shell, and that she might have exulted in the admiring astonishment of the Roman and of Lysias, the Corinthian: and now the most critical instant in the part she meant to play that evening had proved a failure, and it suggested itself to her mind that she might be borne back to her roof-tent, and be floated down once more when she was sure of the presence of the company. But there was one thing she dreaded more even than pain and remorse, and that was any appearance of the ridiculous; so she only commanded the bearers to stand still, and while the master of the ceremonies, waiving his dignity, hurried off to announce to her husband that she was approaching, she signed to the nobles highest in rank to approach, that she might address a few gracious words to them, with distant amiability. Only a few however, for the doors of thyia wood leading into the banqueting hall itself, presently opened, and the king with his friends came forward to meet Cleopatra.

"How were we to expect you so early?" cried Philometor to his wife.

"Is it really still early?" asked the queen, "or have I only taken you by surprise, because you had forgotten to expect me?"

"How unjust you are!" replied the king. "Must you now be told that, come as early as you will, you always come too late for my desires."

"But for ours," cried Lysias, "neither too early nor too late, but at the very right time—like returning health and happiness, or the victor's crown."

"Health as taking the place of sickness?" asked Cleopatra, and her eyes sparkled keenly and merrily. "I perfectly understand Lysias," said Publius, intercepting the Greek. "Once, on the field of Mars, I was flung from my horse, and had to lie for weeks on my couch, and I know that there is no more delightful sensation than that of feeling our departed strength returning as we recover. He means to say that in your presence we must feel exceptionally well."

"Nay rather," interrupted Lysias, "our queen seems to come to us like returning health, since so long as she was not in our midst we felt suffering and sick for longing. Thy presence, Cleopatra, is the most effectual remedy, and restores us to our lost health."

Cleopatra politely lowered her fan, as if in thanks, thus rapidly turning the stick of it in her hand, so as to make the diamonds that were set in it sparkle and flash. Then she turned to the friends, and said:

"Your words are most amiable, and your different ways of expressing your meaning remind me of two gems set in a jewel, one of which sparkles because it is skilfully cut, and reflects every light from its mirrorlike facets, while the other shines by its genuine and intrinsic fire. The genuine and the true are one, and the Egyptians have but one word for both, and your kind speech, my Scipio—but I may surely venture to call you Publius—your kind speech, my Publius seems to me to be truer than that of your accomplished friend, which is better adapted to vainer ears than mine. Pray, give me your hand."

The shell in which she was sitting was gently lowered, and, supported by Publius and her husband, the queen alighted and entered the banqueting-hall, accompanied by her guests.

As soon as the curtains were closed, and when Cleopatra had exchanged a few whispered words with her husband, she turned again to the Roman, who had just been joined by Eulaeus, and said:

"You have come from Athens, Publius, but you do not seem to have followed very closely the courses of logic there, else how could it be that you, who regard health as the highest good—that you, who declared that you never felt so well as in my presence—should have quitted me so promptly after the procession, and in spite of our appointment? May I be allowed to ask what business—"

"Our noble friend," answered Eulaeus, bowing low, but not allowing the queen to finish her speech, "would seem to have found some particular charm in the bearded recluses of Serapis, and to be seeking among them the key-stone of his studies at Athens."

"In that he is very right," said the queen. "For from them he can learn to direct his attention to that third division of our existence, concerning which least is taught in Athens—I mean the future—"

"That is in the hands of the gods," replied the Roman. "It will come soon enough, and I did not discuss it with the anchorite. Eulaeus may be informed that, on the contrary, everything I learned from that singular man in the Serapeum bore reference to the things of the past."

"But how can it be possible," said Eulaeus, "that any one to whom Cleopatra had offered her society should think so long of anything else than the beautiful present?"

"You indeed have good reason," retorted Publius quickly, "to enter the lists in behalf of the present, and never willingly to recall the past."

"It was full of anxiety and care," replied Eulaeus with perfect self-possession. "That my sovereign lady must know from her illustrious mother, and from her own experience; and she will also protect me from the undeserved hatred with which certain powerful enemies seem minded to pursue me. Permit me, your majesty, not to make my appearance at the banquet until later. This noble gentleman kept me waiting for hours in the Serapeum, and the proposals concerning the new building in the temple of Isis at Philae must be drawn up and engrossed to-day, in order that they may be brought to-morrow before your royal husband in council and your illustrious brother Euergetes—"

"You have leave, interrupted Cleopatra."

As soon as Eulaeus had disappeared, the queen went closer up to Publius, and said:

"You are annoyed with this man—well, he is not pleasant, but at any rate he is useful and worthy. May I ask whether you only feel his personality repugnant to you, or whether actual circumstances have given rise to your aversion—nay, if I have judged rightly, to a very bitterly hostile feeling against him?"

"Both," replied Publius. "In this unmanly man, from the very first, I expected to find nothing good, and I now know that, if I erred at all, it was in his favor. To-morrow I will ask you to spare me an hour when I can communicate to your majesty something concerning him, but which is too repulsive and sad to be suitable for telling in an evening devoted to enjoyment. You need not be inquisitive, for they are matters that belong to the past, and which concern neither you nor me."

The high-steward and the cup-bearer here interrupted this conversation by calling them to table, and the royal pair were soon reclining with their guests at the festal board.

Oriental splendor and Greek elegance were combined in the decorations of the saloon of moderate size, in which Ptolemy Philometor was wont to prefer to hold high-festival with a few chosen friends. Like the great reception-hall and the men's hall-with its twenty doors and lofty porphyry columns—in which the king's guests assembled, it was lighted from above, since it was only at the sides that the walls—which had no windows—and a row of graceful alabaster columns with Corinthian acanthus-capitals supported a narrow roof; the centre of the hall was quite uncovered. At this hour, when it was blazing with hundreds of lights, the large opening, which by day admitted the bright sunshine, was closed over by a gold net-work, decorated with stars and a crescent moon of rock-crystal, and the meshes were close enough to exclude the bats and moths which at night always fly to the light. But the illumination of the king's banqueting-hall made it almost as light as day, consisting of numerous lamps with many branches held up by lovely little figures of children in bronze and marble. Every joint was plainly visible in the mosaic of the pavement, which represented the reception of Heracles into Olympus, the feast of the gods, and the astonishment of the amazed hero at the splendor of the celestial banquet; and hundreds of torches were reflected in the walls of polished yellow marble, brought from Hippo Regius; these were inlaid by skilled artists with costly stones, such as lapis lazuli and malachite, crystals, blood-stone, jasper, agates and chalcedony, to represent fruit-pieces and magnificent groups of game or of musical instruments; while the pilasters were decorated with masks of the tragic and comic Muses, torches, thyrsi wreathed with ivy and vine, and pan-pipes. These were wrought in silver and gold, and set with costly marbles, and they stood out from the marble background like metal work on a leather shield, or the rich ornamentation on a sword-sheath. The figures of a Dionysiac procession, forming the frieze, looked down upon the feasters—a fine relievo that had been designed and modelled for Ptolemy Soter by the sculptor Bryaxis, and then executed in ivory and gold.

Everything that met the eye in this hall was splendid, costly, and above all of a genial aspect, even before Cleopatra had come to the throne; and she—here as in her own apartments—had added the busts of the greatest Greek philosophers and poets, from Thales of Miletus down to Strato, who raised chance to fill the throne of God, and from Hesiod to Callimachus; she too had placed the tragic mask side by side with the comic, for at her table—she was wont to say—she desired to see no one who could not enjoy grave and wise discourse more than eating, drinking, and laughter.

Instead of assisting at the banquet, as other ladies used, seated on a chair or at the foot of her husband's couch, she reclined on a couch of her own, behind which stood busts of Sappho the poetess, and Aspasia the friend of Pericles.

Though she made no pretensions to be regarded as a philosopher nor even as a poetess, she asserted her right to be considered a finished connoisseur in the arts of poetry and music; and if she preferred reclining to sitting how should she have done otherwise, since she was fully aware how well it became her to extend herself in a picturesque attitude on her cushions, and to support her head on her arm as it rested on the back of her couch; for that arm, though not strictly speaking beautiful, always displayed the finest specimens of Alexandrian workmanship in gem-cutting and goldsmiths' work.

But, in fact, she selected a reclining posture particularly for the sake of showing her feet; not a woman in Egypt or Greece had a smaller or more finely formed foot than she. For this reason her sandals were so made that when she stood or walked they protected only the soles of her feet, and her slender white toes with the roseate nails and their polished white half-moons were left uncovered.

At the banquet she put off her shoes altogether, as the men did; hiding her feet at first however, and not displaying them till she thought the marks left on her tender skin by the straps of the sandals had completely disappeared.

Eulaeus was the greatest admirer of these feet; not, as he averred, on account of their beauty, but because the play of the queen's toes showed him exactly what was passing in her mind, when he was quite unable to detect what was agitating her soul in the expression of her mouth and eyes, well practised in the arts of dissimulation.

Nine couches, arranged three and three in a horseshoe, invited the guests to repose, with their arms of ebony and cushions of dull olive-green brocade, on which a delicate pattern of gold and silver seemed just to have been breathed.

The queen, shrugging her shoulders, and, as it would seem, by no means agreeably surprised at something, whispered to the chamberlain, who then indicated to each guest the place he was to occupy. To the right of the central group reclined the queen, and her husband took his place to the left; the couch between the royal pair, destined for their brother Euergetes, remained unoccupied.

On one of the three couches which formed the right-hand angle with those of the royal family, Publius found a place next to Cleopatra; opposite to him, and next the king, was Lysias the Corinthian. Two places next to him remained vacant, while on the side by the Roman reclined the brave and prudent Hierax, the friend of Ptolemy Euergetes and his most faithful follower.

While the servants strewed the couches with rose leaves, sprinkled perfumed waters, and placed by the couch of each guest a small table-made of silver and of a slab of fine, reddish-brown porphyry, veined with white-the king addressed a pleasant greeting to each guest, apologizing for the smallness of the number.

"Eulaeus," he said, "has been forced to leave us on business, and our royal brother is still sitting over his books with Aristarchus, who came with him from Alexandria; but he promised certainly to come."

"The fewer we are," replied Lysias, bowing low, "the more honorable is the distinction of belonging to so limited a number of your majesty's most select associates."

"I certainly think we have chosen the best from among the good," said the queen. "But even the small number of friends I had invited must have seemed too large to my brother Euergetes, for he—who is accustomed to command in other folks' houses as he does in his own—forbid the chamberlain to invite our learned friends—among whom Agatharchides, my brothers' and my own most worthy tutor, is known to you—as well as our Jewish friends who were present yesterday at our table, and whom I had set down on my list. I am very well satisfied however, for I like the number of the Muses; and perhaps he desired to do you, Publius, particular honor, since we are assembled here in the Roman fashion. It is in your honor, and not in his, that we have no music this evening; you said that you did not particularly like it at a banquet. Euergetes himself plays the harp admirably. However, it is well that he is late in coming as usual, for the day after tomorrow is his birthday, and he is to spend it here with us and not in Alexandria; the priestly delegates assembled in the Bruchion are to come from thence to Memphis to wish him joy, and we must endeavor to get up some brilliant festival. You have no love for Eulaeus, Publius, but he is extremely skilled in such matters, and I hope he will presently return to give us his advice."

"For the morning we will have a grand procession," cried the king. "Euergetes delights in a splendid spectacle, and I should be glad to show him how much pleasure his visit has given us."

The king's fine features wore a most winning expression as he spoke these words with heart-felt warmth, but his consort said thoughtfully: "Aye! if only we were in Alexandria—but here, among all the Egyptian people—"

CHAPTER IX

A loud laugh re-echoing from the marble walls of the state-room interrupted the queen's speech; at first she started, but then smiled with pleasure as she recognized her brother Euergetes, who, pushing aside the chamberlains, approached the company with an elderly Greek, who walked by his side.

"By all the dwellers on Olympus! By the whole rabble of gods and beasts that live in the temples by the Nile!" cried the new-comer, again laughing so heartily that not only his fat cheeks but his whole immensely stout young frame swayed and shook. "By your pretty little feet, Cleopatra, which could so easily be hidden, and yet are always to be seen—by all your gentle virtues, Philometor, I believe you are trying to outdo the great Philadelphus or our Syrian uncle Antiochus, and to get up a most unique procession; and in my honor! Just so! I myself will take a part in the wonderful affair, and my sturdy person shall represent Eros with his quiver and bow. Some Ethiopian dame must play the part of my mother Aphrodite; she will look the part to perfection, rising from the white sea-foam with her black skin. And what do you think of a Pallas with short woolly hair; of the Charities with broad, flat Ethiopian feet; and an Egyptian, with his shaven head mirroring the sun, as Phoebus Apollo?"

With these words the young giant of twenty years threw himself on the vacant couch between his brother and sister, and, after bowing, not without dignity, to the Roman, whom his brother named to him, he called one of the young Macedonians of noble birth who served at the feast as cup-bearers, had his cup filled once and again and yet a third time, drinking it off quickly and without setting it down; then he said in a loud tone, while he pushed his hands through his tossed, light brown hair, till it stood straight up in the air from his broad temples and high brow:

"I must make up for what you have had before I came.—Another cup-full Diocleides."

"Wild boy!" said Cleopatra, holding up her finger at him half in jest and half in grave warning. "How strange you look!"

"Like Silenus without the goat's hoofs," answered Euergetes. "Hand me a mirror here, Diocleides; follow the eyes of her majesty the queen, and you will be sure to find one. There is the thing! And in fact the picture it shows me does not displease me. I see there a head on which besides the two crowns of Egypt a third might well find room, and in which there is so much brains that they might suffice to fill the skulls of four kings to the brim. I see two vulture's eyes which are always keen of sight even when their owner is drunk, and that are in danger of no peril save from the flesh of these jolly cheeks, which, if they continue to increase so fast, must presently exclude the light, as the growth of the wood encloses a piece of money stuck into a rift in a tree-or as a shutter, when it is pushed to, closes up a window. With these hands and arms the fellow I see in the mirror there could, at need, choke a hippopotamus; the chain that is to deck this neck must be twice as long as that worn by a well-fed Egyptian priest. In this mirror I see a man, who is moulded out of a sturdy clay, baked out of more unctuous and solid stuff than other folks; and if the fine creature there on the bright surface wears a transparent robe, what have you to say against it, Cleopatra? The Ptolemaic princes must protect the import trade of Alexandria, that fact was patent even to the great son of Lagus; and what would become of our commerce with Cos if I did not purchase the finest bombyx stuffs, since those who sell it make no profits out of you, the queen—and you cover yourself, like a vestal virgin, in garments of tapestry. Give me a wreath for my head—aye and another to that, and new wine in the cup! To the glory of Rome and to your health, Publius Cornelius Scipio, and to our last critical conjecture, my Aristarchus—to subtle thinking and deep drinking!"

"To deep thinking and subtle drinking!" retorted the person thus addressed, while he raised the cup, looked into the wine with his twinkling eyes and lifted it slowly to his nose—a long, well-formed and slightly aquiline nose—and to his thin lips.

"Oh! Aristarchus," exclaimed Euergetes, and he frowned. "You please me better when you clear up the meaning of your poets and historians than when you criticise the drinking-maxims of a king. Subtle drinking is mere sipping, and sipping I leave to the bitterns and other birds that live content among the reeds. Do you understand me? Among reeds, I say—whether cut for writing, or no."

"By subtle drinking," replied the great critic with perfect indifference, as he pushed the thin, gray hair from his high brow with his slender hand. "By subtle drinking I mean the drinking of choice wine, and did you ever taste anything more delicate than this juice of the vines of Anthylla that your illustrious brother has set before us? Your paradoxical axiom commends you at once as a powerful thinker and as the benevolent giver of the best of drinks."

"Happily turned," exclaimed Cleopatra, clapping her hands, "you here see, Publius, a proof of the promptness of an Alexandrian tongue."

"Yes!" said Euergetes, "if men could go forth to battle with words instead of spears the masters of the Museum in Alexander's city, with Aristarchus at their head, they might rout the united armies of Rome and Carthage in a couple of hours."

"But we are not now in the battle-field but at a peaceful meal," said the king, with suave amiability. "You did in fact overhear our secret Euergetes, and mocked at my faithful Egyptians, in whose place I would gladly set fair Greeks if only Alexandria still belonged to me instead of to you.—However, a splendid procession shall not be wanting at your birthday festival."

"And do you really still take pleasure in these eternal goose-step performances?" asked Euergetes, stretching himself out on his couch, and folding his hands to support the back of his head. "Sooner could I accustom myself to the delicate drinking of Aristarchus than sit for hours watching these empty pageants. On two conditions only can I declare myself ready and willing to remain quiet, and patiently to dawdle through almost half a day, like an ape in a cage: First, if it will give our Roman friend Publius Cornelius Scipio any pleasure to witness such a performance—though, since our uncle Antiochus pillaged our wealth, and since we brothers shared Egypt between us, our processions are not to be even remotely compared to the triumphs of Roman victors—or, secondly, if I am allowed to take an active part in the affair."

"On my account, Sire," replied Publius, "no procession need be arranged, particularly not such a one as I should here be obliged to look on at."

"Well! I still enjoy such things," said Cleopatra's husband. "Well-arranged groups, and the populace pleased and excited are a sight I am never tired of."

"As for me," cried Cleopatra, "I often turn hot and cold, and the tears even spring to my eyes, when the shouting is loudest. A great mass of men all uniting in a common emotion always has a great effect. A drop, a grain of sand, a block of stone are insignificant objects, but millions of them together, forming the sea, the desert or the pyramids, constitute a sublime whole. One man alone, shouting for joy, is like a madman escaped from an asylum, but when thousands of men rejoice together it must have a powerful effect on the coldest heart. How is it that you, Publius Scipio, in whom a strong will seems to me to have found a peculiarly happy development, can remain unmoved by a scene in which the great collective will of a people finds its utterance?"

"Is there then any expression of will, think you," said the Roman, "in this popular rejoicing? It is just in such circumstances that each man becomes the involuntary mimic and duplicate of his neighbor; while I love to make my own way, and to be independent of everything but the laws and duties laid upon me by the state to which I belong."

"And I," said Euergetes, "from my childhood have always looked on at processions from the very best places, and so it is that fortune punishes me now with indifference to them and to everything of the kind; while the poor miserable devil who can never catch sight of anything more than the nose or the tip of a hair or the broad back of those who take part in them, always longs for fresh pageants. As you hear, I need have no consideration for Publius Scipio in this, willing as I should be to do so. Now what would you say, Cleopatra, if I myself took a part in my procession—I say mine, since it is to be in my honor; that really would be for once something new and amusing."

"More new and amusing than creditable, I think," replied Cleopatra dryly.

"And yet even that ought to please you," laughed Euergetes. "Since, besides being your brother, I am your rival, and we would sooner see our rivals lower themselves than rise."

"Do not try to justify yourself by such words," interrupted the king evasively, and with a tone of regret in his soft voice. "We love you truly; we are ready to yield you your dominion side by side with ours, and I beg you to avoid such speeches even in jest, so that bygones may be bygones."

"And," added Cleopatra, "not to detract from your dignity as a king and your fame as a sage by any such fool's pranks."

"Madam teacher, do you know then what I had in my mind? I would appear as Alcibiades, followed by a train of flute-playing women, with Aristarchus to play the part of Socrates. I have often been told that he and I resemble each other—in many points, say the more sincere; in every point, say the more polite of my friends."

At these words Publius measured with his eye the frame of the royal young libertine, enveloped in transparent robes; and recalling to himself, as he gazed, a glorious statue of that favorite of the Athenians, which he had seen in the Ilissus, an ironical smile passed over his lips. It was not unobserved by Euergetes and it offended him, for there was nothing he liked better than to be compared to the nephew of Pericles; but he suppressed his annoyance, for Publius Cornelius Scipio was the nearest relative of the most influential men of Rome, and, though he himself wielded royal power, Rome exercised over him the sovereign will of a divinity.

Cleopatra noticed what was passing in her brother's mind, and in order to interrupt his further speech and to divert his mind to fresh thoughts, she said cheerfully:

"Let us then give up the procession, and think of some other mode of celebrating your birthday. You, Lysias, must be experienced in such matters, for Publius tells me that you were the leader in all the games of Corinth. What can we devise to entertain Euergetes and ourselves?"

The Corinthian looked for a moment into his cup, moving it slowly about on the marble slab of the little table at his side, between an oyster pasty and a dish of fresh asparagus; and then he said, glancing round to win the suffrages of the company:

"At the great procession which took place under Ptolemy Philadelphus—Agatharchides gave me the description of it, written by the eye-witness Kallixenus, to read only yesterday—all kinds of scenes from the lives of the gods were represented before the people. Suppose we were to remain in this magnificent palace, and to represent ourselves the beautiful groups which the great artists of the past have produced in painting or sculpture; but let us choose those only that are least known."

"Splendid," cried Cleopatra in great excitement, "who can be more like Heracles than my mighty brother there—the very son of Alcmene, as Lysippus has conceived and represented him? Let us then represent the life of Heracles from grand models, and in every case assign to Euergetes the part of the hero."

"Oh! I will undertake it," said the young king, feeling the mighty muscles of his breast and arms, "and you may give me great credit for assuming the part, for the demi-god who strangled the snakes was lacking in the most important point, and it was not without due consideration that Lysippus represented him with a small head on his mighty body; but I shall not have to say anything."

"If I play Omphale will you sit at my feet?" asked Cleopatra.

"Who would not be willing to sit at those feet?" answered Euergetes. "Let us at once make further choice among the abundance of subjects offered to us, but, like Lysias, I would warn you against those that are too well-known."

"There are no doubt things commonplace to the eye as well as to the ear," said Cleopatra. "But what is recognized as good is commonly regarded as most beautiful."

"Permit me," said Lysias, "to direct your attention to a piece of sculpture in marble of the noblest workmanship, which is both old and beautiful, and yet which may be known to few among you. It exists on the cistern of my father's house at Corinth, and was executed many centuries since by a great artist of the Peloponnesus. Publius was delighted with the work, and it is in fact beautiful beyond description. It is an exquisite representation of the marriage of Heracles and Hebe—of the hero, raised to divinity, with sempiternal youth. Will Your Majesty allow yourself to be led by Pallas Athene and your mother Alcmene to your nuptials with Hebe?"

"Why not?" said Euergetes. "Only the Hebe must be beautiful. But one thing must be considered; how are we to get the cistern from your father's house at Corinth to this place by to-morrow or next day? Such a group cannot be posed from memory without the original to guide us; and though the story runs that the statue of Serapis flew from Sinope to Alexandria, and though there are magicians still at Memphis—"

"We shall not need them," interrupted Publius, "while I was staying as a guest in the house of my friend's parents—which is altogether more magnificent than the old castle of King Gyges at Sardis—I had some gems engraved after this lovely group, as a wedding-present for my sister. They are extremely successful, and I have them with me in my tent."

"Have you a sister?" asked the queen, leaning over towards the Roman. "You must tell me all about her."

"She is a girl like all other girls," replied Publius, looking down at the ground, for it was most repugnant to his feelings to speak of his sister in the presence of Euergetes.

"And you are unjust like all other brothers," said Cleopatra smiling, "and I must hear more about her, for"—and she whispered the words and looked meaningly at Publius—"all that concerns you must interest me."

During this dialogue the royal brothers had addressed themselves to Lysias with questions as to the marriage of Heracles and Hebe, and all the company were attentive to the Greek as he went on: "This fine work does not represent the marriage properly speaking, but the moment when the bridegroom is led to the bride. The hero, with his club on his shoulder, and wearing the lion's skin, is led by Pallas Athene, who, in performing this office of peace, has dropped her spear and carries her helmet in her hand; they are accompanied by his mother Alcmene, and are advancing towards the bride's train. This is headed by no less a personage than Apollo himself, singing the praises of Hymenaeus to a lute. With him walks his sister Artemis and behind them the mother of Hebe, accompanied by Hermes, the messenger of the gods, as the envoy of Zeus. Then follows the principal group, which is one of the most lovely works of Greek art that I am acquainted with. Hebe comes forward to meet her bridegroom, gently led on by Aphrodite, the queen of love. Peitho, the goddess of persuasion, lays her hand on the bride's arm, imperceptibly urging her forward and turning away her face; for what she had to say has been said, and she smiles to herself, for Hebe has not turned a deaf ear to her voice, and he who has once listened to Peitho must do what she desires."

"And Hebe?" asked Cleopatra.

"She casts down her eyes, but lifts up the arm on which the hand of Peitho rests with a warning movement of her fingers, in which she holds an unopened rose, as though she would say; 'Ah! let me be—I tremble at the man'—or ask: 'Would it not be better that I should remain as I am and not yield to your temptations and to Aphrodite's power?' Oh! Hebe is exquisite, and you, O Queen! must represent her!"

"I!" exclaimed Cleopatra. "But you said her eyes were cast down."

"That is from modesty and timidity, and her gait must also be bashful and maidenly. Her long robe falls to her feet in simple folds, while Peitho holds hers up saucily, between her forefinger and thumb, as if stealthily dancing with triumph over her recent victory. Indeed the figure of Peitho would become you admirably."

"I think I will represent Peitho," said the queen interrupting the Corinthian. "Hebe is but a bud, an unopened blossom, while I am a mother, and I flatter myself I am something of a philosopher—"

"And can with justice assure yourself," interrupted Aristarchus, "that with every charm of youth you also possess the characters attributed to Peitho, the goddess, who can work her spells not only on the heart but on the intellect also. The maiden bud is as sweet to look upon as the rose, but he who loves not merely color but perfume too—I mean refreshment, emotion and edification of spirit—must turn to the full-blown flower; as the rose—growers of lake Moeris twine only the buds of their favorite flower into wreaths and bunches, but cannot use them for extracting the oil of imperishable fragrance; for that they need the expanded blossom. Represent Peitho, my Queen! the goddess herself might be proud of such a representative."

"And if she were so indeed," cried Cleopatra, "how happy am I to hear such words from the lips of Aristarchus. It is settled—I play Peitho. My companion Zoe may take the part of Artemis, and her grave sister that of Pallas Athene. For the mother's part we have several matrons to choose from; the eldest daughter of Epitropes appears to me fitted for the part of Aphrodite; she is wonderfully lovely."

"Is she stupid too?" asked Euergetes. "That is also an attribute of the ever-smiling Cypria."

"Enough so, I think, for our purpose," laughed Cleopatra. "But where are we to find such a Hebe as you have described, Lysias? The daughter of Alimes the Arabarch is a charming child."

"But she is brown, as brown as this excellent wine, and too thoroughly Egyptian," said the high-steward, who superintended the young Macedonian cup-bearers; he bowed deeply as he spoke, and modestly drew the queen's attention to his own daughter, a maiden of sixteen. But Cleopatra objected, that she was much taller than herself, and that she would have to stand by the Hebe, and lay her hand on her arm.

Other maidens were rejected on various grounds, and Euergetes had already proposed to send off a carrier-pigeon to Alexandria to command that some fair Greek girl should be sent by an express quadriga to Memphis— where the dark Egyptian gods and men flourish, and are more numerous than the fair race of Greeks—when Lysias exclaimed:

"I saw to-day the very girl we want, a Hebe that might have stepped out from the marble group at my father's, and have been endued with life and warmth and color by some god. Young, modest, rose and white, and just about as tall as Your Majesty. If you will allow me, I will not tell you who she is, till after I have been to our tent to fetch the gems with the copies of the marble."

"You will find them in an ivory casket at the bottom of my clothes-chest," said Publius; "here is the key."

"Make haste," cried the queen, "for we are all curious to hear where in Memphis you discovered your modest, rose and white Hebe."

CHAPTER X

An hour had slipped by with the royal party, since Lysias had quitted the company; the wine-cups had been filled and emptied many times; Eulaeus had rejoined the feasters, and the conversation had taken quite another turn, since the whole of the company were not now equally interested in the same subject; on the contrary, the two kings were discussing with Aristarchus the manuscripts of former poets and of the works of the sages, scattered throughout Greece, and the ways and means of obtaining them or of acquiring exact transcripts of them for the library of the Museum. Hierax was telling Eulaeus of the last Dionysiac festival, and of the representation of the newest comedy in Alexandria, and Eulaeus assumed the appearance— not unsuccessfully—of listening with both ears, interrupting him several times with intelligent questions, bearing directly on what he had said, while in fact his attention was exclusively directed to the queen, who had taken entire possession of the Roman Publius, telling him in a low tone of her life— which was consuming her strength—of her unsatisfied affections, and her enthusiasm for Rome and for manly vigor. As she spoke her cheeks glowed and her eyes sparkled, for the more exclusively she kept the conversation in her own hands the better she thought she was being entertained; and Publius, who was nothing less than talkative, seldom interrupted her, only insinuating a flattering word now and then when it seemed appropriate; for he remembered the advice given him by the anchorite, and was desirous of winning the good graces of Cleopatra.

In spite of his sharp ears Eulaeus could understand but little of their whispered discourse, for King Euergetes' powerful voice sounded loud above the rest of the conversation; but Eulaeus was able swiftly to supply the links between the disjointed sentences, and to grasp the general sense, at any rate, of what she was saying. The queen avoided wine, but she had the power of intoxicating herself, so to speak, with her own words, and now just as her brothers and Aristarchus were at the height of their excited and eager question and answer—she raised her cup, touched it with her lips and handed it to Publius, while at the same time she took hold of his.

The young Roman knew well enough all the significance of this hasty action; it was thus that in his own country a woman when in love was wont to exchange her cup with her lover, or an apple already bitten by her white teeth.

Publius was seized with a cold shudder—like a wanderer who carelessly pursues his way gazing up at the moon and stars, and suddenly perceives an abyss yawning; at his feet. Recollections of his mother and of her warnings against the seductive wiles of the Egyptian women, and particularly of this very woman, flashed through his mind like lightning; she was looking at him—not royally by any means, but with anxious and languishing gaze, and he would gladly have kept his eyes fixed on the ground, and have left the cup untouched; but her eye held his fast as though fettering it with ties and bonds; and to put aside the cup seemed to the most fearless son of an unconquered nation a deed too bold to be attempted. Besides, how could he possibly repay this highest favor with an affront that no woman could ever forgive—least of all a Cleopatra?

Aye, many a life's happiness is tossed away and many a sin committed, because the favor of women is a grace that does honor to every man, and that flatters him even when it is bestowed by the unloved and unworthy. For flattery is a key to the heart, and when the heart stands half open the voice of the tempter is never wanting to whisper: "You will hurt her feelings if you refuse."

These were the deliberations which passed rapidly and confusedly through the young Roman's agitated brain, as he took the queen's cup and set his lips to the same spot that hers had touched. Then, while he emptied the cup in long draughts, he felt suddenly seized by a deep aversion to the over-talkative, overdressed and capricious woman before him, who thus forced upon him favors for which he had not sued; and suddenly there rose before his soul the image, almost tangibly distinct, of the humble water-bearer; he saw Klea standing before him and looking far more queenly as, proud and repellent, she avoided his gaze, than the sovereign by his side could ever have done, though crowned with a diadem.

Cleopatra rejoiced to mark his long slow draught, for she thought the Roman meant to imply by it that he could not cease to esteem himself happy in the favor she had shown him. She did not take her eyes off him, and observed with pleasure that his color changed to red and white; nor did she notice that Eulaeus was watching, with a twinkle in his eyes, all that was going on between her and Publius. At last the Roman set down the cup, and tried with some confusion to reply to her question as to how he had liked the flavor of the wine.

"Very fine—excellent—" at last he stammered out, but he was no longer looking at Cleopatra but at Euergetes, who just then cried out loudly:

"I have thought over that passage for hours, I have given you all my reasons and have let you speak, Aristarchus, but I maintain my opinion, and whoever denies it does Homer an injustice; in this place 'siu' must be read instead of 'iu'."

Euergetes spoke so vehemently that his voice outshouted all the other guests; Publius however snatched at his words, to escape the necessity for feigning sentiments he could not feel; so he said, addressing himself half to the speaker and half to Cleopatra:

"Of what use can it be to decide whether it is one or the other—'iu' or 'siu'. I find many things justifiable in other men that are foreign to my own nature, but I never could understand how an energetic and vigorous man, a prudent sovereign and stalwart drinker—like you, Euergetes—can sit for hours over flimsy papyrus-rolls, and rack his brains to decide whether this or that in Homer should be read in one way or another."

"You exercise yourself in other things," replied Euergetes. "I consider that part of me which lies within this golden fillet as the best that I have, and I exercise my wits on the minutest and subtlest questions just as I would try the strength of my arms against the sturdiest athletes. I flung five into the sand the last time I did so, and they quake now when they see me enter the gymnasium of Timagetes. There would be no strength in the world if there were no obstacles, and no man would know that he was strong if he could meet with no resistance to overcome. I for my part seek such exercises as suit my idiosyncrasy, and if they are not to your taste I cannot help it. If you were to set these excellently dressed crayfish before a fine horse he would disdain them, and could not understand how foolish men could find anything palatable that tasted so salt. Salt, in fact, is not suited to all creatures! Men born far from the sea do not relish oysters, while I, being a gourmand, even prefer to open them myself so that they may be perfectly fresh, and mix their liquor with my wine."

"I do not like any very salt dish, and am glad to leave the opening of all marine produce to my servants," answered Publius. "Thereby I save both time and unnecessary trouble."

"Oh! I know!" cried Euergetes. "You keep Greek slaves, who must even read and write for you. Pray is there a market where I may purchase men, who, after a night of carousing, will bear our headache for us? By the shores of the Tiber you love many things better than learning."

"And thereby," added Aristarchus, "deprive yourselves of the noblest and subtlest of pleasures, for the purest enjoyment is ever that which we earn at the cost of some pains and effort."

"But all that you earn by this kind of labor," returned Publius, "is petty and unimportant. It puts me in mind of a man who removes a block of stone in the sweat of his brow only to lay it on a sparrow's feather in order that it may not be carried away by the wind."

"And what is great—and what is small?" asked Aristarchus. "Very opposite opinions on that subject may be equally true, since it depends solely on us and our feelings how things appear to us—whether cold or warm; lovely or repulsive—and when Protagoras says that 'man is the measure of all things,' that is the most acceptable of all the maxims of the Sophists; moreover the smallest matter—as you will fully appreciate—acquires an importance all the greater in proportion as the thing is perfect, of which it forms a part. If you slit the ear of a cart-horse, what does it signify? but suppose the same thing were to happen to a thoroughbred horse, a charger that you ride on to battle!

"A wrinkle or a tooth more or less in the face of a peasant woman matters little, or not at all, but it is quite different in a celebrated beauty. If you scrawl all over the face with which the coarse finger of the potter has decorated a water-jar, the injury to the wretched pot is but small, but if you scratch, only with a needle's point, that gem with the portraits of Ptolemy and Arsinoe, which clasps Cleopatra's robe round her fair throat, the richest queen will grieve as though she had suffered some serious loss.

"Now, what is there more perfect or more worthy to be treasured than the noblest works of great thinkers and great poets.

"To preserve them from injury, to purge them from the errors which, in the course of time, may have spotted their immaculate purity, this is our task; and if we do indeed raise blocks of stone it is not to weight a sparrow's feather that it may not be blown away, but to seal the door which guards a precious possession, and to preserve a gem from injury.

"The chatter of girls at a fountain is worth nothing but to be wafted away on the winds, and to be remembered by none; but can a son ever deem that one single word is unimportant which his dying father has bequeathed to him as a clue to his path in life? If you yourself were such a son, and your ear had not perfectly caught the parting counsels of the dying-how many talents of silver would you not pay to be able to supply the missing words? And what are immortal works of the great poets and thinkers but such sacred words of warning addressed, not to a single individual, but to all that are not barbarians, however many they maybe. They will elevate, instruct, and delight our descendants a thousand years hence as they do us at this day, and they, if they are not degenerate and ungrateful will be thankful to those who have devoted the best powers of their life to completing and restoring all that our mighty forefathers have said, as it must have originally stood before it was mutilated, and spoiled by carelessness and folly.

"He who, like King Euergetes, puts one syllable in Homer right, in place of a wrong one, in my opinion has done a service to succeeding generations—aye and a great service."

"What you say," replied Publius, "sounds convincing, but it is still not perfectly clear to me; no doubt because I learned at an early age to prefer deeds to words. I find it more easy to reconcile my mind to your painful and minute labors when I reflect that to you is entrusted the restoration of the literal tenor of laws, whose full meaning might be lost by a verbal error; or that wrong information might be laid before me as to one single transaction in the life of a friend or of a blood-relation, and it might lie with me to clear him of mistakes and misinterpretation."

"And what are the works of the great singers of the deeds of the heroes-of the writers of past history, but the lives of our fathers related either with veracious exactness or with poetic adornments?" cried Aristarchus. "It is to these that my king and companion in study devotes himself with particular zeal."

"When he is neither drinking, nor raving, nor governing, nor wasting his time in sacrificing and processions," interpolated Euergetes. "If I had not been a king perhaps I might have been an Aristarchus; as it is I am but half a king—since half of my kingdom belongs to you, Philometor—and but half a student; for when am I to find perfect quiet for thinking and writing? Everything, everything in me is by halves, for I, if the scale were to turn in my favor"—and here he struck his chest and his forehead, "I should be twice the man I am. I am my whole real self nowhere but at high festivals, when the wine sparkles in the cup, and bright eyes flash from beneath the brows of the flute-players of Alexandria or Cyrene—sometimes too perhaps in council when the risk is great, or when there is something vast and portentous to be done from which my brother and you others, all of you, would shrink—nay perhaps even the Roman. Aye! so it is—and you will learn to know it."

Euergetes had roared rather than spoken the last words; his cheeks were flushed, his eyes rolled, while he took from his head both the garland of flowers and the golden fillet, and once more pushed his fingers through his hair.

His sister covered her ears with her hands, and said: "You positively hurt me! As no one is contradicting you, and you, as a man of culture, are not accustomed to add force to your assertions, like the Scythians, by speaking in a loud tone, you would do well to save your metallic voice for the further speech with which it is to be hoped you will presently favor us. We have had to bow more than once already to the strength of which you boast—but now, at a merry feast, we will not think of that, but rather continue the conversation which entertained us, and which had begun so well. This eager defence of the interests which most delight the best of the Hellenes in Alexandria may perhaps result in infusing into the mind of our friend Publius Scipio—and through him into that of many young Romans—a proper esteem for a line of intellectual effort which he could not have condemned had he not failed to understand it perfectly.

"Very often some striking poetical turn given to a subject makes it, all at once, clear to our comprehension, even when long and learned disquisitions have failed; and I am acquainted with such an one, written by an anonymous author, and which may please you—and you too, Aristarchus. It epitomizes very happily the subject of our discussion. The lines run as follows:

"Behold, the puny Child of Man
Sits by Time's boundless sea,
And gathers in his feeble hand
Drops of Eternity.

"He overhears some broken words
Of whispered mystery
He writes them in a tiny book
And calls it 'History!'

"We owe these verses to an accomplished friend; another has amplified the idea by adding the two that follow:

"If indeed the puny Child of Man
Had not gathered drops from that wide sea,
Those small deeds that fill his little span
Had been lost in dumb Eternity.

"Feeble is his hand, and yet it dare
Seize some drops of that perennial stream;
As they fall they catch a transient gleam—
Lo! Eternity is mirrored there!

"What are we all but puny children? And those of us who gather up the drops surely deserve our esteem no less than those who spend their lives on the shore of that great ocean in mere play and strife—"

"And love," threw in Eulaeus in a low voice, as he glanced towards Publius.

"Your poet's verses are pretty and appropriate," Aristarchus now said, "and I am very happy to find myself compared to the children who catch the falling drops. There was a time—which came to an end, alas! with the great Aristotle—when there were men among the Greeks, who fed the ocean of which you speak with new tributaries; for the gods had bestowed on them the power of opening new sources, like the magician Moses, of whom Onias, the Jew, was lately telling us, and whose history I have read in the sacred books of the Hebrews. He, it is true—Moses I mean—only struck water from the rock for the use of the body, while to our philosophers and poets we owe inexhaustible springs to refresh the mind and soul. The time is now past which gave birth to such divine and creative spirits; as your majesties' forefathers recognized full well when they founded the Museum of Alexandria and the Library, of which I am one of the guardians, and which I may boast of having completed with your gracious assistance. When Ptolemy Soter first created the Museum in Alexandria the works of the greatest period could receive no additions in the form of modern writings of the highest class; but he set us—children of man, gathering the drops—the task of collecting and of sifting them, of eliminating errors in them—and I think we have proved ourselves equal to this task.

"It has been said that it is no less difficult to keep a fortune than to deserve it; and so perhaps we, who are merely 'keepers' may nevertheless make some credit—all the more because we have been able to arrange the wealth we found under hand, to work it profitably, to apply it well, to elucidate it, and to make it available. When anything new is created by one of our circle we always link it on to the old; and in many departments we have indeed even succeeded in soaring above the ancients, particularly in that of the experimental sciences. The sublime intelligence of our forefathers commanded a broad horizon—our narrower vision sees more clearly the objects that lie close to us. We have discovered the sure path for all intellectual labor, the true scientific method; and an observant study of things as they are, succeeds better with us than it did with our predecessors. Hence it follows that in the provinces of the natural sciences, in mathematics, astronomy, mechanics and geography the sages of our college have produced works of unsurpassed merit. Indeed the industry of my associates—"

"Is very great," cried Euergetes. "But they stir up such a dust that all free-thought is choked, and because they value quantity above all things in the results they obtain, they neglect to sift what is great from what is small; and so Publius Scipio and others like him, who shrug their shoulders over the labors of the learned, find cause enough to laugh in their faces. Out of every four of you I should dearly like to set three to some handicraft, and I shall do it too, one of these days—I shall do it, and turn them and all their miserable paraphernalia out of the Museum, and out of my capital. They may take refuge with you, Philometor, you who marvel at everything you cannot do yourself, who are always delighted to possess what I reject, and to make much of those whom I condemn—and Cleopatra I dare say will play the harp, in honor of their entering Memphis."

"I dare say!" answered the queen, laughing bitterly. "Still, it is to be expected that your wrath may fall even on worthy men. Until then I will practise my music, and study the treatise on harmony that you have begun writing. You are giving us proof to-day of how far you have succeeded in attaining unison in your own soul."

"I like you in this mood!" cried Euergetes. "I love you, sister, when you are like this! It ill becomes the eagle's brood to coo like the dove, and you have sharp talons though you hide them never so well under your soft feathers. It is true that I am writing a treatise on harmony, and I am doing it with delight; still it is one of those phenomena which, though accessible to our perception, are imperishable, for no god even could discover it entire and unmixed in the world of realities. Where is harmony to be found in the struggles and rapacious strife of the life of the Cosmos? And our human existence is but the diminished reflection of that process of birth and decease, of evolution and annihilation, which is going on in all that is perceptible to our senses; now gradually and invisibly, now violently and convulsively, but never harmonyously.

"Harmony is at home only in the ideal world—harmony which is unknown even among the gods harmony, whom I may know, and yet may never comprehend—whom I love, and may never possess—whom I long for, and who flies from me.

"I am as one that thirsteth, and harmony as the remote, unattainable well—I am as one swimming in a wide sea, and she is the land which recedes as I deem myself near to it.

"Who will tell me the name of the country where she rules as queen, undisturbed and untroubled? And which is most in earnest in his pursuit of the fair one: He who lies sleeping in her arms, or he who is consumed by his passion for her?

"I am seeking what you deem that you possess.—Possess—!

"Look round you on the world and on life—look round, as I do, on this hall of which you are so proud! It was built by a Greek; but, because the simple melody of beautiful forms in perfect concord no longer satisfies you, and your taste requires the eastern magnificence in which you were born, because this flatters your vanity and reminds you, each time you gaze upon it, that you are wealthy and powerful—you commanded your architect to set aside simple grandeur, and to build this gaudy monstrosity, which is no more like the banqueting-hall of a Pericles than I or you, Cleopatra, in all our finery, are like the simply clad gods and goddesses of Phidias. I mean not to offend you, Cleopatra, but I must say this; I am writing now on the subject of harmony, and perhaps I shall afterwards treat of justice, truth, virtue; although I know full well that they are pure abstractions which occur neither in nature nor in human life, and which in my dealings I wholly set aside; nevertheless they seem to me worthy of investigation, like any other delusion, if by resolving it we may arrive at conditional truth. It is because one man is afraid of another that these restraints—justice, truth, and what else you will—have received these high-sounding names, have been stamped as characteristics of the gods, and placed under the protection of the immortals; nay, our anxious care has gone so far that it has been taught as a doctrine that it is beautiful and good to cloud our free enjoyment of existence for the sake of these illusions. Think of Antisthenes and his disciples, the dog-like Cynics—think of the fools shut up in the temple of Serapis! Nothing is beautiful but what is free, and he only is not free who is forever striving to check his inclinations—for the most part in vain—in order to live, as feeble cowards deem virtuously, justly and truthfully.

"One animal eats another when he has succeeded in capturing it, either in open fight or by cunning and treachery; the climbing plant strangles the tree, the desert-sand chokes the meadows, stars fall from heaven, and earthquakes swallow up cities. You believe in the gods—and so do I after my own fashion—and if they have so ordered the course of this life in every class of existence that the strong triumph over the weak, why should not I use my strength, why let it be fettered by those much-belauded soporifics which our prudent ancestors concocted to cool the hot blood of such men as I, and to paralyze our sinewy fists.

"Euergetes—the well-doer—I was named at my birth; but if men choose to call me Kakergetes—the evil-doer—I do not mind it, since what you call good I call narrow and petty, and what you call evil is the free and unbridled exercise of power. I would be anything rather than lazy and idle, for everything in nature is active and busy; and as, with Aristippus, I hold pleasure to be the highest good, I would fain earn the name of having enjoyed more than all other men; in the first place in my mind, but no less in my body which I admire and cherish."

During this speech many signs of disagreement had found expression, and Publius, who for the first time in his life heard such vicious sentiments spoken, followed the words of the headstrong youth with consternation and surprise. He felt himself no match for this overbearing spirit, trained too in all the arts of argument and eloquence; but he could not leave all he had heard uncontroverted, and so, as Euergetes paused in order to empty his refilled cup, he began:

"If we were all to act on your principles, in a few centuries, it seems to me, there would be no one left to subscribe to them; for the earth would be depopulated; and the manuscripts, in which you are so careful to substitute 'siu' for 'iu', would be used by strong-handed mothers, if any were left, to boil the pot for their children—in this country of yours where there is no wood to burn. Just now you were boasting of your resemblance to Alcibiades, but that very gift which distinguished him, and made him dear to the Athenians—I mean his beauty—is hardly possible in connection with your doctrines, which would turn men into ravening beasts. He who would be beautiful must before all things be able to control himself and to be moderate—as I learnt in Rome before I ever saw Athens, and have remembered well. A Titan may perhaps have thought and talked as you do, but an Alcibiades—hardly!"

At these words the blood flew to Euergetes' face; but he suppressed the keen and insulting reply that rose to his lips, and this little victory over his wrathful impulse was made the more easy as Lysias, at this moment, rejoined the feasters; he excused himself for his long absence, and then laid before Cleopatra and her husband the gems belonging to Publius.

They were warmly admired; even Euergetes was not grudging of his praise, and each of the company admitted that he had rarely seen anything more beautiful and graceful than the bashful Hebe with downcast eyes, and the goddess of persuasion with her hand resting on the bride's arm.

"Yes, I will take the part of Peitho," said Cleopatra with decision.

"And I that of Heracles," cried Euergetes.

"But who is the fair one," asked King Philometor of Lysias, "whom you have in your eye, as fulfilling this incomparably lovely conception of Hebe? While you were away I recalled to memory the aspect of every woman and girl who frequents our festivals, but only to reject them all, one after the other."

"The fair girl whom I mean," replied Lysias, "has never entered this or any other palace; indeed I am almost afraid of being too bold in suggesting to our illustrious queen so humble a child as fit to stand beside her, though only in sport."

"I shall even have to touch her arm with my hand!" said the queen anxiously, and she drew up her fingers as if she had to touch some unclean thing. "If you mean a flower-seller or a flute-player or something of that kind—"

"How could I dare to suggest anything so improper?" Lysias hastily interposed. "The girl of whom I speak may be sixteen years old; she is innocence itself incarnate, and she looks like a bud ready to open perhaps in the morning dew that may succeed this very night, but which as yet is still enfolded in its cup. She is of Greek race, about as tall as you are, Cleopatra; she has wonderful gazelle-like eyes, her little head is covered by a mass of abundant brown hair, when she smiles she has delicious dimples in her cheeks—and she will be sure to smile when such a Peitho speaks to her!"

"You are rousing our curiosity," cried Philometor. "In what garden, pray, does this blossom grow?"

"And how is it," added Cleopatra, "that my husband has not discovered it long since, and transplanted it to our palace."

"Probably," answered Lysias, "because he who possesses Cleopatra, the fairest rose of Egypt, regards the violets by the roadside as too insignificant to be worth glancing at. Besides, the hedge that fences round my bud grows in a gloomy spot; it is difficult of access and suspiciously watched. To be brief: our Hebe is a water-bearer in the temple of Serapis, and her name is Irene."

CHAPTER XI

Lysias was one of those men from whose lips nothing ever sounds as if it were meant seriously. His statement that he regarded a serving girl from the temple of Serapis as fit to personate Hebe, was spoken as naturally and simply as if he were telling a tale for children; but his words produced an effect on his hearers like the sound of waters rushing into a leaky ship.

Publius had turned perfectly white, and it was not till his friend had uttered the name of Irene that he in some degree recovered his composure; Philometor had struck his cup on the table, and called out in much excitement:

"A water-bearer of Serapis to play Hebe in a gay festal performance! Do you conceive it possible, Cleopatra?"

"Impossible—it is absolutely out of the question," replied the queen, decidedly. Euergetes, who also had opened his eyes wide at the Corinthian's proposition, sat for a long time gazing into his cup in silence; while his brother and sister continued to express their surprise and disapprobation and to speak of the respect and consideration which even kings must pay to the priests and servants of Serapis.

At length, once more lifting his wreath and crown, he raised his curls with both hands, and said, quite calmly and decisively;

"We must have a Hebe, and must take her where we find her. If you hesitate to allow the girl to be fetched it shall be done by my orders. The priests of Serapis are for the most part Greeks, and the high-priest is a Hellene. He will not trouble himself much about a half-grown-up girl if he can thereby oblige you or me. He knows as well as the rest of us that one hand washes the other! The only question now is—for I would rather avoid all woman's outcries—whether the girl will come willingly or unwillingly if we send for her. What do you think, Lysias?"

"I believe she would sooner get out of prison to-day than to-morrow," replied Lysias. "Irene is a lighthearted creature, and laughs as clearly and merrily as a child at play—and besides that they starve her in her cage."

"Then I will have her fetched to-morrow!" said Euergetes.

"But," interrupted Cleopatra, "Asclepiodorus must obey us and not you; and we, my husband and I—"

"You cannot spoil sport with the priests," laughed Euergetes. "If they were Egyptians, then indeed! They are not to be taken in their nests without getting pecked; but here, as I have said, we have to deal with Greeks. What have you to fear from them? For aught I care you may leave our Hebe where she is, but I was once much pleased with these representations, and to-morrow morning, as soon as I have slept, I shall return to Alexandria, if you do not carry them into effect, and so deprive me, Heracles, of the bride chosen for me by the gods. I have said what I have said, and I am not given to changing my mind. Besides, it is time that we should show ourselves to our friends feasting here in the next room. They are already merry, and it must be getting late."

With these words Euergetes rose from his couch, and beckoned to Hierax and a chamberlain, who arranged the folds of his transparent robe, while Philometor and Cleopatra whispered together, shrugging their shoulders and shaking their heads; and Publius, pressing his hand on the Corinthian's wrist, said in his ear: "You will not give them any help if you value our friendship; we will leave as soon as we can do so with propriety."

Euergetes did not like to be kept waiting. He was already going towards the door, when Cleopatra called him back, and said pleasantly, but with gentle reproachfulness:

"You know that we are willing to follow the Egyptian custom of carrying out as far as possible the wishes of a friend and brother for his birthday festival; but for that very reason it is not right in you to try to force us into a proceeding which we refuse with difficulty, and yet cannot carry out without exposing ourselves to the most unpleasant consequences. We beg you to make some other demand on us, and we will certainly grant it if it lies in our power."

The young colossus responded to his sister's appeal with a loud shout of laughter, waved his arm with a flourish of his hand expressive of haughty indifference; and then he exclaimed:

"The only thing I really had a fancy for out of all your possessions you are not willing to concede, and so I must abide by my word—or I go on my way."

Again Cleopatra and her husband exchanged a few muttered words and rapid glances, Euergetes watching them the while; his legs straddled apart, his huge body bent forward, and his hands resting on his hips. His attitude expressed so much arrogance and puerile, defiant, unruly audacity, that Cleopatra found it difficult to suppress an exclamation of disgust before she spoke.

"We are indeed brethren," she said, "and so, for the sake of the peace which has been restored and preserved with so much difficulty, we give in. The best way will be to request Asclepiodorus—"

But here Euergetes interrupted the queen, clapping his hands loudly and laughing:

"That is right, sister! only find me my Hebe! How you do it is your affair, and is all the same to me. To-morrow evening we will have a rehearsal, and the day after we will give a representation of which our grandchildren shall repeat the fame. Nor shall a brilliant audience be lacking, for my complimentary visitors with their priestly splendor and array of arms will, it is to be hoped, arrive punctually. Come, my lords, we will go, and see what there is good to drink or to listen to at the table in the next room."

The doors were opened; music, loud talking, the jingle of cups, and the noise of laughter sounded through them into the room where the princes had been supping, and all the king's guests followed Euergetes, with the exception of Eulaeus. Cleopatra allowed them to depart without speaking a word; only to Publius she said: "Till we meet again!" but she detained the Corinthian, saying:

"You, Lysias, are the cause of this provoking business. Try now to repair the mischief by bringing the girl to us. Do not hesitate! I will guard her, protect her with the greatest care, rely upon me."

"She is a modest maiden," replied Lysias, "and will not accompany me willingly, I am sure. When I proposed her for the part of Hebe I certainly supposed that a word from you, the king and queen, would suffice to induce the head of the temple to entrust her to you for a few hours of harmless amusement. Pardon me if I too quit you now; I have the key of my friend's chest still in my possession, and must restore it to him."

"Shall we have her carried off secretly?" asked Cleopatra of her husband, when the Corinthian had followed the other guests.

"Only let us have no scandal, no violence," cried Philometor anxiously. "The best way would be for me to write to Asclepiodorus, and beg him in a friendly manner to entrust this girl—Ismene or Irene, or whatever the ill-starred child's name is—for a few days to you, Cleopatra, for your pleasure. I can offer him a prospect of an addition to the gift of land I made today, and which fell far short of his demands."

"Let me entreat your majesty," interposed Eulaeus, who was now alone with the royal couple, "let me entreat you not to make any great promises on this occasion, for the moment you do so Asclepiodorus will attribute an importance to your desire—"

"Which it is far from having, and must not seem to have," interrupted the queen. "It is preposterous to waste so many words about a miserable creature, a water-carrying girl, and to go through so much disturbance—but how are we to put an end to it all? What is your advice, Eulaeus?"

"I thank you for that enquiry, noble princess," replied Eulaeus. "My lord, the king, in my opinion, should have the girl carried off, but not with any violence, nor by a man—whom she would hardly follow so immediately as is necessary—but by a woman.

"I am thinking of the old Egyptian tale of 'The Two Brothers,' which you are acquainted with. The Pharaoh desired to possess himself of the wife of the younger one, who lived on the Mount of Cedars, and he sent armed men to fetch her away; but only one of them came back to him, for Batau had slain all the others. Then a woman was sent with splendid ornaments, such as women love, and the fair one followed her unresistingly to the palace.

"We may spare the ambassadors, and send only the woman; your lady in waiting, Zoe, will execute this commission admirably. Who can blame us in any way if a girl, who loves finery, runs away from her keepers?"

"But all the world will see her as Hebe," sighed Philometor, "and proclaim us—the sovereign protectors of the worship of Serapis—as violators of the temple, if Asclepiodorus leads the cry. No, no, the high-priest must first be courteously applied to. In the case of his raising any difficulties, but not otherwise, shall Zoe make the attempt."

"So be it then," said the queen, as if it were her part to express her confirmation of her husband's proposition.

"Let your lady accompany me," begged Eulaeus, "and prefer your request to Asclepiodorus. While I am speaking with the high-priest, Zoe can at any rate win over the girl, and whatever we do must be done to-morrow, or the Roman will be beforehand with us. I know that he has cast an eye on Irene, who is in fact most lovely. He gives her flowers, feeds his pet bird with pheasants and peaches and other sweetmeats, lets himself be lured into the Serapeum by his lady-love as often as possible, stays there whole hours, and piously follows the processions, in order to present the violets with which you graciously honored him by giving them to his fair one—who no doubt would rather wear royal flowers than any others—"

"Liar!" cried the queen, interrupting the courtier in such violent excitement and such ungoverned rage, so completely beside herself, that her husband drew back startled.

"You are a slanderer! a base calumniator! The Roman attacks you with naked weapons, but you slink in the dark, like a scorpion, and try to sting your enemy in the heel. Apelles, the painter, warns us—the grandchildren of Lagus—against folks of your kidney in the picture he painted against Antiphilus; as I look at you I am reminded of his Demon of Calumny. The same spite and malice gleam in your eyes as in hers, and the same fury and greed for some victim, fire your flushed face! How you would rejoice if the youth whom Apelles has represented Calumny as clutching by the hair, could but be Publius! and if only the lean and hollow-eyed form of Envy, and the loathsome female figures of Cunning and Treachery would come to your did as they have to hers! But I remember too the steadfast and truthful glance of the boy she has flung to the ground, his arms thrown up to heaven, appealing for protection to the goddess and the king—and though Publius Scipio is man enough to guard himself against open attack, I will protect him against being surprised from an ambush! Leave this room! Go, I say, and you shall see how we punish slanderers!"

At these words Eulaeus flung himself at the queen's feet, but she, breathing hurriedly and with quivering nostrils, looked away over his head as if she did not even see him, till her husband came towards her, and said in a voice of most winning gentleness:

"Do not condemn him unheard, and raise him from his abasement. At least give him the opportunity of softening your indignation by bringing the water-bearer here without angering Asclepiodorus. Carry out this affair well, Eulaeus, and you will find in me an advocate with Cleopatra."

The king pointed to the door, and Eulaeus retired, bowing deeply and finding his way out backwards. Philometer, now alone with his wife, said with mild reproach:

"How could you abandon yourself to such unmeasured anger? So faithful and prudent a servant—and one of the few still living of those to whom our mother was attached—cannot be sent away like a mere clumsy attendant. Besides, what is the great crime he has committed? Is it a slander which need rouse you to such fury when a cautious old man says in all innocence of a young one—a man belonging to a world which knows nothing of the mysterious sanctity of Serapis—that he has taken a fancy to a girl, who is admired by all who see her, that he seeks her out, and gives her flowers—"

"Gives her flowers?" exclaimed Cleopatra, breaking out afresh. "No, he is accused of persecuting a maiden attached to Serapis—to Serapis I say. But it is simply false, and you would be as angry as I am if you were ever capable of feeling manly indignation, and if you did not want to make use of Eulaeus for many things, some of which I know, and others which you choose to conceal from me. Only let him fetch the girl; and when once we have her here, and if I find that the Roman's indictment against Eulaeus— which I will hear to-morrow morning—is well founded, you shall see that I have manly vigor enough for both of us. Come away now; they are waiting for us in the other room."

The queen gave a call, and chamberlains and servants hurried in; her shell-shaped litter was brought, and in a few minutes, with her husband by her side, she was borne into the great peristyle where the grandees of the court, the commanders of the troops, the most prominent of the officials of the Egyptian provinces, many artists and savants, and the ambassadors from foreign powers, were reclining on long rows of couches, and talking over their wine, the feast itself being ended.

The Greeks and the dark-hued Egyptians were about equally represented in this motley assembly; but among them, and particularly among the learned and the fighting men, there were also several Israelites and Syrians.

The royal pair were received by the company with acclamations and marks of respect; Cleopatra smiled as sweetly as ever, and waved her fan graciously as she descended from her litter; still she vouchsafed not the slightest attention to any one present, for she was seeking Publius, at first among those who were nearest to the couch prepared for her, and then among the other Hellenes, the Egyptians, the Jews, the ambassadors—still she found him not, and when at last she enquired for the Roman of the chief chamberlain at her side, the official was sent for who had charge of the foreign envoys. This was an officer of very high rank, whose duty it was to provide for the representatives of foreign powers, and he was now near at hand, for he had long been waiting for an opportunity to offer to the queen a message of leave-taking from Publius Cornelius Scipio, and to tell her from him, that he had retired to his tent because a letter had come to him from Rome.

"Is that true?" asked the queen letting her feather fan droop, and looking her interlocutor severely in the face.

"The trireme Proteus, coming from Brundisium, entered the harbor of Eunostus only yesterday," he replied; "and an hour ago a mounted messenger brought the letter. Nor was it an ordinary letter but a despatch from the Senate—I know the form and seal."

"And Lysias, the Corinthian?"

"He accompanied the Roman."

"Has the Senate written to him too?" asked the queen annoyed, and ironically. She turned her back on the officer without any kind of courtesy, and turning again to the chamberlain she went on, in incisive tones, as if she were presiding at a trial:

"King Euergetes sits there among the Egyptians near the envoys from the temples of the Upper Country. He looks as if he were giving them a discourse, and they hang on his lips. What is he saying, and what does all this mean?"

"Before you came in, he was sitting with the Syrians and Jews, and telling them what the merchants and scribes, whom he sent to the South, have reported of the lands lying near the lakes through which the Nile is said to flow. He thinks that new sources of wealth have revealed themselves not far from the head of the sacred river which can hardly flow in from the ocean, as the ancients supposed."

"And now?" asked Cleopatra. "What information is he giving to the Egyptians?"

The chamberlain hastened towards Euergetes' couch, and soon returned to the queen—who meanwhile had exchanged a few friendly words with Onias, the Hebrew commander—and informed her in a low tone that the king was interpreting a passage from the Timaeus of Plato, in which Solon celebrates the lofty wisdom of the priests of Sais; he was speaking with much spirit, and the Egyptians received it with loud applause.

Cleopatra's countenance darkened more and more, but she concealed it behind her fan, signed to Philometor to approach, and whispered to him:

"Keep near Euergetes; he has a great deal too much to say to the Egyptians. He is extremely anxious to stand well with them, and those whom he really desires to please are completely entrapped by his portentous amiability. He has spoiled my evening, and I shall leave you to yourselves."

"Till to-morrow, then."

"I shall hear the Roman's complaint up on my roof-terrace; there is always a fresh air up there. If you wish to be present I will send for you, but first I would speak to him alone, for he has received letters from the Senate which may contain something of importance. So, till to-morrow."

CHAPTER XII

While, in the vast peristyle, many a cup was still being emptied, and the carousers were growing merrier and noisier—while Cleopatra was abusing the maids and ladies who were undressing her for their clumsiness and unreadiness, because every touch hurt her, and every pin taken out of her dress pricked her—the Roman and his friend Lysias walked up and down in their tent in violent agitation.

"Speak lower," said the Greek, "for the very griffins woven into the tissue of these thin walls seem to me to be lying in wait, and listening.

"I certainly was not mistaken. When I came to fetch the gems I saw a light gleaming in the doorway as I approached it; but the intruder must have been warned, for just as I got up to the lantern in front of the servants' tent, it disappeared, and the torch which usually burns outside our tent had not been lighted at all; but a beam of light fell on the road, and a man's figure slipped across in a black robe sprinkled with gold ornaments which I saw glitter as the pale light of the lantern fell upon them—just as a slimy, black newt glides through a pool. I have good eyes as you know, and I will give one of them at this moment, if I am mistaken, and if the cat that stole into our tent was not Eulaeus."

"And why did you not have him caught?" asked Publius, provoked.

"Because our tent was pitch-dark," replied Lysias, "and that stout villain is as slippery as a badger with the dogs at his heels, Owls, bats and such vermin which seek their prey by night are all hideous to me, and this Eulaeus, who grins like a hyaena when he laughs—"

"This Eulaeus," said Publius, interrupting his friend, "shall learn to know me, and know too by experience that a man comes to no good, who picks a quarrel with my father's son."

"But, in the first instance, you treated him with disdain and discourtesy," said Lysias, "and that was not wise."

"Wise, and wise, and wise!" the Roman broke out. "He is a scoundrel. It makes no difference to me so long as he keeps out of my way; but when, as has been the case for several days now, he constantly sticks close to me to spy upon me, and treats me as if he were my equal, I will show him that he is mistaken. He has no reason to complain of my want of frankness; he knows my opinion of him, and that I am quite inclined to give him a thrashing. If I wanted to meet his cunning with cunning I should get the worst of it, for he is far superior to me in intrigue. I shall fare better with him by my own unconcealed mode of fighting, which is new to him and puzzles him; besides it is better suited to my own nature, and more consonant to me than any other. He is not only sly, but is keen-witted, and he has at once connected the complaint which I have threatened to bring against him with the manuscript which Serapion, the recluse, gave me in his presence. There it lies—only look.

"Now, being not merely crafty, but a daring rascal too—two qualities which generally contradict each other, for no one who is really prudent lives in disobedience to the laws—he has secretly untied the strings which fastened it. But, you see, he had not time enough to tie the roll up again! He has read it all or in part, and I wish him joy of the picture of himself he will have found painted there. The anchorite wields a powerful pen, and paints with a firm outline and strongly marked coloring. If he has read the roll to the end it will spare me the trouble of explaining to him what I purpose to charge him with; if you disturbed him too soon I shall have to be more explicit in my accusation. Be that as it may, it is all the same to me."

"Nay, certainly not," cried Lysias, "for in the first case Eulaeus will have time to meditate his lies, and bribe witnesses for his defence. If any one entrusted me with such important papers—and if it had not been you who neglected to do it—I would carefully seal or lock them up. Where have you put the despatch from the Senate which the messenger brought you just now?"

"That is locked up in this casket," replied Publius, moving his hand to press it more closely over his robe, under which he had carefully hidden it.

"May I not know what it contain?" asked the Corinthian.

"No, there is not time for that now, for we must first, and at once, consider what can be done to repair the last mischief which you have done. Is it not a disgraceful thing that you should betray the sweet creature whose childlike embarrassment charmed us this morning—of whom you yourself said, as we came home, that she reminded you of your lovely sister—that you should betray her, I say, into the power of the wildest of all the profligates I ever met—to this monster, whose pleasures are the unspeakable, whose boast is vice? What has Euergetes—"

"By great Poseidon!" cried Lysias, eagerly interrupting his friend. "I never once thought of this second Alcibiades when I mentioned her. What can the manager of a performance do, but all in his power to secure the applause of the audience? and, by my honor! it was for my own sake that I wanted to bring Irene into the palace—I am mad with love for her—she has undone me."

"Aye! like Callista, and Phryne, and the flute-player Stephanion," interrupted the Roman, shrugging his shoulders.

"How should it be different?" asked the Corinthian, looking at his friend in astonishment. "Eros has many arrows in his quiver; one strikes deeply, another less deeply; and I believe that the wound I have received to-day will ache for many a week if I have to give up this child, who is even more charming than the much-admired Hebe on our cistern."

"I advise you however to accustom yourself to the idea, and the sooner the better," said Publius gravely, as he set himself with his arms crossed, directly in front of the Greek. "What would you feel inclined to do to me if I took a fancy to lure your pretty sister—whom Irene, I repeat it, is said to resemble—to tempt her with base cunning from your parents' house?"

"I protest against any such comparison," cried the Corinthian very positively, and more genuinely exasperated than the Roman had ever seen him.

"You are angry without cause," replied Publius calmly and gravely. "Your sister is a charming girl, the ornament of your illustrious house, and yet I dare compare the humble Irene—"

"With her! do you mean to say?" Lysias shouted again. "That is a poor return for the hospitality which was shown to you by my parents and of which you formally sang the praises. I am a good-natured fellow and will submit to more from you than from any other man—I know not why, myself;—but in a matter like this I do not understand a joke! My sister is the only daughter of the noblest and richest house in Corinth and has many suitors. She is in no respect inferior to the child of your own parents, and I should like to know what you would say if I made so bold as to compare the proud Lucretia with this poor little thing, who carries water like a serving-maid."

"Do so, by all means!" interrupted Publius coolly, "I do not take your rage amiss, for you do not know who these two sisters are, in the temple of Serapis. Besides, they do not fill their jars for men but in the service of a god.

Here—take this roll and read it through while I answer the despatch from Rome. Here! Spartacus, come and light a few more lamps."

In a few minutes the two young men were sitting opposite each other at the table which stood in the middle of their tent. Publius wrote busily, and only looked up when his friend, who was reading the anchorite's document, struck his hand on the table in disgust or sprang from his seat ejaculating bitter words of indignation. Both had finished at the same moment, and when Publius had folded and sealed his letter, and Lysias had flung the roll on to the table, the Roman said slowly, as he looked his friend steadily in the face: "Well?"

"Well!" repeated Lysias. I now find myself in the humiliating position of being obliged to deem myself more stupid than you—I must own you in the right, and beg your pardon for having thought you insolent and arrogant! Never, no never did I hear a story so infernally scandalous as that in that roll, and such a thing could never have occurred but among these accursed Egyptians! Poor little Irene! And how can the dear little girl have kept such a sunny look through it all! I could thrash myself like any school-boy to think that I—a fool among fools—should have directed the attention of Euergetes to this girl, and he, the most powerful and profligate man in the whole country. What can now be done to save Irene from him? I cannot endure the thought of seeing her abandoned to his clutches, and I will not permit it to happen.

"Do not you think that we ought to take the water-bearers under our charge?"

"Not only we ought but we must," said Publius decisively; "and if we did not we should be contemptible wretches. Since the recluse took me into his confidence I feel as if it were my duty to watch over these girls whose parents have been stolen from them, as if I were their guardian—and you, my Lysias, shall help me. The elder sister is not now very friendly towards me, but I do not esteem her the less for that; the younger one seems less grave and reserved than Klea; I saw how she responded to your smile when the procession broke up. Afterwards, you did not come home immediately any more than I did, and I suspect that it was Irene who detained you. Be frank, I earnestly beseech you, and tell me all; for we must act in unison, and with thorough deliberation, if we hope to succeed in spoiling Euergetes' game."

"I have not much to tell you," replied the Corinthian. "After the procession I went to the Pastophorium—naturally it was to see Irene, and in order not to fail in this I allowed the pilgrims to tell me what visions the god had sent them in their dreams, and what advice had been given them in the temple of Asclepius as to what to do for their own complaints, and those of their cousins, male and female.

"Quite half an hour had passed so before Irene came. She carried a little basket in which lay the gold ornaments she had worn at the festival, and which she had to restore to the keeper of the temple-treasure. My pomegranate-flower, which she had accepted in the morning, shone upon me from afar, and then, when she caught sight of me and blushed all over, casting down her eyes, then it was that it first struck me 'just like the Hebe on our cistern.'

"She wanted to pass me, but I detained her, begging her to show me the ornaments in her hand; I said a number of things such as girls like to hear, and then I asked her if she were strictly watched, and whether they gave her delicate little hands and feet—which were worthy of better occupation than water-carrying—a great deal to do. She did not hesitate to answer, but with all she said she rarely raised her eyes. The longer you look at her the lovelier she is—and yet she is still a mere child-though a child certainly who no longer loves staying at home, who has dreams of splendor, and enjoyment, and freedom while she is kept shut up in a dismal, dark place, and left to starve.

"The poor creatures may never quit the temple excepting for a procession, or before sunrise. It sounded too delightful when she said that she was always so horribly tired, and so glad to go to sleep again after she was waked, and had to go out at once just when it is coldest, in the twilight before sunrise. Then she has to draw water from a cistern called the Well of the Sun."

"Do you know where that cistern lies?" asked Publius.

"Behind the acacia-grove," answered Lysias. "The guide pointed it out to me. It is said to hold particularly sacred water, which must be poured as a libation to the god at sunrise, unmixed with any other. The girls must get up so early, that as soon as dawn breaks water from this cistern shall not be lacking at the altar of Serapis. It is poured out on the earth by the priests as a drink-offering."

Publius had listened attentively, and had not lost a word of his friend's narrative. He now quitted him hastily, opened the tent-door, and went out into the night, looking up to discover the hour from the stars which were silently pursuing their everlasting courses in countless thousands, and sparkling with extraordinary brilliancy in the deep blue sky. The moon was already set, and the morning-star was slowly rising—every night since the Roman had been in the land of the Pyramids he had admired its magnificent size and brightness.

A cold breeze fanned the young man's brow, and as he drew his robe across his breast with a shiver, he thought of the sisters, who, before long, would have to go out in the fresh morning air. Once more he raised his eyes from the earth to the firmament over his head, and it seemed to him that he saw before his very eyes the proud form of Klea, enveloped in a mantle sown over with stars. His heart throbbed high, and he felt as if the breeze that his heaving breast inhaled in deep breaths was as fresh and pure as the ether that floats over Elysium, and of a strange potency withal, as if too rare to breathe. Still he fancied he saw before him the image of Klea, but as he stretched out his hand towards the beautiful vision it vanished—a sound of hoofs and wheels fell upon his ear. Publius was not accustomed to abandon himself to dreaming when action was needed, and this reminded him of the purpose for which he had come out into the open air. Chariot after chariot came driving past as he returned into his tent. Lysias, who during his absence had been pacing up and down and reflecting, met him with the question:

"How long is it yet till sunrise?"

"Hardly two hours," replied the Roman. "And we must make good use of them if we would not arrive too late."

"So I think too," said the Corinthian. "The sisters will soon be at the Well of the Sun outside the temple walls, and I will persuade Irene to follow me. You think I shall not be successful? Nor do I myself—but still perhaps she will if I promise to show her something very pretty, and if she does not suspect that she is to be parted from her sister, for she is like a child."

"But Klea," interrupted Publius thoughtfully, "is grave and prudent; and the light tone which you are so ready to adopt will be very little to her taste, Consider that, and dare the attempt—no, you dare not deceive her. Tell her the whole truth, out of Irene's hearing, with the gravity the matter deserves, and she will not hinder her sister when she knows how great and how imminent is the danger that threatens her."

"Good!" said the Corinthian. "I will be so solemnly earnest that the most wrinkled and furrowed graybeard among the censors of your native city shall seem a Dionysiac dancer compared with me. I will speak like your Cato when he so bitterly complained that the epicures of Rome paid more now for a barrel of fresh herrings than for a yoke of oxen. You shall be perfectly satisfied with me!—But whither am I to conduct Irene? I might perhaps make use of one of the king's chariots which are passing now by dozens to carry the guests home."

"I also had thought of that," replied Publius. "Go with the chief of the Diadoches, whose splendid house was shown to us yesterday. It is on the way to the Serapeum, and just now at the feast you were talking with him incessantly. When there, indemnify the driver by the gift of a gold piece, so that he may not betray us, and do not return here but proceed to the harbor. I will await you near the little temple of Isis with our travelling chariot and my own horses, will receive Irene, and conduct her to some new refuge while you drive back Fuergetes' chariot, and restore it to the driver."

"That will not satisfy me by any means," said Lysias very gravely; "I was ready to give up my pomegranate-flower to you yesterday for Irene, but herself—"

"I want nothing of her," exclaimed Publius annoyed. "But you might— it seems to me—be rather more zealous in helping me to preserve her from the misfortune which threatens her through your own blunder. We cannot bring her here, but I think that I have thought of a safe hiding-place for her.

"Do you remember Apollodorus, the sculptor, to whom we were recommended by my father, and his kind and friendly wife who set before us that capital Chios wine? The man owes me a service, for my father commissioned him and his assistants to execute the mosaic pavement in the new arcade he was having built in the capitol; and subsequently, when the envy of rival artists threatened his life, my father saved him. You yourself heard him say that he and his were all at my disposal."

"Certainly, certainly," said Lysias. "But say, does it not strike you as most extraordinary that artists, the very men, that is to say, who beyond all others devote themselves to ideal aims and efforts, are particularly ready to yield to the basest impulses; envy, detraction, and—"

"Man!" exclaimed Publius, angrily interrupting the Greek, "can you never for ten seconds keep on the same subject, and never keep anything to yourself that comes into your head? We have just now, as it seems to me, more important matters to discuss than the jealousy of each other shown by artists—and in my opinion, by learned men too. The sculptor Apollodorus, who is thus beholden to me, has been living here for the last six months with his wife and daughters, for he has been executing for Philometor the busts of the philosophers, and the animal groups to decorate the open space in front of the tomb of Apis. His sons are managers of his large factory in Alexandria, and when he next goes there, down the Nile in his boat, as often happens, he can take Irene with him, and put her on board a ship.

"As to where we can have her taken to keep her safe from Euergetes, we will talk that over afterwards with Apollodorus."

"Good, very good," agreed the Corinthian. "By Heracles! I am not suspicious—still it does not altogether please me that you should yourself conduct Irene to Apollodorus, for if you are seen in her company our whole project may be shipwrecked. Send the sculptor's wife, who is little known in Memphis, to the temple of Isis, and request her to bring a veil and cloak to conceal the girl. Greet the gay Milesian from me too, and tell her—no, tell her nothing—I shall see her myself afterwards at the temple of Isis."

During the last words of this conversation, slaves had been enveloping the two young men in their mantles. They now quitted the tent together, wished each other success, and set out at a brisk pace; the Roman to have his horses harnessed, and Lysias to accompany the chief of the Diadoches in one of the king's chariots, and then to act on the plan he had agreed upon with Publius.

CHAPTER XIII

Chariot after chariot hurried out of the great gate of the king's palace and into the city, now sunk in slumber. All was still in the great banqueting-hall, and dark-hued slaves began with brooms and sponges to clean the mosaic pavement, which was strewed with rose leaves and with those that had fallen from the faded garlands of ivy and poplar; while here and there the spilt wine shone with a dark gleam in the dim light of the few lamps that had not been extinguished.

A young flute-player, overcome with sleep and wine, still sat in one corner. The poplar wreath that had crowned his curls had slipped over his pretty face, but even in sleep he still held his flute clasped fast in his fingers. The servants let him sleep on, and bustled about without noticing him; only an overseer pointed to him, and said laughing:

"His companions went home no more sober than that one. He is a pretty boy, and pretty Chloes lover besides—she will look for him in vain this morning."

"And to-morrow too perhaps," answered another; "for if the fat king sees her, poor Damon will have seen the last of her."

But the fat king, as Euergetes was called by the Alexandrians, and, following their example, by all the rest of Egypt, was not just then thinking of Chloe, nor of any such person; he was in the bath attached to his splendidly fitted residence. Divested of all clothing, he was standing in the tepid fluid which completely filled a huge basin of white marble. The clear surface of the perfumed water mirrored statues of nymphs fleeing from the pursuit of satyrs, and reflected the shimmering light of numbers of lamps suspended from the ceiling. At the upper end of the bath reclined the bearded and stalwart statue of the Nile, over whom the sixteen infant figures—representing the number of ells to which the great Egyptian stream must rise to secure a favorable inundation—clambered and played to the delight of their noble father Nile and of themselves. From the vase which supported the arm of the venerable god flowed an abundant stream of cold water, which five pretty lads received in slender alabaster vases, and poured over the head and the enormously prominent muscles of the breast, the back and the arms of the young king who was taking his bath.

"More, more—again and again," cried Euergetes, as the boys began to pause in bringing and pouring the water; and then, when they threw a fresh stream over him, he snorted and plunged with satisfaction, and a perfect shower of jets splashed off him as the blast of his breath sputtered away the water that fell over his face.

At last he shouted out: "Enough!" flung himself with all his force into the water, that spurted up as if a huge block of stone had been thrown into it, held his head for a long time under water, and then went up the marble steps of the bath shaking his head violently and mischievously in his boyish insolence, so as thoroughly to wet his friends and servants who were standing round the margin of the basin; he suffered himself to be wrapped in snowy-white sheets of the thinnest and finest linen, to be sprinkled with costly essences of delicate odor, and then he withdrew into a small room hung all round with gaudy hangings.

There he flung himself on a mound of soft cushions, and said with a deep-drawn breath: "Now I am happy; and I am as sober again as a baby that has never tasted anything but its mother's milk. Pindar is right! there is nothing better than water! and it slakes that raging fire which wine lights up in our brain and blood. Did I talk much nonsense just now, Hierax?"

The man thus addressed, the commander-in-chief of the royal troops, and the king's particular friend, cast a hesitating glance at the bystanders; but, Euergetes desiring him to speak without reserve, he replied:

"Wine never weakens the mind of such as you are to the point of folly, but you were imprudent. It would be little short of a miracle if Philometor did not remark—"

"Capital!" interrupted the king sitting up on his cushions. "You, Hierax, and you, Komanus, remain here—you others may go. But do not go too far off, so as to be close at hand in case I should need you. In these days as much happens in a few hours as usually takes place in as many years."

Those who were thus dismissed withdrew, only the king's dresser, a Macedonian of rank, paused doubtfully at the door, but Euergetes signed to him to retire immediately, calling after him:

"I am very merry and shall not go to bed. At three hours after sunrise I expect Aristarchus—and for work too. Put out the manuscripts that I brought. Is the Eunuch Eulaeus waiting in the anteroom? Yes—so much the better!

"Now we are alone, my wise friends Hierax and Komanus, and I must explain to you that on this occasion, out of pure prudence, you seem to me to have been anything rather than prudent. To be prudent is to have the command of a wide circle of thought, so that what is close at hand is no more an obstacle than what is remote. The narrow mind can command only that which lies close under observation; the fool and visionary only that which is far off. I will not blame you, for even the wisest has his hours of folly, but on this occasion you have certainly overlooked that which is at hand, in gazing at the distance, and I see you stumble in consequence. If you had not fallen into that error you would hardly have looked so bewildered when, just now, I exclaimed 'Capital!'

"Now, attend to me. Philometor and my sister know very well what my humor is, and what to expect of me. If I had put on the mask of a satisfied man they would have been surprised, and have scented mischief, but as it was I showed myself to them exactly what I always am and even more reckless than usual, and talked of what I wanted so openly that they may indeed look forward to some deed of violence at my hands but hardly to a treacherous surprise, and that tomorrow; for he who falls on his enemy in the rear makes no noise about it.

"If I believed in your casuistry, I might think that to attack the enemy from behind was not a particularly fine thing to do, for even I would rather see a man's face than his rear—particularly in the case of my brother and sister, who are both handsome to look upon. But what can a man do? After all, the best thing to do is what wins the victory and makes the game. Indeed, my mode of warfare has found supporters among the wise. If you want to catch mice you must waste bacon, and if we are to tempt men into a snare we must know what their notions and ideas are, and begin by endeavoring to confuse them.

"A bull is least dangerous when he runs straight ahead in his fury; while his two-legged opponent is least dangerous when he does not know what he is about and runs feeling his way first to the right and then to the left. Thanks to your approval—for I have deserved it, and I hope to be able to return it, my friend Hierax. I am curious as to your report. Shake up the cushion here under my head—and now you may begin."

"All appears admirably arranged," answered the general. "The flower of our troops, the Diadoches and Hetairoi, two thousand-five hundred men, are on their way hither, and by to-morrow will encamp north of Memphis. Five hundred will find their way into the citadel, with the priests and other visitors to congratulate you on your birthday, the other two thousand will remain concealed in the tents. The captain of your brother Philometor's Philobasilistes is bought over, and will stand by us; but his price was high— Komanus was forced to offer him twenty talents before he would bite."

"He shall have them," said the king laughing, "and he shall keep them too, till it suits me to regard him as suspicious, and to reward him according to his deserts by confiscating his estates. Well! proceed."

"In order to quench the rising in Thebes, the day before yesterday Philometor sent the best of the mercenaries with the standards of Desilaus and Arsinoe to the South. Certainly it cost not a little to bribe the ringleaders, and to stir up the discontent to an outbreak."

"My brother will repay us for this outlay," interrupted the king, "when we pour his treasure into our own coffers. Go on."

"We shall have most difficulty with the priests and the Jews. The former cling to Philometor, because he is the eldest son of his father, and has given large bounties to the temples, particularly of Apollinopolis and Philae; the Jews are attached to him, because he favors them more than the Greeks, and he, and his wife—your illustrious sister—trouble themselves with their vain religious squabbles; he disputes with them about the doctrines contained in their book, and at table too prefers conversing with them to any one else."

"I will salt the wine and meat for them that they fatten on here," cried Euergetes vehemently, "I forbade to-day their presence at my table, for they have good eyes and wits as sharp as their noses. And they are most dangerous when they are in fear, or can reckon on any gains.

"At the same time it cannot be denied that they are honest and tenacious, and as most of them are possessed of some property they rarely make common cause with the shrieking mob—particularly here in Alexandria.

"Envy alone can reproach them for their industry and enterprise, for the activity of the Hellenes has improved upon the example set by them and their Phoenician kindred.

"They thrive best in peaceful times, and since the world runs more quietly here, under my brother and sister, than under me, they attach themselves to them, lend my brother money, and supply my sister with cut stones, sapphires and emeralds, selling fine stuffs and other woman's gear for a scrap of written papyrus, which will soon be of no more value than the feather which falls from the wing of that green screaming bird on the perch yonder.

"It is incomprehensible to me that so keen a people cannot perceive that there is nothing permanent but change, nothing so certain as that nothing is certain; and that they therefore should regard their god as the one only god, their own doctrine as absolutely and eternally true, and that they contemn what other peoples believe.

"These darkened views make fools of them, but certainly good soldiers too—perhaps by reason indeed of this very exalted self-consciousness and their firm reliance on their supreme god."

"Yes, they certainly are," assented Hierax. "But they serve your brother more willingly, and at a lower price, than us."

"I will show them," cried the king, "that their taste is a perverted and obnoxious one. I require of the priests that they should instruct the people to be obedient, and to bear their privations patiently; but the Jews," and at these words his eyes rolled with an ominous glare, "the Jews I will exterminate, when the time comes."

"That will be good for our treasury too," laughed Komanus.

"And for the temples in the country," added Euergetes, "for though I seek to extirpate other foes I would rather win over the priests; and I must try to win them if Philometor's kingdom falls into my hands, for the Egyptians require that their king should be a god; and I cannot arrive at the dignity of a real god, to whom my swarthy subjects will pray with thorough satisfaction, and without making my life a burden to me by continual revolts, unless I am raised to it by the suffrages of the priests."

"And nevertheless," replied Hierax, who was the only one of Euergetes' dependents, who dared to contradict him on important questions, "nevertheless this very day a grave demand is to be preferred on your account to the high-priest of Serapis. You press for the surrender of a servant of the god, and Philometor will not neglect—"

"Will not neglect," interrupted Euergetes, "to inform the mighty Asclepiodorus that he wants the sweet creature for me, and not for himself. Do you know that Eros has pierced my heart, and that I burn for the fair Irene, although these eyes have not yet been blessed with the sight of her?

"I see you believe me, and I am speaking the exact truth, for I vow I will possess myself of this infantine Hebe as surely as I hope to win my brother's throne; but when I plant a tree, it is not merely to ornament my garden but to get some use of it. You will see how I will win over both the prettiest of little lady-loves and the high-priest who, to be sure, is a Greek, but still a man hard to bend. My tools are all ready outside there.

"Now, leave me, and order Eulaeus to join me here."

"You are as a divinity," said Komanus, bowing deeply, "and we but as frail mortals. Your proceedings often seem dark and incomprehensible to our weak intellect, but when a course, which to us seems to lead to no good issue, turns out well, we are forced to admit with astonishment that you always choose the best way, though often a tortuous one."

For a short time the king was alone, sitting with his black brows knit, and gazing meditatively at the floor. But as soon as he heard the soft footfall of Eulaeus, and the louder step of his guide, he once more assumed the aspect of a careless and reckless man of the world, shouted a jolly welcome to Eulaeus, reminded him of his, the king's, boyhood, and of how often he, Eulaeus, had helped him to persuade his mother to grant him some wish she had previously refused him.

"But now, old boy," continued the king, "the times are changed, and with you now-a-days it is everything for Philometor and nothing for poor Euergetes, who, being the younger, is just the one who most needs your assistance."

Eulaeus bowed with a smile which conveyed that he understood perfectly how little the king's last words were spoken in earnest, and he said:

"I purposed always to assist the weaker of you two, and that is what I believe myself to be doing now."

"You mean my sister?"

"Our sovereign lady Cleopatra is of the sex which is often unjustly called the weaker. Though you no doubt were pleased to speak in jest when you asked that question, I feel bound to answer you distinctly that it was not Cleopatra that I meant, but King Philometor."

"Philometor? Then you have no faith in his strength, you regard me as stronger than he; and yet, at the banquet to-day, you offered me your services, and told me that the task had devolved upon you of demanding the surrender of the little serving-maiden of Serapis, in the king's name, of Asclepiodorus, the high-priest. Do you call that aiding the weaker? But perhaps you were drunk when you told me that?

"No? You were more moderate than I? Then some other change of views must have taken place in you; and yet that would very much surprise me, since your principles require you to aid the weaker son of my mother—"

"You are laughing at me," interrupted the courtier with gentle reproachfulness, and yet in a tone of entreaty. "If I took your side it was not from caprice, but simply and expressly from a desire to remain faithful to the one aim and end of my life."

"And that is?"

"To provide for the welfare of this country in the same sense as did your illustrious mother, whose counsellor I was."

"But you forget to mention the other—to place yourself to the best possible advantage."

"I did not forget it, but I did not mention it, for I know how closely measured out are the moments of a king; and besides, it seems to me as self-evident that we think of our personal advantage as that when we buy a horse we also buy his shadow."

"How subtle! But I no more blame you than I should a girl who stands before her mirror to deck herself for her lover, and who takes the same opportunity of rejoicing in her own beauty.

"However, to return to your first speech. It is for the sake of Egypt as you think—if I understand you rightly—that you now offer me the services you have hitherto devoted to my brother's interests?"

"As you say; in these difficult times the country needs the will and the hand of a powerful leader."

"And such a leader you think I am?"

"Aye, a giant in strength of will, body and intellect—whose desire to unite the two parts of Egypt in your sole possession cannot fail, if you strike and grasp boldly, and if—"

"If?" repeated the king, looking at the speaker so keenly that his eyes fell, and he answered softly:

"If Rome should raise no objection."

Euergetes shrugged his shoulders, and replied gravely:

"Rome indeed is like Fate, which always must give the final decision in everything we do. I have certainly not been behindhand in enormous sacrifices to mollify that inexorable power, and my representative, through whose hands pass far greater sums than through those of the paymasters of the troops, writes me word that they are not unfavorably disposed towards me in the Senate."

"We have learned that from ours also. You have more friends by the Tiber than Philometor, my own king, has; but our last despatch is already several weeks old, and in the last few days things have occurred—"

"Speak!" cried Euergetes, sitting bolt upright on his cushions. "But if you are laying a trap for me, and if you are speaking now as my brother's tool, I will punish you—aye! and if you fled to the uttermost cave of the

Troglodytes I would have you followed up, and you should be torn in pieces alive, as surely as I believe myself to be the true son of my father."

"And I should deserve the punishment," replied Eulaeus humbly. Then he went on: "If I see clearly, great events lie before us in the next few days."

"Yes—truly," said Euergetes firmly.

"But just at present Philometor is better represented in Rome than he has ever been. You made acquaintance with young Publius Scipio at the king's table, and showed little zeal in endeavoring to win his good graces."

"He is one of the Cornelii," interrupted the king, "a distinguished young man, and related to all the noblest blood of Rome; but he is not an ambassador; he has travelled from Athens to Alexandria, in order to learn more than he need; and he carries his head higher and speaks more freely than becomes him before kings, because the young fellows fancy it looks well to behave like their elders."

"He is of more importance than you imagine."

"Then I will invite him to Alexandria, and there will win him over in three days, as surely as my name is Euergetes."

"It will then be too late, for he has to-day received, as I know for certain, plenipotentiary powers from the Senate to act in their name in case of need, until the envoy who is to be sent here again arrives."

"And I only now learn this for the first time!" cried the king springing up from his couch, "my friends must be deaf, and blind and dull indeed, if still I have any, and my servants and emissaries too! I cannot bear this haughty ungracious fellow, but I will invite him tomorrow morning—nay I will invite him to-day, to a festive entertainment, and send him the four handsomest horses that I have brought with me from Cyrene. I will—"

"It will all be in vain," said Eulaeus calmly and dispassionately. "For he is master, in the fullest and widest meaning of the word, of the queen's favor—nay—if I may permit myself to speak out freely—of Cleopatra's more than warm liking, and he enjoys this sweetest of gifts with a thankful heart. Philometor—as he always does—lets matters go as they may, and Cleopatra and Publius—Publius and Cleopatra triumph even publicly in their love; gaze into each other's eyes like any pair of pastoral Arcadians, exchange cups and kiss the rim on the spot where the lips of the other have touched it. Promise and grant what you will to this man, he will stand by your sister; and if you should succeed in expelling her from the throne he would boldly treat you as Popilius Laenas did your uncle Antiochus: he would draw a circle round your person, and say that if you dared to step beyond it Rome would march against you."

Euergetes listened in silence, then, flinging away the draperies that wrapped his body, he paced up and down in stormy agitation, groaning from time to time, and roaring like a wild bull that feels itself confined with cords and bands, and that exerts all its strength in vain to rend them.

Finally he stood still in front of Eulaeus and asked him:

"What more do you know of the Roman?"

"He, who would not allow you to compare yourself to Alcibiades, is endeavoring to out-do that darling of the Athenian maidens; for he is not content with having stolen the heart of the king's wife, he is putting out his hand to reach the fairest virgin who serves the highest of the gods. The water-bearer whom Lysias, the Roman's friend, recommended for a Hebe is beloved by Publius, and he hopes to enjoy her favors more easily in your gay palace than he can in the gloomy temple of Serapis."

At these words the king struck his forehead with his hand, exclaiming: "Oh! to be a king—a man who is a match for any ten! and to be obliged to submit with a patient shrug like a peasant whose grain my horsemen crush into the ground!

"He can spoil everything; mar all my plans and thwart all my desires— and I can do nothing but clench my fist, and suffocate with rage. But this fuming and groaning are just as unavailing as my raging and cursing by the death-bed of my mother, who was dead all the same and never got up again.

"If this Publius were a Greek, a Syrian, an Egyptian—nay, were he my own brother—I tell you, Eulaeus, he should not long stand in my way; but he is plenipotentiary from Rome, and Rome is Fate—Rome is Fate."

The king flung himself back on to his cushions with a deep sigh, and as if crushed with despair, hiding his face in the soft pillows; but Eulaeus crept noiselessly up to the young giant, and whispered in his ear with solemn deliberateness:

"Rome is Fate, but even Rome can do nothing against Fate. Publius Scipio must die because he is ruining your mother's daughter, and stands in the way of your saving Egypt. The Senate would take a terrible revenge if he were murdered, but what can they do if wild beasts fall on their plenipotentiary, and tear him to pieces?"

"Grand! splendid!" cried Euergetes, springing again to his feet, and opening his large eyes with radiant surprise and delight, as if heaven itself had opened before them, revealing the sublime host of the gods feasting at golden tables.

"You are a great man, Eulaeus, and I shall know how to reward you; but do you know of such wild beasts as we require, and do they know how to conduct themselves so that no one shall dare to harbor even the shadow of a suspicion that the wounds torn by their teeth and claws were inflicted by daggers, pikes or spearheads?"

"Be perfectly easy," replied Eulaeus. "These beasts of prey have already had work to do here in Memphis, and are in the service of the king—"

"Aha! of my gentle brother!" laughed Euergetes. "And he boasts of never having killed any one excepting in battle—and now—"

"But Philometor has a wife," interposed Eulaeus; and Euergetes went on.

"Aye, woman, woman! what is there that a man may not learn from a woman?"

Then he added in a lower tone: "When can your wild beasts do their work?"

"The sun has long since risen; before it sets I will have made my preparations, and by about midnight, I should think, the deed may be done. We will promise the Roman a secret meeting, lure him out to the temple of Serapis, and on his way home through the desert—"

"Aye, then,—" cried the king, making a thrust at his own breast as though his hand held a dagger, and he added in warning: "But your beasts must be as powerful as lions, and as cautious-as cautious, as cats. If you want gold apply to Komanus, or, better still, take this purse. Is it enough? Still I must ask you; have you any personal ground of hatred against the Roman?"

"Yes," answered Eulaeus decisively. "He guesses that I know all about him and his doings, and he has attacked me with false accusations which may bring me into peril this very day. If you should hear that the queen has decided on throwing me into prison, take immediate steps for my liberation."

"No one shall touch a hair of your head; depend upon that. I see that it is to your interest to play my game, and I am heartily glad of it, for a man works with all his might for no one but himself. And now for the last thing: When will you fetch my little Hebe?"

"In an hour's time I am going to Asclepiodorus; but we must not demand the girl till to-morrow, for today she must remain in the temple as a decoy-bird for Publius Scipio."

"I will take patience; still I have yet another charge to give you. Represent the matter to the high-priest in such a way that he shall think my brother wishes to gratify one of my fancies by demanding—absolutely demanding—the water-bearer on my behalf. Provoke the man as far as is possible without exciting suspicion, and if I know him rightly, he will stand upon his rights, and refuse you persistently. Then, after you, will come Komanus from me with greetings and gifts and promises.

"To-morrow, when we have done what must be done to the Roman, you shall fetch the girl in my brother's name either by cunning or by force; and the day after, if the gods graciously lend me their aid in uniting the two realms of Egypt under my own hand, I will explain to Asclepiodorus that I have punished Philometor for his sacrilege against his temple, and have deposed him from the throne. Serapis shall see which of us is his friend.

"If all goes well, as I mean that it shall, I will appoint you Epitropon of the re-united kingdom—that I swear to you by the souls of my deceased ancestors. I will speak with you to-day at any hour you may demand it."

Eulaeus departed with a step as light as if his interview with the king had restored him to youth.

When Hierax, Komanus, and the other officers returned to the room, Euergetes gave orders that his four finest horses from Cyrene should be led before noonday to his friend Publius Cornelius Scipio, in token of his affection and respect. Then he suffered himself to be dressed, and went to Aristarchus with whom he sat down to work at his studies.

CHAPTER XIV

The temple of Serapis lay in restful silence, enveloped in darkness, which so far hid its four wings from sight as to give it the aspect of a single rock-like mass wrapped in purple mist.

Outside the temple precincts too all had been still; but just now a clatter of hoofs and rumble of wheels was audible through the silence, otherwise so profound that it seemed increased by every sound. Before the vehicle which occasioned this disturbance had reached the temple, it stopped, just outside the sacred acacia-grove, for the neighing of a horse was now audible in that direction.

It was one of the king's horses that neighed; Lysias, the Greek, tied him up to a tree by the road at the edge of the grove, flung his mantle over the loins of the smoking beast; and feeling his way from tree to tree soon found himself by the Well of the Sun where he sat down on the margin.

Presently from the east came a keen, cold breeze, the harbinger of sunrise; the gray gloaming began by degrees to pierce and part the tops of the tall trees, which, in the darkness, had seemed a compact black roof. The crowing of cocks rang out from the court-yard of the temple, and, as the Corinthian rose with a shiver to warm himself by a rapid walk backwards and forwards, he heard a door creak near the outer wall of the temple, of which the outline now grew sharper and clearer every instant in the growing light.

He now gazed with eager observation down the path which, as the day approached, stood out with increasing clearness from the surrounding shades, and his heart began to beat faster as he perceived a figure approaching the well, with rapid steps. It was a human form that advanced towards him—only one—no second figure accompanied it; but it was not a man—no, a woman in a long robe. Still, she for whom he waited was surely smaller than the woman, who now came near to him. Was it the elder and not the younger sister, whom alone he was anxious to speak with, who came to the well this morning?

He could now distinguish her light foot-fall—now she was divided from him by a young acacia-shrub which hid her from his gaze-now she set down two water-jars on the ground—now she briskly lifted the bucket and filled the vessel she held in her left hand—now she looked towards the eastern horizon, where the dim light of dawn grew broader and brighter, and Lysias thought he recognized Irene—and now—Praised be the gods! he was sure; before him stood the younger and not the elder sister; the very maiden whom he sought.

Still half concealed by the acacia-shrub, and in a soft voice so as not to alarm her, he called Irene's name, and the poor child's blood froze with terror, for never before had she been startled by a man here, and at this hour. She stood as if rooted to the spot, and, trembling with fright, she pressed the cold, wet, golden jar, sacred to the god, closely to her bosom.

Lysias repeated her name, a little louder than before, and went on, but in a subdued voice:

"Do not be frightened, Irene; I am Lysias, the Corinthian—your friend, whose pomegranate-blossom you wore yesterday, and who spoke to you after the procession. Let me bid you good morning!"

At these words the girl let her hand fall by her side, still holding the jar, and pressing her right hand to her heart, she exclaimed, drawing a deep breath:

"How dreadfully you frightened me! I thought some wandering soul was calling me that had not yet returned to the nether world, for it is not till the sun rises that spirits are scared away."

"But it cannot scare men of flesh and blood whose purpose is good. I, you may believe me, would willingly stay with you, till Helios departs again, if you would permit me."

"I can neither permit nor forbid you anything," answered Irene. "But, how came you here at this hour?"

"In a chariot," replied Lysias smiling.

"That is nonsense—I want to know what you came to the Well of the Sun for at such an hour."

"I What but for you yourself? You told me yesterday that you were glad to sleep, and so am I; still, to see you once more, I have been only to glad to shorten my night's rest considerably."

"But, how did you know?"

"You yourself told me yesterday at what time you were allowed to leave the temple."

"Did I tell you? Great Serapis! how light it is already. I shall be punished if the water-jar is not standing on the altar by sunrise, and there is Klea's too to be filled."

"I will fill it for you directly—there—that is done; and now I will carry them both for you to the end of the grove, if you will promise me to return soon, for I have many things to ask you."

"Go on—only go on," said the girl; "I know very little; but ask away, though you will not find much to be made of any answers that I can give."

"Oh! yes, indeed, I shall—for instance, if I asked you to tell me all about your parents. My friend Publius, whom you know, and I also have heard how cruelly and unjustly they were punished, and we would gladly do much to procure their release."

"I will come—I will be sure to come," cried Irene loudly and eagerly, "and shall I bring Klea with me? She was called up in the middle of the night by the gatekeeper, whose child is very ill. My sister is very fond of it, and Philo will only take his medicine from her. The little one had gone to sleep in her lap, and his mother came and begged me to fetch the water for us both. Now give me the jars, for none but we may enter the temple."

"There they are. Do not disturb your sister on my account in her care of the poor little boy, for I might indeed have one or two things to say to you which she need not hear, and which might give you pleasure. Now, I am going back to the well, so farewell! But do not let me have to wait very long for you." He spoke in a tender tone of entreaty, and the girl answered low and rapidly as she hurried away from him:

"I will come when the sun is up."

The Corinthian looked after her till she had vanished within the temple, and his heart was stirred—stirred as it had not been for many years. He could not help recalling the time when he would teaze his younger sister, then still quite a child, putting her to the test by asking her, with a perfectly grave face, to give him her cake or her apple which he did not really want at all. The little one had almost always put the thing he asked for to his mouth with her tiny hands, and then he had often felt exactly as he felt now.

Irene too was still but a child, and no less guileless than his darling in his own home; and just as his sister had trusted him—offering him the best she had to give—so this simple child trusted him; him, the profligate Lysias, before whom all the modest women of Corinth cast down their eyes, while fathers warned their growing-up sons against him; trusted him with her virgin self—nay, as he thought, her sacred person.

"I will do thee no harm, sweet child!" he murmured to himself, as he presently turned on his heel to return to the well. He went forward quickly at first, but after a few steps he paused before the marvellous and glorious picture that met his gaze. Was Memphis in flames? Had fire fallen to burn up the shroud of mist which had veiled his way to the temple?

The trunks of the acacia-trees stood up like the blackened pillars of a burning city, and behind them the glow of a conflagration blazed high up to the heavens. Beams of violet and gold slipped and sparkled between the boughs, and danced among the thorny twigs, the white racemes of flowers, and the tufts of leaves with their feathery leaflets; the clouds above were fired with tints more pure and tender than those of the roses with which Cleopatra had decked herself for the banquet.

Not like this did the sun rise in his own country! Or, was it perhaps only that in Corinth or in Athens at break of day, as he staggered home drunk from some feast, he had looked more at the earth than at the heavens?

His horses began now to neigh loudly as if to greet the steeds of the coming Sun-god. Lysias hurried to them through the grove, patted their shining necks with soothing words, and stood looking down at the vast city at his feet, over which hung a film of violet mist—at the solemn Pyramids, over which the morning glow flung a gay robe of rose-color—on the huge temple of Ptah, with the great colossi in front of its pylons—on the Nile, mirroring the glory of the sky, and on the limestone hills behind the villages of Babylon and Troy, about which he had, only yesterday, heard a Jew at the king's table relating a legend current among his countrymen to the effect that these hills had been obliged to give up all their verdure to grace the mounts of the sacred city Hierosolyma.

The rocky cliffs of this barren range glowed at this moment like the fire in the heart of the great ruby which had clasped the festal robe of King Euergetes across his bull-neck, as it reflected the shimmer of the tapers: and Lysias saw the day-star rising behind the range with blinding radiance, shooting forth rays like myriads of golden arrows, to rout and destroy his foe, the darkness of night.

Eos, Helios, Phoebus Apollo—these had long been to him no more than names, with which he associated certain phenomena, certain processes and ideas; for he when he was not luxuriating in the bath, amusing himself in the gymnasium, at cock or quail-fights, in the theatre or at Dionysiac processions—was wont to exercise his wits in the schools of the philosophers, so as to be able to shine in bandying words at entertainments; but to-day, and face to face with this sunrise, he believed as in the days of his childhood—he saw in his mind's eye the god riding in his golden chariot, and curbing his foaming steeds, his shining train floating lightly round him, bearing torches or scattering flowers—he threw up his arms with an impulse of devotion, praying aloud:

"To-day I am happy and light of heart. To thy presence do I owe this, O! Phoebus Apollo, for thou art light itself. Oh! let thy favors continue—"

But he here broke off in his invocation, and dropped his arms, for he heard approaching footsteps. Smiling at his childish weakness—for such he deemed it that he should have prayed—and yet content from his pious impulse, he turned his back on the sun, now quite risen, and stood face to face with Irene who called out to him:

"I was beginning to think that you had got out of patience and had gone away, when I found you no longer by the well. That distressed me—but you were only watching Helios rise. I see it every day, and yet it always grieves me to see it as red as it was to-day, for our Egyptian nurse used to tell me that when the east was very red in the morning it was because the Sun-god had slain his enemies, and it was their blood that colored the heavens, and the clouds and the hills."

"But you are a Greek," said Lysias, "and you must know that it is Eos that causes these tints when she touches the horizon with her rosy fingers before Helios appears. Now to-day you are, to me, the rosy dawn presaging a fine day."

"Such a ruddy glow as this," said Irene, "forebodes great heat, storms, and perhaps heavy rain, so the gatekeeper says; and he is always with the astrologers who observe the stars and the signs in the heavens from the towers near the temple-gates. He is poor little Philo's father. I wanted to bring Klea with me, for she knows more about our parents than I do; but he begged me not to call her away, for the child's throat is almost closed up, and if it cries much the physician says it will choke, and yet it is never quiet but when it is lying in Klea's arms. She is so good—and she never thinks of herself; she has been ever since midnight till now rocking that heavy child on her lap."

"We will talk with her presently," said the Corinthian. "But to-day it was for your sake that I came; you have such merry eyes, and your little mouth looks as if it were made for laughing, and not to sing lamentations. How can you bear being always in that shut up dungeon with all those solemn men in their black and white robes?"

"There are some very good and kind ones among them. I am most fond of old Krates, he looks gloomy enough at every one else; but with me only he jokes and talks, and he often shows me such pretty and elegantly wrought things."

"Ah! I told you just now you are like the rosy dawn before whom all darkness must vanish."

"If only you could know how thoughtless I can be, and how often I give trouble to Klea, who never scolds me for it, you would be far from comparing me with a goddess. Little old Krates, too, often compares me to all sorts of pretty things, but that always sounds so comical that I cannot help laughing. I had much rather listen to you when you flatter me."

"Because I am young and youth suits with youth. Your sister is older, and so much graver than you are. Have you never had a companion of your own age whom you could play with, and to whom you could tell everything?"

"Oh! yes when I was still very young; but since my parents fell into trouble, and we have lived here in the temple, I have always been alone with Klea. What do you want to know about my father?"

"That I will ask you by-and-by. Now only tell me, have you never played at hide and seek with other girls? May you never look on at the merry doings in the streets at the Dionysiac festivals? Have you ever ridden in a chariot?"

"I dare say I have, long ago—but I have forgotten it. How should I have any chance of such things here in the temple? Klea says it is no good even to think of them. She tells me a great deal about our parents—how my mother took care of us, and what my father used to say. Has anything happened that may turn out favorably for him? Is it possible that the king should have learned the truth? Make haste and ask your questions at once, for I have already been too long out here."

The impatient steeds neighed again as she spoke, and Lysias, to whom this chat with Irene was perfectly enchanting, but who nevertheless had not for a moment lost sight of his object, hastily pointed to the spot where his horses were standing, and said:

"Did you hear the neighing of those mettlesome horses? They brought me hither, and I can guide them well; nay, at the last Isthmian games I won the crown with my own quadriga. You said you had never ridden standing in a chariot. How would you like to try for once how it feels? I will drive you with pleasure up and down behind the grove for a little while."

Irene heard this proposal with sparkling eyes and cried, as she clapped her hands:

"May I ride in a chariot with spirited horses, like the queen? Oh! impossible! Where are your horses standing?"

In this instant she had forgotten Klea, the duty which called her back to the temple, even her parents, and she followed the Corinthian with winged steps, sprang into the two-wheeled chariot, and clung fast to the breastwork, as Lysias took his place by her side, seized the reins, and with a strong and practised hand curbed the mettle of his spirited steeds.

She stood perfectly guileless and undoubting by his side, and wholly at his mercy as the chariot rattled off; but, unknown to herself, beneficent powers were shielding her with buckler and armor—her childlike innocence, and that memory of her parents which her tempter himself had revived in her mind, and which soon came back in vivid strength.

Breathing deep with excitement, and filled with such rapture as a bird may feel when it first soars from its narrow nest high up into the ether she cried out again and again:

"Oh, this is delightful! this is splendid!" and then:

"How we rush through the air as if we were swallows! Faster, Lysias, faster! No, no—that is too fast; wait a little that I may not fall! Oh, I am not frightened; it is too delightful to cut through the air just as a Nile boat cuts through the stream in a storm, and to feel it on my face and neck."

Lysias was very close to her; when, at her desire, he urged his horses to their utmost pace, and saw her sway, he involuntarily put out his hand to hold her by the girdle; but Irene avoided his grasp, pressing close against the side of the chariot next her, and every time he touched her she drew her arm close up to her body, shrinking together like the fragile leaf of a sensitive plant when it is touched by some foreign object.

She now begged the Corinthian to allow her to hold the reins for a little while, and he immediately acceded to her request, giving them into her hand, though, stepping behind her, he carefully kept the ends of them in his own. He could now see her shining hair, the graceful oval of her head, and her white throat eagerly bent forward; an indescribable longing came over him to press a kiss on her head; but he forbore, for he remembered his friend's words that he would fulfil the part of a guardian to these girls. He too would be a protector to her, aye and more than that, he would care for her as a father might. Still, as often as the chariot jolted over a stone, and he touched her to support her, the suppressed wish revived, and once when her hair was blown quite close to his lips he did indeed kiss it—but only as a friend or a brother might. Still, she must have felt the breath from his lips, for she turned round hastily, and gave him back the reins; then, pressing her hand to her brow, she said in a quite altered voice—not unmixed with a faint tone of regret:

"This is not right—please now to turn the horses round."

Lysias, instead of obeying her, pulled at the reins to urge the horses to a swifter pace, and before he could find a suitable answer, she had glanced up at the sun, and pointing to the east she exclaimed:

"How late it is already! what shall I say if I have been looked for, and they ask me where I have been so long? Why don't you turn round—nor ask me anything about my parents?"

The last words broke from her with vehemence, and as Lysias did not immediately reply nor make any attempt to check the pace of the horses, she herself seized the reins exclaiming:

"Will you turn round or no?"

"No!" said the Greek with decision. "But—"

"And this is what you intended!" shrieked the girl, beside herself. "You meant to carry me off by stratagem—but wait, only wait—"

And before Lysias could prevent her she had turned round, and was preparing to spring from the chariot as it rushed onwards; but her companion was quicker than she; he clutched first at her robe and then her girdle, put his arm round her waist, and in spite of her resistance pulled her back into the chariot.

Trembling, stamping her little feet and with tears in her eyes, she strove to free her girdle from his grasp; he, now bringing his horses to a stand-still, said kindly but earnestly:

"What I have done is the best that could happen to you, and I will even turn the horses back again if you command it, but not till you have heard me; for when I got you into the chariot by stratagem it was because I was afraid that you would refuse to accompany me, and yet I knew that every delay would expose you to the most hideous peril. I did not indeed take a base advantage of your father's name, for my friend Publius Scipio, who is very influential, intends to do everything in his power to procure his freedom and to reunite you to him. But, Irene, that could never have happened if I had left you where you have hitherto lived."

During this discourse the girl had looked at Lysias in bewilderment, and she interrupted him with the exclamation:

"But I have never done any one an injury! Who can gain any benefit by persecuting a poor creature like me:

"Your father was the most righteous of men," replied Lysias, "and nevertheless he was carried off into torments like a criminal. It is not only the unrighteous and the wicked that are persecuted. Have you ever heard of King Euergetes, who, at his birth, was named the 'well-doer,' and who has earned that of the 'evil doer' by his crimes? He has heard that you are fair, and he is about to demand of the high-priest that he should surrender you to him. If Asclepiodorus agrees—and what can he do against the might of a king—you will be made the companion of flute-playing girls and painted women, who riot with drunken men at his wild carousals and orgies, and if your parents found you thus, better would it be for them—"

"Is it true, all you are telling me?" asked Irene with flaming cheeks.

"Yes," answered Lysias firmly. "Listen Irene—I have a father and a dear mother and a sister, who is like you, and I swear to you by their heads—by those whose names never passed my lips in the presence of any other woman I ever sued to—that I am speaking the simple truth; that I seek nothing but only to save you; that if you desire it, as soon as I have hidden you I will never see you again, terribly hard as that would be to me—for I love you so dearly, so deeply—poor sweet little Irene—as you can never imagine."

Lysias took the girl's hand, but she withdrew it hastily, and raising her eyes, full of tears, to meet his she said clearly and firmly:

"I believe you, for no man could speak like that and betray another. But how do you know all this? Where are you taking me? Will Klea follow me?"

"At first you shall be concealed with the family of a worthy sculptor. We will let Klea know this very day of all that has happened to you, and when we have obtained the release of your parents then—but—Help us, protecting Zeus! Do you see the chariot yonder? I believe those are the white horses of the Eunuch Eulaeus, and if he were to see us here, all would be lost! Hold tight, we must go as fast as in a chariot race. There, now the hill hides us, and down there, by the little temple of Isis, the wife of your future host is already waiting for you; she is no doubt sitting in the closed chariot near the palm-trees.

"Yes, certainly, certainly, Klea shall hear all, so that she may not be uneasy about you! I must say farewell to you directly and then, afterwards, sweet Irene, will you sometimes think of the unhappy Lysias; or did Aurora, who greeted him this morning, so bright and full of happy promise, usher in a day not of joy but of sorrow and regret?" The Greek drew in rein as he spoke, bringing his horses to a sober pace, and looked tenderly in Irene's eyes. She returned his gaze with heart-felt emotion, but her gunny glance was dimmed with tears.

"Say something," entreated the Greek. "Will you not forget me? And may I soon visit you in your new retreat?"

Irene would so gladly have said yes—and yes again, a thousand times yes; and yet she, who was so easily carried away by every little emotion of her heart, in this supreme moment found strength enough to snatch her hand from that of the Greek, who had again taken it, and to answer firmly:

"I will remember you for ever and ever, but you must not come to see me till I am once more united to my Klea."

"But Irene, consider, if now—" cried Lysias much agitated.

"You swore to me by the heads of your nearest kin to obey my wishes," interrupted the girl. "Certainly I trust you, and all the more readily because you are so good to me, but I shall not do so any more if you do not keep your word. Look, here comes a lady to meet us who looks like a friend. She is already waving her hand to me. Yes, I will go with her gladly, and yet I am so anxious—so troubled, I cannot tell you—but I am so thankful too! Think of me sometimes, Lysias, and of our journey here, and of our talk, and of my parents: I entreat you, do for them all you possibly can. I wish I could help crying—but I cannot!"

CHAPTER XV

Lysias eyes had not deceived him. The chariot with white horses which he had evaded during his flight with Irene belonged to Eulaeus. The morning being cool—and also because Cleopatra's lady-in-waiting was with him—he had come out in a closed chariot, in which he sat on soft cushions side by side with the Macedonian lady, endeavoring to win her good graces by a conversation, witty enough in its way.

"On the way there," thought he, "I will make her quite favorable to me, and on the way back I will talk to her of my own affairs."

The drive passed quickly and pleasantly for both, and they neither of them paid any heed to the sound of the hoofs of the horses that were bearing away Irene.

Eulaeus dismounted behind the acacia-grove, and expressed a hope that Zoe would not find the time very long while he was engaged with the high-priest; perhaps indeed, he remarked, she might even make some use of the time by making advances to the representative of Hebe.

But Irene had been long since warmly welcomed in the house of Apollodorus, the sculptor, by the time they once more found themselves together in the chariot; Eulaeus feigning, and Zoe in reality feeling, extreme dissatisfaction at all that had taken place in the temple. The high-priest had rejected Philometor's demand that he should send the water-bearer to the palace on King Euergetes' birthday, with a decisiveness which Eulaeus would never have given him credit for, for he had on former occasions shown a disposition to measures of compromise; while Zoe had not even seen the waterbearer.

"I fancy," said the queen's shrewd friend, "that I followed you somewhat too late, and that when I entered the temple about half an hour after you—having been detained first by Imhotep, the old physician, and then by an assistant of Apollodorus, the sculptor, with some new busts of the philosophers—the high-priest had already given orders that the girl should be kept concealed; for when I asked to see her, I was conducted first to her miserable room, which seemed more fit for peasants or goats than for a Hebe, even for a sham one—but I found it perfectly deserted.

"Then I was shown into the temple of Serapis, where a priest was instructing some girls in singing, and then sent hither and thither, till at last, finding no trace whatever of the famous Irene, I came to the dwelling-house of the gate-keeper of the temple.

"An ungainly woman opened the door, and said that Irene had been gone from thence for some long time, but that her elder sister was there, so I desired she might be fetched to speak with me. And what, if you please, was the answer I received? The goddess Klea—I call her so as being sister to a Hebe—had to nurse a sick child, and if I wanted to see her I might go in and find her.

"The tone of the message quite conveyed that the distance from her down to me was as great as in fact it is the other way. However, I thought it worth the trouble to see this supercilious water-bearing girl, and I went into a low room—it makes me sick now to remember how it smelt of poverty—and there she sat with an idiotic child, dying on her lap. Everything that surrounded me was so revolting and dismal that it will haunt my dreams with terror for weeks to come and spoil all my cheerful hours.

"I did not remain long with these wretched creatures, but I must confess that if Irene is as like to Hebe as her elder sister is to Hera, Euergetes has good grounds for being angry if Asclepiodorus keeps the girl from him.

"Many a queen—and not least the one whom you and I know so intimately-would willingly give half of her kingdom to possess such a figure and such a mien as this serving-girl. And then her eyes, as she looked at me when she rose with that little gasping corpse in her arms, and asked me what I wanted with her sister!

"There was an impressive and lurid glow in those solemn eyes, which looked as if they had been taken out of some Medusa's head to be set in her beautiful face. And there was a sinister threat in them too which seemed to say: 'Require nothing of her that I do not approve of, or you will be turned into stone on the spot.' She did not answer twenty words to my questions, and when I once more tasted the fresh air outside, which never seemed to me so pleasant as by contrast with that horrible hole, I had learnt no more than that no one knew—or chose to know—in what corner the fair Irene was hidden, and that I should do well to make no further enquiries.

"And now, what will Philometor do? What will you advise him to do?"

"What cannot be got at by soft words may sometimes be obtained by a sufficiently large present," replied Eulaeus. "You know very well that of all words none is less familiar to these gentry than the little word 'enough'; but who indeed is really ready to say it?

"You speak of the haughtiness and the stern repellent demeanor of our Hebe's sister. I have seen her too, and I think that her image might be set up in the Stoa as a happy impersonation of the severest virtue: and yet children generally resemble their parents, and her father was the veriest peculator and the most cunning rascal that ever came in my way, and was sent off to the gold-mines for very sufficient reasons. And for the sake of the daughter of a convicted criminal you have been driven through the dust and the scorching heat, and have had to submit to her scorn and contemptuous airs, while I am threatened with grave peril on her account, for you know that Cleopatra's latest whim is to do honor to the Roman, Publius Scipio; he, on the other hand, is running after our Hebe, and, having promised her that he will obtain an unqualified pardon for her father, he will do his utmost to throw the odium of his robbery upon me.

"The queen is to give him audience this very day, and you cannot know how many enemies a man makes who, like me, has for many years been one of the leading men of a great state. The king acknowledges, and with gratitude, all that I have done for him and for his mother; but if, at the moment when Publius Scipio accuses me, he is more in favor with her than ever, I am a lost man.

"You are always with the queen; do you tell her who these girls are, and what motives the Roman has for loading me with their father's crimes; and some opportunity must offer for doing you and your belongings some friendly office or another."

"What a shameless crew!" exclaimed Zoe. "Depend upon it I will not be silent, for I always do what is just. I cannot bear seeing others suffering an injustice, and least of all that a man of your merit and distinction should be wounded in his honor, because a haughty foreigner takes a fancy to a pretty little face and a conceited doll of a girl."

Zoe was in the right when she found the air stifling in the gate-keeper's house, for poor Irene, unaccustomed to such an atmosphere, could no more endure it than the pretentious maid of honor. It cost even Klea an effort to remain in the wretched room, which served as the dwelling-place of the whole family; where the cooking was carried on at a smoky hearth, while, at night, it also sheltered a goat and a few fowls; but she had endured even severer trials than this for the sake of what she deemed right, and she was so fond of little Philo—her anxious care in arousing by degrees his slumbering intelligence had brought her so much soothing satisfaction, and the child's innocent gratitude had been so tender a reward—that she wholly forgot the repulsive surroundings as soon as she felt that her presence and care were indispensable to the suffering little one.

Imhotep, the most famous of the priest-physicians of the temple of Asclepius—a man who was as learned in Greek as in Egyptian medical lore, and who had been known by the name of "the modern Herophilus" since King Philometor had summoned him from Alexandria to Memphis— had long since been watchful of the gradual development of the dormant intelligence of the gate-keeper's child, whom he saw every day in his visits to the temple. Now, not long after Zoe had quitted the house, he came in to see the sick child for the third time. Klea was still holding the boy on her lap when he entered. On a wooden stool in front of her stood a brazier of charcoal, and on it a small copper kettle the physician had brought with him; to this a long tube was attached. The tube was in two parts, joined together by a leather joint, also tubular, in such a way that the upper portion could be turned in any direction. Klea from time to time applied it to the breast of the child, and, in obedience to Imhotep's instructions, made the little one inhale the steam that poured out of it.

"Has it had the soothing effect it ought to have?" asked the physician.

"Yes, indeed, I think so," replied Klea, "There is not so much noise in the chest when the poor little fellow draws his breath."

The old man put his ear to the child's mouth, laid his hand on his brow, and said:

"If the fever abates I hope for the best. This inhaling of steam is an excellent remedy for these severe catarrhs, and a venerable one besides; for in the oldest writings of Hermes we find it prescribed as an application in such cases. But now he has had enough of it. Ah! this steam—this steam! Do you know that it is stronger than horses or oxen, or the united strength of a whole army of giants? That diligent enquirer Hero of Alexandria discovered this lately.

"But our little invalid has had enough of it, we must not overheat him. Now, take a linen cloth—that one will do though it is not very fine. Fold it together, wet it nicely with cold water—there is some in that miserable potsherd there—and now I will show you how to lay it on the child's throat.

"You need not assure me that you understand me, Klea, for you have hands—neat hands—and patience without end! Sixty-five years have I lived, and have always had good health, but I could almost wish to be ill for once, in order to be nursed by you. That poor child is well off better than many a king's child when it is sick; for him hireling nurses, no doubt, fetch and do all that is necessary, but one thing they cannot give, for they have it not; I mean the loving and indefatigable patience by which you have worked a miracle on this child's mind, and are now working another on his body. Aye, aye, my girl; it is to you and not me that this woman will owe her child if it is preserved to her. Do you hear me, woman? and tell your husband so too; and if you do not reverence Klea as a goddess, and do not lay your hands beneath her feet, may you be—no—I will wish you no ill, for you have not too much of the good things of life as it is!"

As he spoke the gate-keeper's wife came timidly up to the physician and the sick child, pushed her rough and tangled hair off her forehead a little, crossed her lean arms at full length behind her back, and, looking down with out-stretched neck at the boy, stared in dumb amazement at the wet cloths. Then she timidly enquired:

"Are the evil spirits driven out of the child?"

"Certainly," replied the physician. "Klea there has exorcised them, and I have helped her; now you know."

"Then I may go out for a little while? I have to sweep the pavement of the forecourt."

Klea nodded assent, and when the woman had disappeared the physician said:

"How many evil demons we have to deal with, alas! and how few good ones. Men are far more ready and willing to believe in mischievous spirits than in kind or helpful ones; for when things go ill with them—and it is generally their own fault when they do—it comforts them and flatters their vanity if only they can throw the blame on the shoulders of evil spirits; but when they are well to do, when fortune smiles on them of course, they like to ascribe it to themselves, to their own cleverness or their superior insight, and they laugh at those who admonish them of the gratitude they owe to the protecting and aiding demons. I, for my part, think more of the good than of the evil spirits, and you, my child, without doubt are one of the very best.

"You must change the compress every quarter of an hour, and between whiles go out into the open air, and let the fresh breezes fan your bosom— your cheeks look pale. At mid-day go to your own little room, and try to sleep. Nothing ought to be overdone, so you are to obey me."

Klea replied with a friendly and filial nod, and Imhotep stroked down her hair; then he left; she remained alone in the stuffy hot room, which grew hotter every minute, while she changed the wet cloths for the sick child, and watched with delight the diminishing hoarseness and difficulty of his breathing. From time to time she was overcome by a slight drowsiness, and closed her eyes for a few minutes, but only for a short while; and this half-awake and half-asleep condition, chequered by fleeting dreams, and broken only by an easy and pleasing duty, this relaxation of the tension of mind and body, had a certain charm of which, through it all, she remained perfectly conscious. Here she was in her right place; the physicians kind words had done her good, and her anxiety for the little life she loved was now succeeded by a well-founded hope of its preservation.

During the night she had already come to a definite resolution, to explain to the high-priest that she could not undertake the office of the twin-sisters, who wept by the bier of Osiris, and that she would rather endeavor to earn bread by the labor of her hands for herself and Irene—for that Irene should do any real work never entered her mind—at Alexandria, where even the blind and the maimed could find occupation. Even this prospect, which only yesterday had terrified her, began now to smile upon her, for it opened to her the possibility of proving independently the strong energy which she felt in herself.

Now and then the figure of the Roman rose before her mind's eye, and every time that this occurred she colored to her very forehead. But to-day she thought of this disturber of her peace differently from yesterday; for yesterday she had felt herself overwhelmed by him with shame, while to-day it appeared to her as though she had triumphed over him at the procession, since she had steadily avoided his glance, and when he had dared to approach her she had resolutely turned her back upon him. This was well, for how could the proud foreigner expose himself again to such humiliation.

"Away, away—for ever away!" she murmured to herself, and her eyes and brow, which had been lighted up by a transient smile, once more assumed the expression of repellent sternness which, the day before, had so startled and angered the Roman. Soon however the severity of her features relaxed, as she saw in fancy the young man's beseeching look, and remembered the praise given him by the recluse, and as—in the middle of this train of thought—her eyes closed again, slumber once more falling upon her spirit for a few minutes, she saw in her dream Publius himself, who approached her with a firm step, took her in his arms like a child, held her wrists to stop her struggling hands, gathered her up with rough force, and then flung her into a canoe lying at anchor by the bank of the Nile.

She fought with all her might against this attack and seizure, screamed aloud with fury, and woke at the sound of her own voice. Then she got up, dried her eyes that were wet with tears, and, after laying a freshly wetted cloth on the child's throat, she went out of doors in obedience to the physician's advice.

The sun was already at the meridian, and its direct rays were fiercely reflected from the slabs of yellow sandstone that paved the forecourt. On one side only of the wide, unroofed space, one of the colonnades that surrounded it threw a narrow shade, hardly a span wide; and she would not go there, for under it stood several beds on which lay pilgrims who, here in the very dwelling of the divinity, hoped to be visited with dreams which might give them an insight into futurity.

Klea's head was uncovered, and, fearing the heat of noon, she was about to return into the door-keeper's house, when she saw a young white-robed scribe, employed in the special service of Asclepiodorus, who came across the court beckoning eagerly to her. She went towards him, but before he had reached her he shouted out an enquiry whether her sister Irene was in the gate-keeper's lodge; the high-priest desired to speak with her, and she was nowhere to be found. Klea told him that a grand lady from the queen's court had already enquired for her, and that the last time she had seen her had been before daybreak, when she was going to fill the jars for the altar of the god at the Well of the Sun.

"The water for the first libation," answered the priest, "was placed on the altar at the right time, but Doris and her sister had to fetch it for the second and third. Asclepiodorus is angry—not with you, for he knows from Imhotep that you are taking care of a sick child—but with Irene. Try and think where she can be. Something serious must have occurred that the high-priest wishes to communicate to her."

Klea was startled, for she remembered Irene's tears the evening before, and her cry of longing for happiness and freedom. Could it be that the thoughtless child had yielded to this longing, and escaped without her knowledge, though only for a few hours, to see the city and the gay life there?

She collected herself so as not to betray her anxiety to the messenger, and said with downcast eyes:

"I will go and look for her."

She hurried back into the house, once more looked to the sick child, called his mother and showed her how to prepare the compresses, urging her to follow Imhotep's directions carefully and exactly till she should return; she pressed one loving kiss on little Philo's forehead—feeling as she did so that he was less hot than he had been in the morning—and then she left, going first to her own dwelling.

There everything stood or lay exactly as she had left it during the night, only the golden jars were wanting. This increased Klea's alarm, but the thought that Irene should have taken the precious vessels with her, in order to sell them and to live on the proceeds, never once entered her mind, for her sister, she knew, though heedless and easily persuaded, was incapable of any base action.

Where was she to seek the lost girl? Serapion, the recluse, to whom she first addressed herself, knew nothing of her.

On the altar of Serapis, whither she next went, she found both the vessels, and carried them back to her room.

Perhaps Irene had gone to see old Krates, and while watching his work and chattering to him, had forgotten the flight of time—but no, the priest-smith, whom she sought in his workshop, knew nothing of the vanished maiden. He would willingly have helped Klea to seek for his favorite, but the new lock for the tombs of the Apis had to be finished by mid-day, and his swollen feet were painful.

Klea stood outside the old man's door sunk in thought, and it occurred to her that Irene had often, in her idle hours, climbed up into the dove-cot belonging to the temple, to look out from thence over the distant landscape, to visit the sitting birds, to stuff food into the gaping beaks of the young ones, or to look up at the cloud of soaring doves. The pigeon-house, built up of clay pots and Nile-mud, stood on the top of the storehouse, which lay adjoining the southern boundary wall of the temple.

She hastened across the sunny courts and slightly shaded alleys, and mounted to the flat roof of the storehouse, but she found there neither the old dove-keeper nor his two grandsons who helped him in his work, for all three were in the anteroom to the kitchen, taking their dinner with the temple-servants.

Klea shouted her sister's name; once, twice, ten times—but no one answered. It was just as if the fierce heat of the sun burnt up the sound as it left her lips. She looked into the first pigeon-house, the second, the third, all the way to the last. The numberless little clay tenements of the brisk little birds threw out a glow like a heated oven; but this did not hinder her from hunting through every nook and corner. Her cheeks were burning, drops of perspiration stood on her brow, and she had much difficulty in freeing herself from the dust of the pigeon-houses, still she was not discouraged.

Perhaps Irene had gone into the Anubidium, or sanctuary of Asclepius, to enquire as to the meaning of some strange vision, for there, with the priestly physicians, lived also a priestess who could interpret the dreams of those who sought to be healed even better than a certain recluse who also could exercise that science. The enquirers often had to wait a long time outside the temple of Asclepius, and this consideration encouraged Klea, and made her insensible to the burning southwest wind which was now rising, and to the heat of the sun; still, as she returned to the Pastophorium—slowly, like a warrior returning from a defeat—she suffered severely from the heat, and her heart was wrung with anguish and suspense.

Willingly would she have cried, and often heaved a groan that was more like a sob, but the solace of tears to relieve her heart was still denied to her.

Before going to tell Asclepiodorus that her search had been unsuccessful, she felt prompted once more to talk with her friend, the anchorite; but before she had gone far enough even to see his cell, the high-priest's scribe once more stood in her way, and desired her to follow him to the temple. There she had to wait in mortal impatience for more than an hour in an ante room. At last she was conducted into a room where Asclepiodorus was sitting with the whole chapter of the priesthood of the temple of Serapis.

Klea entered timidly, and had to wait again some minutes in the presence of the mighty conclave before the high-priest asked her whether she could give any information as to the whereabouts of the fugitive, and whether she had heard or observed anything that could guide them on her track, since he, Asclepiodorus, knew that if Irene had run away secretly from the temple she must be as anxious about her as he was.

Klea had much difficulty in finding words, and her knees shook as she began to speak, but she refused the seat which was brought for her by order of Asclepiodorus. She recounted in order all the places where she had in vain sought her sister, and when she mentioned the sanctuary of Asclepius, and a recollection came suddenly and vividly before her of the figure of a lady of distinction, who had come there with a number of slaves and waiting-maids to have a dream interpreted, Zoe's visit to herself flashed upon her memory; her demeanor—at first so over-friendly and then so supercilious—and her haughty enquiries for Irene.

She broke off in her narrative, and exclaimed:

"I am sure, holy father, that Irene has not fled of her own free impulse, but some one perhaps may have lured her into quitting the temple and me; she is still but a child with a wavering mind. Could it possibly be that a lady of rank should have decoyed her into going with her? Such a person came to-day to see me at the door-keeper's lodge. She was richly dressed and wore a gold crescent in her light wavy hair, which was plaited with a silk ribband, and she asked me urgently about my sister. Imhotep, the physician, who often visits at the king's palace, saw her too, and told me her name is Zoe, and that she is lady-in-waiting to Queen Cleopatra."

These words occasioned the greatest excitement throughout the conclave of priests, and Asclepiodorus exclaimed:

"Oh! women, women! You indeed were right, Philammon; I could not and would not believe it! Cleopatra has done many things which are forgiven only in a queen, but that she should become the tool of her brother's basest passions, even you, Philammon, could hardly regard as likely, though you are always prepared to expect evil rather than good. But now, what is to be done? How can we protect ourselves against violence and superior force?"

Klea had appeared before the priests with cheeks crimson and glowing from the noontide heat, but at the high-priest's last words the blood left her face, she turned ashy-pale, and a chill shiver ran through her trembling limbs. Her father's child—her bright, innocent Irene—basely stolen for Euergetes, that licentious tyrant of whose wild deeds Serapion had told her only last evening, when he painted the dangers that would threaten her and Irene if they should quit the shelter of the sanctuary.

Alas, it was too true! They had tempted away her darling child, her comfort and delight, lured her with splendor and ease, only to sink her in shame! She was forced to cling to the back of the chair she had disdained, to save herself from falling.

But this weakness overmastered her for a few minutes only; she boldly took two hasty steps up to the table behind which the high-priest was sitting, and, supporting herself with her right hand upon it, she exclaimed, while her voice, usually so full and sonorous, had a hoarse tone:

"A woman has been the instrument of making another woman unworthy of the name of woman! and you—you, the protectors of right and virtue—you who are called to act according to the will and mind of the gods whom you serve—you are too weak to prevent it? If you endure this, if you do not put a stop to this crime you are not worthy—nay, I will not be interrupted—you, I say, are unworthy of the sacred title and of the reverence you claim, and I will appeal—"

"Silence, girl!" cried Asclepiodorus to the terribly excited Klea. "I would have you imprisoned with the blasphemers, if I did not well understand the anguish which has turned your brain. We will interfere on behalf of the abducted girl, and you must wait patiently in silence. You, Callimachus, must at once order Ismael, the messenger, to saddle the horses, and ride to Memphis to deliver a despatch from me to the queen; let us all combine to compose it, and subscribe our names as soon as we are perfectly certain that Irene has been carried off from these precincts. Philammon, do you command that the gong be sounded which calls together all the inhabitants of the temple; and you, my girl, quit this hall, and join the others."

CHAPTER XVI

Klea obeyed the high-priest's command at once, and wandered—not knowing exactly whither—from one corridor to another of the huge pile, till she was startled by the sound of the great brazen plate, struck with mighty blows, which rang out to the remotest nook and corner of the precincts. This call was for her too, and she went forthwith into the great court of assembly, which at every moment grew fuller and fuller. The temple-servants and the keepers of the beasts, the gate-keepers, the litter-bearers, the water-carriers- all streamed in from their interrupted meal, some wiping their mouths as they hurried in, or still holding in their hands a piece of bread, a radish, or a date which they hastily munched; the washer-men and women came in with hands still wet from washing the white robes of the priests, and the cooks arrived with brows still streaming from their unfinished labors. Perfumes floated round from the unwashed hands of the pastophori, who had been busied in the laboratories in the preparation of incense, while from the library and writing-rooms came the curators and scribes and the officials of the temple counting-house, their hair in disorder, and their light working-dress stained with red or black. The troop of singers, male and female, came in orderly array, just as they had been assembled for practice, and with them came the faded twins to whom Klea and Irene had been designated as successors by Asclepiodorus. Then came the pupils of the temple-school, tumbling noisily into the court-yard in high delight at this interruption to their lessons. The eldest of these were sent to bring in the great canopy under which the heads of the establishment might assemble.

Last of all appeared Asclepiodorus, who handed to a young scribe a complete list of all the inhabitants and members of the temple, that he might read it out. This he proceeded to do; each one answered with an audible "Here" as his name was called, and for each one who was absent information was immediately given as to his whereabouts.

Klea had joined the singing-women, and awaited in breathless anxiety a long-endlessly long-time for the name of her sister to be called; for it was not till the very smallest of the school-boys and the lowest of the neat-herds had answered, "Here," that the scribe read out, "Klea, the water-bearer," and nodded to her in answer as she replied "Here!"

Then his voice seemed louder than before as he read. "Irene, the water-bearer."

No answer following on these words, a slight movement, like the bowing wave that flies over a ripe cornfield when the morning breeze sweeps across the ears, was evident among the assembled inhabitants of the temple, who waited in breathless silence till Asclepiodorus stood forth, and said in a distinct and audible voice:

"You have all met here now at my call. All have obeyed it excepting those holy men consecrated to Serapis, whose vows forbid their breaking their seclusion, and Irene, the water-bearer. Once more I call, 'Irene,' a second, and a third time—and still no answer; I now appeal to you all assembled here, great and small, men and women who serve Serapis. Can any one of you give any information as to the whereabouts of this young girl? Has any one seen her since, at break of day, she placed the first libation from the Well of the Sun on the altar of the god? You are all silent! Then no one has met her in the course of this day? Now, one question more, and whoever can answer it stand forth and speak the words of truth.

"By which gate did this lady of rank depart who visited the temple early this morning?—By the eastern gate—good.

"Was she alone?—She was.

"By which gate did the epistolographer Eulaeus depart?—By the east.

"Was he alone?—He was.

"Did any one here present meet the chariot either of the lady or of Eulaeus?"

"I did," cried a car-driver, whose daily duty it was to go to Memphis with his oxen and cart to fetch provisions for the kitchen, and other necessaries.

"Speak," said the high-priest.

"I saw," replied the man, "the white horses of my Lord Eulaeus hard by the vineyard of Khakem; I know them well. They were harnessed to a closed chariot, in which besides himself sat a lady."

"Was it Irene?" asked Asclepiodorus.

"I do not know," replied the tarter, "for I could not see who sat in the chariot, but I heard the voice of Eulaeus, and then a woman's laugh. She laughed so heartily that I had to screw my mouth up myself, it tickled me so."

While Klea supposed this description to apply to Irene's merry laugh-which she had never thought of with regret till this moment—the high-priest exclaimed:

"You, keeper of the eastern gate, did the lady and Eulaeus enter and leave this sanctuary together?"

"No," was the answer. "She came in half an hour later than he did, and she quitted the temple quite alone and long after the eunuch."

"And Irene did not pass through your gate, and cannot have gone out by it?—I ask you in the name of the god we serve!"

"She may have done so, holy father," answered the gate-keeper in much alarm. "I have a sick child, and to look after him I went into my room several times; but only for a few minutes at a time-still, the gate stands open, all is quiet in Memphis now."

"You have done very wrong," said Asclepiodorus severely, "but since you have told the truth you may go unpunished. We have learned enough. All you gate-keepers now listen to me. Every gate of the temple must be carefully shut, and no one—not even a pilgrim nor any dignitary from Memphis, however high a personage he may be—is to enter or go out without my express permission; be as alert as if you feared an attack, and now go each of you to his duties."

The assembly dispersed; these to one side, those to another.

Klea did not perceive that many looked at her with suspicion as though she were responsible for her sister's conduct, and others with compassion; she did not even notice the twin-sisters, whose place she and Irene were to have filled, and this hurt the feelings of the good elderly maidens, who had to perform so much lamenting which they did not feel at all, that they eagerly seized every opportunity of expressing their feelings when, for once in a way, they were moved to sincere sorrow. But neither these sympathizing persons nor any other of the inhabitants of the temple, who approached Klea with the purpose of questioning or of pitying her, dared to address her, so stern and terrible was the solemn expression of her eyes which she kept fixed upon the ground.

At last she remained alone in the great court; her heart beat faster unusual, and strange and weighty thoughts were stirring in her soul. One thing was clear to her: Eulaeus—her father's ruthless foe and destroyer—was now also working the fall of the child of the man he had ruined, and, though she knew it not, the high-priest shared her suspicions. She, Klea, was by no means minded to let this happen without an effort at defence, and it even became clearer and clearer to her mind that it was her duty to act, and without delay. In the first instance she would ask counsel of her friend Serapion; but as she approached his cell the gong was sounded which summoned the priests to service, and at the same time warned her of her duty of fetching water.

Mechanically, and still thinking of nothing but Irene's deliverance, she fulfilled the task which she was accustomed to perform every day at the sound of this brazen clang, and went to her room to fetch the golden jars of the god.

As she entered the empty room her cat sprang to meet her with two leaps of joy, putting up her back, rubbing her soft head against her feet with her fine bushy tail ringed with black stripes set up straight, as cats are wont only when they are pleased. Klea was about to stroke the coaxing animal, but it sprang back, stared at her shyly, and, as she could not help thinking, angrily with its green eyes, and then shrank back into the corner close to Irene's couch.

"She mistook me!" thought Klea. "Irene is more lovable than I even to a beast, and Irene, Irene—" She sighed deeply at the name, and would have sunk down on her trunk there to consider of new ways and means—all of which however she was forced to reject as foolish and impracticable—but on the chest lay a little shirt she had begun to make for little Philo, and this reminded her again of the sick child and of the duty of fetching the water.

Without further delay she took up the jars, and as she went towards the well she remembered the last precepts that had been given her by her father, whom she had once been permitted to visit in prison. Only a few detached sentences of this, his last warning speech, now came into her mind, though no word of it had escaped her memory; it ran much as follows:

"It may seem as though I had met with an evil recompense from the gods for my conduct in adhering to what I think just and virtuous; but it only seems so, and so long as I succeed in living in accordance with nature, which obeys an everlasting law, no man is justified in accusing me. My own peace of mind especially will never desert me so long as I do not set myself to act in opposition to the fundamental convictions of my inmost being, but obey the doctrines of Zeno and Chrysippus. This peace every one may preserve, aye, even you, a woman, if you constantly do what you recognize to be right, and fulfil the duties you take upon yourself. The very god himself is proof and witness of this doctrine, for he grants to him who obeys him that tranquillity of spirit which must be pleasing in his eyes, since it is the only condition of the soul in which it appears to be neither fettered and hindered nor tossed and driven; while he, on the contrary, who wanders from the paths of virtue and of her daughter, stern duty, never attains peace, but feels the torment of an unsatisfied and hostile power, which with its hard grip drags his soul now on and now back.

"He who preserves a tranquil mind is not miserable, even in misfortune, and thankfully learns to feel contented in every state of life; and that because he is filled with those elevated sentiments which are directly related to the noblest portion of his being—those, I mean—of justice and goodness. Act then, my child, in conformity with justice and duty, regardless of any ulterior object, without considering whether your action will bring you pleasure or pain, without fear of the judgment of men or the envy of the gods, and you will win that peace of mind which distinguishes the wise from the unwise, and may be happy even in adverse circumstances; for the only real evil is the dominion of wickedness, that is to say the unreason which rebels against nature, and the only true happiness consists in the possession of virtue. He alone, however, can call virtue his who possesses it wholly, and sins not against it in the smallest particular; for there is no difference of degrees either in good or in evil, and even the smallest action opposed to duty, truth or justice, though punishable by no law, is a sin, and stands in opposition to virtue.

"Irene," thus Philotas had concluded his injunctions, "cannot as yet understand this doctrine, but you are grave and have sense beyond your years. Repeat this to her daily, and when the time comes impress on your sister—towards whom you must fill the place of a mother—impress on her heart these precepts as your father's last will and testament."

And now, as Klea went towards the well within the temple-wall to fetch water, she repeated to herself many of these injunctions; she felt herself encouraged by them, and firmly resolved not to give her sister up to the seducer without a struggle.

As soon as the vessels for libation at the altar were filled she returned to little Philo, whose state seemed to her to give no further cause for anxiety; after staying with him for more than an hour she left the gate-keeper's dwelling to seek Serapion's advice, and to divulge to him all she had been able to plan and consider in the quiet of the sick-room.

The recluse was wont to recognize her step from afar, and to be looking out for her from his window when she went to visit him; but to-day he heard her not, for he was stepping again and again up and down the few paces which the small size of his tiny cell allowed him to traverse. He could reflect best when he walked up and down, and he thought and thought again, for he had heard all that was known in the temple regarding Irene's disappearance; and he would, he must rescue her—but the more he tormented his brain the more clearly he saw that every attempt to snatch the kidnapped girl from the powerful robber must in fact be vain.

"And it must not, it shall not be!" he had cried, stamping his great foot, a few minutes before Klea reached his cell; but as soon as he was aware of her presence he made an effort to appear quite easy, and cried out with the vehemence which characterized him even in less momentous circumstances:

"We must consider, we must reflect, we must puzzle our brains, for the gods have been napping this morning, and we must be doubly wide-awake. Irene—our little Irene—and who would have thought it yesterday! It is a good-for-nothing, unspeakably base knave's trick—and now, what can we do to snatch the prey from the gluttonous monster, the savage wild beast, before he can devour our child, our pet little one?

"Often and often I have been provoked at my own stupidity, but never, never have I felt so stupid, such a godforsaken blockhead as I do now. When I try to consider I feel as if that heavy shutter had been nailed clown on my head. Have you had any ideas? I have not one which would not disgrace the veriest ass—not a single one."

"Then you know everything?" asked Klea, "even that it is probably our father's enemy, Eulaeus, who has treacherously decoyed the poor child to go away with him?"

"Yes, Yes!" cried Serapion, "wherever there is some scoundrel's trick to be played he must have a finger in the pie, as sure as there must be meal for bread to be made. But it is a new thing to me that on this occasion he should be Euergetes' tool. Old Philammon told me all about it. Just now the messenger came back from Memphis, and brought a paltry scrap of papyrus on which some wretched scribbler had written in the name of Philometer, that nothing was known of Irene at court, and complaining deeply that Asclepiodorus had not hesitated to play an underhand game with the king. So they have no idea whatever of voluntarily releasing our child."

"Then I shall proceed to do my duty," said Klea resolutely. "I shall go to Memphis, and fetch my sister."

The anchorite stared at the girl in horror, exclaiming: "That is folly, madness, suicide! Do you want to throw two victims into his jaws instead of one?"

"I can protect myself, and as regards Irene, I will claim the queen's assistance. She is a woman, and will never suffer—"

"What is there in this world that she will not suffer if it can procure her profit or pleasure? Who knows what delightful thing Euergetes may not have promised her in return for our little maid? No, by Serapis! no, Cleopatra will not help you, but—and that is a good idea—there is one who will to a certainty. We must apply to the Roman Publius Scipio, and he will have no difficulty in succeeding."

"From him," exclaimed Klea, coloring scarlet, "I will accept neither good nor evil; I do not know him, and I do not want to know him."

"Child, child!" interrupted the recluse with grave chiding. "Does your pride then so far outweigh your love, your duty, and concern for Irene? What, in the name of all the gods, has Publius done to you that you avoid him more anxiously than if he were covered with leprosy? There is a limit to all things, and now—aye, indeed—I must out with it come what may, for this is not the time to pretend to be blind when I see with both eyes what is going on—your heart is full of the Roman, and draws you to him; but you are an honest girl, and, in order to remain so, you fly from him because you distrust yourself, and do not know what might happen if he were to tell you that he too has been hit by one of Eros' darts. You may turn red and white, and look at me as if I were your enemy, and talking contemptible nonsense. I have seen many strange things, but I never saw any one before you who was a coward out of sheer courage, and yet of all the women I know there is not one to whom fear is less known than my bold and resolute Klea. The road is a hard one that you must take, but only cover your poor little heart with a coat of mail, and venture in all confidence to meet the Roman, who is an excellent good fellow. No doubt it will be hard to you to crave a boon, but ought you to shrink from those few steps over sharp stones? Our poor child is standing on the edge of the abyss; if you do not arrive at the right time, and speak the right words to the only person who is able to help in this matter, she will be thrust into the foul bog and sink in it, because her brave sister was frightened at—herself!"

Klea had cast down her eyes as the anchorite addressed her thus; she stood for some time frowning at the ground in silence, but at last she said, with quivering lips and as gloomily as if she were pronouncing a sentence on herself.

"Then I will ask the Roman to assist me; but how can I get to him?"

"Ah!—now my Klea is her father's daughter once more," answered Serapion, stretching out both his arms towards her from the little window of his cell; and then he went on: "I can make the painful path somewhat smoother for you. My brother Glaucus, who is commander of the civic guard in the palace, you already know; I will give you a few words of recommendation to him, and also, to lighten your task, a little letter to Publius Scipio, which shall contain a short account of the matter in hand. If

Publius wishes to speak with you yourself go to him and trust him, but still more trust yourself.

"Now go, and when you have once more filled the water-jars come back to me, and fetch the letters. The sooner you can go the better, for it would be well that you should leave the path through the desert behind you before nightfall, for in the dark there are often dangerous tramps about. You will find a friendly welcome at my sister Leukippa's; she lives in the toll-house by the great harbor—show her this ring and she will give you a bed, and, if the gods are merciful, one for Irene too."

"Thank you, father," said Klea, but she said no more, and then left him with a rapid step.

Serapion looked lovingly after her; then he took two wooden tablets faced with wax out of his chest, and, with a metal style, he wrote on one a short letter to his brother, and on the other a longer one to the Roman, which ran as follows:

"Serapion, the recluse of Serapis, to Publius Cornelius Scipio Nasica, the Roman.

"Serapion greets Publius Scipio, and acquaints him that Irene, the younger sister of Klea, the water-bearer, has disappeared from this temple, and, as Serapion suspects, by the wiles of the epistolographer Eulaeus, whom we both know, and who seems to have acted under the orders of King Ptolemy Euergetes. Seek to discover where Irene can be. Save her if thou canst from her ravishers, and conduct her back to this temple or deliver her in Memphis into the hands of my sister Leukippa, the wife of the overseer of the harbor, named Hipparchus, who dwells in the toll-house. May Serapis preserve thee and thine."

The recluse had just finished his letters when Klea returned to him. The girl hid them in the folds of the bosom of her robe, said farewell to her friend, and remained quite grave and collected, while Serapion, with tears in his eyes, stroked her hair, gave her his parting blessing, and finally even hung round her neck an amulet for good luck, that his mother had worn—it was an eye in rock-crystal with a protective inscription. Then, without any further delay, she set out towards the temple gate, which, in obedience to the commands of the high priest, was now locked. The gate-keeper—little Philo's father—sat close by on a stone bench, keeping guard. In a friendly tone Klea asked him to open the gate; but the anxious official would not immediately comply with her request, but reminded her of Asclepiodorus' strict injunctions, and informed her that the great Roman had demanded admission to the temple about three hours since, but had been refused by the high-priest's special orders. He had asked too for her, and had promised to return on the morrow.

The hot blood flew to Klea's face and eyes as she heard this news. Could Publius no more cease to think of her than she of him? Had Serapion guessed rightly? "The darts of Eros"—the recluse's phrase flashed through her mind, and struck her heart as if it were itself a winged arrow; it frightened her and yet she liked it, but only for one brief instant, for the utmost distrust of her own weakness came over her again directly, and she told herself with a shudder that she was on the high-road to follow up and seek out the importunate stranger.

All the horrors of her undertaking stood vividly before her, and if she had now retraced her steps she would not have been without an excuse to offer to her own conscience, since the temple-gate was closed, and might not be opened to any one, not even to her.

For a moment she felt a certain satisfaction in this flattering reflection, but as she thought again of Irene her resolve was once more confirmed, and going closer up to the gate-keeper she said with great determination:

"Open the gate to me without delay; you know that I am not accustomed to do or to desire anything wrong. I beg of you to push back the bolt at once."

The man to whom Klea had done many kindnesses, and whom Imhotep had that very day told that she was the good spirit of his house, and that he ought to venerate her as a divinity—obeyed her orders, though with some doubt and hesitation. The heavy bolt flew back, the brazen gate opened, the water-bearer stepped out, flung a dark veil over her head, and set out on her walk.

CHAPTER XVII

A paved road, with a row of Sphinxes on each side, led from the Greek temple of Serapis to the rock-hewn tombs of Apis, and the temples and chapels built over them, and near them; in these the Apis bull after its death— or "in Osiris" as the phrase went—was worshipped, while, so long as it lived, it was taken care of and prayed to in the temple to which it belonged, that of the god Ptah at Memphis. After death these sacred bulls, which were distinguished by peculiar marks, had extraordinarily costly obsequies; they were called the risen Ptah, and regarded as the symbol of the soul of Osiris, by whose procreative power all that dies or passes away is brought to new birth and new life—the departed soul of man, the plant that has perished, and the heavenly bodies that have set. Osiris-Sokari, who was worshipped as the companion of Osiris, presided over the wanderings which had to be performed by the seemingly extinct spirit before its resuscitation as another being in a new form; and Egyptian priests governed in the temples of these gods, which were purely Egyptian in style, and which had been built at a very early date over the tomb-cave of the sacred bulls. And even the Greek ministers of Serapis, settled at Memphis, were ready to follow the example of their rulers and to sacrifice to Osiris-Apis, who was closely allied to Serapis—not only in name but in his essential attributes. Serapis himself indeed was a divinity introduced from Asia into the Nile valley by the Ptolemies, in order to supply to their Greek and Egyptian subjects alike an object of adoration, before whose altars they could unite in a common worship. They devoted themselves to the worship of Apis in Osiris at the shrines, of Greek architecture, and containing stone images of bulls, that stood outside the Egyptian sanctuary, and they were very ready to be initiated into the higher significance of his essence; indeed, all religious mysteries in their Greek home bore reference to the immortality of the soul and its fate in the other world.

Just as two neighboring cities may be joined by a bridge, so the Greek temple of Serapis—to which the water-bearers belonged—was connected with the Egyptian sanctuary of Osiris-Apis by the fine paved road for processions along which Klea now rapidly proceeded. There was a shorter way to Memphis, but she chose this one, because the mounds of sand on each side of the road bordered by Sphinxes—which every day had to be cleared of the desert-drift—concealed her from the sight of her companions in the temple; besides the best and safest way into the city was by a road leading from a crescent, decorated with busts of the philosophers, that lay near the principal entrance to the new Apis tombs.

She looked neither at the lion-bodies with men's heads that guarded the way, nor at the images of beasts on the wall that shut it in; nor did she heed the dusky-hued temple-slaves of Osiris-Apis who were sweeping the sand from the paved way with large brooms, for she thought of nothing but Irene and the difficult task that lay before her, and she walked swiftly onwards with her eyes fixed on the ground.

But she had taken no more than a few steps when she heard her name called quite close to her, and looking up in alarm she found herself standing opposite Krates, the little smith, who came close up to her, took hold of her veil, threw it back a little before she could prevent him, and asked:

"Where are you off to, child?"

"Do not detain me," entreated Klea. "You know that Irene, whom you are always so fond of, has been carried off; perhaps I may be able to save her, but if you betray me, and if they follow me—"

"I will not hinder you," interrupted the old man. "Nay, if it were not for these swollen feet I would go with you, for I can think of nothing else but the poor dear little thing; but as it is I shall be glad enough when I am sitting still again in my workshop; it is exactly as if a workman of my own trade lived in each of my great toes, and was dancing round in them with hammer and file and chisel and nails. Very likely you may be so fortunate as to find your sister, for a crafty woman succeeds in many things which are too difficult for a wise man. Go on, and if they seek for you old Krates will not betray you."

He nodded kindly at Klea, and had already half turned his back on her when he once more looked round, and called out to her:

"Wait a minute, girl—you can do me a little service. I have just fitted a new lock to the door of the Apis-tomb down there. It answers admirably, but the one key to it which I have made is not enough; we require four, and you shall order them for me of the locksmith Heri, to be sent the day after to-morrow; he lives opposite the gate of Sokari—to the left, next the bridge over the canal—you cannot miss it. I hate repeating and copying as much as I like inventing and making new things, and Heri can work from a pattern just as well as I can. If it were not for my legs I would give the man my commission myself, for he who speaks by the lips of a go-between is often misunderstood or not understood at all."

"I will gladly save you the walk," replied Klea, while the Smith sat down on the pedestal of one of the Sphinxes, and opening the leather wallet which hung by his side shook out the contents. A few files, chisels, and nails fell out into his lap; then the key, and finally a sharp, pointed knife with which Krates had cut out the hollow in the door for the insertion of the lock; Krates touched up the pattern-key for the smith in Memphis with a few strokes of the file, and then, muttering thoughtfully and shaking his head doubtfully from side to side, he exclaimed:

"You still must come with me once more to the door, for I require accurate workmanship from other people, and so I must be severe upon my own."

"But I want so much to reach Memphis before dark," besought Klea.

"The whole thing will not take a minute, and if you will give me your arm I shall go twice as fast. There are the files, there is the knife."

"Give it me," Klea requested. "This blade is sharp and bright, and as soon as I saw it I felt as if it bid me take it with me. Very likely I may have to come through the desert alone at night."

"Aye," said the smith, "and even the weakest feels stronger when he has a weapon. Hide the knife somewhere about you, my child, only take care not to hurt yourself with it. Now let me take your arm, and on we will go—but not quite so fast."

Klea led the smith to the door he indicated, and saw with admiration how unfailingly the bolt sprang forward when one half of the door closed upon the other, and how easily the key pushed it back again; then, after conducting Krates back to the Sphinx near which she had met him, she went on her way at her quickest pace, for the sun was already very low, and it seemed scarcely possible to reach Memphis before it should set.

As she approached a tavern where soldiers and low people were accustomed to resort, she was met by a drunken slave. She went on and past him without any fear, for the knife in her girdle, and on which she kept her hand, kept up her courage, and she felt as if she had thus acquired a third hand which was more powerful and less timid than her own. A company of soldiers had encamped in front of the tavern, and the wine of Kbakem, which was grown close by, on the eastern declivity of the Libyan range, had an excellent savor. The men were in capital spirits, for at noon today—after they had been quartered here for months as guards of the tombs of Apis and of the temples of the Necropolis—a commanding officer of the Diadoches had arrived at Memphis, who had ordered them to break up at once, and to withdraw into the capital before nightfall. They were not to be relieved by other mercenaries till the next morning.

All this Klea learned from a messenger from the Egyptian temple in the Necropolis, who recognized her, and who was going to Memphis, commissioned by the priests of Osiris-Apis and Sokari to convey a petition to the king, praying that fresh troops might be promptly sent to replace those now withdrawn.

For some time she went on side by side with this messenger, but soon she found that she could not keep up with his hurried pace, and had to fall behind. In front of another tavern sat the officers of the troops, whose noisy mirth she had heard as she passed the former one; they were sitting over their wine and looking on at the dancing of two Egyptian girls, who screeched like cackling hens over their mad leaps, and who so effectually riveted the attention of the spectators, who were beating time for them by clapping their hands, that Klea, accelerating her step, was able to slip unobserved past the wild crew. All these scenes, nay everything she met with on the high-road, scared the girl who was accustomed to the silence and the solemn life of the temple of Serapis, and she therefore struck into a side path that probably also led to the city which she could already see lying before her with its pylons, its citadel and its houses, veiled in evening mist. In a quarter of an hour at most she would have crossed the desert, and reach the fertile meadow land, whose emerald hue grew darker and darker every moment. The sun was already sinking to rest behind the Libyan range, and soon after, for twilight is short in Egypt, she was wrapped in the darkness of night. The westwind, which had begun to blow even at noon, now rose higher, and seemed to pursue her with its hot breath and the clouds of sand it carried with it from the desert.

She must certainly be approaching water, for she heard the deep pipe of the bittern in the reeds, and fancied she breathed a moister air. A few steps more, and her foot sank in mud; and she now perceived that she was standing on the edge of a wide ditch in which tall papyrus-plants were growing. The side path she had struck into ended at this plantation, and there was nothing to be done but to turn about, and to continue her walk against the wind and with the sand blowing in her face.

The light from the drinking-booth showed her the direction she must follow, for though the moon was up, it is true, black clouds swept across it, covering it and the smaller lights of heaven for many minutes at a time. Still she felt no fatigue, but the shouts of the men and the loud cries of the women that rang out from the tavern filled her with alarm and disgust. She made a wide circuit round the hostelry, wading through the sand hillocks and tearing her dress on the thorns and thistles that had boldly struck deep root in the desert, and had grown up there like the squalid brats in the hovel of a beggar. But still, as she hurried on by the high-road, the hideous laughter and the crowing mirth of the dancing-girls still rang in her mind's ear.

Her blood coursed more swiftly through her veins, her head was on fire, she saw Irene close before her, tangibly distinct — with flowing hair and fluttering garments, whirling in a wild dance like a Moenad at a Dionysiac festival, flying from one embrace to another and shouting and shrieking in unbridled folly like the wretched girls she had seen on her way. She was seized with terror for her sister — an unbounded dread such as she had never felt before, and as the wind was now once more behind her she let herself be driven on by it, lifting her feet in a swift run and flying, as if pursued by the Erinnyes, without once looking round her and wholly forgetful of the smith's commission, on towards the city along the road planted with trees, which as she knew led to the gate of the citadel.

CHAPTER XVIII

In front of the gate of the king's palace sat a crowd of petitioners who were accustomed to stay here from early dawn till late at night, until they were called into the palace to receive the answer to the petition they had drawn up. When Klea reached the end of her journey she was so exhausted and bewildered that she felt the imperative necessity of seeking rest and quiet reflection, so she seated herself among these people, next to a woman from Upper Egypt. But hardly had she taken her place by her with a silent greeting, when her talkative neighbor began to relate with particular minuteness why she had come to Memphis, and how certain unjust judges had conspired with her bad husband to trick her—for men were always ready to join against a woman—and to deprive her of everything which had been secured to her and her children by her marriage-contract. For two months now, she said, she had been waiting early and late before the sublime gate, and was consuming her last ready cash in the city where living was so dear; but it was all one to her, and at a pinch she would sell even her gold ornaments, for sooner or later her cause must come before the king, and then the wicked villain and his accomplices would be taught what was just.

Klea heard but little of this harangue; a feeling had come over her like that of a person who is having water poured again and again on the top of his head. Presently her neighbor observed that the new-comer was not listening at all to her complainings; she slapped her shoulder with her hand, and said:

"You seem to think of nothing but your own concerns; and I dare say they are not of such a nature as that you should relate them to any one else; so far as mine are concerned the more they are discussed, the better."

The tone in which these remarks were made was so dry, and at the same time so sharp, that it hurt Klea, and she rose hastily to go closer to the gate. Her neighbor threw a cross word after her; but she did not heed it, and drawing her veil closer over her face, she went through the gate of the palace into a vast courtyard, brightly lighted up by cressets and torches, and crowded with foot-soldiers and mounted guards.

The sentry at the gate perhaps had not observed her, or perhaps had let her pass unchallenged from her dignified and erect gait, and the numerous armed men through whom she now made her way seemed to be so much occupied with their own affairs, that no one bestowed any notice on her. In a narrow alley, which led to a second court and was lighted by lanterns, one of the body-guard known as Philobasilistes, a haughty young fellow in yellow riding-boots and a shirt of mail over his red tunic, came riding towards her on his tall horse, and noticing her he tried to squeeze her between his charger and the wall, and put out his hand to raise her veil; but Klea slipped aside, and put up her hands to protect herself from the horse's head which was almost touching her.

The cavalier, enjoying her alarm, called out: "Only stand still—he is not vicious."

"Which, you or your horse?" asked Klea, with such a solemn tone in her deep voice that for an instant the young guardsman lost his self-possession, and this gave her time to go farther from the horse. But the girl's sharp retort had annoyed the conceited young fellow, and not having time to follow her himself, he called out in a tone of encouragement to a party of mercenaries from Cyprus, whom the frightened girl was trying to pass:

"Look under this girl's veil, comrades, and if she is as pretty as she is well-grown, I wish you joy of your prize." He laughed as he pressed his knees against the flanks of his bay and trotted slowly away, while the Cypriotes gave Klea ample time to reach the second court, which was more brightly lighted even than the first, that they might there surround her with insolent importunity.

The helpless and persecuted girl felt the blood run cold in her veins, and for a few minutes she could see nothing but a bewildering confusion of flashing eyes and weapons, of beards and hands, could hear nothing but words and sounds, of which she understood and felt only that they were revolting and horrible, and threatened her with death and ruin. She had crossed her arms over her bosom, but now she raised her hands to hide her face, for she felt a strong hand snatch away the veil that covered her head. This insolent proceeding turned her numb horror to indignant rage, and, fixing her sparkling eyes on her bearded opponents, she exclaimed:

"Shame upon you, who in the king's own house fall like wolves on a defenceless woman, and in a peaceful spot snatch the veil from a young girl's head. Your mothers would blush for you, and your sisters cry shame on you—as I do now!"

Astonished at Klea's distinguished beauty, startled at the angry glare in her eyes, and the deep chest-tones of her voice which trembled with excitement, the Cypriotes drew back, while the same audacious rascal that had pulled away her veil came closer to her, and cried:

"Who would make such a noise about a rubbishy veil! If you will be my sweetheart I will buy you a new one, and many things besides."

At the same time he tried to throw his arm round her; but at his touch Klea felt the blood leave her cheeks and mount to her bloodshot eyes, and at that instant her hand, guided by some uncontrollable inward impulse, grasped the handle of the knife which Krates had lent her; she raised it high in the air though with an unsteady arm, exclaiming:

"Let me go or, by Serapis whom I serve, I will strike you to the heart!"

The soldier to whom this threat was addressed, was not the man to be intimidated by a blade of cold iron in a woman's hand; with a quick movement he seized her wrist in order to disarm her; but although Klea was forced to drop the knife she struggled with him to free herself from his clutch, and this contest between a man and a woman, who seemed to be of superior rank to that indicated by her very simple dress, seemed to most of the Cypriotes so undignified, so much out of place within the walls of a palace, that they pulled their comrade back from Klea, while others on the contrary came to the assistance of the bully who defended himself stoutly. And in the midst of the fray, which was conducted with no small noise, stood Klea with flying breath. Her antagonist, though flung to the ground, still held her wrist with his left hand while he defended himself against his comrades with the right, and she tried with all her force and cunning to withdraw it; for at the very height of her excitement and danger she felt as if a sudden gust of wind had swept her spirit clear of all confusion, and she was again able to contemplate her position calmly and resolutely.

If only her hand were free she might perhaps be able to take advantage of the struggle between her foes, and to force her way out between their ranks.

Twice, thrice, four times, she tried to wrench her hand with a sudden jerk through the fingers that grasped it; but each time in vain. Suddenly, from the man at her feet there broke a loud, long-drawn cry of pain which re-echoed from the high walls of the court, and at the same time she felt the fingers of her antagonist gradually and slowly slip from her arm like the straps of a sandal carefully lifted by the surgeon from a broken ankle.

"It is all over with him!" exclaimed the eldest of the Cypriotes. "A man never calls out like that but once in his life! True enough—the dagger is sticking here just under the ninth rib! This is mad work! That is your doing again, Lykos, you savage wolf!"

"He bit deep into my finger in the struggle—"

"And you are for ever tearing each other to pieces for the sake of the women," interrupted the elder, not listening to the other's excuses. "Well, I was no better than you in my time, and nothing can alter it! You had better be off now, for if the Epistrategist learns we have fallen to stabbing each other again—"

The Cypriote had not ceased speaking, and his countrymen were in the very act of raising the body of their comrade when a division of the civic watch rushed into the court in close order and through the passage near which the fight for the girl had arisen, thus stopping the way against those who were about to escape, since all who wished to get out of the court into the open street must pass through the doorway into which Klea had been forced by the horseman. Every other exit from this second court of the citadel led into the strictly guarded gardens and buildings of the palace itself.

The noisy strife round Klea, and the cry of the wounded man had attracted the watch; the Cypriotes and the maiden soon found themselves surrounded, and they were conducted through a narrow side passage into the court-yard of the prison. After a short enquiry the men who had been taken were allowed to return under an escort to their own phalanx, and Klea gladly followed the commander of the watch to a less brilliantly illuminated part of the prison-yard, for in him she had recognized at once Serapion's brother Glaucus, and he in her the daughter of the man who had done and suffered so much for his father's sake; besides they had often exchanged greetings and a few words in the temple of Serapis.

"All that is in my power," said Glaucus—a man somewhat taller but not so broadly built as his brother—when he had read the recluse's note and when Klea had answered a number of questions, "all that is in my power I will gladly do for you and your sister, for I do not forget all that I owe to your father; still I cannot but regret that you have incurred such risk, for it is always hazardous for a pretty young girl to venture into this palace at a late hour, and particularly just now, for the courts are swarming not only with Philometor's fighting men but with those of his brother, who have come here for their sovereign's birthday festival. The people have been liberally entertained, and the soldier who has been sacrificing to Dionysus seizes the gifts of Eros and Aphrodite wherever he may find them. I will at once take charge of my brother's letter to the Roman Publius Cornelius Scipio, but when you have received his answer you will do well to let yourself be escorted to my wife or my sister, who both live in the city, and to remain till to-morrow morning with one or the other. Here you cannot remain a minute unmolested while I am away—Where now—Aye! The only safe shelter I can offer you is the prison down there; the room where they lock up the subaltern officers when they have committed any offence is quite unoccupied, and I will conduct you thither. It is always kept clean, and there is a bench in it too."

Klea followed her friend who, as his hasty demeanor plainly showed, had been interrupted in important business. In a few steps they reached the prison; she begged Glaucus to bring her the Roman's answer as quickly as possible, declared herself quite ready to remain in the dark—since she perceived that the light of a lamp might betray her, and she was not afraid of the dark—and suffered herself to be locked in.

As she heard the iron bolt creak in its brass socket a shiver ran through her, and although the room in which she found herself was neither worse nor smaller than that in which she and her sister lived in the temple, still it oppressed her, and she even felt as if an indescribable something hindered her breathing as she said to herself that she was locked in and no longer free to come and to go. A dim light penetrated into her prison through the single barred window that opened on to the court, and she could see a little bench of palm-branches on which she sat down to seek the repose she so sorely needed. All sense of discomfort gradually vanished before the new feeling of rest and refreshment, and pleasant hopes and anticipations were just beginning to mingle themselves with the remembrance of the horrors she had just experienced when suddenly there was a stir and a bustle just in front of the prison—and she could hear, outside, the clatter of harness and words of command. She rose from her seat and saw that about twenty horsemen, whose golden helmets and armor reflected the light of the lanterns, cleared the wide court by driving the men before them, as the flames drive the game from a fired hedge, and by forcing them into a second court from which again they proceeded to expel them. At least Klea could hear them shouting 'In the king's name' there as they had before done close to her. Presently the horsemen returned and placed themselves, ten and ten, as guards at each of the passages leading into the court. It was not without interest that Klea looked on at this scene which was perfectly new to her; and when one of the fine horses, dazzled by the light of the lanterns, turned restive and shied, leaping and rearing and threatening his rider with a fall—when the horseman checked and soothed it, and brought it to a stand-still—the Macedonian warrior was transfigured in her eyes to Publius, who no doubt could manage a horse no less well than this man.

No sooner was the court completely cleared of men by the mounted guard than a new incident claimed Klea's attention. First she heard footsteps in the room adjoining her prison, then bright streaks of light fell through the cracks of the slight partition which divided her place of retreat from the other room, then the two window-openings close to hers were closed with heavy shutters, then seats or benches were dragged about and various objects were laid upon a table, and finally the door of the adjoining room was thrown open and slammed to again so violently, that the door which closed hers and the bench near which she was standing trembled and jarred.

At the same moment a deep sonorous voice called out with a loud and hearty shout of laughter:

"A mirror—give me a mirror, Eulaeus. By heaven! I do not look much like prison fare—more like a man in whose strong brain there is no lack of deep schemes, who can throttle his antagonist with a grip of his fist, and who is prompt to avail himself of all the spoil that comes in his way, so that he may compress the pleasures of a whole day into every hour, and enjoy them to the utmost! As surely as my name is Euergetes my uncle Antiochus was right in liking to mix among the populace. The splendid puppets who surround us kings, and cover every portion of their own bodies in wrappings and swaddling bands, also stifle the expression of every genuine sentiment; and it is enough to turn our brain to reflect that, if we would not be deceived, every word that we hear—and, oh dear! how many words we must needs hear-must be pondered in our minds. Now, the mob on the contrary—who think themselves beautifully dressed in a threadbare cloth hanging round their brown loins—are far better off. If one of them says to another of his own class—a naked wretch who wears about him everything he happens to possess—that he is a dog, he answers with a blow of his fist in the other's face, and what can be plainer than that! If on the other hand he tells him he is a splendid fellow, he believes it without reservation, and has a perfect right to believe it.

"Did you see how that stunted little fellow with a snub-nose and bandy-legs, who is as broad as he is long, showed all his teeth in a delighted grin when I praised his steady hand? He laughs just like a hyena, and every respectable father of a family looks on the fellow as a god-forsaken monster; but the immortals must think him worth something to have given him such magnificent grinders in his ugly mouth, and to have preserved him mercifully for fifty years—for that is about the rascal's age. If that fellow's dagger breaks he can kill his victim with those teeth, as a fox does a duck, or smash his bones with his fist."

"But, my lord," replied Eulaeus dryly and with a certain matter-of-fact gravity to King Euergetes—for he it was who had come with him into the room adjoining Klea's retreat, "the dry little Egyptian with the thin straight hair is even more trustworthy and tougher and nimbler than his companion, and, so far, more estimable. One flings himself on his prey with a rush like a block of stone hurled from a roof, but the other, without being seen, strikes his poisoned fang into his flesh like an adder hidden in the sand. The third, on whom I had set great hopes, was beheaded the day before yesterday without my knowledge; but the pair whom you have condescended to inspect with your own eyes are sufficient. They must use neither dagger nor lance, but they will easily achieve their end with slings and hooks and poisoned needles, which leave wounds that resemble the sting of an adder. We may safely depend on these fellows."

Once more Euergetes laughed loudly, and exclaimed: What criticism! Exactly as if these blood-hounds were tragic actors of which one could best produce his effects by fire and pathos, and the other by the subtlety of his conception. I call that an unprejudiced judgment. And why should not a man be great even as a murderer? From what hangman's noose did you drag out the neck of one, and from what headsman's block did you rescue the other when you found them?

"It is a lucky hour in which we first see something new to us, and, by Heracles! I never before in the whole course of my life saw such villains as these. I do not regret having gone to see them and talked to them as if I were their equal. Now, take this torn coat off me, and help me to undress. Before I go to the feast I will take a hasty plunge in my bath, for I twitch in every limb, I feel as if I had got dirty in their company.

"There lie my clothes and my sandals; strap them on for me, and tell me as you do it how you lured the Roman into the toils."

Klea could hear every word of this frightful conversation, and clasped her hand over her brow with a shudder, for she found it difficult to believe in the reality of the hideous images that it brought before her mind. Was she awake or was she a prey to some horrid dream?

She hardly knew, and, indeed, she scarcely understood half of all she heard till the Roman's name was mentioned. She felt as if the point of a thin, keen knife was being driven obliquely through her brain from right to left, as it now flashed through her mind that it was against him, against Publius, that the wild beasts, disguised in human form, were directed by Eulaeus, and face to face with this—the most hideous, the most incredible of horrors—she suddenly recovered the full use of her senses. She softly slipped close to that rift in the partition through which the broadest beam of light fell into the room, put her ear close to it, and drank in, with fearful attention, word for word the report made by the eunuch to his iniquitous superior, who frequently interrupted him with remarks, words of approval or a short laugh-drank them in, as a man perishing in the desert drinks the loathsome waters of a salt pool.

And what she heard was indeed well fitted to deprive her of her senses, but the more definite the facts to which the words referred that she could overhear, the more keenly she listened, and the more resolutely she collected her thoughts. Eulaeus had used her own name to induce the Roman to keep an assignation at midnight in the desert close to the Apistombs. He repeated the words that he had written to this effect on a tile, and which requested Publius to come quite alone to the spot indicated, since she dare not speak with him in the temple. Finally he was invited to write his answer on the other side of the square of clay. As Klea heard these words, put into her own mouth by a villain, she could have sobbed aloud heartily with anguish, shame, and rage; but the point now was to keep her ears wide open, for Euergetes asked his odious tool:

"And what was the Roman's answer?" Eulaeus must have handed the tile to the king, for he laughed loudly again, and cried out:

"So he will walk into the trap—will arrive by half an hour after midnight at the latest, and greets Klea from her sister Irene. He carries on love-making and abduction wholesale, and buys water-bearers by the pair, like doves in the market or sandals in a shoe maker's stall. Only see how the simpleton writes Greek; in these few words there are two mistakes, two regular schoolboys' blunders.

"The fellow must have had a very pleasant day of it, since he must have been reckoning on a not unsuccessful evening—but the gods have an ugly habit of clenching the hand with which they have long caressed their favorites, and striking him with their fist.

"Amalthea's horn has been poured out on him today; first he snapped up, under my very nose, my little Hebe, the Irene of Irenes, whom I hope tomorrow to inherit from him; then he got the gift of my best Cyrenaan horses, and at the same time the flattering assurance of my valuable friendship; then he had audience of my fair sister—and it goes more to the heart of a republican than you would believe when crowned heads are graciously disposed towards him—finally the sister of his pretty sweetheart invites him to an assignation, and she, if you and Zoe speak the truth, is a beauty in the grand style. Now these are really too many good things for one inhabitant of this most stingily provided world; and in one single day too, which, once begun, is so soon ended; and justice requires that we should lend a helping hand to destiny, and cut off the head of this poppy that aspires to rise above its brethren; the thousands who have less good fortune than he would otherwise have great cause to complain of neglect."

"I am happy to see you in such good humor," said Eulaeus.

"My humor is as may be," interrupted the king. "I believe I am only whistling a merry tune to keep up my spirits in the dark. If I were on more familiar terms with what other men call fear I should have ample reason to be afraid; for in the quail-fight we have gone in for I have wagered a crown-aye, and more than that even. To-morrow only will decide whether the game is lost or won, but I know already to-day that I would rather see my enterprise against Philometor fail, with all my hopes of the double crown, than our plot against the life of the Roman; for I was a man before I was a king, and a man I should remain, if my throne, which now indeed stands on only two legs, were to crash under my weight.

"My sovereign dignity is but a robe, though the costliest, to be sure, of all garments. If forgiveness were any part of my nature I might easily forgive the man who should soil or injure that—but he who comes too near to Euergetes the man, who dares to touch this body, and the spirit it contains, or to cross it in its desires and purposes—him I will crush unhesitatingly to the earth, I will see him torn in pieces. Sentence is passed on the Roman, and if your ruffians do their duty, and if the gods accept the holocaust that I had slain before them at sunset for the success of my project, in a couple of hours Publius Cornelius Scipio will have bled to death.

"He is in a position to laugh at me—as a man—but I therefore—as a man—have the right, and—as a king—have the power, to make sure that that laugh shall be his last. If I could murder Rome as I can him how glad should I be! for Rome alone hinders me from being the greatest of all the great kings of our time; and yet I shall rejoice to-morrow when they tell me Publius Cornelius Scipio has been torn by wild beasts, and his body is so mutilated that his own mother could not recognize it more than if a messenger were to bring me the news that Carthage had broken the power of Rome."

Euergetes had spoken the last words in a voice that sounded like the roll of thunder as it growls in a rapidly approaching storm, louder, deeper, and more furious each instant. When at last he was silent Eulaeus said: "The immortals, my lord, will not deny you this happiness. The brave fellows whom you condescended to see and to talk to strike as certainly as the bolt of our father Zeus, and as we have learned from the Roman's horse-keeper where he has hidden Irene, she will no more elude your grasp than the crowns of Upper and Lower Egypt.—Now, allow me to put on your mantle, and then to call the body-guard that they may escort you as you return to your residence."

"One thing more," cried the king, detaining Eulaeus. "There are always troops by the Tombs of Apis placed there to guard the sacred places; may not they prove a hindrance to your friends?"

"I have withdrawn all the soldiers and armed guards to Memphis down to the last man," replied Eulaeus, "and quartered them within the White Wall. Early tomorrow, before you proceed to business, they will be replaced by a stronger division, so that they may not prove a reinforcement to your brother's troops here if things come to fighting."

"I shall know how to reward your foresight," said Euergetes as Eulaeus quitted the room.

Again Klea heard a door open, and the sound of many hoofs on the pavement of the court-yard, and when she went, all trembling, up to the window, she saw Euergetes himself, and the powerfully knit horse that was led in for him. The tyrant twisted his hand in the mane of the restless and pawing steed, and Klea thought that the monstrous mass could never mount on to the horse's back without the aid of many men; but she was mistaken, for with a mighty spring the giant flung himself high in the air and on to the horse, and then, guiding his panting steed by the pressure of his knees alone, he bounded out of the prison-yard surrounded by his splendid train.

For some minutes the court-yard remained empty, then a man hurriedly crossed it, unlocked the door of the room where Klea was, and informed her that he was a subaltern under Glaucus, and had brought her a message from him.

"My lord," said the veteran soldier to the girl, "bid me greet you, and says that he found neither the Roman Publius Scipio, nor his friend the Corinthian at home. He is prevented from coming to you himself; he has his hands full of business, for soldiers in the service of both the kings are quartered within the White Wall, and all sorts of squabbles break out between them. Still, you cannot remain in this room, for it will shortly be occupied by a party of young officers who began the fray. Glaucus proposes for your choice that you should either allow me to conduct you to his wife or return to the temple to which you are attached. In the latter case a chariot shall convey you as far as the second tavern in Khakem on the borders of the desert-for the city is full of drunken soldiery. There you may probably find an escort if you explain to the host who you are. But the chariot must be back again in less than an hour, for it is one of the king's, and when the banquet is over there may be a scarcity of chariots."

"Yes—I will go back to the place I came from," said Klea eagerly, interrupting the messenger. "Take me at once to the chariot."

"Follow me, then," said the old man.

"But I have no veil," observed Klea, "and have only this thin robe on. Rough soldiers snatched my wrapper from my face, and my cloak from off my shoulders."

"I will bring you the captain's cloak which is lying here in the orderly's room, and his travelling-hat too; that will hide your face with its broad flap. You are so tall that you might be taken for a man, and that is well, for a woman leaving the palace at this hour would hardly pass unmolested. A slave shall fetch the things from your temple to-morrow. I may inform you that my master ordered me take as much care of you as if you were his own daughter. And he told me too—and I had nearly forgotten it—to tell you that your sister was carried off by the Roman, and not by that other dangerous man, you would know whom he meant. Now wait, pray, till I return; I shall not be long gone."

In a few minutes the guard returned with a large cloak in which he wrapped Klea, and a broad-brimmed travelling-hat which she pressed down on her head, and he then conducted her to that quarter of the palace where the king's stables were. She kept close to the officer, and was soon mounted on a chariot, and then conducted by the driver—who took her for a young Macedonian noble, who was tempted out at night by some assignation—as far as the second tavern on the road back to the Serapeum.

CHAPTER XIX

While Klea had been listening to the conversation between Euergetes and Eulaeus, Cleopatra had been sitting in her tent, and allowing herself to be dressed with no less care than on the preceding evening, but in other garments.

It would seem that all had not gone so smoothly as she wished during the day, for her two tire-women had red eyes. Her lady-in-waiting, Zoe, was reading to her, not this time from a Greek philosopher but from a Greek translation of the Hebrew Psalms: a discussion as to their poetic merit having arisen a few days previously at the supper-table. Onias, the Israelite general, had asserted that these odes might be compared with those of Alcman or of Pindar, and had quoted certain passages that had pleased the queen. To-day she was not disposed for thought, but wanted something strange and out of the common to distract her mind, so she desired Zoe to open the book of the Hebrews, of which the translation was considered by the Hellenic Jews in Alexandria as an admirable work—nay, even as inspired by God himself; it had long been known to her through her Israelite friends and guests.

Cleopatra had been listening for about a quarter of an hour to Zoe's reading when the blast of a trumpet rang out on the steps which led up her tent, announcing a visitor of the male sex. The queen glanced angrily round, signed to her lady to stop reading, and exclaimed:

"I will not see my husband now! Go, Thais, and tell the eunuchs on the steps, that I beg Philometor not to disturb me just now. Go on, Zoe."

Ten more psalms had been read, and a few verses repeated twice or thrice by Cleopatra's desire, when the pretty Athenian returned with flaming cheeks, and said in an excited tone:

"It is not your husband, the king, but your brother Euergetes, who asks to speak with you."

"He might have chosen some other hour," replied Cleopatra, looking round at her maid. Thais cast down her eyes, and twitched the edge of her robe between her fingers as she addressed her mistress; but the queen, whom nothing could escape that she chose to see, and who was not to-day in the humor for laughing or for letting any indiscretion escape unreproved, went on at once in an incensed and cutting tone, raising her voice to a sharp pitch:

"I do not choose that my messengers should allow themselves to be detained, be it by whom it may—do you hear! Leave Me this instant and go to your room, and stay there till I want you to undress me this evening. Andromeda—do you hear, old woman?—you can bring my brother to me, and he will let you return quicker than Thais, I fancy. You need not leer at yourself in the glass, you cannot do anything to alter your wrinkles. My head-dress is already done. Give me that linen wrapper, Olympias, and then he may come! Why, there he is already! First you ask permission, brother, and then disdain to wait till it is given you."

"Longing and waiting," replied Euergetes, "are but an ill-assorted couple. I wasted this evening with common soldiers and fawning flatterers; then, in order to see a few noble countenances, I went into the prison, after that I hastily took a bath, for the residence of your convicts spoils one's complexion more, and in a less pleasant manner, than this little shrine, where everything looks and smells like Aphrodite's tiring-room; and now I have a longing to hear a few good words before supper-time comes."

"From my lips?" asked Cleopatra.

"There are none that can speak better, whether by the Nile or the Ilissus."

"What do you want of me?"

"I—of you?"

"Certainly, for you do not speak so prettily unless you want something."

"But I have already told you! I want to hear you say something wise, something witty, something soul-stirring."

"We cannot call up wit as we would a maid-servant. It comes unbidden, and the more urgently we press it to appear the more certainly it remains away."

"That may be true of others, but not of you who, even while you declare that you have no store of Attic salt, are seasoning your speech with it. All yield obedience to grace and beauty, even wit and the sharp-tongued Momus who mocks even at the gods."

"You are mistaken, for not even my own waiting-maids return in proper time when I commission them with a message to you."

"And may we not to be allowed to sacrifice to the Charites on the way to the temple of Aphrodite?"

"If I were indeed the goddess, those worshippers who regarded my hand-maidens as my equals would find small acceptance with me."

"Your reproof is perfectly just, for you are justified in requiring that all who know you should worship but one goddess, as the Jews do but one god. But I entreat you do not again compare yourself to the brainless Cyprian dame. You may be allowed to do so, so far as your grace is concerned; but who ever saw an Aphrodite philosophizing and reading serious books? I have disturbed you in grave studies no doubt; what is the book you are rolling up, fair Zoe?"

"The sacred book of the Jews, Sire," replied Zoe; "one that I know you do not love."

"And you—who read Homer, Pindar, Sophocles, and Plato—do you like it?" asked Euergetes.

"I find passages in it which show a profound knowledge of life, and others of which no one can dispute the high poetic flight," replied Cleopatra. "Much of it has no doubt a thoroughly barbarian twang, and it is particularly in the Psalms—which we have now been reading, and which might be ranked with the finest hymns—that I miss the number and rhythm of the syllables, the observance of a fixed metre—in short, severity of form. David, the royal poet, was no less possessed by the divinity when he sang to his lyre than other poets have been, but he does not seem to have known that delight felt by our poets in overcoming the difficulties they have raised for themselves. The poet should slavishly obey the laws he lays down for himself of his own free-will, and subordinate to them every word, and yet his matter and his song should seem to float on a free and soaring wing. Now, even the original Hebrew text of the Psalms has no metrical laws."

"I could well dispense with them," replied Euergetes; "Plato too disdained to measure syllables, and I know passages in his works which are nevertheless full of the highest poetic beauty. Besides, it has been pointed out to me that even the Hebrew poems, like the Egyptian, follow certain rules, which however I might certainly call rhetorical rather than poetical. The first member in a series of ideas stands in antithesis to the next, which either re-states the former one in a new form or sets it in a clearer light by suggesting some contrast. Thus they avail themselves of the art of the orator—or indeed of the painter—who brings a light color into juxtaposition with a dark one, in order to increase its luminous effect. This method and style are indeed not amiss, and that was the least of all the things that filled me with aversion for this book, in which besides, there is many a proverb which may be pleasing to kings who desire to have submissive subjects, and to fathers who would bring up their sons in obedience to themselves and to the laws. Even mothers must be greatly comforted by them,—who ask no more than that their children may get through the world without being jostled or pushed, and unmolested if possible, that they may live longer than the oaks or ravens, and be blessed with the greatest possible number of descendants. Aye! these ordinances are indeed precious to those who accept them, for they save them the trouble of thinking for themselves. Besides, the great god of the Jews is said to have dictated all that this book contains to its writers, just as I dictate to Philippus, my hump-backed secretary, all that I want said. They regard everyone as a blasphemer and desecrator who thinks that anything written in that roll is erroneous, or even merely human. Plato's doctrines are not amiss, and yet Aristotle had criticised them severely and attempted to confute them. I myself incline to the views of the Stagyrite, you to those of the noble Athenian, and how many good and instructive hours we owe to our discussions over this difference of opinion! And how amusing it is to listen when the Platonists on the one hand and the Aristotelians on the other, among the busy threshers of straw in the Museum at Alexandria, fall together by the ears so vehemently that they would both enjoy flinging their metal cups at each others' heads—if the loss of the wine, which I pay for, were not too serious to bear. We still seek for truth; the Jews believe they possess it entirely.

"Even those among them who most zealously study our philosophers believe this; and yet the writers of this book know of nothing but actual present, and their god—who will no more endure another god as his equal than a citizen's wife will admit a second woman to her husband's house—is said to have created the world out of nothing for no other purpose but to be worshipped and feared by its inhabitants.

"Now, given a philosophical Jew who knows his Empedocles—and I grant there are many such in Alexandria, extremely keen and cultivated men—what idea can he form in his own mind of 'creation out of nothing?' Must he not pause to think very seriously when he remembers the fundamental axiom that 'out of nothing, nothing can come,' and that nothing which has once existed can ever be completely annihilated? At any rate the necessary deduction must be that the life of man ends in that nothingness whence everything in existence has proceeded. To live and to die according to this book is not highly profitable. I can easily reconcile myself to the idea of annihilation, as a man who knows how to value a dreamless sleep after a day brimful of enjoyment—as a man who if he must cease to be Euergetes would rather spring into the open jaws of nothingness—but as a philosopher, no, never!"

"You, it is true," replied the queen, "cannot help measuring all and everything by the intellectual standard exclusively; for the gods, who endowed you with gifts beyond a thousand others, struck with blindness or deafness that organ which conveys to our minds any religious or moral sentiment. If that could see or hear, you could no more exclude the conviction that these writings are full of the deepest purport than I can, nor doubt that they have a powerful hold on the mind of the reader.

"They fetter their adherents to a fixed law, but they take all bitterness out of sorrow by teaching that a stern father sends us suffering which is represented as being sometimes a means of education, and sometimes a punishment for transgressing a hard and clearly defined law. Their god, in his infallible but stern wisdom, sets those who cling to him on an evil and stony path to prove their strength, and to let them at last reach the glorious goal which is revealed to them from the beginning."

"How strange such words as these sound in the mouth of a Greek," interrupted Euergetes. "You certainly must be repeating them after the son of the Jewish high-priest, who defends the cause of his cruel god with so much warmth and skill."

"I should have thought," retorted Cleopatra, "that this overwhelming figure of a god would have pleased you, of all men; for I know of no weakness in you. Quite lately Dositheos, the Jewish centurion—a very learned man—tried to describe to my husband the one great god to whom his nation adheres with such obstinate fidelity, but I could not help thinking of our beautiful and happy gods as a gay company of amorous lords and pleasure-loving ladies, and comparing them with this stern and powerful being who, if only he chose to do it, might swallow them all up, as Chronos swallowed his own children."

"That," exclaimed Euergetes, "is exactly what most provokes me in this superstition. It crushes our light-hearted pleasure in life, and whenever I have been reading the book of the Hebrews everything has come into my mind that I least like to think of. It is like an importunate creditor that reminds us of our forgotten debts, and I love pleasure and hate an importunate reminder. And you, pretty one, life blooms for you—"

"But I," interrupted Cleopatra, "I can admire all that is great; and does it not seem a bold and grand thing even to you, that the mighty idea that it is one single power that moves and fills the world, should be freely and openly declared in the sacred writings of the Jews—an idea which the Egyptians carefully wrap up and conceal, which the priests of the Nile only venture to divulge to the most privileged of those who are initiated into their mysteries, and which—though the Greek philosophers indeed have fearlessly uttered it—has never been introduced by any Hellene into the religion of the people? If you were not so averse to the Hebrew nation, and if you, like my husband and myself, had diligently occupied yourself with their concerns and their belief you would be juster to them and to their scriptures, and to the great creating and preserving spirit, their god—"

"You are confounding this jealous and most unamiable and ill-tempered tyrant of the universe with the Absolute of Aristotle!" cried Euergetes; "he stigmatises most of what you and I and all rational Greeks require for the enjoyment of life as sin—sin upon sin. And yet if my easily persuadable brother governed at Alexandria, I believe the shrewd priests might succeed in stamping him as a worshipper of that magnified schoolmaster, who punishes his untutored brood with fire and torment."

"I cannot deny," replied Cleopatra, "that even to me the doctrine of the Jews has something very fearful in it, and that to adopt it seems to me tantamount to confiscating all the pleasures of life.—But enough of such things, which I should no more relish as a daily food than you do. Let us rejoice in that we are Hellenes, and let us now go to the banquet. I fear you have found a very unsatisfactory substitute for what you sought in coming up here."

"No—no. I feel strangely excited to-day, and my work with Aristarchus would have led to no issue. It is a pity that we should have begun to talk of that barbarian rubbish; there are so many other subjects more pleasing and more cheering to the mind. Do you remember how we used to read the great tragedians and Plato together?"

"And how you would often interrupt our tutor Agatharchides in his lectures on geography, to point out some mistake! Did you prosecute those studies in Cyrene?"

"Of course. It really is a pity, Cleopatra, that we should no longer live together as we did formerly. There is no one, not even Aristarchus, with whom I find it more pleasant and profitable to converse and discuss than with you. If only you had lived at Athens in the time of Pericles, who knows if you might not have been his friend instead of the immortal Aspasia. This Memphis is certainly not the right place for you; for a few months in the year you ought to come to Alexandria, which has now risen to be superior to Athens."

"I do not know you to-day!" exclaimed Cleopatra, gazing at her brother in astonishment. "I have never heard you speak so kindly and brotherly since the death of my mother. You must have some great request to make of us."

"You see how thankless a thing it is for me to let my heart speak for once, like other people. I am like the boy in the fable when the wolf came!

I have so often behaved in an unbrotherly fashion that when I show the aspect of a brother you think I have put on a mask. If I had had anything special to ask of you I should have waited till to-morrow, for in this part of the country even a blind beggar does not like to refuse his lame comrade anything on his birthday."

"If only we knew what you wish for! Philometor and I would do it more than gladly, although you always want something monstrous. Our performance to-morrow will—at any rate—but—Zoe, pray be good enough to retire with the maids; I have a few words to say to my brother alone."

As soon as the queen's ladies had withdrawn, she went on:

"It is a real grief to use, but the best part of the festival in honor of your birthday will not be particularly successful, for the priests of Serapis spitefully refuse us the Hebe about whom Lysias has made us so curious. Asclepiodorus, it would seem, keeps her in concealment, and carries his audacity so far as to tell us that someone has carried her off from the temple. He insinuates that we have stolen her, and demands her restitution in the name of all his associates."

"You are doing the man an injustice; our dove has followed the lure of a dove-catcher who will not allow me to have her, and who is now billing and cooing with her in his own nest. I am cheated, but I can scarcely be angry with the Roman, for his claim was of older standing than mine."

"The Roman?" asked Cleopatra, rising from her seat and turning pale. "But that is impossible. You are making common cause with Eulaeus, and want to set me against Publius Scipio. At the banquet last night you showed plainly enough your ill-feeling against him."

"You seem to feel more warmly towards him. But before I prove to you that I am neither lying nor joking, may I enquire what has this man, this many-named Publius Cornelius Scipio Nasica, to recommend him above any handsome well-grown Macedonian, who is resolute in my cause, in the whole corps of your body guard, excepting his patrician pride? He is as bitter and ungenial as a sour apple, and all the very best that you—a subtle thinker, a brilliant and cultivated philosopher—can find to say is no more appreciated by his meanly cultivated intellect than the odes of Sappho by a Nubian boatman."

"It is exactly for that," cried the queen, "that I value him; he is different from all of us; we who—how shall I express myself—who always think at second-hand, and always set our foot in the rut trodden by the master of the school we adhere to; who squeeze our minds into the moulds that others have carved out, and when we speak hesitate to step beyond the outlines of those figures of rhetoric which we learned at school! You have burst these bonds, but even your mighty spirit still shows traces of them. Publius Scipio, on the contrary, thinks and sees and speaks with perfect independence, and his upright sense guides him to the truth without any trouble or special training. His society revives me like the fresh air that I breathe when I come out into the open air from the temple filled with the smoke of incense—like the milk and bread which a peasant offered us during our late excursion to the coast, after we had been living for a year on nothing but dainties."

"He has all the admirable characteristics of a child!" interrupted Euergetes. "And if that is all that appears estimable to you in the Roman your son may soon replace the great Cornelius."

"Not soon! no, not till he shall have grown older than you are, and a man, a thorough man, from the crown of his head to the sole of his foot, for such a man is Publius! I believe—nay, I am sure—that he is incapable of any mean action, that he could not be false in word or even in look, nor feign a sentiment be did not feel."

"Why so vehement, sister? So much zeal is quite unnecessary on this occasion! You know well enough that I have my easy days, and that this excitement is not good for you; nor has the Roman deserved that you should be quite beside yourself for his sake. The fellow dared in my presence to look at you as Paris might at Helen before he carried her off, and to drink out of your cup; and this morning he no doubt did not contradict what he conveyed to you last night with his eyes—nay, perhaps by his words. And yet, scarcely an hour before, he had been to the Necropolis to bear his sweetheart away from the temple of the gloomy Serapis into that of the smiling Eros."

"You shall prove this!" cried the queen in great excitement. "Publius is my friend—"

"And I am yours!"

"You have often proved the reverse, and now again with lies and cheating—"

"You seem," interrupted Euergetes, "to have learned from your unphilosophical favorite to express your indignation with extraordinary frankness; to-day however I am, as I have said, as gentle as a kitten—"

"Euergetes and gentleness!" cried Cleopatra with a forced laugh. "No, you only step softly like a cat when she is watching a bird, and your gentleness covers some ruthless scheme, which we shall find out soon enough to our cost. You have been talking with Eulaeus to-day; Eulaeus, who fears and hates Publius, and it seems to me that you have hatched some conspiracy against him; but if you dare to cast a single stone in his path, to touch a single hair of his head, I will show you that even a weak woman can be terrible. Nemesis and the Erinnyes from Alecto to Megaera, the most terrible of all the gods, are women!"

Cleopatra had hissed rather than spoken these words, with her teeth set with rage, and had raised her small fist to threaten her brother; but Euergetes preserved a perfect composure till she had ceased speaking. Then he took a step closer to her, crossed his arms over his breast, and asked her in the deepest bass of his fine deep voice:

"Are you idiotically in love with this Publius Cornelius Scipio Nasica, or do you purpose to make use of him and his kith and kin in Rome against me?"

Transported with rage, and without blenching in the least at her brother's piercing gaze, she hastily retorted: "Up to this moment only the first perhaps—for what is my husband to me? But if you go on as you have begun I shall begin to consider how I may make use of his influence and of his liking for me, on the shores of the Tiber."

"Liking!" cried Euergetes, and he laughed so loud and violently that Zoe, who was listening at the tent door, gave a little scream, and Cleopatra drew back a step. "And to think that you—the most prudent of the prudent— who can hear the dew fall and the grass grow, and smell here in Memphis the smoke of every fire that is lighted in Alexandria or in Syria or even in Rome—that you, my mother's daughter, should be caught over head and ears by a broad-shouldered lout, for all the world like a clumsy town-girl or a wench at a loom. This ignorant Adonis, who knows so well how to make use of his own strange and resolute personality, and of the power that stands in his background, thinks no more of the hearts he sets in flames than I of the earthen jar out of which water is drawn when I am thirsty. You think to make use of him by the 'Tiber; but he has anticipated you, and learns from you all that is going on by the Nile and everything they most want to know in the Senate.

"You do not believe me, for no one ever is ready to believe anything that can diminish his self-esteem—and why should you believe me? I frankly confess that I do not hesitate to lie when I hope to gain more by untruth than by that much-belauded and divine truth, which, according to your favorite Plato, is allied to all earthly beauty; but it is often just as useless as beauty itself, for the useful and the beautiful exclude each other in a thousand cases, for ten when they coincide. There, the gong is sounding for the third time. If you care for plain proof that the Roman, only an hour before he visited you this morning, had our little Hebe carried off from the temple, and conveyed to the house of Apollodorus, the sculptor, at Memphis, you have only to come to see me in my rooms early to-morrow after the first morning sacrifice. You will at any rate wish to come and congratulate me; bring your children with you, as I propose making them presents. You might even question the Roman himself at the banquet to-day, but he will hardly appear, for the sweetest gifts of Eros are bestowed at night, and as the temple of Serapis is closed at sunset Publius has never yet seen his Irene in the evening. May I expect you and the children after morning sacrifice?"

Before Cleopatra had time to answer this question another trumpet-blast was heard, and she exclaimed: "That is Philometor, come to fetch us to the banquet. I will ere long give the Roman the opportunity of defending himself, though—in spite of your accusations—I trust him entirely. This morning I asked him solemnly whether it was true that he was in love with his friend's charming Hebe, and he denied it in his firm and manly way, and his replies were admirable and worthy of the noblest mind, when I ventured to doubt his sincerity. He takes truth more seriously than you do. He regards it not only as beautiful and right to be truthful, he says, but as prudent too; for lies can only procure us a small short-lived advantage, as transitory as the mists of night which vanish as soon as the sun appears, while truth is like the sunlight itself, which as often as it is dimmed by clouds reappears again and again. And, he says, what makes a liar so particularly contemptible in his eyes is, that to attain his end, he must be constantly declaring and repeating the horror he has of those who are and do the very same thing as he himself. The ruler of a state cannot always be truthful, and I often have failed in truth; but my intercourse with Publius has aroused much that is good in me, and which had been slumbering with closed eyes; and if this man should prove to be the same as all the rest of you, then I will follow your road, Euergetes, and laugh at virtue and truth, and set the busts of Aristippus and Strato on the pedestals where those of Zeno and Antisthenes now stand."

"You mean to have the busts of the philosophers moved again?" asked King Philometor, who, as he entered the tent, had heard the queen's last words. "And Aristippus is to have the place of honor? I have no objection—though he teaches that man must subjugate matter and not become subject to it.—['Mihi res, non me rebus subjungere.']—This indeed is easier to say than to do, and there is no man to whom it is more impossible than to a king who has to keep on good terms with Greeks and Egyptians, as we have, and with Rome as well. And besides all this to avoid quarrelling with a jealous brother, who shares our kingdom! If men could only know how much they would have to do as kings only in reading and writing, they would take care never to struggle for a crown! Up to this last half hour I have been examining and deciding applications and petitions. Have you got through yours, Euergetes? Even more had accumulated for you than for us."

"All were settled in an hour," replied the other promptly. "My eye is quicker than the mouth of your reader, and my decisions commonly consist of three words while you dictate long treatises to your scribes. So I had done when you had scarcely begun, and yet I could tell you at once, if it were not too tedious a matter, every single case that has come before me for months, and explain it in all its details."

"That I could not indeed," said Philometor modestly, "but I know and admire your swift intelligence and accurate memory."

"You see I am more fit for a king than you are;" laughed Euergetes. "You are too gentle and debonair for a throne! Hand over your government to me. I will fill your treasury every year with gold. I beg you now, come to Alexandria with Cleopatra for good, and share with me the palace and the gardens in the Bruchion. I will nominate your little Philopator heir to the throne, for I have no wish to contract a permanent tie with any woman, as Cleopatra belongs to you. This is a bold proposal, but reflect, Philometor, if you were to accept it, how much time it would give you for your music, your disputations with the Jews, and all your other favorite occupations."

"You never know how far you may go with your jest!" interrupted Cleopatra. "Besides, you devote quite as much time to your studies in philology and natural history as he does to music and improving conversations with his learned friends."

"Just so," assented Philometor, "and you may be counted among the sages of the Museum with far more reason than I."

"But the difference between us," replied Euergetes, "is that I despise all the philosophical prattlers and rubbish-collectors in Alexandria almost to the point of hating them, while for science I have as great a passion as for a lover. You, on the contrary, make much of the learned men, but trouble yourself precious little about science."

"Drop the subject, pray," begged Cleopatra. "I believe that you two have never yet been together for half an hour without Euergetes having begun some dispute, and Philometor having at last given in, to pacify him. Our guests must have been waiting for us a long time. Had Publius Scipio made his appearance?"

"He had sent to excuse himself," replied the king as he scratched the poll of Cleopatra's parrot, parting its feathers with the tips of his fingers. "Lysias, the Corinthian, is sitting below, and he says he does not know where his friend can be gone."

"But we know very well," said Euergetes, casting an ironical glance at the queen. "It is pleasant to be with Philometor and Cleopatra, but better still with Eros and Hebe. Sister, you look pale—shall I call for Zoe?"

Cleopatra shook her head in negation, but she dropped into a seat, and sat stooping, with her head bowed over her knees as if she were dreadfully tired. Euergetes turned his back on her, and spoke to his brother of indifferent subjects, while she drew lines, some straight and some crooked, with her fan-stick through the pile of the soft rug on the floor, and sat gazing thoughtfully at her feet. As she sat thus her eye was caught by her sandals, richly set with precious stones, and the slender toes she had so often contemplated with pleasure; but now the sight of them seemed to vex her, for in obedience to a swift impulse she loosened the straps, pushed off her right sandal with her left foot, kicked it from her, and said, turning to her husband:

"It is late and I do not feel well, and you may sup without me."

"By the healing Isis!" exclaimed Philometor, going up to her. "You look suffering. Shall I send for the physicians? Is it really nothing more than your usual headache? The gods be thanked! But that you should be unwell just to-day! I had so much to say to you; and the chief thing of all was that we are still a long way from completeness in our preparations for our performance. If this luckless Hebe were not—"

"She is in good hands," interrupted Euergetes. "The Roman, Publius Scipio, has taken her to a place of safety; perhaps in order to present her to me to morrow morning in return for the horses from Cyrene which I sent him to-day. How brightly your eyes sparkle, sister—with joy no doubt at this good idea. This evening, I dare say he is rehearsing the little one in her part that she may perform it well to-morrow. If we are mistaken— if Publius is ungrateful and proposes keeping the dove, then Thais, your pretty Athenian waiting-woman, may play the part of Hebe. What do you think of that suggestion, Cleopatra?"

"That I forbid such jesting with me!" cried the queen vehemently. "No one has any consideration for me—no one pities me, and I suffer fearfully! Euergetes scorns me—you, Philometor, would be glad to drag me down! If only the banquet is not interfered with, and so long as nothing spoils your pleasure!—Whether I die or no, no one cares!"

With these words the queen burst into tears, and roughly pushed away her husband as he endeavored to soothe her. At last she dried her eyes, and said: "Go down-the guests are waiting."

"Immediately, my love," replied Philometor. "But one thing I must tell you, for I know that it will arouse your sympathy. The Roman read to you the petition for pardon for Philotas, the chief of the Chrematistes and 'relative of the king,' which contains such serious charges against Eulaeus. I was ready with all my heart to grant your wish and to pardon the man who is the father of these miserable water-bearers; but, before having the decree drawn up, I had the lists of the exiles to the gold-mines carefully looked through, and there it was discovered that Philotas and his wife have both been dead more than half a year. Death has settled this question, and I cannot grant to Publius the first service he has asked of me—asked with great urgency too. I am sorry for this, both for his sake and for that of poor Philotas, who was held in high esteem by our mother."

"May the ravens devour them!" answered Cleopatra, pressing her forehead against the ivory frame which surrounded the stuffed back of her seat. "Once more I beg of you excuse me from all further speech." This time the two kings obeyed her wishes. When Euergetes offered her his hand she said with downcast eyes, and poking her fan-stick into the wool of the carpet:

"I will visit you early to-morrow."

"After the first sacrifice," added Euergetes. "If I know you well, something that you will then hear will please you greatly; very greatly indeed, I should think. Bring the children with you; that I ask of you as a birthday request."

CHAPTER XX

The royal chariot in which Klea was standing, wrapped in the cloak and wearing the hat of the captain of the civic guard, went swiftly and without stopping through the streets of Memphis. As long as she saw houses with lighted windows on each side of the way, and met riotous soldiers and quiet citizens going home from the taverns, or from working late in their workshops, with lanterns in their hands or carried by their slaves—so long her predominant feeling was one of hatred to Publius; and mixed with this was a sentiment altogether new to her—a sentiment that made her blood boil, and her heart now stand still and then again beat wildly—the thought that he might be a wretched deceiver. Had he not attempted to entrap one of them—whether her sister or herself it was all the same—wickedly to betray her, and to get her into his power!

"With me," thought she, "he could not hope to gain his evil ends, and when he saw that I knew how to protect myself he lured the poor unresisting child away with him, in order to ruin her and to drag her into shame and misery. Just like Rome herself, who seizes on one country after another to make them her own, so is this ruthless man. No sooner had that villain Eulaeus' letter reached him, than he thought himself justified in believing that I too was spellbound by a glance from his eyes, and would spread my wings to fly into his arms; and so he put out his greedy hand to catch me too, and threw aside the splendor and delights of a royal banquet to hurry by night out into the desert, and to risk a hideous death—for the avenging deities still punish the evildoer."

By this time she was shrouded in total darkness, for the moon was still hidden by black clouds. Memphis was already behind her, and the chariot was passing through a tall-stemmed palm-grove, where even at mid-day deep shades intermingled with the sunlight. When, just at this spot, the thought once more pierced her soul that the seducer was devoted to death, she felt as though suddenly a bright glaring light had flashed up in her and round her, and she could have broken out into a shout of joy like one who, seeking retribution for blood, places his foot at last on the breast of his fallen foe. She clenched her teeth tightly and grasped her girdle, in which she had stuck the knife given her by the smith.

If the charioteer by her side had been Publius, she would have stabbed him to the heart with the weapon with delight, and then have thrown herself under the horses' hoofs and the brazen wheels of the chariot.

But no! Still more gladly would she have found him dying in the desert, and before his heart had ceased to beat have shouted in his ear how much she hated him; and then, when his breast no longer heaved a breath—then she would have flung herself upon him, and have kissed his dimmed eyes.

Her wildest thoughts of vengeance were as inseparable from tender pity and the warmest longings of a heart overflowing with love, as the dark waters of a river are from the brighter flood of a stream with which it has recently mingled. All the passionate impulses which had hitherto been slumbering in her soul were set free, and now raised their clamorous voices as she was whirled across the desert through the gloom of night. The wishes roused in her breast by her hatred appealing to her on one side and her love singing in her ear, in tempting flute-tones, on the other, jostled and hustled one another, each displacing the other as they crowded her mind in wild confusion. As she proceeded on her journey she felt that she could have thrown herself like a tigress on her victim, and yet—like an outcast woman—have flung herself at Publius' knees in supplication for the love that was denied her. She had lost all idea of time and distance, and started as from a wild and bewildering dream when the chariot suddenly halted, and the driver said in his rough tones:

"Here we are, I must turn back again."

She shuddered, drew the cloak more closely round her, sprang out on to the road, and stood there motionless till the charioteer said:

"I have not spared my horses, my noble gentleman. Won't you give me something to get a drop of wine?" Klea's whole possessions were two silver drachma, of which she herself owned one and the other belonged to Irene. On the last anniversary but one of his mother's death, the king had given at the temple a sum to be divided among all the attendants, male and female, who served Serapis, and a piece of silver had fallen to the share of herself and her sister. Klea had them both about her in a little bag, which also contained a ring that her mother had given her at parting, and the amulet belonging to Serapion. The girl took out the two silver coins and gave them to the driver, who, after testing the liberal gift with his fingers, cried out as he turned his horses:

"A pleasant night to you, and may Aphrodite and all the Loves be favorable!"

"Irene's drachma!" muttered Klea to herself, as the chariot rolled away. The sweet form of her sister rose before her mind; she recalled the hour when the girl—still but a child—had entrusted it to her, because she lost everything unless Klea took charge of it for her.

"Who will watch her and care for her now?" she asked herself, and she stood thinking, trying to defend herself against the wild wishes which again began to stir in her, and to collect her scattered thoughts. She had involuntarily avoided the beam of light which fell across the road from the tavern-window, and yet she could not help raising her eyes and looking along it, and she found herself looking through the darkness which enveloped her, straight into the faces of two men whose gaze was directed to the very spot where she was standing. And what faces they were that she saw! One, a fat face, framed in thick hair and a short, thick and ragged beard, was of a dusky brown and as coarse and brutal as the other was smooth, colorless and lean, cruel and crafty. The eyes of the first of these ruffians were prominent, weak and bloodshot, with a fixed glassy stare, while those of the other seemed always to be on the watch with a restless and uneasy leer.

These were Euergetes' assassins—they must be! Spellbound with terror and revulsion she stood quite still, fearing only that the ruffians might hear the beating of her heart, for she felt as if it were a hammer swung up and down in an empty space, and beating with loud echoes, now in her bosom and now in her throat.

"The young gentleman must have gone round behind the tavern—he knows the shortest way to the 'tombs. Let us go after him, and finish off the business at once," said the broad-shouldered villain in a hoarse whisper that broke down every now and then, and which seemed to Klea even more repulsive than the monster's face.

"So that he may hear us go after him-stupid!" answered the other. "When he has been waiting for his sweetheart about a quarter of an hour I will call his name in a woman's voice, and at his first step towards the desert do you break his neck with the sand-bag. We have plenty of time yet, for it must still be a good half hour before midnight."

"So much the better," said the other. "Our wine-jar is not nearly empty yet, and we paid the lazy landlord for it in advance, before he crept into bed."

"You shall only drink two cups more," said the punier villain. "For this time we have to do with a sturdy fellow, Setnam is not with us now to lend a hand in the work, and the dead meat must show no gaping thrusts or cuts. My teeth are not like yours when you are fasting—even cooked food must not be too tough for them to chew it, now-a-days. If you soak yourself in drink and fail in your blow, and I am not ready with the poisoned stiletto the thing won't come off neatly. But why did not the Roman let his chariot wait?"

"Aye! why did he let it go away?" asked the other staring open-mouthed in the direction where the sound of wheels was still to be heard. His companion mean while laid his hand to his ear, and listened. Both were silent for a few minutes, then the thin one said:

"The chariot has stopped at the first tavern. So much the better. The Roman has valuable cattle in his shafts, and at the inn down there, there is a shed for horses. Here in this hole there is hardly a stall for an ass, and nothing but sour wine and mouldy beer. I don't like the rubbish, and save my coin for Alexandria and white Mariotic; that is strengthening and purifies the blood. For the present I only wish we were as well off as those horses; they will have plenty of time to recover their breath."

"Yes, plenty of time," answered the other with a broad grin, and then he with his companion withdrew into the room to fill his cup.

Klea too could hear that the chariot which had brought her hither, had halted at the farther tavern, but it did not occur to her that the driver had gone in to treat himself to wine with half of Irene's drachma. The horses should make up for the lost time, and they could easily do it, for when did the king's banquets ever end before midnight?

As soon as Plea saw that the assassins were filling their earthen cups, she slipped softly on tiptoe behind the tavern; the moon came out from behind the clouds for a few minutes, she sought and found the short way by the desert-path to the Apis-tombs, and hastened rapidly along it. She looked straight before her, for whenever she glanced at the road-side, and her eye was caught by some dried up shrub of the desert, silvery in the pale moonlight, she fancied she saw behind it the face of a murderer.

The skeletons of fallen beasts standing up out of the dust, and the bleached jawbones of camels and asses, which shone much whiter than the desert-sand on which they lay, seemed to have come to life and motion, and made her think of the tiger-teeth of the bearded ruffian.

The clouds of dust driven in her face by the warm west wind, which had risen higher, increased her alarm, for they were mingled with the colder current of the night-breeze; and again and again she felt as if spirits were driving her onwards with their hot breath, and stroking her face with their cold fingers. Every thing that her senses perceived was transformed by her heated imagination into a fearful something; but more fearful and more horrible than anything she heard, than any phantom that met her eye in the ghastly moonlight, were her own thoughts of what was to be done now, in the immediate future—of the fearful fate that threatened the Roman and Irene; and she was incapable of separating one from the other in her mind, for one influence alone possessed her, heart and soul: dread, dread; the same boundless, nameless, deadly dread—alike of mortal peril and irremediable shame, and of the airiest phantoms and the merest nothings.

A large black cloud floated slowly across the moon and utter darkness hid everything around, even the undefined forms which her imagination had turned to images of dread. She was forced to moderate her pace, and find her way, feeling each step; and just as to a child some hideous form that looms before him vanishes into nothingness when he covers his eyes with his hand, so the profound darkness which now enveloped her, suddenly released her soul from a hundred imaginary terrors.

She stood still, drew a deep breath, collected the whole natural force of her will, and asked herself what she could do to avert the horrid issue.

Since seeing the murderers every thought of revenge, every wish to punish the seducer with death, had vanished from her mind; one desire alone possessed her now—that of rescuing him, the man, from the clutches of these ravening beasts. Walking slowly onwards she repeated to herself every word she had heard that referred to Publius and Irene as spoken by Euergetes, Eulaeus, the recluse, and the assassins, and recalled every step she had taken since she left the temple; thus she brought herself back to the consciousness that she had come out and faced danger and endured terror, solely and exclusively for Irene's sake. The image of her sister rose clearly before her mind in all its bright charm, undimmed by any jealous grudge which, indeed, ever since her passion had held her in its toils had never for the smallest fraction of a minute possessed her.

Irene had grown up under her eye, sheltered by her care, in the sunshine of her love. To take care of her, to deny herself, and bear the severest fatigue for her had been her pleasure; and now as she appealed to her father—as she wont to do—as if he were present, and asked him in an inaudible cry: "Tell me, have I not done all for her that I could do?" and said to herself that he could not possibly answer her appeal but with assent, her eyes filled with tears; the bitterness and discontent which had lately filled her breast gradually disappeared, and a gentle, calm, refreshing sense of satisfaction came over her spirit, like a cooling breeze after a scorching day.

As she now again stood still, straining her eyes which were growing more accustomed to the darkness, to discover one of the temples at the end of the alley of sphinxes, suddenly and unexpectedly at her right hand a solemn and many-voiced hymn of lamentation fell upon her ear. This was from the priests of Osiris-Apis who were performing the sacred mysteries of their god, at midnight, on the roof of the temple. She knew the hymn well—a lament for the deceased Osiris which implored him with urgent supplication to break the power of death, to rise again, to bestow new light and new vitality on the world and on men, and to vouchsafe to all the departed a new existence.

The pious lament had a powerful effect on her excited spirit. Her parents too perhaps had passed through death, and were now taking part in the conduct of the destiny of the world and of men in union with the life giving God. Her breath came fast, she threw up her arms, and, for the first time since in her wrath she had turned her back on the holy of holies in the temple of Serapis, she poured forth her whole soul with passionate fervor in a deep and silent prayer for strength to fulfil her duty to the end,—for some sign to show her the way to save Irene from misfortune, and Publius from death. And as she prayed she felt no longer alone—no, it seemed to her that she stood face to face with the invincible Power which protects the good, in whom she now again had faith, though for Him she knew no name; as a daughter, pursued by foes, might clasp her powerful father's knees and claim his succor.

She had not stood thus with uplifted arms for many minutes when the moon, once more appearing, recalled her to herself and to actuality. She now perceived close to her, at hardly a hundred paces from where she stood, the line of sphinxes by the side of which lay the tombs of Apis near which she was to await Publius. Her heart began to beat faster again, and her dread of her own weakness revived. In a few minutes she must meet the Roman, and, involuntarily putting up her hand to smooth her hair, she was reminded that she still wore Glaucus' hat on her head and his cloak wrapped round her shoulders. Lifting up her heart again in a brief prayer for a calm and collected mind, she slowly arranged her dress and its folds, and as she did so the key of the tomb-cave, which she still had about her, fell under her hand. An idea flashed through her brain—she caught at it, and with hurried breath followed it out, till she thought she had now hit upon the right way to preserve from death the man who was so rich and powerful, who had given her nothing but taken everything from her, and to whom, nevertheless, she—the poor water-bearer whom he had thought to trifle with—could now bestow the most precious of the gifts of the immortals, namely, life.

Serapion had said, and she was willing to believe, that Publius was not base, and he certainly was not one of those who could prove ungrateful to a preserver. She longed to earn the right to demand something of him, and that could be nothing else but that he should give up her sister and bring Irene back to her.

When could it be that he had come to an understanding with the inexperienced and easily wooed maiden? How ready she must have been to clasp the hand held out to her by this man! Nothing surprised her in Irene, the child of the present; she could comprehend too that Irene's charm might quickly win the heart even of a grave and serious man.

And yet—in all the processions it was never Irene that he had gazed at, but always herself, and how came it to pass that he had given a prompt and ready assent to the false invitation to go out to meet her in the desert at midnight? Perhaps she was still nearer to his heart than Irene, and if gratitude drew him to her with fresh force then—aye then—he might perhaps woo her, and forget his pride and her lowly position, and ask her to be his wife.

She thought this out fully, but before she had reached the half circle enclosed by the Philosophers' busts the question occurred to her mind. And Irene?

Had she gone with him and quitted her without bidding her farewell because the young heart was possessed with a passionate love for Publius—who was indeed the most lovable of men? And he? Would he indeed, out of gratitude for what she hoped to do for him, make up his mind, if she demanded it, to make her Irene his wife—the poor but more than lovely daughter of a noble house?

And if this were possible, if these two could be happy in love and honor, should she Klea come between the couple to divide them? Should she jealously snatch Irene from his arms and carry her back to the gloomy temple which now—after she had fluttered awhile in sportive freedom in the sunny air—would certainly seem to her doubly sinister and unendurable? Should she be the one to plunge Irene into misery—Irene, her child, the treasure confided to her care, whom she had sworn to cherish?

"No, and again no," she said resolutely. "She was born for happiness, and I for endurance, and if I dare beseech thee to grant me one thing more, O thou infinite Divinity! it is that Thou wouldst cut out from my soul this love which is eating into my heart as though it were rotten wood, and keep me far from envy and jealousy when I see her happy in his arms. It is hard—very hard to drive one's own heart out into the desert in order that spring may blossom in that of another: but it is well so—and my mother would commend me and my father would say I had acted after his own heart, and in obedience to the teaching of the great men on these pedestals. Be still, be still my aching heart—there—that is right!"

Thus reflecting she went past the busts of Zeno and Chrysippus, glancing at their features distinct in the moonlight: and her eyes falling on the smooth slabs of stone with which the open space was paved, her own shadow caught her attention, black and sharply defined, and exactly resembling that of some man travelling from one town to another in his cloak and broad-brimmed hat.

"Just like a man!" she muttered to herself; and as, at the same moment, she saw a figure resembling her own, and, like herself, wearing a hat, appear near the entrance to the tombs, and fancied she recognized it as Publius, a thought, a scheme, flashed through her excited brain, which at first appalled her, but in the next instant filled her with the ecstasy which an eagle may feel when he spreads his mighty wings and soars above the dust of the earth into the pure and infinite ether. Her heart beat high, she breathed deeply and slowly, but she advanced to meet the Roman, drawn up to her full height like a queen, who goes forward to receive some equal sovereign; her hat, which she had taken off, in her left hand, and the Smith's key in her right-straight on towards the door of the Apis-tombs.

CHAPTER XXI

The man whom Klea had seen was in fact none other than Publius. He was now at the end of a busy day, for after he had assured himself that Irene had been received by the sculptor and his wife, and welcomed as if she were their own child, he had returned to his tent to write once more a dispatch to Rome. But this he could not accomplish, for his friend Lysias paced restlessly up and down by him as he sat, and as often as he put the reed to the papyrus disturbed him with enquiries about the recluse, the sculptor, and their rescued protegee.

When, finally, the Corinthian desired to know whether he, Publius, considered Irene's eyes to be brown or blue, he had sprung up impatiently, and exclaimed indignantly:

"And supposing they were red or green, what would it matter to me!"

Lysias seemed pleased rather than vexed with this reply, and he was on the point of confessing to his friend that Irene had caused in his heart a perfect conflagration—as of a forest or a city in flames—when a master of the horse had appeared from Euergetes, to present the four splendid horses from Cyrene, which his master requested the noble Roman Publius Cornelius Scipio Nasica to accept in token of his friendship.

The two friends, who both were judges and lovers of horses, spent at least an hour in admiring the fine build and easy paces of these valuable beasts. Then came a chamberlain from the queen to invite Publius to go to her at once.

The Roman followed the messenger after a short delay in his tent, in order to take with him the gems representing the marriage of Hebe, for on his way from the sculptor's to the palace it had occurred to him that he would offer them to the queen, after he had informed her of the parentage of the two water-carriers. Publius had keen eyes, and the queen's weaknesses had not escaped him, but he had never suspected her of being capable of abetting her licentious brother in forcibly possessing himself of the innocent daughter of a noble father. He now purposed to make her a present—as in some degree a substitute for the representation his friend had projected, and which had come to nothing—of the picture which she had hoped to find pleasure in reproducing.

Cleopatra received him on her roof, a favor of which few could boast; she allowed him to sit at her feet while she reclined on her couch, and gave him to understand, by every glance of her eyes and every word she spoke, that his presence was a happiness to her, and filled her with passionate delight. Publius soon contrived to lead the conversation to the subject of the innocent parents of the water-bearers, who had been sent off to the goldmines; but Cleopatra interrupted his speech in their favor and asked him plainly, undisguisedly, and without any agitation, whether it was true that he himself desired to win the youthful Hebe. And she met his absolute denial with such persistent and repeated expressions of disbelief, assuming at last a tone of reproach, that he grew vexed and broke out into a positive declaration that he regarded lying as unmanly and disgraceful, and could endure any insult rather than a doubt of his veracity.

Such a vehement and energetic remonstrance from a man she had distinguished was a novelty to Cleopatra, and she did not take it amiss, for she might now believe—what she much wished to believe—that Publius wanted to have nothing to do with the fair Hebe, that Eulaeus had slandered her friend, and that Zoe had been in error when, after her vain expedition to the temple—from which she had then just returned—she had told her that the Roman was Irene's lover, and must at the earliest hour have betrayed to the girl herself, or to the priests in the Serapeum, what was their purpose regarding her.

In the soul of this noble youth there was nothing false—there could be nothing false! And she, who was accustomed never to hear a word from the men who surrounded her without asking herself with what aim it was spoken, and how much of it was dissimulation or downright falsehood, trusted the Roman, and was so happy in her trust that, full of gracious gaiety, she herself invited Publius to give her the recluse's petition to read. The Roman at once gave her the roll, saying that since it contained so much that was sad, much as he hoped she would make herself acquainted with it, he felt himself called upon also to give her some pleasure, though in truth but a very small one. Thus speaking he produced the gems, and she showed as much delight over this little work of art as if, instead of being a rich queen and possessed of the finest engraved gems in the world, she were some poor girl receiving her first gift of some long-desired gold ornament.

"Exquisite, splendid!" she cried again and again. "And besides, they are an imperishable memorial of you, dear friend, and of your visit to Egypt. I will have them set with the most precious stones; even diamonds will seem worthless to me compared with this gift from you. This has already decided my sentence as to Eulaeus and his unhappy victims before I read your petition. Still I will read that roll, and read it attentively, for my husband regards Eulaeus as a useful—almost an indispensable-tool, and I must give good reasons for my verdict and for the pardon. I believe in the innocence of the unfortunate Philotas, but if he had committed a hundred murders, after this present I would procure his freedom all the same."

The words vexed the Roman, and they made her who had spoken them in order to please him appear to him at that moment more in the light of a corruptible official than of a queen. He found the time hang heavy that he spent with Cleopatra, who, in spite of his reserve, gave him to understand with more and more insistence how warmly she felt towards him; but the more she talked and the more she told him, the more silent he became, and he breathed a sigh of relief when her husband at last appeared to fetch him and Cleopatra away to their mid-day meal.

At table Philometor promised to take up the cause of Philotas and his wife, both of whom he had known, and whose fate had much grieved him; still he begged his wife and the Roman not to bring Eulaeus to justice till Euergetes should have left Memphis, for, during his brother's presence, beset as he was with difficulties, he could not spare him; and if he might judge of Publius by himself he cared far more to reinstate the innocent in their rights, and to release them from their miserable lot—a lot of which he had only learned the full horrors quite recently from his tutor Agatharchides—than to drag a wretch before the judges to-morrow or the day after, who was unworthy of his anger, and who at any rate should not escape punishment.

Before the letter from Asclepiodorus—stating the mistaken hypothesis entertained by the priests of Serapis that Irene had been carried off by the king's order—could reach the palace, Publius had found an opportunity of excusing himself and quitting the royal couple. Not even Cleopatra herself could raise any objection to his distinct assurance that he must write to Rome today on matters of importance. Philometor's favor was easy to win, and as soon as he was alone with his wife he could not find words enough in praise of the noble qualities of the young man, who seemed destined in the future to be of the greatest service to him and to his interests at Rome, and whose friendly attitude towards himself was one more advantage that he owed—as he was happy to acknowledge—to the irresistible talents and grace of his wife.

When Publius had quitted the palace and hurried back to his tent, he felt like a journeyman returning from a hard day's labor, or a man acquitted from a serious charge; like one who had lost his way, and has found the right road again.

The heavy air in the arbors and alleys of the embowered gardens seemed to him easier to breathe than the cool breeze that fanned Cleopatra's raised roof. He felt the queen's presence to be at once exciting and oppressive, and in spite of all that was flattering to himself in the advances made to him by the powerful princess, it was no more gratifying to his taste than an elegantly prepared dish served on gold plate, which we are forced to partake of though poison may be hidden in it, and which when at last we taste it is sickeningly sweet.

Publius was an honest man, and it seemed to him—as to all who resemble him—that love which was forced upon him was like a decoration of honor bestowed by a hand which we do not respect, and that we would rather refuse than accept; or like praise out of all proportion to our merit, which may indeed delight a fool, but rouses the indignation rather than the gratitude of a wise man. It struck him too that Cleopatra intended to make use of him, in the first place as a toy to amuse herself, and then as a useful instrument or underling, and this so gravely incensed and discomfited the serious and sensitive young man that he would willingly have quitted Memphis and Egypt at once and without any leave-taking. However, it was not quite easy for him to get away, for all his thoughts of Cleopatra were mixed up with others of Klea, as inseparably as when we picture to ourselves the shades of night, the tender light of the calm moon rises too before our fancy.

Having saved Irene, his present desire was to restore her parents to liberty; to quit Egypt without having seen Klea once more seemed to him absolutely impossible. He endeavored once more to revive in his mind the image of her proud tall figure; he felt he must tell her that she was beautiful, a woman worthy of a king—that he was her friend and hated injustice, and was ready to sacrifice much for justice's sake and for her own in the service of her parents and herself. To-day again, before the banquet, he purposed to go to the temple, and to entreat the recluse to help him to an interview with his adopted daughter.

If only Klea could know beforehand what he had been doing for Irene and their parents she must surely let him see that her haughty eyes could look kindly on him, must offer him her hand in farewell, and then he should clasp it in both his, and press it to his breast. Then would he tell her in the warmest and most inspired words he could command how happy he was to have seen her and known her, and how painful it was to bid her farewell; perhaps she might leave her hand in his, and give him some kind word in return. One kind word—one phrase of thanks from Klea's firm but beautiful mouth—seemed to him of higher value than a kiss or an embrace from the great and wealthy Queen of Egypt.

When Publius was excited he could be altogether carried away by a sudden sweep of passion, but his imagination was neither particularly lively nor glowing. While his horses were being harnessed, and then while he was driving to the Serapeum, the tall form of the water-bearer was constantly before him; again and again he pictured himself holding her hand instead of the reins, and while he repeated to himself all he meant to say at parting, and in fancy heard her thank him with a trembling voice for his valuable help, and say that she would never forget him, he felt his eyes moisten— unused as they had been to tears for many years. He could not help recalling the day when he had taken leave of his family to go to the wars for the first time. Then it had not been his own eyes but his mother's that had sparkled through tears, and it struck him that Klea, if she could be compared to any other woman, was most like to that noble matron to whom he owed his life, and that she might stand by the side of the daughter of the great Scipio Africanus like a youthful Minerva by the side of Juno, the stately mother of the gods.

His disappointment was great when he found the door of the temple closed, and was forced to return to Memphis without having seen either Klea or the recluse.

He could try again to-morrow to accomplish what had been impossible to-day, but his wish to see the girl he loved, rose to a torturing longing, and as he sat once more in his tent to finish his second despatch to Rome the thought of Klea came again to disturb his serious work. Twenty times he started up to collect his thoughts, and as often flung away his reed as the figure of the water-bearer interposed between him and the writing under his hand; at last, out of patience with himself, he struck the table in front of him with some force, set his fists in his sides hard enough to hurt himself, and held them there for a minute, ordering himself firmly and angrily to do his duty before he thought of anything else.

His iron will won the victory; by the time it was growing dusk the despatch was written. He was in the very act of stamping the wax of the seal with the signet of his family—engraved on the sardonyx of his ring—when one of his servants announced a black slave who desired to speak with him. Publius ordered that he should be admitted, and the negro handed him the tile on which Eulaeus had treacherously written Klea's invitation to meet her at midnight near the Apis-tombs. His enemy's crafty-looking emissary seemed to the young man as a messenger from the gods; in a transport of haste and, without the faintest shadow of a suspicion he wrote, "I will be there," on the luckless piece of clay.

Publius was anxious to give the letter to the Senate, which he had just finished, with his own hand, and privately, to the messenger who had yesterday brought him the despatch from Rome; and as he would rather have set aside an invitation to carry off a royal treasure that same night than have neglected to meet Klea, he could not in any case be a guest at the king's banquet, though Cleopatra would expect to see him there in accordance with his promise. At this juncture he was annoyed to miss his friend Lysias, for he wished to avoid offending the queen; and the Corinthian, who at this moment was doubtless occupied in some perfectly useless manner, was as clever in inventing plausible excuses as he himself was dull in such matters. He hastily wrote a few lines to the friend who shared his tent, requesting him to inform the king that he had been prevented by urgent business from appearing among his guests that evening; then he threw on his cloak, put on his travelling-hat which shaded his face, and proceeded on foot and without any servant to the harbor, with his letter in one hand and a staff in the other.

The soldiers and civic guards which filled the courts of the palace, taking him for a messenger, did not challenge him as he walked swiftly and firmly on, and so, without being detained or recognized, he reached the inn by the harbor, where he was forced to wait an hour before the messenger came home from the gay strangers' quarter where he had gone to amuse himself. He had a great deal to talk of with this man, who was to set out next morning for Alexandria and Rome; but Publius hardly gave himself the necessary time, for he meant to start for the meeting place in the Necropolis indicated by Klea, and well-known to himself, a full hour before midnight, although he knew that he could reach his destination in a very much shorter time.

The sun seems to move too slowly to those who long and wait, and a planet would be more likely to fail in punctuality than a lover when called by love.

In order to avoid observation he did not take a chariot but a strong mule which the host of the inn lent him with pleasure; for the Roman was so full of happy excitement in the hope of meeting Klea that he had slipped a gold piece into the small, lightly-closed fingers of the innkeeper's pretty child, which lay asleep on a bench by the side of the table, besides paying double as much for the country wine he had drunk as if it had been fine Falernian and without asking for his reckoning. The host looked at him in astonishment when, finally, he sprang with a grand leap on to the back of the tall beast, without laying his hand on it; and it seemed even to Publius himself as though he had never since boyhood felt so fresh, so extravagantly happy as at this moment.

The road to the tombs from the harbor was a different one to that which led thither from the king's palace, and which Klea had taken, nor did it lead past the tavern in which she had seen the murderers. By day it was much used by pilgrims, and the Roman could not miss it even by night, for the mule he was riding knew it well. That he had learned, for in answer to his question as to what the innkeeper kept the beast for he had said that it was wanted every day to carry pilgrims arriving from Upper Egypt to the temple of Serapis and the tombs of the sacred bulls; he could therefore very decidedly refuse the host's offer to send a driver with the beast. All who saw him set out supposed that he was returning to the city and the palace.

Publius rode through the streets of the city at an easy trot, and, as the laughter of soldiers carousing in a tavern fell upon his ear, he could have joined heartily in their merriment. But when the silent desert lay around him, and the stars showed him that he would be much too early at the appointed place, he brought the mule to a slower pace, and the nearer he came to his destination the graver he grew, and the stronger his heart beat. It must be something important and pressing indeed that Klea desired to tell him in such a place and at such an hour. Or was she like a thousand other women—was he now on the way to a lover's meeting with her, who only a few days before had responded to his glance and accepted his violets?

This thought flashed once through his mind with importunate distinctness, but he dismissed it as absurd and unworthy of himself. A king would be more likely to offer to share his throne with a beggar than this girl would be to invite him to enjoy the sweet follies of love-making with her in a secret spot.

Of course she wanted above all things to acquire some certainty as to her sister's fate, perhaps too to speak to him of her parents; still, she would hardly have made up her mind to invite him if she had not learned to trust him, and this confidence filled him with pride, and at the same time with an eager longing to see her, which seemed to storm his heart with more violence with every minute that passed.

While the mule sought and found its way in the deep darkness with slow and sure steps, he gazed up at the firmament, at the play of the clouds which now covered the moon with their black masses, and now parted, floating off in white sheeny billows while the silver crescent of the moon showed between them like a swan against the dark mirror of a lake.

And all the time he thought incessantly of Klea—thinking in a dreamy way that he saw her before him, but different and taller than before, her form growing more and more before his eyes till at last it was so tall that her head touched the sky, the clouds seemed to be her veil, and the moon a brilliant diadem in her abundant dark hair. Powerfully stirred by this vision he let the bridle fall on the mule's neck, and spread open his arms to the beautiful phantom, but as he rode forwards it ever retired, and when presently the west wind blew the sand in his face, and he had to cover his eyes with his hand it vanished entirely, and did not return before he found himself at the Apis-tombs.

He had hoped to find here a soldier or a watchman to whom he could entrust the beast, but when the midnight chant of the priests of the temple of Osiris-Apis had died away not a sound was to be heard far or near; all that lay around him was as still and as motionless as though all that had ever lived there were dead. Or had some demon robbed him of his hearing? He could hear the rush of his own swift pulses in his ears-not the faintest sound besides.

Such silence is there nowhere but in the city of the dead and at night, nowhere but in the desert.

He tied the mule's bridle to a stela of granite covered with inscriptions, and went forward to the appointed place. Midnight must be past—that he saw by the position of the moon, and he was beginning to ask himself whether he should remain standing where he was or go on to meet the water-bearer when he heard first a light footstep, and then saw a tall erect figure wrapped in a long mantle advancing straight towards him along the avenue of sphinxes. Was it a man or a woman—was it she whom he expected? and if it were she, was there ever a woman who had come to meet a lover at an assignation with so measured, nay so solemn, a step? Now he recognized her face—was it the pale moonlight that made it look so bloodless and marble-white? There was something rigid in her features, and yet they had never—not even when she blushingly accepted his violets—looked to him so faultlessly beautiful, so regular and so nobly cut, so dignified, nay impressive.

For fully a minute the two stood face to face, speechless and yet quite near to each other. Then Publius broke the silence, uttering with the warmest feeling and yet with anxiety in his deep, pure voice, only one single word; and the word was her name "Klea."

The music of this single word stirred the girl's heart like a message and blessing from heaven, like the sweetest harmony of the siren's song, like the word of acquittal from a judge's lips when the verdict is life or death, and her lips were already parted to say 'Publius' in a tone no less deep and heartfelt-but, with all the force of her soul, she restrained herself, and said softly and quickly:

"You are here at a late hour, and it is well that you have come."

"You sent for me," replied the Roman.

"It was another that did that, not I," replied Klea in a slow dull tone, as if she were lifting a heavy weight, and could hardly draw her breath. "Now—follow me, for this is not the place to explain everything in."

With these words Klea went towards the locked door of the Apis-tombs, and tried, as she stood in front of it, to insert into the lock the key that Krates had given her; but the lock was still so new, and her fingers shook so much, that she could not immediately succeed. Publius meanwhile was standing close by her side, and as he tried to help her his fingers touched hers.

And when he—certainly not by mistake—laid his strong and yet trembling hand on hers, she let it stay for a moment, for she felt as if a tide of warm mist rose up in her bosom dimming her perceptions, and paralyzing her will and blurring her sight.

"Klea," he repeated, and he tried to take her left hand in his own; but she, like a person suddenly aroused to consciousness after a short dream, immediately withdrew the hand on which his was resting, put the key into the lock, opened the door, and exclaimed in a voice of almost stern command, "Go in first."

Publius obeyed and entered the spacious antechamber of the venerable cave, hewn out of the rock and now dimly lighted. A curved passage of which he could not see the end lay before him, and on both sides, to the right and left of him, opened out the chambers in which stood the sarcophagi of the deceased sacred bulls. Over each of the enormous stone coffins a lamp burnt day and night, and wherever a vault stood open their glimmer fell across the deep gloom of the cave, throwing a bright beam of light on the dusky path that led into the heart of the rock, like a carpet woven of rays of light.

What place was this that Klea had chosen to speak with him in.

But though her voice sounded firm, she herself was not cool and insensible as Orcus—which this place, which was filled with the fumes of incense and weighed upon his senses, much resembled—for he had felt her fingers tremble under his, and when he went up to her, to help her, her heart beat no less violently and rapidly than his own. Ah! the man who should succeed in touching that heart of hard, but pure and precious crystal would indeed enjoy a glorious draught of the most perfect bliss.

"This is our destination," said Klea; and then she went on in short broken sentences. "Remain where you are. Leave me this place near the door. Now, answer me first one question. My sister Irene has vanished from the temple. Did you cause her to be carried off?"

"I did," replied Publius eagerly. "She desired me to greet you from her, and to tell you how much she likes her new friends. When I shall have told you—"

"Not now," interrupted Klea excitedly. "Turn round—there where you see the lamp-light." Publius did as he was desired, and a slight shudder shook even his bold heart, for the girl's sayings and doings seemed to him not solemn merely, but mysterious like those of a prophetess. A violent crash sounded through the silent and sacred place, and loud echoes were tossed from side to side, ringing ominously throughout the grotto. Publius turned anxiously round, and his eye, seeking Klea, found her no more; then, hurrying to the door of the cave, he heard her lock it on the outside.

The water-bearer had escaped him, had flung the heavy door to, and imprisoned him; and this idea was to the Roman so degrading and unendurable that, lost to every feeling but rage, wounded pride, and the wild desire to be free, he kicked the door with all his might, and called out angrily to Klea:

"Open this door—I command you. Let me free this moment or, by all the gods—"

He did not finish his threat, for in the middle of the right-hand panel of the door a small wicket was opened through which the priests were wont to puff incense into the tomb of the sacred bulls—and twice, thrice, finally, when he still would not be pacified, a fourth time, Klea called out to him:

"Listen to me—listen to me, Publius." Publius ceased storming, and she went on:

"Do not threaten me, for you will certainly repent it when you have heard what I have to tell you. Do not interrupt me; I may tell you at once this door is opened every day before sunrise, so your imprisonment will not last long; and you must submit to it, for I shut you in to save your life—yes, your life which was in danger. Do you think my anxiety was folly? No, Publius, it is only too well founded, and if you, as a man, are strong and bold, so am I as a woman. I never was afraid of an imaginary nothing. Judge yourself whether I was not right to be afraid for you.

"King Euergetes and Eulaeus have bribed two hideous monsters to murder you. When I went to seek out Irene I overheard all, and I have seen with my own eyes the two horrible wolves who are lurking to fall upon you, and heard with these ears their scheme for doing it. I never wrote the note on the tile which was signed with my name; Eulaeus did it, and you took his bait and came out into the desert by night. In a few minutes the ruffians will have stolen up to this place to seek their victim, but they will not find you,

Publius, for I have saved you—I, Klea, whom you first met with smiles—whose sister you have stolen away—the same Klea that you a minute since were ready to threaten. Now, at once, I am going into the desert, dressed like a traveller in a coat and hat, so that in the doubtful light of the moon I may easily be taken for you—going to give my weary heart as a prey to the assassins' knife."

"You are mad!" cried Publius, and he flung himself with his whole weight on the door, and kicked it with all his strength. "What you purpose is pure madness open the door, I command you! However strong the villains may be that Euergetes has bribed, I am man enough to defend myself."

"You are unarmed, Publius, and they have cords and daggers."

"Then open the door, and stay here with me till day dawns. It is not noble, it is wicked to cast away your life. Open the door at once, I entreat you, I command you!"

At any other time the words would not have failed of their effect on Klea's reasonable nature, but the fearful storm of feeling which had broken over her during the last few hours had borne away in its whirl all her composure and self-command. The one idea, the one resolution, the one desire, which wholly possessed her was to close the life that had been so full of self-sacrifice by the greatest sacrifice of all—that of life itself, and not only in order to secure Irene's happiness and to save the Roman, but because it pleased her—her father's daughter—to make a noble end; because she, the maiden, would fain show Publius what a woman might be capable of who loved him above all others; because, at this moment, death did not seem a misfortune; and her mind, overwrought by hours of terrific tension, could not free itself from the fixed idea that she would and must sacrifice herself.

She no longer thought these things—she was possessed by them; they had the mastery, and as a madman feels forced to repeat the same words again and again to himself, so no prayer, no argument at this moment would have prevailed to divert her from her purpose of giving up her young life for Publius and Irene. She contemplated this resolve with affection and pride as justifying her in looking up to herself as to some nobler creature. She turned a deaf ear to the Roman's entreaty, and said in a tone of which the softness surprised him:

"Be silent Publius, and hear me further. You too are noble, and certainly you owe me some gratitude for having saved your life."

"I owe you much, and I will pay it," cried Publius, "as long as there is breath in this body—but open the door, I beseech you, I implore you—"

"Hear me to the end, time presses; hear me out, Publius. My sister Irene went away with you. I need say nothing about her beauty, but how bright, how sweet her nature is you do not know, you cannot know, but you will find out. She, you must be told, is as poor as I am, but the child of freeborn and noble parents. Now swear to me, swear—no, do not interrupt me—swear by the head of your father that you will never, abandon her, that you will never behave to her otherwise than as if she were the daughter of your dearest friend or of your own brother."

"I swear it and I will keep my oath—by the life of the man whose head is more sacred to me than the names of all the gods. But now I beseech you, I command you open this door, Klea—that I may not lose you—that I may tell you that my whole heart is yours, and yours alone—that I love you, love you unboundedly."

"I have your oath," cried the girl in great excitement, for she could now see a shadow moving backwards and forwards at some distance in the desert. "You have sworn by the head of your father. Never let Irene repent having gone with you, and love her always as you fancy now, in this moment, that you love me, your preserver. Remember both of you the hapless Klea who would gladly have lived for you, but who now gladly dies for you. Do not forget me, Publius, for I have never but this once opened my heart to love, but I have loved you Publius, with pain and torment, and with sweet delight—as no other woman ever yet revelled in the ecstasy of love or was consumed in its torments." She almost shouted the last words at the Roman as if she were chanting a hymn of triumph, beside herself, forgetting everything and as if intoxicated.

Why was he now silent, why had he nothing to answer, since she had confessed to him the deepest secret of her breast, and allowed him to look into the inmost sanctuary of her heart? A rush of burning words from his lips would have driven her off at once to the desert and to death; his silence held her back—it puzzled her and dropped like cool rain on the soaring flames of her pride, fell on the raging turmoil of her soul like oil on troubled water. She could not part from him thus, and her lips parted to call him once more by his name.

While she had been making confession of her love to the Roman as if it were her last will and testament, Publius felt like a man dying of thirst, who has been led to a flowing well only to be forbidden to moisten his lips with the limpid fluid. His soul was filled with passionate rage approaching to despair, and as with rolling eyes he glanced round his prison an iron crow-bar leaning against the wall met his gaze; it had been used by the workmen to lift the sarcophagus of the last deceased Apis into its right place. He seized upon this tool, as a drowning man flings himself on a floating plank: still he heard Klea's last words, and did not lose one of them, though the sweat poured from his brow as he inserted the metal lever like a wedge between the two halves of the door, just above the threshold.

All was now silent outside; perhaps the distracted girl was already hurrying towards the assassins—and the door was fearfully heavy and would not open nor yield. But he must force it—he flung himself on the earth and thrust his shoulder under the lever, pushing his whole body against the iron bar, so that it seemed to him that every joint threatened to give way and every sinew to crack; the door rose—once more he put forth the whole strength of his manly vigor, and now the seam in the wood cracked, the door flew open, and Klea, seized with terror, flew off and away—into the desert—straight towards the murderers.

Publius leaped to his feet and flung himself out of his prison; as he saw Klea escape he flew after her with, hasty leaps, and caught her in a few steps, for her mantle hindered her in running, and when she would not obey his desire that she should stand still he stood in front of her and said, not tenderly but sternly and decidedly:

"You do not go a step farther, I forbid it."

"I am going where I must go," cried the girl in great agitation. "Let me go, at once!"

"You will stay here—here with me," snarled Publius, and taking both her hands by the wrists he clasped them with his iron fingers as with handcuffs. "I am the man and you are the woman, and I will teach you who is to give orders here and who is to obey."

Anger and rage prompted these quite unpremeditated words, and as Klea—while he spoke them with quivering lips—had attempted with the exertion of all her strength, which was by no means contemptible, to wrench her hands from his grasp, he forced her—angry as he still was, but nevertheless with due regard for her womanliness—forced her by a gentle and yet irresistible pressure on her arms to bend before him, and compelled her slowly to sink down on both knees.

As soon as she was in this position, Publius let her free; she covered her eyes with her aching hands and sobbed aloud, partly from anger, and because she felt herself bitterly humiliated.

"Now, stand up," said Publius in an altered tone as he heard her weeping. "Is it then such a hard matter to submit to the will of a man who will not and cannot let you go, and whom you love, besides?" How gentle and kind the words sounded! Klea, when she heard them, raised her eyes to Publius, and as she saw him looking down on her as a supplicant her anger melted and turned to grateful emotion—she went closer to him on her knees, laid her head against him and said:

"I have always been obliged to rely upon myself, and to guide another person with loving counsel, but it must be sweeter far to be led by affection and I will always, always obey you."

"I will thank you with heart and soul henceforth from this hour!" cried Publius, lifting her up. "You were ready to sacrifice your life for me, and now mine belongs to you. I am yours and you are mine—I your husband, you my wife till our life's end!"

He laid his hands on her shoulders, and turned her face round to his; she resisted no longer, for it was sweet to her to yield her will to that of this strong man. And how happy was she, who from her childhood had taken it upon herself to be always strong, and self-reliant, to feel herself the weaker, and to be permitted to trust in a stronger arm than her own. Somewhat thus a young rose-tree might feel, which for the first time receives the support of the prop to which it is tied by the careful gardener.

Her eyes rested blissfully and yet anxiously on his, and his lips had just touched hers in a first kiss when they started apart in terror, for Klea's name was clearly shouted through the still night-air, and in the next instant a loud scream rang out close to them followed by dull cries of pain.

"The murderers!" shrieked Klea, and trembling for herself and for him she clung closely to her lover's breast. In one brief moment the self-reliant heroine—proud in her death-defying valor—had become a weak, submissive, dependent woman.

CHAPTER XXII

On the roof of the tower of the pylon by the gate of the Serapeum stood an astrologer who had mounted to this, the highest part of the temple, to observe the stars; but it seemed that he was not destined on this occasion to fulfil his task, for swiftly driving black clouds swept again and again across that portion of the heavens to which his observations were principally directed. At last he impatiently laid aside his instruments, his waxed tablet and style, and desired the gate-keeper—the father of poor little Philo—whose duty it was to attend at night on the astrologers on the tower, to carry down all his paraphernalia, as the heavens were not this evening favorable to his labors.

"Favorable!" exclaimed the gate-keeper, catching up the astrologer's words, and shrugging his shoulders so high that his head disappeared between them.

"It is a night of horror, and some great disaster threatens us for certain. Fifteen years have I been in my place, and I never saw such a night but once before, and the very next day the soldiers of Antiochus, the Syrian king, came and plundered our treasury. Aye—and to-night is worse even than that was; when the dog-star first rose a horrible shape with a lion's mane flew across the desert, but it was not till midnight that the fearful uproar began, and even you shuddered when it broke out in the Apis-cave. Frightful things must be coming on us when the sacred bulls rise from the dead and butt and storm at the door with their horns to break it open. Many a time have I seen the souls of the dead fluttering and wheeling and screaming above the old mausoleums, and rock-tombs of ancient times. Sometimes they would soar up in the air in the form of hawks with men's heads, or like ibises with a slow lagging flight, and sometimes sweep over the desert like gray shapeless shadows, or glide across the sand like snakes; or they would creep out of the tombs, howling like hungry dogs. I have often heard them barking like jackals or laughing like hyenas when they scent carrion, but to-night is the first time I ever heard them shrieking like furious men, and then groaning and wailing as if they were plunged in the lake of fire and suffering horrible torments.

"Look there—out there—something is moving again! Oh! holy father, exorcise them with some mighty bann. Do you not see how they are growing larger? They are twice the size of ordinary mortals." The astronomer took an amulet in his hand, muttered a few sentences to himself, seeking at the same time to discover the figures which had so scared the gate-keeper.

"They are indeed tall," he said when he perceived them. "And now they are melting into one, and growing smaller and smaller—however, perhaps they are only men come to rob the tombs, and who happen to be particularly tall, for these figures are not of supernatural height."

"They are twice as tall as you, and you are not short," cried the gate-keeper, pressing his lips devoutly to the amulet the astrologer held in his hand, "and if they are robbers why has no watchman called out to stop them? How is it their screams and groans have not waked the sentinels that are posted there every night? There—that was another fearful cry! Did you ever hear such tones from any human breast? Great Serapis, I shall die of fright! Come down with me, holy father, that I may look after my little sick boy, for those who have seen such sights do not escape unstricken."

The peaceful silence of the Necropolis had indeed been disturbed, but the spirits of the departed had no share in the horrors which had been transacted this night in the desert, among the monuments and rocktombs. They were living men that had disturbed the calm of the sacred place, that had conspired with darkness in cold-blooded cruelty, greater than that of evil spirits, to achieve the destruction of a fellow-man; but they were living men too who, in the midst of the horrors of a most fearful night, had experienced the blossoming in their own souls of the divinest germ which heaven implants in the bosom of its mortal children. Thus in a day of battle amid blood and slaughter may a child be born that shall grow up blessed and blessing, the comfort and joy of his family.

The lion-maned monster whose appearance and rapid disappearance in the desert had first alarmed the gate-keeper, had been met by several travellers on its way to Memphis, and each and all, horrified by its uncanny aspect, had taken to flight or tried to hide themselves—and yet it was no more than a man with warm pulses, an honest purpose, and a true and loving heart. But those who met him could not see into his soul, and his external aspect certainly bore little resemblance to that of other men.

His feet, unused to walking, moved but clumsily, and had a heavy body to carry, and his enormous beard and the mass of gray hair on his head—which he turned now this way and now that—gave him an aspect that might well scare even a bold man who should meet him unexpectedly. Two stall-keepers who, by day, were accustomed to offer their wares for sale near the Serapeum to the pilgrims, met him close to the city.

"Did you see that panting object?" said one to the other as they looked after him. "If he were not shut up fast in his cell I could declare it was Serapion, the recluse."

"Nonsense," replied the other. "He is tied faster by his oath than by chains and fetters. It must be one of the Syrian beggars that besiege the temple of Astarte."

"Perhaps," answered his companion with indifference. "Let us get on now, my wife has a roast goose for supper this evening."

Serapion, it is true, was fast tied to his cell, and yet the pedler had judged rightly, for he it was who hurried along the high-road frightening all he met. After his long captivity walking was very painful to him; besides, he was barefoot, and every stone in the path hurt the soles of his feet which had grown soft; nevertheless he contrived to make a by no means contemptible pace when in the distance he caught sight of a woman's figure which he could fancy to be Klea. Many a man, who in his own particular sphere of life can cut a very respectable figure, becomes a laughing-stock for children when he is taken out of his own narrow circle, and thrown into the turmoil of the world with all his peculiarities clinging to him. So it was with Serapion; in the suburbs the street-boys ran after him mocking at him, but it was not till three smart hussys, who were resting from their dance in front of a tavern, laughed loudly as they caught sight of him, and an insolent soldier drove the point of his lance through his flowing mane, as if by accident, that he became fully conscious of his wild appearance, and it struck him forcibly that he could never in this guise find admission to the king's palace.

With prompt determination he turned into the first barber's stall that he saw lighted up; at his appearance the barber hastily retreated behind his counter, but he got his hair and beard cut, and then, for the first time for many years, he saw his own face in the mirror that the barber held before him. He nodded, with a melancholy smile, at the face—so much aged—that looked at him from the bright surface, paid what was asked, and did not heed the compassionate glance which the barber and his assistant sent after him. They both thought they had been exercising their skill on a lunatic, for he had made no answer to all their questions, and had said nothing but once in a deep and fearfully loud voice:

"Chatter to other people—I am in a hurry."

In truth his spirit was in no mood for idle gossip; no, it was full of gnawing anxiety and tender fears, and his heart bled when he reflected that he had broken his vows, and forsworn the oath he had made to his dying mother.

When he reached the palace-gate he begged one of the civic guard to conduct him to his brother, and as he backed his request with a gift of money he was led at once to the man whom he sought. Glaucus was excessively startled to recognize Serapion, but he was so much engaged that he could only give up a few minutes to his brother, whose proceedings he considered as both inexplicable and criminal.

Irene, as the anchorite now learned, had been carried off from the temple, not by Euergetes but by the Roman, and Klea had quitted the palace only a few minutes since in a chariot and would return about midnight and on foot from the second tavern to the temple. And the poor child was so utterly alone, and her way lay through the desert where she might be attacked by dissolute soldiery or tomb-robbers or jackals and hyenas. Her walk was to begin from the second tavern, and that was the very spot where low rioters were wont to assemble—and his darling was so young, so fair, and so defenceless!

He was once more a prey to the same unendurable dread that had come over him, in his cell, after Klea had left the temple and darkness had closed in. At that moment he had felt all that a father could feel who from his prison-window sees his beloved and defenceless child snatched away by some beast of prey. All the perils that could threaten her in the palace or in the city, swarming with drunken soldiers, had risen before his mind with fearful vividness, and his powerful imagination had painted in glaring colors all the dangers to which his favorite—the daughter of a noble and respected man—might be exposed.

He rushed up and down his cell like a wounded tiger, he flung himself against the walls, and then, with his body hanging far out of the window, had looked out to see if the girl—who could not possibly have returned yet—were not come back again. The darker it grew, the more his anguish rose, and the more hideous were the pictures that stood before his fancy; and when, presently, a pilgrim in the Pastophorium who had fallen into convulsions screamed out loud, he was no longer master of himself—he kicked open the door which, locked on the outside and rotten from age, had been closed for years, hastily concealed about him some silver coins he kept in his chest, and let himself down to the ground.

There he stood, between his cell and the outer wall of the temple, and now it was that he remembered his vows, and the oath he had sworn, and his former flight from his retreat. Then he had fled because the pleasures and joys of life had tempted him forth—then he had sinned indeed; but now the love, the anxious care that urged him to quit his prison were the same as had brought him back to it. It was to keep faith that he now broke faith, and mighty Serapis could read his heart, and his mother was dead, and while she lived she had always been ready and willing to forgive.

He fancied so vividly that he could see her kind old face looking at him that he nodded at her as if indeed she stood before him.

Then, he rolled an empty barrel to the foot of the wall, and with some difficulty mounted on it. The sweat poured down him as he climbed up the wall built of loose unbaked bricks to the parapet, which was much more than a man's height; then, sliding and tumbling, he found himself in the ditch which ran round it on the outside, scrambled up its outer slope, and set out at last on his walk to Memphis.

What he had afterwards learned in the palace concerning Klea had but little relieved his anxiety on her account; she must have reached the border of the desert so much sooner than he, and quick walking was so difficult to him, and hurt the soles of his feet so cruelly! Perhaps he might be able to procure a staff, but there was just as much bustle outside the gate of the citadel as by day. He looked round him, feeling the while in his wallet, which was well filled with silver, and his eye fell on a row of asses whose drivers were crowding round the soldiers and servants that streamed out of the great gate.

He sought out the strongest of the beasts with an experienced eye, flung a piece of silver to the owner, mounted the ass, which panted under its load, and promised the driver two drachmm in addition if he would take him as quickly as possible to the second tavern on the road to the Serapeum. Thus—he belaboring the sides of the unhappy donkey with his sturdy bare legs, while the driver, running after him snorting and shouting, from time to time poked him up from behind with a stick—Serapion, now going at a short trot, and now at a brisk gallop, reached his destination only half an hour later than Klea.

In the tavern all was dark and empty, but the recluse desired no refreshment. Only his wish that he had a staff revived in his mind, and he soon contrived to possess himself of one, by pulling a stake out of the fence that surrounded the innkeeper's little garden. This was a somewhat heavy walking-stick, but it eased the recluse's steps, for though his hot and aching feet carried him but painfully the strength of his arms was considerable.

The quick ride had diverted his mind, had even amused him, for he was easily pleased, and had recalled to him his youthful travels; but now, as he walked on alone in the desert, his thoughts reverted to Klea, and to her only.

He looked round for her keenly and eagerly as soon as the moon came out from behind the clouds, called her name from time to time, and thus got as far as the avenue of sphinxes which connected the Greek and Egyptian temples; a thumping noise fell upon his ear from the cave of the Apis-tombs. Perhaps they were at work in there, preparing for the approaching festival. But why were the soldiers, which were always on guard here, absent from their posts to-night? Could it be that they had observed Klea, and carried her off?

On the farther side of the rows of sphinxes too, which he had now reached, there was not a man to be seen—not a watchman even though the white limestone of the tombstones and the yellow desert-sand shone as clear in the moonlight as if they had some internal light of their own.

At every instant he grew more and more uneasy, he climbed to the top of a sand-hill to obtain a wider view, and loudly called Klea's name.

There—was he deceived? No—there was a figure visible near one of the ancient tomb-shrines—a form that seemed wrapped in a long robe, and when once more he raised his voice in a loud call it came nearer to him and to the row of sphinxes. In great haste and as fast as he could he got down again to the roadway, hurried across the smooth pavement, on both sides of which the long perspective of man-headed lions kept guard, and painfully clambered up a sand-heap on the opposite side. This was in truth a painful effort, for the sand crumbled away again and again under his feet, slipping down hill and carrying him with it, thus compelling him to find a new hold with hand and foot. At last he was standing on the outer border of the sphinx-avenue and opposite the very shrine where he fancied he had seen her whom he sought; but during his clamber it had become perfectly dark again, for a heavy cloud had once more veiled the moon. He put both hands to his mouth, and shouted as loud as he could, "Klea!"—and then again, "Klea!"

Then, close at his feet he heard a rustle in the sand, and saw a figure moving before him as though it had risen out of the ground. This could not be Klea, it was a man—still, perhaps, he might have seen his darling—but before he had time to address him he felt the shock of a heavy blow that fell with tremendous force on his back between his shoulders. The assassin's sand-bag had missed the exact spot on the nape of the neck, and Serapion's strongly-knit backbone would have been able to resist even a stronger blow.

The conviction that he was attacked by robbers flashed on his consciousness as immediately as the sense of pain, and with it the certainty that he was a lost man if he did not defend himself stoutly.

Behind him he heard another rustle in the sand. As quickly as he could he turned round with an exclamation of "Accursed brood of vipers!" and with his heavy staff he fell upon the figure before him like a smith beating cold iron, for his eye, now more accustomed to the darkness, plainly saw it to be a man. Serapion must have hit straight, for his foe fell at his feet with a hideous roar, rolled over and over in the sand, groaning and panting, and then with one shrill shriek lay silent and motionless.

The recluse, in spite of the dim light, could see all the movements of the robber he had punished so severely, and he was bending over the fallen man anxiously and compassionately when he shuddered to feel two clammy hands touching his feet, and immediately after two sharp pricks in his right heel, which were so acutely painful that he screamed aloud, and was obliged to lift up the wounded foot. At the same time, however, he did not overlook the need to defend himself. Roaring like a wounded bull, cursing and raging, he laid about him on all sides with his staff, but hit nothing but the ground. Then as his blows followed each other more slowly, and at last his wearied arms could no longer wield the heavy stake, and he found himself compelled to sink on his knees, a hoarse voice addressed him thus:

"You have taken my comrade's life, Roman, and a two-legged serpent has stung you for it. In a quarter of an hour it will be all over with you, as it is with that fellow there. Why does a fine gentleman like you go to keep an appointment in the desert without boots or sandals, and so make our work so easy? King Euergetes and your friend Eulaeus send you their greetings. You owe it to them that I leave you even your ready money; I wish I could only carry away that dead lump there!"

During this rough speech Serapion was lying on the ground in great agony; he could only clench his fists, and groan out heavy curses with his lips which were now getting parched. His sight was as yet undimmed, and he could distinctly see by the light of the moon, which now shone forth from a broad cloudless opening in the sky, that the murderer attempted to carry away his fallen comrade, and then, after raising his head to listen for a moment sprang off with flying steps away into the desert. But the recluse now lost consciousness, and when some minutes later he once more opened his eyes his head was resting softly in the lap of a young girl, and it was the voice of his beloved Klea that asked him tenderly.

"You poor dear father! How came you here in the desert, and into the hands of these murderers? Do you know me—your Klea? And he who is looking for your wounds—which are not visible at all—he is the Roman Publius Scipio. Now first tell us where the dagger hit you that I may bind it up quickly—I am half a physician, and understand these things as you know."

The recluse tried to turn his head towards Klea's, but the effort was in vain, and he said in a low voice: "Prop me up against the slanting wall of the tomb shrine yonder; and you, child, sit down opposite to me, for I would fain look at you while I die. Gently, gently, my friend Publius, for I feel as if all my limbs were made of Phoenician glass, and might break at the least touch. Thank you, my young friend—you have strong arms, and you may lift me a little higher yet. So—now I can bear it; nay, I am well content, I am to be envied—for the moon shows me your dear face, my child, and I see tears on your cheeks, tears for me, a surly old man. Aye, it is good, it is very good to die thus."

"Oh, father, father!" cried Klea. "You must not speak so. You must live, you must not die; for see, Publius here asks me to be his wife, and the Immortals only can know how glad I am to go with him, and Irene is to stay with us, and be my sister and his. That must make you happy, father.—But tell us, pray tell us where the wound hurts that the murderer gave you?"

"Children, children," murmured the anchorite, and a happy smile parted his lips. "The gracious gods are merciful in permitting me to see that—aye, merciful to me, and to effect that end I would have died twenty deaths."

Klea pressed his now cold hand to her lips as he spoke and again asked, though hardly able to control her voice for tears:

"But the wound, father—where is the wound?" "Let be, let be," replied Serapion. "It is acrid poison, not a dagger or dart that has undone my strength. And I can depart in peace, for I am no longer needed for anything. You, Publius, must now take my place with this child, and will do it better than I. Klea, the wife of Publius Scipio! I indeed have dreamt that such a thing might come to pass, and I always knew, and have said to myself a thousand times that I now say to you my son: This girl here, this Klea is of a good sort, and worthy only of the noblest. I give her to you, my son Publius, and now join your hands before me here—for I have always been like a father to her."

"That you have indeed," sobbed Klea. "And it was no doubt for my sake, and to protect me, that you quitted your retreat, and have met your death."

"It was fate, it was fate," stammered the old man.

"The assassins were in ambush for me," cried Publius, seizing Serapion's hand, "the murderers who fell on you instead of me. Once more, where is your wound?"

"My destiny fulfils itself," replied the recluse. "No locked-up cell, no physician, no healing herb can avail against the degrees of Fate. I am dying of a serpent's sting as it was foretold at my birth; and if I had not gone out to seek Klea a serpent would have slipped into my cage, and have ended my life there. Give me your hands, my children, for a deadly chill is creeping over me, and its cold hand already touches my heart."

For a few minutes his voice failed him, and then he said softly:

"One thing I would fain ask of you. My little possessions, which were intended for you and Irene, you will now use to bury me. I do not wish to be burnt, as they did with my father—no, I should wish to be finely embalmed, and my mummy to be placed with my mother's. If indeed we may meet again after death—and I believe we shall—I would rather see her once more than any one, for she loved me so much—and I feel now as if I were a child again, and could throw my arms round her neck. In another life, perhaps, I may not be the child of misfortune that I have been in this—in another life— now it grips my heart—in another——Children whatever joys have smiled on me in this, children, it was to you I have owed it—Klea, to you—and there is my little Irene too——"

These were the last words of Serapion the recluse; he fell back with a deep sigh and was dead. Klea and Publius tenderly closed his faithful eyes.

CHAPTER XXIII

The unwonted tumult that had broken the stillness of the night had not been unobserved in the Greek Serapeum any more than in the Egyptian temple adjoining the Apis-tombs; but perfect silence once more reigned in the Necropolis, when at last the great gate of the sanctuary of Osiris-Apis was thrown open, and a little troop of priests arranged in a procession came out from it with a vanguard of temple servants, who had been armed with sacrificial knives and axes.

Publius and Klea, who were keeping faithful watch by the body of their dead friend, saw them approaching, and the Roman said:

"It would have been even less right in such a night as this to let you proceed to one of the temples with out my escort than to have let our poor friend remain unwatched."

"Once more I assure you," said Klea eagerly "that we should have thrown away every chance of fulfilling Serapion's last wish as he intended, if during our absence a jackal or a hyena had mutilated his body, and I am happy to be able at least to prove to my friend, now he is dead, how grateful I am for all the kindness he showed us while he lived. We ought to be grateful even to the departed, for how still and blissful has this hour been while guarding his body. Storm and strife brought us together—"

"And here," interrupted Publius, "we have concluded a happy and permanent treaty of peace for the rest of our lives."

"I accept it willingly," replied Klea, looking down, "for I am the vanquished party."

"But you have already confessed," said Publius, "that you were never so unhappy as when you thought you had asserted your strength against mine, and I can tell you that you never seemed to me so great and yet so lovable as when in the midst of your triumph, you gave up the battle for lost. Such an hour as that, a man experiences but once in his lifetime. I have a good memory, but if ever I should forget it, and be angry and passionate— as is sometimes my way—remind me of this spot, or of this our dead friend, and my hard mood will melt, and I shall remember that you once were ready to give your life for mine. I will make it easy for you, for in honor of this man, who sacrificed his life for yours and who was actually murdered in my stead, I promise to add his name of Serapion to my own, and I will confirm this vow in Rome. He has behaved to us as a father, and it behoves me to reverence his memory as though I had been his son. An obligation was always unendurable to me, and how I shall ever make full restitution to you for what you have done for me this night I do not yet know—and yet I should be ready and willing every day and every hour to accept from you some new gift of love. 'A debtor,' says the proverb, 'is half a prisoner,' and so I must entreat you to deal mercifully with your conquerer."

He took her hand, stroked back the hair from her forehead, and touched it lightly with his lips. Then he went on:

"Come with me now that we may commit the dead into the hands of these priests."

Klea once more bent over the remains of the anchorite, she hung the amulet he had given her for her journey round his neck, and then silently obeyed her lover. When they came up with the little procession Publius informed the chief priest how he had found Serapion, and requested him to fetch away the corpse, and to cause it to be prepared for interment in the costliest manner in the embalming house attached to their temple. Some of the temple-servants took their places to keep watch over the body, and after many questions addressed to Publius, and after examining too the body of the assassin who had been slain, the priests returned to the temple.

As soon as the two lovers were left alone again Klea seized the Roman's hand, and said passionately: "You have spoken many tender words to me, and I thank you for them; but I am wont always to be honest, and less than any one could I deceive you. Whatever your love bestows upon me will always be a free gift, since you owe me nothing at all and I owe you infinitely much; for I know now that you have snatched my sister from the clutches of the mightiest in the land while I, when I heard that Irene had gone away with you, and that murder threatened your life, believed implicitly that on the contrary you had lured the child away to become your sweetheart, and then—then I hated you, and then—I must confess it\ —in my horrible distraction I wished you dead!"

"And you think that wish can offend me or hurt me?" said Publius. "No, my child; it only proves to me that you love me as I could wish to be loved. Such rage under such circumstances is but the dark shadow cast by love, and is as inseparable from love as from any tangible body. Where it is absent there is no such thing as real love present—only an airy vision, a phantom, a mockery. Such an one as Klea does not love nor hate by halves; but there are mysterious workings in your soul as in that of every other woman. How did the wish that you could see me dead turn into the fearful resolve to let yourself be killed in my stead?"

"I saw the murderers," answered Klea, "and I was overwhelmed with horror of them and of their schemes, and of all that had to do with them; I would not destroy Irene's happiness, and I loved you even more deeply than I hated you; and then—but let us not speak of it."

"Nay-tell me all."

"Then there was a moment—"

"Well, Klea?"

"Then—in these last hours, while we have been sitting hand in hand by the body of poor Serapion, and hardly speaking, I have felt it all over again—then the midnight hymn of the priests fell upon my heart, and as I lifted up my soul in prayer at their pious chant I felt as if all my inmost heart had been frozen and hardened, and was reviving again to new life and tenderness and warmth. I could not help thinking of all that is good and right, and I made up my mind to sacrifice myself for you and for Irene's happiness far more quickly and easily than I could give it up afterwards. My father was one of the followers of Zeno—"

"And you," interrupted Publius, "thought you were acting in accordance with the doctrine of the Stoa. I also am familiar with it, but I do not know the man who is so virtuous and wise that he can live and act, as that teaching prescribes, in the heat of the struggle of life, or who is the living representative in flesh and blood of the whole code of ethics, not sinning against one of its laws and embodying it in himself. Did you ever hear of the peace of mind, the lofty indifference and equanimity of the Stoic sages? You look as if the question offended you, but you did not by any means know how to attain that magnanimity, for I have seen you fail in it; indeed it is contrary to the very nature of woman, and—the gods be thanked—you are not a Stoic in woman's dress, but a woman—a true woman, as you should be. You have learned nothing from Zeno and Chrysippus but what any peasant girl might learn from an honest father, to be true I mean and to love virtue. Be content with that; I am more than satisfied."

"Oh, Publius," exclaimed the girl, grasping her friend's hand. "I understand you, and I know that you are right. A woman must be miserable so long as she fancies herself strong, and imagines and feels that she needs no other support than her own firm will and determination, no other counsel than some wise doctrines which she accepts and adheres to. Before I could call you mine, and went on my own way, proud of my own virtue, I was—I cannot bear to think of it—but half a soul, and took it for a whole; but now—if now fate were to snatch you from me, I should still know where to seek the support on which I might lean in need and despair. Not in the Stoa, not in herself can a woman find such a stay, but in pious dependence on the help of the gods."

"I am a man," interrupted Publius, "and yet I sacrifice to them and yield ready obedience to their decrees."

"But," cried Klea, "I saw yesterday in the temple of Serapis the meanest things done by his ministers, and it pained me and disgusted me, and I lost my hold on the divinity; but the extremest anguish and deepest love have led me to find it again. I can no longer conceive of the power that upholds the universe as without love nor of the love that makes men happy as other than divine. Any one who has once prayed for a being they love as I prayed for you in the desert can never again forget how to pray. Such prayers indeed are not in vain. Even if no god can hear them there is a strengthening virtue in such prayer itself.

"Now I will go contentedly back to our temple till you fetch me, for I know that the discreetest, wisest, and kindest Beings will watch over our love."

"You will not accompany me to Apollodorus and Irene?" asked Publius in surprise.

"No," answered Klea firmly. "Rather take me back to the Serapeum. I have not yet been released from the duties I undertook there, and it will be more worthy of us both that Asclepiodorus should give you the daughter of Philotas as your wife than that you should be married to a runaway serving-maid of Serapis."

Publius considered for a moment, and then he said eagerly:

"Still I would rather you should come with me. You must be dreadfully tired, but I could take you on my mule to Apollodorus. I care little for what men say of me when I am sure I am doing right, and I shall know how to protect you against Euergetes whether you wish to be readmitted to the temple or accompany me to the sculptor. But do come—it will be hard on me to part from you again. The victor does not lay aside the crown when he has just won it in hard fight."

"Still I entreat you to take me back to the Serapeum," said Klea, laying her hand in that of Publius.

"Is the way to Memphis too long, are you utterly tired out?"

"I am much wearied by agitation and terror, by anxiety and happiness, still I could very well bear the ride; but I beg of you to take me back to the temple."

"What—although you feel strong enough to remain with me, and in spite of my desire to conduct you at once to Apollodorus and Irene?" asked Publius astonished, and he withdrew his hand. "The mule is waiting out there. Lean on my arm. Come and do as I request you."

"No, Publius, no. You are my lord and master, and I will always obey you unresistingly. In one thing only let me have my own way, now and in the future. As to what becomes a woman I know better than you, it is a thing that none but a woman can decide."

Publius made no reply to these words, but he kissed her, and threw his arm round her; and so, clasped in each other's embrace, they reached the gate of the Serapeum, there to part for a few hours.

Klea was let into the temple, and as soon as she had learned that little Philo was much better, she threw herself on her humble bed.

How lonely her room seemed, how intolerably empty without Irene. In obedience to a hasty impulse she quitted her own bed, lay herself down on her sister's, as if that brought her nearer to the absent girl, and closed her eyes; but she was too much excited and too much exhausted to sleep soundly. Swiftly-changing visions broke in again and again on her sincerely devotional thoughts and her restless half-sleep, painting to her fancy now wondrously bright images, and now most horrible ones—now pictures of exquisite happiness, and again others of dismal melancholy. And all the time she imagined she heard distant music and was being rocked up and down by unseen hands.

Still the image of the Roman overpowered all the rest.

At last a refreshing sleep sealed her eyes more closely, and in her dream she saw her lover's house in Rolne, his stately father, his noble mother—who seemed to her to bear a likeness to her own mother—and the figures of a number of tall and dignified senators. She felt herself much embarrassed among all these strangers, who looked enquiringly at her, and then kindly held out their hands to her. Even the dignified matron came to meet her with effusion, and clasped her to her breast; but just as Publius had opened his to her and she flew to his heart, and she fancied she could feel his lips pressed to hers, the woman, who called her every morning, knocked at her door and awoke her.

This time she had been happy in her dream and would willingly have slept again; but she forced herself to rise from her bed, and before the sun was quite risen she was standing by the Well of the Sun and, not to neglect her duty, she filled both the jars for the altar of the god.

Tired and half-overcome by sleep, she set the golden vessels in their place, and sat down to rest at the foot of a pillar, while a priest poured out the water she had brought, as a drink-offering on the ground.

It was now broad daylight as she looked out into the forecourt through the many-pillared hall of the temple; the early sunlight played round the columns, and its slanting rays, at this hour, fell through the tall doorway far into the great hall which usually lay in twilight gloom.

The sacred spot looked very solemn in her eyes, sublime, and as it were reconsecrated, and obeying an irresistible impulse she leaned against a column, and lifting up her arms, and raising her eyes, she uttered her thankfulness to the god for his loving kindness, and found but one thing to pray for, namely that he would preserve Publius and Irene, and all mankind, from sorrow and anxiety and deception.

She felt as if her heart had till now been benighted and dark, and had just disclosed some latent light—as if it had been withered and dry, and was now blossoming in fresh verdure and brightly-colored flowers.

To act virtuously is granted even to those who, relying on themselves. earnestly strive to lead moral, just and honest lives; but the happy union of virtue and pure inner happiness is solemnized only in the heart which is able to seek and find a God—be it Serapis or Jehovah.

At the door of the forecourt Klea was met by Asclepiodorus, who desired her to follow him. The high-priest had learned that she had secretly quitted the temple: when she was alone with him in a quiet room he asked her gravely and severely, why she had broken the laws and left the sanctuary without his permission. Klea told him, that terror for her sister had driven her to Memphis, and that she there had heard that Publics Cornelius Scipio, the Roman who had taken up her father's cause, had saved Irene from king Euergetes, and placed her in safety, and that then she had set out on her way home in the middle of the night.

The high-priest seemed pleased at her news, and when she proceeded to inform him that Serapion had forsaken his cell out of anxiety for her, and had met his death in the desert, he said:

"I knew all that, my child. May the gods forgive the recluse, and may Serapis show him mercy in the other world in spite of his broken oath! His destiny had to be fulfilled. You, child, were born under happier stars than he, and it is within my power to let you go unpunished. This I do willingly; and Klea, if my daughter Andromeda grows up, I can only wish that she may resemble you; this is the highest praise that a father can bestow on another man's daughter. As head of this temple I command you to fill your jars to-day, as usual, till one who is worthy of you comes to me, and asks you for his wife. I suspect he will not be long to wait for."

"How do you know, father,—" asked Klea, coloring.

"I can read it in your eyes," said Asclepiodorus, and he gazed kindly after her as, at a sign from him, she quitted the room.

As soon as he was alone he sent for his secretary and said:

"King Philometor has commanded that his brother Euergetes' birthday shall be kept to-day in Memphis. Let all the standards be hoisted, and the garlands of flowers which will presently arrive from Arsinoe be fastened up on the pylons; have the animals brought in for sacrifice, and arrange a procession for the afternoon. All the dwellers in the temple must be carefully attired. But there is another thing; Komanus has been here, and has promised us great things in Euergetes' name, and declares that he intends to punish his brother Philometor for having abducted a girl—Irene—attached to our temple. At the same time he requests me to send Klea the water-bearer, the sister of the girl who was carried off, to Memphis to be examined—but this may be deferred. For to-day we will close the temple gates, solemnize the festival among ourselves, and allow no one to enter our precincts for sacrifice and prayer till the fate of the sisters is made certain. If the kings themselves make their appearance, and want to bring their troops in, we will receive them respectfully as becomes us, but we will not give up Klea, but consign her to the holy of holies, which even Euergetes dare not enter without me; for in giving up the girl we sacrifice our dignity, and with that ourselves."

The secretary bowed, and then announced that two of the prophets of Osiris-Apis desired to speak with Asclepiodorus.

Klea had met these men in the antechamber as she quitted the high-priest, and had seen in the hand of one of them the key with which she had opened the door of the rock-tomb. She had started, and her conscience urged her to go at once to the priest-smith, and tell him how ill she had fulfilled her errand.

When she entered his room Krates was sitting at his work with his feet wrapped up, and he was rejoiced to see her, for his anxiety for her and for Irene had disturbed his night's rest, and towards morning his alarm had been much increased by a frightful dream.

Klea, encouraged by the friendly welcome of the old man, who was usually so surly, confessed that she had neglected to deliver the key to the smith in the city, that she had used it to open the Apis-tombs, and had then forgotten to take it out of the new lock. At this confession the old man broke out violently, he flung his file, and the iron bolt at which he was working, on to his work-table, exclaiming:

"And this is the way you executed your commission. It is the first time I ever trusted a woman, and this is my reward! All this will bring evil on you and on me, and when it is found out that the sanctuary of Apis has been desecrated through my fault and yours, they will inflict all sorts of penance on me, and with very good reason—as for you, they will punish you with imprisonment and starvation."

"And yet, father," Klea calmly replied, "I feel perfectly guiltless, and perhaps in the same fearful situation you might not have acted differently."

"You think so—you dare to believe such a thing?" stormed the old man. "And if the key and perhaps even the lock have been stolen, and if I have done all that beautiful and elaborate work in vain?"

"What thief would venture into the sacred tombs?" asked Klea doubtfully.

"What! are they so unapproachable?" interrupted Krates. "Why, a miserable creature like you even dared to open them. But only wait—only wait; if only my feet were not so painful—"

"Listen to me," said the girl, going closer up to the indignant smith. "You are discreet, as you proved to me only yesterday; and if I were to tell you all I went through and endured last night you would certainly forgive me, that I know."

"If you are not altogether mistaken!" shouted the smith. "Those must be strange things indeed which could induce me to let such neglect of duty and such a misdemeanor pass unpunished."

And strange things they were indeed which the old man now had to hear, for when Klea had ended her narrative of all that had occurred during the past night, not her eyes only but those of the old smith too were wet with tears.

"These accursed legs!" he muttered, as his eyes met the enquiring glance of the young girl, and he wiped the salt dew from his cheeks with the sleeve of his coat. "Aye-a swelled foot like mine is painful, child, and a cripple such as I am is not always strong-minded. Old women grow like men, and old men grow like women. Ah! old age—it is bad to have such feet as mine, but what is worse is that memory fades as years advance. I believe now that I left the key myself in the door of the Apis-tombs last evening, and I will send at once to Asclepiodorus, so that he may beg the Egyptians up there to forgive me—they are indebted to me for many small jobs."

CHAPTER XXIV

All the black masses of clouds which during the night had darkened the blue sky and hidden the light of the moon had now completely disappeared. The north-east wind which rose towards morning had floated them away, and Zeus, devourer of the clouds, had swallowed them up to the very last. It was a glorious morning, and as the sun rose in the heavens, and pierced and burnt up with augmenting haste the pale mist that hovered over the Nile, and the vapor that hung—a delicate transparent veil of bluish-grey bombyx-gauze—over the eastern slopes, the cool shades of night vanished too from the dusky nooks of the narrow town which lay, mile-wide, along the western bank of the river. And the intensely brilliant sunlight which now bathed the streets and houses, the palaces and temples, the gardens and avenues, and the innumerable vessels in the harbor of Memphis, was associated with a glow of warmth which was welcome even there in the early morning of a winter's day.

Boats' captains and sailors—were hurrying down to the shore of the Nile to avail themselves of the northeast breeze to travel southwards against the current, and sails were being hoisted and anchors heaved, to an accompaniment of loud singing. The quay was so crowded with ships that it was difficult to understand how those that were ready could ever disentangle themselves, and find their way through those remaining behind; but each somehow found an outlet by which to reach the navigable stream, and ere long the river was swarming with boats, all sailing southwards, and giving it the appearance of an endless perspective of camp tents set afloat.

Long strings of camels with high packs, of more lightly laden asses, and of dark-colored slaves, were passing down the road to the harbor; these last were singing, as yet unhurt by the burden of the day, and the overseers' whips were still in their girdles.

Ox-carts were being laden or coming down to the landing-place with goods, and the ship's captains were already beginning to collect round the different great merchants—of whom the greater number were Greeks, and only a few dressed in Egyptian costume—in order to offer their freight for sale, or to hire out their vessels for some new expedition.

The greatest bustle and noise were at a part of the quay where, under large tents, the custom-house officials were busily engaged, for most vessels first cast anchor at Memphis to pay duty or Nile-toll on the "king's table." The market close to the harbor also was a gay scene; there dates and grain, the skins of beasts, and dried fish were piled in great heaps, and bleating and bellowing herds of cattle were driven together to be sold to the highest bidder.

Soldiers on foot and horseback in gaudy dresses and shining armor, mingled with the busy crowd, like peacocks and gaudy cocks among the fussy swarm of hens in a farm yard; lordly courtiers, in holiday dresses of showy red, blue and yellow stuffs, were borne by slaves in litters or standing on handsome gilt chariots; garlanded priests walked about in long white robes, and smartly dressed girls were hurrying down to the taverns near the harbor to play the flute or to dance.

The children that were playing about among this busy mob looked covetously at the baskets piled high with cakes, which the bakers' boys were carrying so cleverly on their heads. The dogs innumerable, put up their noses as the dealers in such dainties passed near them, and many of them set up longing howls when a citizen's wife came by with her slaves, carrying in their baskets freshly killed fowls, and juicy meats to roast for the festival, among heaps of vegetables and fruits.

Gardeners' boys and young girls were bearing garlands of flowers, festoons and fragrant nosegays, some piled on large trays which they carried two and two, some on smaller boards or hung on cross poles for one to carry; at that part of the quay where the king's barge lay at anchor numbers of workmen were busily employed in twining festoons of greenery and flowers round the flag-staffs, and in hanging them with lanterns.

Long files of the ministers of the god-representing the five phyla or orders of the priesthood of the whole country—were marching, in holiday attire, along the harbor-road in the direction of the palace, and the jostling crowd respectfully made way for them to pass. The gleams of festal splendor seemed interwoven with the laborious bustle on the quay like scraps of gold thread in a dull work-a-day garment.

Euergetes, brother of the king, was keeping his birthday in Memphis to-day, and all the city was to take part in the festivities.

At the first hour after sunrise victims had been sacrificed in the temple of Ptah, the most ancient, and most vast of the sanctuaries of the venerable capital of the Pharaohs; the sacred Apis-bull, but recently introduced into the temple, was hung all over with golden ornaments; early in the morning

Euergetes had paid his devotions to the sacred beast—which had eaten out of his hand, a favorable augury of success for his plans; and the building in which the Apis lived, as well as the stalls of his mother and of the cows kept for him, had been splendidly decked with flowers.

The citizens of Memphis were not permitted to pursue their avocations or ply their trades beyond the hour of noon; then the markets, the booths, the workshops and schools were to be closed, and on the great square in front of the temple of Ptah, where the annual fair was held, dramas both sacred and profane, and shows of all sorts were to be seen, heard and admired by men, women and children—provided at the expense of the two kings.

Two men of Alexandria, one an Æolian of Lesbos, and the other a Hebrew belonging to the Jewish community, but who was not distinguishable by dress or accent from his Greek fellow-citizens, greeted each other on the quay opposite the landing-place for the king's vessels, some of which were putting out into the stream, spreading their purple sails and dipping their prows inlaid with ivory and heavily gilt.

"In a couple of hours," said the Jew, "I shall be travelling homewards. May I offer you a place in my boat, or do you propose remaining here to assist at the festival and not starting till to-morrow morning? There are all kinds of spectacles to be seen, and when it is dark a grand illumination is to take place."

"What do I care for their barbarian rubbish?" answered the Lesbian. "Why, the Egyptian music alone drives me to distraction. My business is concluded. I had inspected the goods brought from Arabia and India by way of Berenice and Coptos, and had selected those I needed before the vessel that brought them had moored in the Mariotic harbor, and other goods will have reached Alexandria before me. I will not stay an hour longer than is necessary in this horrible place, which is as dismal as it is huge. Yesterday I visited the gymnasium and the better class of baths—wretched, I call them! It is an insult to the fish-market and the horse-ponds of Alexandria to compare them with them."

"And the theatre!" exclaimed the Jew. "The exterior one can bear to look at—but the acting! Yesterday they gave the 'Thals' of Menander, and I assure you that in Alexandria the woman who dared to impersonate the bewitching and cold-hearted Hetaira would have been driven off the stage—they would have pelted her with rotten apples. Close by me there sat a sturdy, brown Egyptian, a sugar-baker or something of the kind, who held his sides with laughing, and yet, I dare swear, did not understand a word of the comedy. But in Memphis it is the fashion to know Greek, even among the artisans. May I hope to have you as my guest?"

"With pleasure, with pleasure!" replied the Lesbian. "I was about to look out for a boat. Have you done your business to your satisfaction?"

"Tolerably!" answered the Jew. "I have purchased some corn from Upper Egypt, and stored it in the granaries here. The whole of that row yonder were to let for a mere song, and so we get off cheaply when we let the wheat lie here instead of at Alexandria where granaries are no longer to be had for money."

"That is very clever!" replied the Greek. "There is bustle enough here in the harbor, but the many empty warehouses and the low rents prove how Memphis is going down. Formerly this city was the emporium for all vessels, but now for the most part they only run in to pay the toll and to take in supplies for their crews. This populous place has a big stomach, and many trades drive a considerable business here, but most of those that fail here are still carried on in Alexandria."

"It is the sea that is lacking," interrupted the Jew; "Memphis trades only with Egypt, and we with the whole world. The merchant who sends his goods here only load camels, and wretched asses, and flat-bottomed Nile-boats, while we in our harbors freight fine seagoing vessels. When the winter-storms are past our house alone sends twenty triremes with Egyptian wheat to Ostia and to Pontus; and your Indian and Arabian goods, your imports from the newly opened Ethiopian provinces, take up less room, but I should like to know how many talents your trade amounted to in the course of the past year. Well then, farewell till we meet again on my boat; it is called the Euphrosyne, and lies out there, exactly opposite the two statues of the old king—who can remember these stiff barbarian names? In three hours we start. I have a good cook on board, who is not too particular as to the regulations regarding food by which my countrymen in Palestine live, and you will find a few new books and some capital wine from Byblos."

"Then we need not dread a head-wind," laughed the Lesbian. "We meet again in three hours."

The Israelite waved his hand to his travelling companion, and proceeded at first along the shore under the shade of an alley of sycamores with their broad unsymmetrical heads of foliage, but presently he turned aside into a narrow street which led from the quay to the city. He stood still for a moment opposite the entrance of the corner house, one side of which lay parallel to the stream while the other—exhibiting the front door, and a small oil-shop—faced the street; his attention had been attracted to it by a strange scene; but he had still much to attend to before starting on his journey, and he soon hurried on again without noticing a tall man who came towards him, wearing a travelling-hat and a cloak such as was usually adapted only for making journeys.

The house at which the Jew had gazed so fixedly was that of Apollodorus, the sculptor, and the man who was so strangely dressed for a walk through the city at this hour of the day was the Roman, Publius Scipio. He seemed to be still more attracted by what was going on in the little stall by the sculptor's front door, than even the Israelite had been; he leaned against the fence of the garden opposite the shop, and stood for some time gazing and shaking his head at the strange things that were to be seen within.

A wooden counter supported by the wall of the house-which was used by customers to lay their money on and which generally held a few oil-jars-projected a little way into the street like a window-board, and on this singular couch sat a distinguished looking youth in a light blue, sleeveless chiton, turning his back on the stall itself, which was not much bigger than a good sized travelling-chariot. By his side lay a "Himation" —[A long square cloak, and an indispensable part of the dress of the Greeks.]—of fine white woolen stuff with a blue border. His legs hung out into the street, and his brilliant color stood out in wonderful contrast to the dark skin of a naked Egyptian boy, who crouched at his feet with a cage full of doves.

The young Greek sitting on the window-counter had a golden fillet on his oiled and perfumed curls, sandals of the finest leather on his feet, and even in these humble surroundings looked elegant—but even more merry than elegant—for the whole of his handsome face was radiant with smiles while he tied two small rosy-grey turtle doves with ribands of rose-colored bombyx-silk to the graceful basket in which they were sitting, and then slipped a costly gold bracelet over the heads of the frightened birds, and attached it to their wings with a white silk tie.

When he had finished this work he held the basket up, looked at it with a smile of satisfaction, and he was in the very act of handing it to the black boy when he caught sight of Publius, who went up to him from the garden-fence.

"In the name of all the gods, Lysias," cried the Roman, without greeting his friend, "what fool's trick are you at there again! Are you turned oil-seller, or have you taken to training pigeons?"

"I am the one, and I am doing the other," answered the Corinthian with a laugh, for he it was to whom the Roman's speech was addressed. "How do you like my nest of young doves? It strikes me as uncommonly pretty, and how well the golden circlet that links their necks becomes the little creatures!"

"Here, put out your claws, you black crocodile," he continued, turning to his little assistant, "carry the basket carefully into the house, and repeat what I say, 'From the love-sick Lysias to the fair Irene'—Only look, Publius, how the little monster grins at me with his white teeth. You shall hear that his Greek is far less faultless than his teeth. Prick up your ears, you little ichneumon—now once more repeat what you are to say in there—do you see where I am pointing with my finger?—to the master or to the lady who shall take the doves from you."

With much pitiful stammering the boy repeated the Corinthian's message to Irene, and as he stood there with his mouth wide open, Lysias, who was an expert at "ducks and drakes" on the water, neatly tossed into it a silver drachma. This mouthful was much to the little rascal's taste, for after he had taken the coin out of his mouth he stood with wide-open jaws opposite his liberal master, waiting for another throw; Lysias however boxed him lightly on his ears, and chucked him under the chin, saying as he snapped the boy's teeth together:

"Now carry up the birds and wait for the answer." "This offering is to Irene, then?" said Publius. "We have not met for a long time; where were you all day yesterday?"

"It will be far more entertaining to hear what you were about all the night long. You are dressed as if you had come straight here from Rome. Euergetes has already sent for you once this morning, and the queen twice; she is over head and ears in love with you."

"Folly! Tell me now what you were doing all yesterday."

"Tell me first where you have been."

"I had to go some distance and will tell you all about it later, but not now; and I encountered strange things on my way—aye, I must say extraordinary things. Before sunrise I found a bed in the inn yonder, and to my own great surprise I slept so soundly that I awoke only two hours since."

"That is a very meagre report; but I know of old that if you do not choose to speak no god could drag a syllable from you. As regards myself I should do myself an injury by being silent, for my heart is like an overloaded beast of burden and talking will relieve it. Ah! Publius, my fate to-day is that of the helpless Tantalus, who sees juicy pears bobbing about under his nose and tempting his hungry stomach, and yet they never let him catch hold of them, only look—in there dwells Irene, the pear, the peach, the pomegranate, and my thirsting heart is consumed with longing for her. You may laugh—but to-day Paris might meet Helen with impunity, for Eros has shot his whole store of arrows into me. You cannot see them, but I can feel them, for not one of them has he drawn out of the wound. And the darling little thing herself is not wholly untouched by the winged boy's darts. She has confessed so much to me myself. It is impossible for me to refuse her any thing, and so I was fool enough to swear a horrible oath that I would not try to see her till she was reunited to her tall solemn sister, of whom I am exceedingly afraid. Yesterday I lurked outside this house just as a hungry wolf in cold weather sneaks about a temple where lambs are being sacrificed, only to see her, or at least to hear a word from her lips, for when she speaks it is like the song of nightingales—but all in vain. Early this morning I came back to the city and to this spot; and as hanging about forever was of no use, I bought up the stock of the old oil-seller, who is asleep there in the corner, and settled myself in his stall, for here no one can escape me, who enters or quits Apollodorus' house—and, besides, I am only forbidden to visit Irene; she herself allows me to send her greetings, and no one forbids me, not even Apollodorus, to whom I spoke an hour ago."

"And that basket of birds that your dusky errand-boy carried into the house just now, was such a 'greeting?'"

"Of course—that is the third already. First I sent her a lovely nosegay of fresh pomegranate-blossoms, and with it a few verses I hammered out in the course of the night; then a basket of peaches which she likes very much, and now the doves. And there lie her answers—the dear, sweet creature! For my nosegay I got this red riband, for the fruit this peach with a piece bitten out. Now I am anxious to see what I shall get for my doves. I bought that little brown scamp in the market, and I shall take him with me to Corinth as a remembrance of Memphis, if he brings me back something pretty this time. There, I hear the door, that is he; come here youngster, what have you brought?" Publius stood with his arms crossed behind his back, hearing and watching the excited speech and gestures of his friend who seemed to him, to-day more than ever, one of those careless darlings of the gods, whose audacious proceedings give us pleasure because they match with their appearance and manner, and we feel they can no more help their vagaries than a tree can help blossoming. As soon as Lysias spied a small packet in the boy's hand he did not take it from him but snatched up the child, who was by no means remarkably small, by the leather belt that fastened up his loin-cloth, tossed him up as if he were a plaything, and set him down on the table by his side, exclaiming:

"I will teach you to fly, my little hippopotamus! Now, show me what you have got."

He hastily took the packet from the hand of the youngster, who looked quite disconcerted, weighed it in his hand and said, turning to Publius:

"There is something tolerably heavy in this—what can it contain?"

"I am quite inexperienced in such matters," replied the Roman.

"And I much experienced," answered Lysias. "It might be, wait-it might be the clasp of her girdle in here. Feel, it is certainly something hard."

Publius carefully felt the packet that the Corinthian held out to him, with his fingers, and then said with a smile:

"I can guess what you have there, and if I am right I shall be much pleased. Irene, I believe, has returned you the gold bracelet on a little wooden tablet."

"Nonsense!" answered Lysias. "The ornament was prettily wrought and of some value, and every girl is fond of ornaments."

"Your Corinthian friends are, at any rate. But look what the wrapper contains."

"Do you open it," said the Corinthian.

Publius first untied a thread, then unfolded a small piece of white linen, and came at last to an object wrapped in a bit of flimsy, cheap papyrus. When this last envelope was removed, the bracelet was in fact discovered, and under it lay a small wax tablet.

Lysias was by no means pleased with this discovery, and looked disconcerted and annoyed at the return of his gift; but he soon mastered his vexation, and said turning to his friend, who was not in the least maliciously triumphant, but who stood looking thoughtfully at the ground.

"Here is something on the little tablet—the sauce no doubt to the peppered dish she has set before me."

"Still, eat it," interrupted Publius. "It may do you good for the future."

Lysias took the tablet in his hand, and after considering it carefully on both sides he said:

"It belongs to the sculptor, for there is his name. And there—why she has actually spiced the sauce or, if you like it better the bitter dose, with verses. They are written more clearly than beautifully, still they are of the learned sort."

"Well?" asked the Roman with curiosity, as Lysias read the lines to himself; the Greek did not look up from the writing but sighed softly, and rubbing the side of his finely-cut nose with his finger he replied:

"Very pretty, indeed, for any one to whom they are not directly addressed. Would you like to hear the distich?"

"Read it to me, I beg of you."

"Well then," said the Corinthian, and sighing again he read aloud;

> 'Sweet is the lot of the couple whom love has united;
> But gold is a debt, and needs must at once be restored.'

"There, that is the dose. But doves are not human creatures, and I know at once what my answer shall be. Give me the fibula, Publius, that clasps that cloak in which you look like one of your own messengers. I will write my answer on the wax."

The Roman handed to Lysias the golden circlet armed with a strong pin, and while he stood holding his cloak together with his hands, as he was anxious to avoid recognition by the passers-by that frequented this street, the Corinthian wrote as follows:

> "When doves are courting the lover adorns himself only;
> But when a youth loves, he fain would adorn his beloved."

"Am I allowed to hear it?" asked Publius, and his friend at once read him the lines; then he gave the tablet to the boy, with the bracelet which he hastily wrapped up again, and desired him to take it back immediately to the fair Irene. But the Roman detained the lad, and laying his hand on the Greek's shoulder, he asked him: "And if the young girl accepts this gift, and after it many more besides—since you are rich enough to make her presents to her heart's content—what then, Lysias?"

"What then?" repeated the other with more indecision and embarrassment than was his wont. "Then I wait for Klea's return home and—Aye! you may laugh at me, but I have been thinking seriously of marrying this girl, and taking her with me to Corinth. I am my father's only son, and for the last three years he has given me no peace. He is bent on my mother's finding me a wife or on my choosing one for myself. And if I took him the pitch-black sister of this swarthy lout I believe he would be glad. I never was more madly in love with any girl than with this little Irene, as true as I am your friend; but I know why you are looking at me with a frown like Zeus the Thunderer. You know of what consequence our family is in Corinth, and when I think of that, then to be sure—"

"Then to be sure?" enquired the Roman in sharp, grave tone.

"Then I reflect that a water-bearer—the daughter of an outlawed man, in our house—"

"And do you consider mine as being any less illustrious in Rome than your own is in Corinth?" asked Publius sternly.

"On the contrary, Publius Cornelius Scipio Nasica. We are important by our wealth, you by your power and estates."

"So it is—and yet I am about to conduct Irene's sister Klea as my lawful wife to my father's house."

"You are going to do that!" cried Lysias springing from his seat, and flinging himself on the Roman's breast, though at this moment a party of Egyptians were passing by in the deserted street. "Then all is well, then—oh! what a weight is taken off my mind!—then Irene shall be my wife as sure as I live! Oh Eros and Aphrodite and Father Zeus and Apollo! how happy I am! I feel as if the biggest of the Pyramids yonder had fallen off my heart. Now, you rascal, run up and carry to the fair Irene, the betrothed of her faithful Lysias—mark what I say—carry her at once this tablet and bracelet. But you will not say it right; I will write here above my distich: 'From the faithful Lysias to the fair Irene his future wife.' There—and now I think she will not send the thing back again, good girl that she is! Listen, rascal, if she keeps it you may swallow cakes to-day out on the Grand Square till you burst—and yet I have only just paid five gold pieces for you. Will she keep the bracelet, Publius—yes or no?"

"She will keep it."

A few minutes later the boy came hurrying back, and pulling the Greek vehemently by his dress, he cried:

"Come, come with me, into the house." Lysias with a light and graceful leap sprang right over the little fellow's head, tore open the door, and spread out his arms as he caught sight of Irene, who, though trembling like a hunted gazelle, flew down the narrow ladder-like stairs to meet him, and fell on his breast laughing and crying and breathless.

In an instant their lips met, but after this first kiss she tore herself from his arms, rushed up the stairs again, and then, from the top step, shouted joyously:

"I could not help seeing you this once! now farewell till Klea comes, then we meet again," and she vanished into an upper room.

Lysias turned to his friend like one intoxicated, he threw himself down on his bench, and said:

"Now the heavens may fall, nothing can trouble me! Ye immortal gods, how fair the world is!"

"Strange boy!" exclaimed the Roman, interrupting his friend's rapture. "You can not stay for ever in this dingy stall."

"I will not stir from this spot till Klea comes. The boy there shall fetch me victuals as an old sparrow feeds his young; and if necessary I will lie here for a week, like the little sardines they preserve in oil at Alexandria."

"I hope you will have only a few hours to wait; but I must go, for I am planning a rare surprise for King Euergetes on his birthday, and must go to the palace. The festival is already in full swing. Only listen how they are shouting and calling down by the harbor; I fancy I can hear the name of Euergetes."

"Present my compliments to the fat monster! May we meet again soon— brother-in-law!"

CHAPTER XXV

King Euergetes was pacing restlessly up and down the lofty room which his brother had furnished with particular magnificence to be his reception-room. Hardly had the sun risen on the morning of his birthday when he had betaken himself to the temple of Ptah with a numerous suite—before his brother Philometor could set out—in order to sacrifice there, to win the good graces of the high-priest of the sanctuary, and to question of the oracle of Apis. All had fallen out well, for the sacred bull had eaten out of his hand; and yet he would have been more glad—though it should have disdained the cake he offered it, if only Eulaeus had brought him the news that the plot against the Roman's life had been successful.

Gift after gift, addresses of congratulation from every district of the country, priestly decrees drawn up in his honor and engraved on tablets of hard stone, lay on every table or leaned against the walls of the vast ball which the guests had just quitted. Only Hierax, the king's friend, remained with him, supporting himself, while he waited for some sign from his sovereign, on a high throne made of gold and ivory and richly decorated with gems, which had been sent to the king by the Jewish community of Alexandria.

The great commander knew his master well and knew too that it was not prudent to address him when he looked as he did now. But Euergetes himself was aware of the need for speech, and he began, without pausing in his walk or looking at his dignified friend:

"Even the Philobasilistes have proved corrupt; my soldiers in the citadel are more numerous and are better men too than those that have remained faithful to Philometor, and there ought to be nothing more for me to do but to stir up a brief clatter of swords on shields, to spring upon the throne, and to have myself proclaimed king; but I will never go into the field with the strongest division of the enemy in my rear. My brother's head is on my sister's shoulders, and so long as I am not certain of her—"

A chamberlain rushed into the room as the king spoke, and interrupted him by shouting out:

"Queen Cleopatra."

A smile of triumph flashed across the features of the young giant; he flung himself with an air of indifference on to a purple divan, and desired that a magnificent lyre made of ivory, and presented to him by his sister, should be brought to him; on it was carved with wonderful skill and delicacy a representation of the first marriage, that of Cadmus with Harmonia, at which all the gods had attended as guests.

Euergetes grasped the chords with wonderful vigor and mastery, and began to play a wedding march, in which eager triumph alternated with tender whisperings of love and longing.

The chamberlain, whose duty it was to introduce the queen to her brother's presence, wished to interrupt this performance of his sovereign's; but Cleopatra held him back, and stood listening at the door with her children till Euergetes had brought the air to a rapid conclusion with a petulant sweep of the strings, and a loud and ear-piercing discord; then he flung his lute on the couch and rose with well-feigned surprise, going forward to meet the queen as if, absorbed in playing, he had not heard her approach.

He greeted his sister affectionately, holding out both his hands to her, and spoke to the children—who were not afraid of him, for he knew how to play madcap games with them like a great frolicsome boy—welcoming them as tenderly as if he were their own father.

He could not weary of thanking Cleopatra for her thoughtful present—so appropriate to him, who like Cadmus longed to boast of having mastered Harmonia, and finally—she not having found a word to say—he took her by the hand to exhibit to her the presents sent him by her husband and from the provinces. But Cleopatra seemed to take little pleasure in all these things, and said:

"Yes, everything is admirable, just as it has always been every year for the last twenty years; but I did not come here to see but to listen."

Her brother was radiant with satisfaction; she on the contrary was pale and grave, and, could only now and then compel herself to a forced smile.

"I fancied," said Euergetes, "that your desire to wish me joy was the principal thing that had brought you here, and, indeed, my vanity requires me to believe it. Philometor was with me quite early, and fulfilled that duty with touching affection. When will he go into the banqueting-hall?"

"In half an hour; and till then tell me, I entreat you, what yesterday you—"

"The best events are those that are long in preparing," interrupted her brother. "May I ask you to let the children, with their attendants, retire for a few minutes into the inner rooms?"

"At once!" cried Cleopatra eagerly, and she pushed her eldest boy, who clamorously insisted on remaining with his uncle, violently out of the door without giving his attendant time to quiet him or take him in her arms.

While she was endeavoring, with angry scolding and cross words, to hasten the children's departure, Eulaeus came into the room. Euergetes, as soon as he saw him, set every limb with rigid resolve, and drew breath so deeply that his broad chest heaved high, and a strong respiration parted his lips as he went forward to meet the eunuch, slowly but with an enquiring look.

Eulaeus cast a significant glance at Hierax and Cleopatra, went quite close up to the king, whispered a few words into his ear, and answered his brief questions in a low voice.

"It is well," said Euergetes at last, and with a decisive gesture of his hand he dismissed Eulaeus and his friend from the room.

Then he stood, as pale as death, his teeth set in his under-lip, and gazing blankly at the ground.

He had his will, Publius Cornelius Scipio lived no more; his ambition might reach without hindrance the utmost limits of his desires, and yet he could not rejoice; he could not escape from a deep horror of himself, and he struck his broad forehead with his clenched fists. He was face to face with his first dastardly murder.

"And what news does Eulaeus bring?" asked Cleopatra in anxious excitement, for she had never before seen her brother like this; but he did not hear these words, and it was not till she had repeated them with more insistence that he collected himself, stared at her from head to foot with a fixed, gloomy expression, and then, letting his hand fall on her shoulder so heavily that her knees bent under her and she gave a little cry, asked her in a low but meaning tone:

"Are you strong enough to bear to hear great news?"

"Speak," she said in a low voice, and her eyes were fixed on his lips while she pressed her hand on her heart. Her anxiety to hear fettered her to him, as with a tangible tie, and he, as if he must burst it by the force of his utterance, said with awful solemnity, in his deepest tones and emphasizing every syllable:

"Publius Cornelius Scipio Nasica is dead."

At these words Cleopatra's pale cheeks were suddenly dyed with a crimson glow, and clenching her little hands she struck them together, and exclaimed with flashing eyes:

"I hoped so!"

Euergetes withdrew a step from his sister, and said: "You were right. It is not only among the race of gods that the most fearful of all are women!"

"What have you to say?" retorted Cleopatra. "And am I to believe that a toothache has kept the Roman away from the banquet yesterday, and again from coming to see me to-day? Am I to repeat, after you, that he died of it? Now, speak out, for it rejoices my heart to hear it; where and how did the insolent hypocrite meet his end?"

"A serpent stung him," replied Euergetes, turning from his sister. "It was in the desert, not far from the Apis-tombs."

"He had an assignation in the Necropolis at midnight—it would seem to have begun more pleasantly than it ended?"

Euergetes nodded assent to the question, and added gravely:

"His fate overtook him—but I cannot see anything very pleasing in the matter."

"No?" asked the queen. "And do you think that I do not know the asp that ended that life in its prime? Do you think that I do not know, who set the poisoned serpent on the Roman? You are the assassin, and Eulaeus and his accomplices have helped you! Only yesterday I would have given my heart's blood for Publius, and would rather have carried you to the grave than him; but to-day, now that I know the game that the wretch has been playing with me, I would even have taken on myself the bloody deed which, as it is, stains your hands. Not even a god should treat your sister with such contempt—should insult her as he has done—and go unpunished! Another has already met the same fate, as you know—Eustorgos, Hipparchon of Bithynia, who, while he seemed to be dying of love for me, was courting Kallistrata my lady in waiting; and the wild beasts and serpents exercised their dark arts on him too. Eulaeus' intelligence has fallen on you, who are powerful, like a cold hand on your heart; in me, the weak woman, it rouses unspeakable delight. I gave him the best of all a woman has to bestow, and he dared to trample it in the dust; and had I no right to require of him that he should pour out the best that he had, which was his life, in the same way as he had dared to serve mine, which is my love? I have a right to rejoice at his death. Aye! the heavy lids now close those bright eyes which could be falser than the stern lips that were so apt to praise truth. The faithless heart is forever still which could scorn the love of a queen—and for what? For whom? Oh, ye pitiful gods!"

With these words the queen sobbed aloud, hastily lifting her hands to cover her eyes, and ran to the door by which she had entered her brother's rooms.

But Euergetes stood in her way, and said sternly and positively:

"You are to stay here till I return. Collect yourself, for at the next event which this momentous day will bring forth it will be my turn to laugh while your blood shall run cold." And with a few swift steps he left the hall.

Cleopatra buried her face in the soft cushions of the couch, and wept without ceasing, till she was presently startled by loud cries and the clatter of arms. Her quick wit told her what was happening. In frantic haste she flew to the door but it was locked; no shaking, no screaming, no thumping seemed to reach the ears of the guard whom she heard monotonously walking up and down outside her prison.

And now the tumult and clang of arms grew louder and louder, and the rattle of drums and blare of trumpets began to mingle with the sound. She rushed to the window in mortal fear, and looked down into the palace-yard; at that same instant the door of the great banqueting-hall was flung open, and a flying crowd streamed out in distracted confusion—then another, and a third—all troops in King Philometor's uniform. She ran to the door of the room into which she had thrust her children; that too was locked. In her desperation she once more sprang to the window, shouted to the flying Macedonians to halt and make a stand—threatening and entreating; but no one heard her, and their number constantly increased, till at length she saw her husband standing on the threshold of the great hall with a gaping wound on his forehead, and defending himself bravely and stoutly with buckler and sword against the body-guard of his own brother, who were pressing him sorely. In agonized excitement she shouted encouraging words to him, and he seemed to hear her, for with a strong sweep of his shield he struck his nearest antagonist to the earth, sprang with a mighty leap into the midst of his flying adherents, and vanished with them through the passage which led to the palace-stables.

The queen sank fainting on her knees by the window, and, through the gathering shades of her swoon her dulled senses still were conscious of the trampling of horses, of a shrill trumpet-blast, and at last of a swelling and echoing shout of triumph with cries of, "Hail: hail to the son of the Sun—Hail to the uniter of the two kingdoms; Hail to the King of Upper and Lower Egypt, to Euergetes the god."

But at the last words she recovered consciousness entirely and started up. She looked down into the court again, and there saw her brother borne along on her husband's throne-litter by dignitaries and nobles. Side by side with the traitor's body-guard marched her own and Philometor's Philobasilistes and Diadoches.

The magnificent train went out of the great court of the palace, and then—as she heard the chanting of priests—she realized that she had lost her crown, and knew whither her faithless brother was proceeding.

She ground her teeth as her fancy painted all that was now about to happen. Euergetes was being borne to the temple of Ptah, and proclaimed by its astonished chief-priests, as King of Upper and Lower Egypt, and successor to Philometor. Four pigeons would be let fly in his presence to announce to the four quarters of the heavens that a new sovereign had mounted the throne of his fathers, and amid prayer and sacrifice a golden sickle would be presented to him with which, according to ancient custom, he would cut an ear of corn.

Betrayed by her brother, abandoned by her husband, parted from her children, scorned by the man she had loved, dethroned and powerless, too weak and too utterly crushed to dream of revenge—she spent two interminably long hours in the keenest anguish of mind, shut up in her prison which was overloaded with splendor and with gifts. If poison had been within her reach, in that hour she would unhesitatingly have put an end to her ruined life. Now she walked restlessly up and down, asking herself what her fate would be, and now she flung herself on the couch and gave herself up to dull despair.

There lay the lyre she had given to her brother; her eye fell on the relievo of the marriage of Cadmus and Harmonia, and on the figure of a woman who was offering a jewel to the bride. The bearer of the gift was the goddess of love, and the ornament she gave—so ran the legend—brought misfortune on those who inherited it. All the darkest hours of her life revived in her memory, and the blackest of them all had come upon her as the outcome of Aphrodite's gifts. She thought with a shudder of the murdered Roman, and remembered the moment when Eulaeus had told her that her Bithynian lover had been killed by wild beasts. She rushed from one door to another— the victim of the avenging Eumenides—shrieked from the window for rescue and help, and in that one hour lived through a whole year of agonies and terrors.

At last—at last, the door of the room was opened, and Euergetes came towards her, clad in the purple, with the crown of the two countries on his grand head, radiant with triumph and delight.

"All hail to you, sister!" he exclaimed in a cheerful tone, and lifting the heavy crown from his curling hair. "You ought to be proud to-day, for your own brother has risen to high estate, and is now King of Upper and Lower Egypt."

Cleopatra turned from him, but he followed her and tried to take her hand. She however snatched it away, exclaiming:

"Fill up the measure of your deeds, and insult the woman whom you have robbed and made a widow. It was with a prophecy on your lips that you went forth just now to perpetrate your greatest crime; but it falls on your own head, for you laugh over our misfortune—and it cannot regard me, for my blood does not run cold; I am not overwhelmed nor hopeless, and I shall—"

"You," interrupted Euergetes, at first with a loud voice, which presently became as gentle as though he were revealing to her the prospect of a future replete with enjoyment, "You shall retire to your roof-tent with your children, and there you shall be read to as much as you like, eat as many dainties as you can, wear as many splendid dresses as you can desire, receive my visits and gossip with me as often as my society may seem agreeable to you—as yours is to me now and at all times. Besides all this you may display your sparkling wit before as many Greek and Jewish men of letters or learning as you can command, till each and all are dazzled to blindness. Perhaps even before that you may win back your freedom, and with it a full treasury, a stable full of noble horses, and a magnificent residence in the royal palace on the Bruchion in gay Alexandria. It depends only on how soon our brother Philometor—who fought like a lion this morning—perceives that he is more fit to be a commander of horse, a lute-player, an attentive host of word-splitting guests—than the ruler of a kingdom. Now, is it not worthy of note to those who, like you and me, sister, love to investigate the phenomena of our spiritual life, that this man—who in peace is as yielding as wax, as week as a reed—is as tough and as keen in battle as a finely tempered sword? We hacked bravely at each other's shields, and I owe this slash here on my shoulder to him. If Hierax—who is in pursuit of him with his horsemen—is lucky and catches him in time, he will no doubt give up the crown of his own free will."

"Then he is not yet in your power, and he had time to mount a horse!" cried Cleopatra, her eyes sparkling with satisfaction; "then all is not yet lost for us. If Philometor can but reach Rome, and lay our case before the Senate—"

"Then he might certainly have some prospect of help from the Republic, for Rome does not love to see a strong king on the throne of Egypt," said Euergetes. "But you have lost your mainstay by the Tiber, and I am about to make all the Scipios and the whole gens Cornelia my stanch allies, for I mean to have the deceased Roman burnt with the finest cedar-wood and Arabian spices; sacrifices shall be slaughtered at the same time as if he had been a reigning king, and his ashes shall be sent to Ostia and Rome in the costliest specimen of Vasa murrina that graces my treasure-house, and on a ship specially fitted, and escorted by the noblest of my friends. The road to the rampart of a hostile city lies over corpses, and I, as general and king—"

Euergetes suddenly broke off in his sentence, for a loud noise and vehement talking were heard outside the door. Cleopatra too had not failed to observe it, and listened with alert attention; for on such a day and in these apartments every dialogue, every noise in the king's antechamber might be of grave purport.

Euergetes did not deceive himself in this matter any more than his sister, and he went towards the door holding the sacrificial sickle, which formed part of his regalia, in his right hand. But he had not crossed the room when Eulaeus rushed in, as pale as death, and calling out to his sovereign:

"The murderers have betrayed us; Publius Scipio is alive, and insists on being admitted to speak with you."

The king's armed hand fell by his side, and for a moment he gazed blankly into vacancy, but the next instant he had recovered himself, and roared in a voice which filled the room like rolling thunder:

"Who dares to hinder the entrance of my friend Publius Cornelius Scipio? And are you still here, Eulaeus—you scoundrel and you villain! The first case that I, as King of Upper and Lower Egypt, shall open for trial will be that which this man—who is your foe and my friend—proposes to bring against you. Welcome! most welcome on my birthday, my noble friend!"

The last words were addressed to Publius, who now entered the room with stately dignity, and clad in the ample folds of the white toga worn by Romans of high birth. He held a sealed roll or despatch in his right hand, and, while he bowed respectfully to Cleopatra, he seemed entirely to overlook the hands King Euergetes held out in welcome. After his first greeting had been disdained by the Roman, Euergetes would not have offered him a second if his life had depended on it. He crossed his arms with royal dignity, and said:

"I am grieved to receive your good wishes the last of all that have been offered me on this happy day."

"Then you must have changed your mind," replied Publius, drawing up his slight figure, which was taller than the king's, "You have no lack of docile instruments, and last night you were fully determined to receive my first congratulations in the realm of shades."

"My sister," answered Euergetes, shrugging his shoulders, "was only yesterday singing the praises of your uncultured plainness of speech; but to-day it is your pleasure to speak in riddles like an Egyptian oracle."

"They cannot, however, be difficult to solve by you and your minions," replied Publius coldly, as he pointed to Eulaeus. "The serpents which you command have powerful poisons and sharp fangs at their disposal; this time, however, they mistook their victim, and have sent a poor recluse of Serapis to Hades instead of one of their king's guests."

"Your enigma is harder than ever," cried the king. "My intelligence at least is unequal to solve it, and I must request you to speak in less dark language or else to explain your meaning."

"Later, I will," said Publius emphatically, "but these things concern myself alone, and I stand here now commissioned by the State of Rome which I serve. To-day Juventius Thalna will arrive here as ambassador from the Republic, and this document from the Senate accredits me as its representative until his arrival."

Euergetes took the sealed roll which Publius offered to him. While he tore it open, and hastily looked through its contents, the door was again thrown open and Hierax, the king's trusted friend, appeared on the threshold with a flushed face and hair in disorder.

"We have him!" he cried before he came in. "He fell from his horse near Heliopolis."

"Philometor?" screamed Cleopatra, flinging herself upon Hierax. "He fell from his horse—you have murdered him?"

The tone in which the words were said, so full of grief and horror that the general said compassionately:

"Calm yourself, noble lady; your husband's wound in the forehead is not dangerous. The physicians in the great hall of the temple of the Sun bound it up, and allowed me to bring him hither on a litter."

Without hearing Hierax to the end Cleopatra flew towards the door, but Euergetes barred her way and gave his orders with that decision which characterized him, and which forbade all contradiction:

"You will remain here till I myself conduct you to him. I wish to have you both near me."

"So that you may force us by every torment to resign the throne!" cried Cleopatra. "You are in luck to-day, and we are your prisoners."

"You are free, noble queen," said the Roman to the poor woman, who was trembling in every limb. "And on the strength of my plenipotentiary powers I here demand the liberty of King Philometor, in the name of the Senate of Rome."

At these words the blood mounted to King Euergetes' face and eyes, and, hardly master of himself, he stammered out rather than said:

"Popilius Laenas drew a circle round my uncle Antiochus, and threatened him with the enmity of Rome if he dared to overstep it. You might excel the example set you by your bold countryman—whose family indeed was far less illustrious than yours—but I—I—"

"You are at liberty to oppose the will of Rome," interrupted Publius with dry formality, "but, if you venture on it, Rome, by me, will withdraw her friendship. I stand here in the name of the Senate, whose purpose it is to uphold the treaty which snatched this country from the Syrians, and by which you and your brother pledged yourselves to divide the realm of Egypt between you. It is not in my power to alter what has happened here; but it is incumbent on me so to act as to enable Rome to distribute to each of you that which is your due, according to the treaty ratified by the Republic.

"In all questions which bear upon that compact Rome alone must decide, and it is my duty to take care that the plaintiff is not prevented from appearing alive and free before his protectors. So, in the name of the Senate, King Euergetes, I require you to permit King Philometor your brother, and Queen Cleopatra your sister, to proceed hence, whithersoever they will." Euergetes, breathing hard in impotent fury, alternately doubling his fists, and extending his quivering fingers, stood opposite the Roman who looked enquiringly in his face with cool composure; for a short space both were silent. Then Euergetes, pushing his hands through his hair, shook his head violently from side to side, and exclaimed:

"Thank the Senate from me, and say that I know what we owe to it, and admire the wisdom which prefers to see Egypt divided rather than united in one strong hand—Philometor is free, and you also Cleopatra."

For a moment he was again silent, then he laughed loudly, and cried to the queen:

"As for you sister—your tender heart will of course bear you on the wings of love to the side of your wounded husband."

Cleopatra's pale cheeks had flushed scarlet at the Roman's speech; she vouchsafed no answer to her brother's ironical address, but advanced proudly to the door. As she passed Publius she said with a farewell wave of her pretty hand.

"We are much indebted to the Senate."

Publius bowed low, and she, turning away from him, quitted the room.

"You have forgotten your fan, and your children!" the king called after her; but Cleopatra did not hear his words, for, once outside her brother's apartment, all her forced and assumed composure flew to the winds; she clasped her hands on her temples, and rushed down the broad stairs of the palace as if she were pursued by fiends.

When the sound of her steps had died away, Euergetes turned to the Roman and said:

"Now, as you have fulfilled what you deem to be your duty, I beg of you to explain the meaning of your dark speeches just now, for they were addressed to Euergetes the man, and not the king. If I understood you rightly you meant to imply that your life had been attempted, and that one of those extraordinary old men devoted to Serapis had been murdered instead of you."

"By your orders and those of your accomplice Eulaeus," answered Publius coolly.

"Eulaeus, come here!" thundered the king to the trembling courtier, with a fearful and threatening glare in his eyes. "Have you hired murderers to kill my friend—this noble guest of our royal house—because he threatened to bring your crimes to light?"

"Mercy!" whimpered Eulaeus sinking on his knees before the king.

"He confesses his crime!" cried Euergetes; he laid his hand on the girdle of his weeping subordinate, and commanded Hierax to hand him over without delay to the watch, and to have him hanged before all beholders by the great gate of the citadel. Eulaeus tried to pray for mercy and to speak, but the powerful officer, who hated the contemptible wretch, dragged him up, and out of the room.

"You were quite right to lay your complaint before me," said Euergetes while Eulaeus cries and howls were still audible on the stairs. "And you see that I know how to punish those who dare to offend a guest."

"He has only met with the portion he has deserved for years," replied Publius. "But now that we stand face to face, man to man, I must close my account with you too. In your service and by your orders Eulaeus set two assassins to lie in wait for me—"

"Publius Cornelius Scipio!" cried the king, interrupting his enemy in an ominous tone; but the Roman went on, calmly and quietly:

"I am saying nothing that I cannot support by witnesses; and I have truly set forth, in two letters, that king Euergetes during the past night has attempted the life of an ambassador from Rome. One of these despatches is addressed to my father, the other to Popilius Lamas, and both are already on their way to Rome. I have given instructions that they are to be opened if, in the course of three months reckoned from the present date, I have not demanded them back. You see you must needs make it convenient to protect my life, and to carry out whatever I may require of you. If you obey my will in everything I may demand, all that has happened this night shall remain a secret between you and me and a third person, for whose silence I will be answerable; this I promise you, and I never broke my word."

"Speak," said the king flinging himself on the couch, and plucking the feathers from the fan Cleopatra had forgotten, while Publius went on speaking.

"First I demand a free pardon for Philotas of Syracuse, 'relative of the king,' and president of the body of the Chrematistes, his immediate release, with his wife, from their forced labor, and their return from the mines."

"They both are dead," said Euergetes, "my brother can vouch for it."

"Then I require you to have it declared by special decree that Philotas was condemned unjustly, and that he is reinstated in all the dignities he was deprived of. I farther demand that you permit me and my friend Lysias of Corinth, as well as Apollodorus the sculptor, to quit Egypt without let or hindrance, and with us Klea and Irene, the daughters of Philotas, who serve as water-bearers in the temple of Serapis.—Do you hesitate as to your reply?"

"No," answered the king, and he tossed up his hand. "For this once I have lost the game."

"The daughters of Philotas, Klea and Irene," continued Publius with imperturbable coolness, "are to have the confiscated estates of their parents restored to them."

"Then your sweetheart's beauty does not satisfy you!" interposed Euergetes satirically.

"It amply satisfies me. My last demand is that half of this wealth shall be assigned to the temple of Serapis, so that the god may give up his serving-maidens willingly, and without raising any objections. The other half shall be handed over to Dicearchus, my agent in Alexandria, because it is my will that Klea and Irene shall not enter my own house or that of Lysias in Corinth as wives, without the dowry that beseems their rank. Now, within one hour, I must have both the decree and the act of restitution in my hands, for as soon as Juventius Thalna arrives here—and I expect him, as I told you this very day—we propose to leave Memphis, and to take ship at Alexandria."

"A strange conjuncture!" cried Euergetes. "You deprive me alike of my revenge and my love, and yet I see myself compelled to wish you a pleasant journey. I must offer a sacrifice to Poseidon, to the Cyprian goddess, and to the Dioscurides that they may vouchsafe your ship a favorable voyage, although it will carry the man who in the future, can do us more injury at Rome by his bitter hostility, than any other."

"I shall always take the part of which ever of you has justice on his side."

Publius quitted the room with a proud wave of his hand, and Euergetes, as soon as the door had closed behind the Roman, sprang from his couch, shook his clenched fist in angry threat, and cried:

You, you obstinate fellow and your haughty patrician clan may do me mischief enough by the Tiber; and yet perhaps I may win the game in spite of you!

"You cross my path in the name of the Roman Senate. If Philometor waits in the antechambers of consuls and senators we certainly may chance to meet there, but I shall also try my luck with the people and the tribunes.

"It is very strange! This head of mine hits upon more good ideas in an hour than a cool fellow like that has in a year, and yet I am beaten by him—and if I am honest I can not but confess that it was not his luck alone, but his shrewdness that gained the victory. He may be off as soon as he likes with his proud Hera—I can find a dozen Aphrodites in Alexandria in her place!

"I resemble Hellas and he Rome, such as they are at present. We flutter in the sunshine, and seize on all that satisfies our intellect or gratifies our senses: they gaze at the earth, but walk on with a firm step to seek power and profit. And thus they get ahead of us, and yet—I would not change with them."